nothing
but
trouble

ALSO BY AMY ANDREWS

NAUGHTY OR NICE SERIES

No More Mr. Nice Guy
Ask Me Nicely

SYDNEY SMOKE RUGBY SERIES

Playing By Her Rules
Playing It Cool
Playing the Player
Playing with Forever
Playing House
Playing Dirty

OTHER BOOKS BY AMY ANDREWS

Hanky Spanky Christmas
The DILF
Taming the Tycoon
Seducing the Colonel's Daughter
Tis the Season to Be Kissed

nothing
but
trouble

AMY
ANDREWS

Copyright © 2019 by Amy Andrews. All rights reserved, including the right to reproduce, distribute, or transmit in any form or by any means. For information regarding subsidiary rights, please contact the Publisher.

Entangled Publishing, LLC
2614 South Timberline Road
Suite 109
Fort Collins, CO 80525
Visit our website at www.entangledpublishing.com.

Amara is an imprint of Entangled Publishing, LLC.

Edited by Liz Pelletier
Cover design by Liz Pelletier, Bree Archer,
and Heather Howland
Interior design by Heather Howland

Print ISBN 978-1-64063-537-1
ebook ISBN 978-1-64063-538-8

Manufactured in the United States of America

First Edition May 2019

AMARA

To Liz Pelletier, for not only believing in my writing but for championing it, for opening doors and giving me opportunities I haven't had before, and for going to bat for me. And for her friendship.

CHAPTER ONE

There were some days Cecilia Morgan would gladly shove her boss off the top of Mile High Stadium in downtown Denver. This was one of them. Wade "The Catapult" Carter may have been QB royalty, but he was lousy at relationships. *Allergic* to them, actually. And today, like so many days, that was a giant pain in *her* ass.

"But I thought he really liked me," came the forlorn voice of another jilted Wade Carter conquest.

"Of course he did."

CC straightened her pen and her drink coaster as she sipped on her Red Bull. Comforting slightly hysterical women was all part of her job description, and she'd become a pro. This one's name was Annabel. CC knew that because Annabel had called her frequently the last few weeks, chasing Wade. God forbid he should ever give out *his* cell number.

Plus, she'd supplied it to the florist this morning. The florist who had a standing order for a letting-her-down-gently floral arrangement. And a drawer full of cards that all said the same thing.

> *I've enjoyed our time together. Unfortunately, I can't commit to further dates. Thanks for your company. —WC*

For crying out loud—the man didn't even personalize it with his full damn name!

"He took me to that flashy new restaurant three

nights ago. You don't take just *anyone* there, CC. *There's a waiting list*."

CC stifled a sigh. Waiting lists didn't matter when you were more famous than God *and* John Denver in Broncos country. Celebrity opened doors. Wade didn't use his obnoxiously, but he didn't have to.

People knew who he was.

Restaurants ushered him to tables, fancy watch companies sent him exclusive timepieces, car salesmen handed over keys.

And women opened their legs.

"Oh God." There was a long groan on the other end of the line. "He was just using me for sex, wasn't he?"

CC blinked at Annabel's candor. She drew in a deep breath and thought about a warm SoCal beach. The Pacific Ocean. Blond surfer dudes with tans and abs.

Six months. Just six more months left on her employment contract.

No more twenty-four seven availability. No more midnight runs to the nearest gas station for Wonka Nerds. No more phone calls from emotional women she barely knew.

Technically, after the call from her broker this morning, she could walk her ass out of Wade's apartment right now. One of her investments had paid off, and while it hadn't made her rich, she now had the money she needed—she didn't need any more of his. But she'd signed a contract, and Wade's lawyers did not screw around. She'd seen them in action too often.

"Wade doesn't discuss his dates with me."

CC stuck to the company line instead of saying

what she wanted to say, which was, *Ya think?* And also, *Weren't you using him, too? Bagging a famous jock for some social capital?*

Bragging rights with the gal pals?

Because she knew Wade would have given Annabel the usual spiel up front. He didn't go out with any woman unless he had.

He wasn't interested in anything more than a few dates.

He wasn't interested in anything long-term.

He wasn't interested in a wife.

How many times had she heard Wade say that, either over the phone or face-to-face? "Don't fall for me, darlin'. I don't do past next week."

And as much as CC really hated this part of her job and thought Wade needed to stop treating the women of the world like he was in a candy shop and they were the buffet, he was always up-front with them.

Always.

But…as usual, there were some who thought they'd be different.

They'd be the one.

"Don't get me wrong—it was really freaking awesome sex. I mean…holy cow, CC, that man knows things about a woman's body. Like, *knows* things."

Oh God! Palm trees. Seagulls. The sound of the surf.

"He does this thing with his tongue—"

"Oookay!" CC was quick to interrupt.

Too. Much. Information. CC might have pretty much run Wade Carter's life, but there were some things she just didn't want to know about the man.

Some things you just couldn't *un*hear.

"I'm telling you, that man has *stamina.*"

Well, yes. He'd been the star quarterback of the Broncos for thirteen years. There were three Super Bowl rings in his safe to prove it. He had stamina.

Throw the man a parade.

"Okay, well, thank you for calling."

"No. Wait! *CC?*"

CC sighed. She'd never perfected the art of the polite hang-up. Wade was excellent at it, but these women broke her heart.

"*You* know the man. What did I do wrong? What could I have done differently?"

A humorless laugh rose in CC's throat, and she quashed it ruthlessly. What could she have done differently?

How about not putting out?

It was that simple. Her boss was a man—one with stamina and apparently crazy-good skills with his tongue she *did not want to know about.* One who used sex for recreation with absolutely no intention of follow-through.

In other words, he was a total, unashamed, card-carrying horn dog.

What did a woman do differently with such a man? How did she get *that* guy's attention? She said the one thing Mr. Hotshot Quarterback wasn't used to hearing. The one word women just didn't say to His Royal Sexiness.

No.

Sure. He might walk away without doing *that thing he did.* But it might just make him work a little harder, too.

Seriously, what was wrong with these women?

She'd known treat-them-mean, keep-them-keen since she was six years old. But maybe that was just a result of having five older, very protective brothers.

Not that she'd had a chance to treat anyone mean since she'd taken up this job. Being Wade Carter's PA-cum-*servant* for the last five and a half years had pretty much decimated her social life and killed her sex life dead.

Not only did Wade always know where she was, thanks to that annoying app he insisted she install on her phone, he was also uncannily attuned to when she was about to get lucky in her rare moments of free time. It was like he'd shoved an estrogen monitor under her skin one day when she'd been too exhausted to protest and called her when it hit the red zone.

"CC?"

CC dragged her attention back to the woman waiting on the other end of the phone. She should have pulled out her usual line about not discussing Wade with anybody. But she didn't. There was something in the pitch of Annabel's voice that tugged at CC's heartstrings.

She sighed as she fingered the neat stack of Post-its sitting at an exact right angle to her pen. She was tired of clucking and soothing Wade's women, of being fucking *Switzerland*. It felt like a betrayal of *all* women. "Annabel, you're perfect just the way you are. Don't change for any man, okay?"

And she hung up the phone, thunking her forehead against the desk. That was it. She was done. She *couldn't* do it anymore. Deal with Wade's women.

She *wouldn't*. And, thanks to her windfall, she didn't *have* to. Yesterday, she hadn't had quite enough money to leave. Today—she did.

It was as simple as that.

It was time. Time to go. Not in six months, not at the end of her contract. *Now*.

CC pulled her head off the desk, cheered by the thought. She was…free. She smiled and then she grinned. She could just…walk away. A laugh pressed itself against her vocal chords, and she gave it voice.

Of course, Wade *could* be an asshole about it, and the thought of his lawyers sobered her laughter. She had to be smart about this, *really* smart. Not walk in there and tell him to shove his job and his women up his ass—no matter how tempting. Confrontation was *not* the way to approach the situation.

She had to pick her moment. She had to be composed and reasonable. State her intentions with clarity and sincerity and calmly hand in her notice. Appeal to him for understanding. Assure him she'd find him a top-notch replacement.

Hold his damn man-baby hand a little bit longer…

But it *had* to be today because her mind was made up and frankly, one more weepy phone call was going to see her spiking her Red Bull with vodka. And CC had no intentions of making a side trip to rehab on her way to California.

• • •

Wade glared at the blinking cursor on the blank screen. It'd been doing that for the last three hours. Sitting there. Blinking. Defying him.

Not too many things defied Wade Carter. Mostly, they just saw him coming and got out of his way. Everything from a three-hundred-pound linebacker to a three-hundred-pound hog.

Well…everything except his mother. His PA. And this fucking annoying cursor.

When he'd been approached by a publishing house immediately after his retirement three years ago to write a book about his life, he'd dismissed it out of hand. But so many people had asked for his memoir since—fans and sports commentators and NFL execs—that he'd started to think about it seriously. The publishing house, who had coughed up a million-dollar advance, had offered to get a ghost writer, but Wade had refused.

He might not have graduated summa cum laude, but he was capable of writing his own story. He'd read all the great American classics and could get his head around algebra. He'd actually been a reasonable student—he just hadn't seen the point of wasting time inside the classroom when he could be out on the field, where his true vocation lay.

And now, here he was. Just him and the cursor.

Wade had no idea why it was taking him so long to write the first word. He and CC had prepared copious, detailed notes about his life and career to be included in the book.

But he didn't know where to start.

Where was he *supposed* to start? At the beginning? Back on the hog farm in Credence? Or when he started playing college ball for the CU Buffs? Or when he was drafted by the Denver Broncos? He'd had a long and illustrious career in the NFL before his knee had blown out for the last time a few years back.

And yet he couldn't figure out where to start.

He glanced up from his screen, seeking inspiration through the floor-to-ceiling windows throwing summer light into his office. From his penthouse vantage point, he could see the gleaming curves of the horseshoe-shaped bowl belonging to Mile High—or whatever the hell it was called these days—and, even now, he could still hear the roar of the crowd inside his head.

Behind the stadium, in the distance, stood the jagged outline of the Rocky Mountains. They rose majestically—strong and indomitable. As strong and indomitable as the spirit within Mile High on game night.

It was a view that always awed him. The juxtaposition of the modern and the ancient, the man-made and the natural. These two great megaliths had shaped him, and the sight of them both humbled and strengthened him.

It was inspirational stuff. Except today. Today, he had nothin'.

He groaned as he plonked his head on the desk, disturbing one of the many piles of neatly stacked papers CC had meticulously printed out and compiled, each marked with Post-its and labeled clearly in her legible, no-nonsense handwriting.

That handwriting irritated him more than usual right now.

"You should have gotten a ghost writer."

Wade lifted his head off the desk and shot an annoyed look at his PA lounging in his open doorway.

She was in her regulation blue jeans. She always wore jeans, whether it was cold enough for them or not. It'd been one of the few things she'd insisted on when she'd agreed to be his PA almost six years ago—no more ridiculous corporate wear.

Today, she'd teamed it with a red stripy T-shirt. She thought it made her look Parisian. He thought it made her look like a tiny female version of *Where's Waldo*.

"There is nobody more equipped than *me* to write about *me*."

Wade tried and failed to keep the exasperation out of his voice. It was the same argument he'd had with the publisher. And won. And he was in no mood to have it with CC—again.

"Yes. But." A slice of her mahogany bangs fell across one eye, and she brushed it away. She wore them longer than the rest of her hair, which was super short and choppy all over. "Writing is a different skill than throwing a ball."

Leave it to CC to point out the fucking obvious. But still, Wade hated how this was already kicking his ass. He succeeded at everything he did. Nothing defeated The Catapult.

Not even the blinking cursor of doom.

"So I should spend weeks talking to someone else so they can tell my story?"

"Sure, why not?" She shrugged. "You do like talking about yourself."

Wade grunted as he returned his attention to the screen. "Why do I pay you so much money, again?"

"Because I'm the only PA on the face of the planet who doesn't quit after you wake me at three in the morning to go and buy you Nerds and condoms."

He grinned at the memory. Yeah, she'd been *really* pissed about that. But it'd been the deal they'd made. Six years of twenty-four seven. He paid her a shitload of money—because he could afford it and a good PA was worth their weight in gold—and her time was his. *All* of it.

"That was an emergency."

She folded her arms. "Your apartment burning down is an emergency."

Wade laughed. He loved how CC didn't try to flatter him *or* pussyfoot around. And he appreciated it. She was like a cranky, bossy older sister—except at thirty-two, she was six years younger than him. His mother always said men needed someone to call them on their horseshit.

Well, his mother never said "horseshit" because not even forty-plus years in rural Colorado could coax the Texan Southern belle out of her. But when she said balooey, they all knew what she meant.

CC wandered into his office. "I also don't complain when I have to provide regular phone counseling to distraught women."

Wade flicked his gaze up from the damn blinking cursor. "It sounds like you're about to, though."

"Seriously, Wade." She sighed as she pulled to a stop on the opposite side of his desk, crossing her arms under her breasts.

She totally wasn't his type. He was the full jock cliché—into tall, busty blondes. And CC was his PA, and he'd promised her all those years ago, when he'd seen her knee her then-boss in the balls for making a pass, that he would *never*, *ever* go there with her.

But you couldn't beat biology. He was a man; he was genetically wired to notice boobs.

"Just give them your damn cell number already."

CC seemed testier than usual, but she was hardly a ray of sunshine at the best of times. He shook his head. *Hell no*. Being able to abdicate all the unpleasant things was one of the perks of being seriously fucking rich. "Annabel?"

"Yes. Annabel. And before that, it was Chrissie. And before that, Shondra."

Yeah. He'd been picking some doozies lately. It didn't seem to matter how many times he told the women he took to his bed that he wasn't looking for a wife—they were getting more determined. It had taken a lot of fun out of dating. And frankly, he was wondering if dating was more trouble than it was worth.

For him *and* CC.

Between women and this book, he was going a little stir-crazy. Maybe he was losing his mojo?

"Can't you be a little more…discerning?"

He propped his feet up on his desk and raised his arms to tuck his hands behind his head, the back of his chair reclining slightly. "What can I say? Women like me." Then he smiled that smile he knew would make her roll her eyes.

She didn't disappoint. He half expected her to mimic a gag reflex, but she opened her mouth to speak, instead, her face suddenly intent and serious as she took a step closer to his desk. "Do you have a moment to discuss something, Wade?"

Wade's scalp prickled at the grave note in her voice—he didn't like the sound of that. The last time she'd been this serious, there'd been a major Nerd shortage two Christmases ago. Thankfully his phone rang, cutting her off, and he grabbed it quickly, holding up his hand, indicating for her to hold her thought. He couldn't cope with a Nerd shortage and the blink, blink, blink of the taunting cursor.

Noticing the word *Mom* displayed on the screen, he pushed back in his chair again. Few people had this number. His parents, his brother, some old NFL buddies, and CC.

He put her on speaker. "Hey, Mom."

"Wade." The soft lilt of her Southern accent was as soothing as it'd always been. "How's my baby?"

CC rolled her eyes again, and Wade stifled a laugh. He was thirty-eight years old, filthy rich, and about as close to sporting royalty as it was possible for an ex-quarterback to be, but he'd always be her baby.

"Same old, same old."

"Staying outta trouble?"

"Always," he said and ignored CC's not-so-quiet snort.

"You're going to church?"

"Every Sunday."

CC mouthed, *You're going to hell*, and Wade grinned.

His mother laughed, obviously not fooled. "Well, now listen, darlin', don't go getting all worked up, just calling to let you know your dad had a bit of a… funny turn, and he's in the hospital."

Wade sat up abruptly, his feet hitting the floor with a *thud*. "What kind of a funny turn?"

His father was as strong as an ox, but he was almost

seventy. Sure, Wyatt, Wade's older brother, did most of the heavy lifting on the farm these days, but his dad was still in the thick of it.

Why in hell hadn't Wyatt contacted him?

CC took two steps closer to the desk, her forehead furrowed, her phone already out of her pocket.

"He went all dizzy and short of breath yesterday. He had some kind of arrhythmia or something. But Doc McNally sent him to Denver to be sure, and the heart specialist here says he needs a pacemaker."

"A pacemaker?"

Wade felt a little dizzy himself. And maybe like throwing up. His father had something wrong with his *heart*. His father, who'd first tossed a ball to Wade when he'd been four years old.

"You're at St. Luke's?"

"Now, darlin', there's no need to rush over; your father's fine. Cussin' up a storm."

"I'll be there in twenty." Wade hung up, pushing to his feet, meeting CC's gaze. "Fuck."

She nodded. CC's father had walked out on her mother when she was three, and she'd made damn sure Wade had kept in close contact with his since she'd been in his employ. Last week, a Post-it on his desk had reminded Wade it was his father's birthday. And he'd gotten distracted and forgotten to call.

Fuck.

"Just ordered an Uber. It'll be here in five."

He shook his head. "I'll drive." It'd give him something to do. Something to concentrate on.

"Okay. I'll cancel." Her thumbs got busy on her phone. She glanced up from the screen. "Go."

Her urging sliced into his inertia. Right. Yes. *Go.*

And he was moving. "Send me some info on pace-makers."

"Already on it."

Of course she was. "I'll call from the hospital."

"Yep," she said, not looking up from her phone.

He was at the door when CC called his name. He turned back in time to intercept a packet of Nerds she'd just pulled from her pocket and tossed in his direction. He caught them in his right hand, out of pure instinct, the packet rattling with familiar, sugary goodness.

"Thanks."

She nodded dismissively but she was all intent again as she watched him, which put an unpleasant itch up his spine. He had a feeling whatever she'd wanted to talk about was way more serious than a Nerd shortage, and he could only cope with one crisis at a time.

Wade did not multi-task. That's why he had CC. *Thank God.*

CHAPTER TWO

Wade did not spare the horses as he drove his Mustang to St Luke's. About a hundred different scenarios chased their way through his head as he navigated red lights, pedestrians, and roadworks. All of them ended up with his father being dead when Wade arrived at the hospital.

Why hadn't he fucking picked up the phone and called him on his birthday?

Twenty minutes later, it was a massive relief to find his father alive and well. But it still punched Wade in the gut to stand at his bedside and see such a big, strong man with drips and wires and a monitor that reduced his heart rate to a green squiggle and a continuous series of blips.

Cal Carter had always towered in Wade's mind, yet today he seemed smaller. Older.

Mortal.

"Son...I told your mother to tell you I was fine. There's no need to go interrupting your day over this."

Wade felt lower than a snake's belly that both of his parents apparently felt something as serious as this would be some kind of *inconvenience* in his life. He knew it wasn't intended as a criticism, but it sunk like a barb into his chest.

He'd been neglecting his family responsibilities. Showing up for Christmas and Thanksgiving wasn't enough. His parents were both getting older.

"Dad. You're in the hospital. You need a pacemaker."

His father waved it aside. "Doctor Cranforth says I'll be right as rain once it's in."

Wade glanced at his mother. Veronica—Ronnie—Carter nodded reassuringly. Her blond hair had turned silver over the last decade, and there were lines on her face, but she looked good for sixty-four. She still helped out on the farm, contributed to their church, and had a seat on the Credence town council.

"What do we know about him?"

"He's the heart doctor and the loveliest man. Seems very competent. Don't fret now, darlin'."

Wade didn't give one fuck how lovely the doctor was. He cared how experienced he was, how many people had tried to sue him, and how steady the guy's hand was. He pulled out his phone. There was a text from CC with a bunch of links for him to check out pacemakers. He sent a quick reply.

Find out about Doctor Cranforth. He's a cardiologist at St Luke's.

He also sent a text to Doug Schumann, the team doctor when he was playing for the Broncos, but it could be a while before Doug got back to him. CC'd be quicker.

"When are they doing it?"

"Tomorrow."

That was good. It would give Wade time to check out the doctor and make arrangements to get his father somewhere else if needed. "How long will you be in for?"

"Doc reckons I can go home the next day if everything goes well. Day after at the most."

"But he has to take it easy for six weeks," Ronnie interjected. "No lifting. No driving."

Christ, his father would *hate* that. Wade had never seen his father idle in his entire life. "Any hogs due to farrow in that time?"

His father snorted. "There's always hogs farrowing."

"It's okay," Ronnie soothed. "Wyatt'll pick up the slack."

Wade nodded. His brother was more than capable of running the entire operation by himself. "I could get him some extra help while Dad recovers."

"Nah, son." His father patted his hand with his big paw. It was easy to see where Wade had inherited his giant, safe quarterback hands from. "We'll be fine."

Which probably meant his father wasn't planning on being very compliant. He opened his mouth to say as much, but his phone buzzed, and a message from CC flashed onto the screen.

Dr. Richard Jonathon Cranforth is the best cardiologist in Colorado. Possibly the world.

Tension in Wade's shoulders—tension he hadn't even realized was there—eased suddenly.

"Dad…" He glanced at his mom, who was apparently as unconcerned about his heart requiring an *external force to keep beating* as his father. That was the problem with his parents' generation—they put too much faith in doctors. "Have you thought about retiring?"

"Retiring?"

Wade couldn't help but smile. His father was

looking at him as if he'd just muttered the "v" word in his presence.

Vegetarian.

"Yeah, you know. Stop working. Pass the farm over to Wyatt and…I don't know. Go on a vacation or something. I can send you on that Caribbean cruise Mom's always been talking about."

His parents had worked all their lives, why shouldn't they get to relax in their old age?

"Hell, you can go live somewhere else if you want. Come to Denver. Or Florida. Mom likes Florida. I'll buy you a place there. Some place with a view of the ocean. Some place where you're not freezing your ass off half the year or up at three in the morning with a sow."

The blipping of the heart monitor picked up a little as his father gaped at him. "*Florida?*"

That suggestion drew an even more virulent response than the retirement suggestion. Wade might as well have uttered *vegan* this time.

"What in hell would we do in Florida?"

Wade shrugged. "Go deep-sea diving. Learn how to salsa."

His father snorted. "You want me to move to a state where one of the football teams is called *the Dolphins*?" His father looked scandalized. "I'm a Broncos man."

Wade had to concede his father's point with that one.

"Fine." He sighed. "But you could move into the house I bought you in Credence. You'd still be in town, still be close to the farm, but you wouldn't have to work so hard every day."

Wade had earned a lot of money over his career and had invested it wisely. He'd cleared the debt on the family farm many years ago. Every few years he upgraded the farm vehicles, and whatever new tech came along that Wyatt considered a worthwhile purchase, he bought.

He might not have been mucking in with the day-to-day work, but with Wade's money and his brother's savvy, they'd turned the farm into a modern agri-business.

"Son, if you think I'm ever living in that god-awful Southern horror show—" He glanced at his wife. "Sorry honey, no offense."

Ronnie smiled at her husband. "None taken."

His father turned his attention back to Wade. "—then you've fallen off the tater wagon."

A couple of hundred years ago, back when Credence had been a thriving outpost, a snake oil salesman had settled in town and built a replica Southern-style mansion for his sweetheart, who had come from a plantation near Atlanta.

It wasn't the full *Gone with the Wind* catastrophe, but it sure as hell stuck out like a pimple on a pumpkin in Credence.

As a kid, Wade'd been fascinated with the house. He used to pass it on his way to school, and it had seemed very elegant and grand. When it had come up for sale a decade ago, he'd snapped it up. Wade had thought his mother might appreciate some Southern influence, and it was a good solid building—big and roomy with amazing attention to detail in the interior.

"It's got character."

"I'm not living in a house that looks like a damn wedding cake," his father bitched. "I'd rather move to Florida."

"So." Wade shoved a hand through his hair, exasperated. "I'll buy you another one."

"Darlin.'" His mother's soft Southern drawl cut into the father/son verbal tussle. She squeezed her husband's hand. "That's so generous. We're very lucky to have such a generous son. But your dad and I are happy on the farm. Your great-grandfather bought the land just before the depression. Your father was born there, and I've been living there for over forty years. It's our home, and we're not fixin' to move."

And that was that. His father might think he wore the pants in their relationship, but he was the only one under that illusion. Her voice may have been quiet, but when Veronica Carter spoke—everyone listened. She even had all the old dudes on the town council totally snowed.

She smiled at Wade reassuringly. "I won't let your dad do anything he's not supposed to be doing. Neither will Wyatt."

His father scowled, none too happy to hear that. Wade wasn't particularly happy about it, either. His father was having a pacemaker put in, and his brother and sixty-four-year-old mother were going to be picking up the slack and bearing the brunt of his father's frustrations at being idle.

He suddenly felt like an outsider in his own family. He only had himself to blame for that, but it didn't make it any easier to face.

Maybe it was time he stepped up and took on some

parental responsibility instead of leaving everything to Wyatt? Being able to abdicate stuff *was* awesome, but he shouldn't abdicate *this*.

Not any longer.

The kernel of an idea formed and took root in his brain. By the time he headed back to his apartment two hours later, it was fully-fledged.

He and CC and that annoying fucking cursor were moving to Credence to write his damn memoir.

• • •

CC was finishing her fifth Red Bull of the day—she was going to kick the habit the second she moved to SoCal—when she heard Wade let himself into the apartment. She'd been juggling research into cardiac conditions requiring pacemakers and clearing his schedule for the next couple of days while she'd waited to hear from him.

She knew this unexpected development was going to throw a wrench into her resignation plans but, right now, that wasn't important. Wade needed her to do her job, and CC was in full organizational mode.

Wade looked good when he appeared in the doorway—better than when he'd hightailed it out of here a couple of hours ago. His father must have been okay. She'd been trying not to think about the older man, but it'd been hard. She'd met him on several occasions and had always liked him. He reminded her of Wade in a lot of ways.

Physically, there were many similarities. Both men were big and broad and had hands like meat cleavers.

Not to mention that loose-hipped swagger and the aura of restless energy that seemed to vibrate off both of them. But it was in the attitude as well. She'd seen Wade's masculine confidence in Cal, too.

CC opened her mouth to ask Wade about his father, but he didn't give her a chance.

"How long would it take you to pack for Credence?"

CC blinked, alarmed. Oh God. Was his father *that* sick? "Is it bad? Your father?"

"Oh no." He shook his head. "I spoke with the cardiologist. Barring unforeseen complications, he should be out in a couple of days."

"Okay." A surge of relief flushed through CC's veins. "So…you're going there for a few days? A week?"

Normally he went overnight and packed his own bag. If he wanted her to do it for him, she'd need to know how long he was planning on staying away.

"Three months. Thinking of going for the summer."

Three months? The longest Wade had ever spent in his hometown since she'd been with him had been two nights, and that usually had him mad as a cut snake on his return, mumbling about country drivers and the appalling lack of good coffee.

"The *summer*?" Her brain quickly rattled through the logistics of possibly having to cancel three months of speaking engagements and public appearances and board meetings. Or most of them, anyway. She glanced at his schedule on the screen of her desktop, running her eyes over the heavily booked months. "Like, *all* of it?"

"CC." He shoved his hands on his hips, the epitome of exaggerated patience. "My dad's having a pacemaker put in. He'll be out of action for six weeks, and I want to be there to help Wyatt around the farm. Neither of my parents is getting any younger, and I think this is a good opportunity to spend some time with them."

Obviously seeing his father in the hospital had shaken him, but…"Wade *The Catapult* Carter is going to help muck out pigsties?"

The man couldn't even buy his own condoms.

One winged eyebrow lifted. "I spent a lotta years mucking out pigsties, thank you very much. I'm pretty sure nothing's changed. Plus, I have a book to write. And I think going home to my roots might be good for the process. It'll sure as hell be a lot easier doing it in Credence, away from all the distractions in Denver."

CC snorted. She knew what *distraction* was code for. She clicked the schedule closed because her head hurt even thinking about reshuffling everything. "I hate to break this to you, Wade, but wherever you go, there'll be women."

"Nope." He shook his head. "Not Credence. It's had a declining female population for decades. Girls go off to college and don't come back. My mother tells me that very few women of marriageable and child-bearing years can be found in Credence these days, and the rest are snapped up pretty damn quick. Apparently, the school will be facing closure in a few years' time because of low enrollment. No babies being born in Credence."

CC didn't care how many women of marriageable age there might or might not be in Credence. She'd been around Wade long enough to know that wherever he was, women followed. He was like the pied freaking piper of women.

She'd lay money on a busload of Playboy Bunnies pulling into town the day after he arrived.

"So…let me get this straight." Folding her arms, she leaned back in her desk chair. "*You're* moving to a town with *no women*? For three whole months?"

"I *can* go without, CC."

"Yeah, but…when was the last time you *had* to?" *Mercy.* The man was delusional. He wasn't like other mere mortals—women threw themselves at him.

"You think I can't be celibate?"

CC laughed at the very suggestion. "I think a rabbit on Viagra has more of a chance at celibacy than you."

He looked like he was going to dispute it for a moment, then grimaced and clearly thought better of it. "Well, yeah…maybe. But it won't kill me."

"*I* know that." If lack of sex killed, she'd have been dead five years ago.

"It'll be better for my concentration."

"Absolutely." She didn't doubt it for a moment. Wade was not a multi-tasker. He did well when he concentrated on one thing to the exclusion of everything else. His football career being a case in point.

"Good. So…how soon can you get us ready to go?"

"Well…your schedule might take a while to wrangle, but—" Wait… CC blinked as her brain zeroed in on what he'd just said. *Us?* She sat forward abruptly. "What do you mean, *us*?"

He frowned at her as he wandered over to her desk, stopping right in front, all that swagger and confidence even more potent up close. "Well…*I'm* going to Credence for the summer, and you, as my PA who *always goes wherever I go*, will be coming with me."

CC gaped at him. *What?* Had he lost his mind? *No.* Absolutely not. No way, no how.

No sirrreeee.

She was leaving his employ and yes, she'd have to serve out her notice, but there was no way Wade was taking her any farther away from California than she already was. Even for a couple of weeks. Moving to Denver had been hard enough. As pretty as those mountains were, give her a beach any day.

Sure, she'd been to a lot of different places with him far from a beach. A day here, two days there. But *never* three months. And he'd *never* taken her to Credence. Something that wasn't about to change— not for three damn months *or* two lousy weeks.

He could take that to the bank.

"You don't need me there," CC hedged. She really didn't want to dump a resignation on him when his father was facing heart surgery. She'd wait until his dad had been discharged and was safely home in Credence.

He folded his arms. His forearms bunched in an annoyingly distracting way. "You're my PA, of course I need you there."

Not for much longer. Surely the man could figure out how to buy his own Nerds?

CC shook her head. "I can manage things perfectly well from here. Especially if I'm canceling your schedule for three months. There'll be nothing much for me to do, anyway. No Wade to wrangle, no schedule to juggle. Hell, there won't even be any florists to call with no women, right?"

He shot her a doleful look at her attempt at a joke. "You're my assistant." He said it like she was his indentured servant and, standing there as implacable and unmoving as the ridged outline of mountains behind him, he kinda made her feel that way.

Her resolve to keep quiet about her intention to resign took a serious hit.

"You go where I go. You've *always* gone where I've gone."

CC clenched her jaw. "Not for *three* months. To Credence."

"Jesus, CC, anybody would think I was asking you to come with me to Siberia. It's rural Colorado. It's two hours down the road."

She swung her head determinedly from side to side. "It's practically Nebraska."

"You're *from* Nebraska."

"My point exactly." She'd gotten out of Nebraska as soon as she'd been able. A broken home, thanks to a father who'd left for another woman and a vengeful, needy mother who hadn't coped with the betrayal, had amplified CC's dislike of cornfields and snow. Nebraska was heartbreak and bitterness and stifling dependence. California was warmth and sunshine and freedom.

"You have a problem with small towns?"

"Not as long as there's a beach."

"There's a lake."

"Doesn't count." Everybody knew that.

"CC." He sighed in that way he had that signaled his patience was wearing thin.

"Wade." CC stood, although, as usual, he still dwarfed her. It felt good to have a desk between them. "You don't *need* me there with you."

"I'm writing my memoir. You're supposed to be

helping me with that."

"I can do that from Denver." She could edit and proof and be his research assistant from anywhere. He could call her, text her, Snapchat, or message her as much as he liked—just as he did every other day of his life.

Hell, she could handle all that from *California*. The thought was slightly cheering.

"Okay." He took a breath, pinching the bridge of his nose momentarily before continuing. "Let me rephrase it. You work for me. I pay you very good money to go wherever the hell I want. And for the next three months, we're going to Credence. End of story."

He did. He did pay her very good money. She had close to a million in her bank account from almost six years with Wade and some astute investments. Almost enough to buy a place right on a beach somewhere in California. But that money had come with a certain price, and she'd known that.

She'd known she'd be at his beck and call twenty-four seven. That life would be fast-paced and busy, and there would be travel and all kinds of demands made on her time. He'd told her as much when he'd outlined his expectations almost six years ago.

If I call you at three in the morning for toothpaste, I expect you to say which brand. If I ask you to help me bury a body, I expect you to bring the shovels.

She'd understood. She'd sold her soul.

Something she'd been willing to take on the chin for six years. He'd wanted ten, but CC had done the math—she hadn't needed that long on the salary he'd been offering. She'd countered at six, been adamant that it was her limit, and they'd signed on the dotted line.

So, yeah, basically, she'd known she wouldn't have a life. She hadn't known she'd develop a serious Red Bull addiction, but she'd been fine with both.

Not anymore.

Her broker had given her the means to walk away. Annabel had been the last straw. And Credence was her line in the sand. The ocean was calling. She really didn't want to resign this way, but his arrogance wasn't leaving her much choice.

"Okay. Fine." Her decision crystallized inside her head, and CC knew it was the right thing to do. For her. She doubted Wade would be happy, but he was a grown-ass man—he'd get over it. Hopefully without the involvement of his lawyers.

He nodded. "Good."

To his credit, he didn't look smug. Wade never did smug. He just accepted that people would eventually bend to his will.

"I quit."

CHAPTER THREE

CC wasn't sure who was more stunned, Wade or herself. She'd tried hard not to land this in his lap with his dad in the hospital, but all of a sudden, a giant weight lifted from her shoulders.

Not working for Wade? What a novelty. It'd only been five and a half years but, in a lot of ways, it felt like she'd been working for him forever. That he'd always been in her life. This hulking force of nature creating all her weather—the good and the bad.

She could…put herself first. She could sleep in. Her phone number would be hers alone.

Hell, she could get laid.

"You've got six months left on your contract," he said through stiff lips.

CC wasn't surprised he knew this little fact. Wade was no dumb jock—he kept on top of his business stuff. Still, she fought the urge to swallow at the steel in his voice. Maybe he wouldn't just *get over it*. "I know."

She wasn't sure if it was the set to her jaw or the lack of emotion in her voice, but Wade was taking notice. There was a sudden alertness in his stance, the likes of which she'd only ever seen on the football field.

The truth was, if he wanted to sic his attack-dog lawyers on her, she'd lose. It was, after all, a very straightforward breach of contract. Not to mention how court costs could very well wipe out a chunk of her money.

But, deep down inside, in her heart of hearts, she didn't think Wade would stoop that low. She hoped, anyway…

Without missing a beat, Wade changed tack. "I'll give you a fifty thousand bonus at the end of the summer."

CC blinked. *Was he serious?* He could hire a secretary for a shitload less. Not that he had to worry about money. And frankly, prior to this morning, this would have been an offer she probably wouldn't have refused. But with one phone call, everything had changed, and CC couldn't deny the perverse kind of pleasure she was going to get from showing Wade that *she* was holding the trump card.

"I don't need your bonus, Wade. My broker called earlier. One of my investments just hit the jackpot. I have the money I need. I don't need *any* of yours."

The angle of his jaw ticked as he ground his teeth together, and strangely, CC didn't feel as triumphant as she'd imagined.

"Congratulations," he said in a way that gave her absolutely zero pleasure. "But there's still the small matter of your contract."

There was a hardness in his tone that sent a little chill skating up her spine. This was Wade the quarterback, not giving an inch. "You wouldn't sue me for breach of contract, Wade."

She was calling his bluff, because she had to believe that deep down Wade wasn't the vengeful type. He certainly hadn't been in the time she'd been with him. Sure, he was tough, he could play hardball, but he wasn't mean.

His jaw ticked harder. "Try me."

CC stared at him, his face carved from granite,

as hard and unforgiving as the Rockies behind him. This was all kinds of ridiculous. The man didn't *need* her. "You don't need me."

"Maybe not."

He was conceding her point, but it didn't lessen the impact. When it all boiled down to it, he *didn't* need her. She *wasn't* indispensable just because she knew what brand of breakfast cereal he ate and the number of his dentist. When she was gone, someone else would be doing her job.

Because God forbid Wade make his own dental appointments.

He'd developed a severe case of learned helplessness because she took care of every single detail of his life. Christ on a cracker, he was a thirty-eight-year-old *toddler*.

"But I want you."

CC blinked. She'd never heard those words from Wade before. She knew he didn't mean them like *that*, but he was watching her so intently, it felt like a possibility for a moment.

The thought made her early departure more desirable. Wade Carter was sex on a stick, but she'd never let herself go there because she'd absolutely no desire to be on the receiving end of one of WC's floral arrangements.

"Okay, fine…" Her continued silence was obviously getting on his nerves as he changed tack again. "What about if we meet each other halfway?"

She eyed him warily. "O…kay."

"Come to Credence with me, help me with the book, and I'll release you from your contract at the end of summer. That's three months early. No lawyers, no recriminations, no hard feelings."

CC regarded him for a long moment. It was a good compromise, she had to give him that, even though she knew Wade was playing on her sense of honor and duty. She should tell him to stick it, but his offer was too tempting. She may have been a pushover, but avoiding a messy end to what had been, despite the exasperating moments, a solid professional relationship was important. If nothing else, her reputation was at stake, and that was important in this industry. She wasn't rich enough that she wouldn't have to work again.

But seriously, the man should have taken the publisher up on their offer of help. "I told you, you should have gotten a ghost writer."

He ignored her grumbling. "Is that a yes?"

She narrowed her eyes. The man was impossible.

"Come on, CC. You know that's a good deal."

It was. On many levels. Wade got what he wanted—someone to hold his hand. And CC got what she wanted—light at the end of the tunnel without being sued.

Win. Win.

But why did it *have* to be Credence?

"So...how soon to clear my schedule and get things organized on this end?"

CC gritted her teeth. Typical that he could see her prevaricating and pounce. A person didn't waver in front of The Catapult. "I guess it'll take me...a few days."

Her brain had already turned to the task of rearranging Wade's life. Maybe she had Stockholm syndrome after all these years?

He nodded briskly, smart enough not to smirk. "Make it happen."

Make it happen. Like she had a magic freaking wand. No *thanks CC.* No *I really appreciate this, CC.* Wade Carter had gotten his way—again—and he was moving inexorably forward, as ever.

"Where will I be staying while I'm there?" She didn't think Credence had that many hotels or short-term rentals, so she needed to get on it.

"With me."

CC frowned. *With him?* She'd never lived with Wade. Her apartment, which he paid for, was about a ten-minute drive from his place, so she came and went each day when he was in Denver. When they traveled, it was hotel rooms. Him in his. Her in hers. Sure, there was usually an interconnected door in between, which he generally abused, but it wasn't the same as being under one roof.

"At…the farm?" With his parents and his brother. She tried not to think about all her SoCal sensibilities trapped on a rural Colorado hog farm.

"No, in town."

A flood of relief swept through her. "So you want me to book a hotel?"

"No, I have a place there I bought years ago for Mom and Dad. We'll stay there."

Her relief was instantly tempered. *We'll* stay there. "Yeah, but, you'll want me at the hotel?"

He laughed. "There's one Motel 6 about fifty miles out on the interstate. You're staying at my house."

A dark sense of foreboding dripped into her bloodstream. Escaping the overwhelming presence of Wade every day had been the one thing that had kept her in this job so long. He had the kind of personality—and good looks—a woman needed to take a break from.

For reasons of sanity. And to catch her breath.

"I don't mind the drive."

"CC." He pinched the bridge of his nose again, his patience clearly at an end.

He didn't have to say anything else. She could read his thoughts from the exasperation in his voice, and she took pity on him. He sounded tired, and she reminded herself that he was dealing with a lot today. Plus, he *was* letting her out of her contract early— she'd sleep in the damn henhouse if he wanted.

"Yeah, yeah." She waved her hand at him in surrender. "But don't think I'm cooking or cleaning for you. That is *not* part of my job description."

CC had hired a woman named Mrs. Duncan when she'd first started with Wade to take care of the apartment and cook for him when he was in Denver. She was worth her weight in gold. For any parties or events, she hired a reputable firm.

He smiled. "I'm sure you'll find someone local who can take care of that."

"And I'm not touching your dirty underwear, either."

He laughed this time. "I do know how to use a washing machine, you know?"

CC snorted. She sincerely doubted Wade had ever used such a contraption in his life. "You're going to give them to your mother, aren't you?"

He shrugged with that smile of his, revealing his even teeth and the deep brackets on either side of his mouth like long-ass dimples. "She's going to insist."

Oi... Did the man have no shame? "I'll make sure whoever I get is fine with all domestic chores."

Reaching for the can of Red Bull, CC brought it to her lips and drained it, wishing it had been spiked with vodka. She hoped they sold the energy drink in Credence, because she couldn't live under Wade's roof while going cold turkey on her favorite pick-me-up.

She might not be responsible for her actions, and being thrown in the local jail cell for strangling Credence's blue-eyed boy in his sleep would not be a smart move.

Wade paced around his office. He'd left CC frowning at her computer screen and clicking madly as she made the first of what he knew had to be many calls to rearrange his schedule. He'd told her he was going to try and get some words down. She clearly didn't believe him but had waved him away distractedly anyway. It soon became evident, however, that between worry about his father and the unsettling thought of his PA deciding she was going to *just randomly resign on him*, there was no way he could stare down that prick of a cursor.

He was *not* in the mood.

So he stared at the mountains instead as he paced. It was amazing how often just looking at their jagged outline gave him a sense of peace and, more importantly, clarity.

To say CC's announcement had been a bomb-shell was an insult to bombs. It had come completely out of the blue, and he'd been…shocked. Also, pretty fucking ticked. She couldn't *resign*, damn it. She had six more months on her contract, and…truth be told…he'd been hoping to convince her to stay for a couple more years.

He'd already had his lawyer draw up the contract and had planned to bring it up in a few months. Obviously, that was going to need to be rethought…

Yes, she'd made it perfectly clear when they'd negotiated her contract she'd be leaving after six years. He'd pushed for more but had ceded to her stipulation, and he'd been fine with it at the time. Six years had seemed an age back then, when his career had been riding an all-time high. But, looking into the past, through the crazy highs and lows of football and the even crazier years since, it had *flown* by.

And she'd been there for *all* of it. There'd been plenty of women in and out of his life, but she'd been his only constant. The woman knew everything about him. Well, almost everything. She sure as hell knew him better than most.

Better maybe than even his *mother.*

CC was an asset impossible to replace, and Wade didn't want to just let go without at least trying to convince her to stay a little longer. Sure, he knew there were parts of her job she didn't like, and she whined and bitched about them, but she *did* them. Because she was damn good at her job, and she liked her paycheck and the perks that came with being in his employ.

Exactly what he needed in a PA.

The problem was, when CC set her mind on something, she was fiercely focused. She didn't change her direction easily. And she had set her mind on moving to California. He knew in a factoid kind of way—she didn't really talk much about her past—that she'd come from a broken home, that her childhood had been unhappy, and that escape had been a beautiful, shiny dream to cling to during those years. And escape, for CC, was the ocean.

But maybe he could get his lawyer to negotiate a different kind of contract? One that gave them both what they wanted. That had her working in Denver part of the week but allowed her to work remotely from California for the other part. And he'd just…fly her back and forth.

Actually, he'd hate that—he'd gotten used to seeing her face every day and grown accustomed to the Red Bull in his fridge and the little v that formed between her eyebrows when she was pissed at him—but it was better than losing her, than not seeing her at all.

And her air miles would be through the roof.

He wasn't sure how it might work right now. All he knew for sure was Cecilia Morgan was the best damn PA in the country—he'd had plenty of doozies to make that judgment call—and he didn't want anyone else. He didn't want to have to break someone else in. He didn't want to get used to someone else's foibles. He liked that little v, damn it.

So…he had to try and persuade her to stay.

Easy. *Not.*

It was frustrating for him that ultimately, he had no say in the matter. Especially now that she was more set financially. Money wasn't a carrot he could use like it had been in the past, and he doubted CC would respond well to blatant attempts at persuasion.

But he'd bought himself three months. And there was no crying in football.

• • •

Four days later, CC stood on the sidewalk, blinking at the white facade of the replica Southern plantation–style house, complete with fluted Corinthian columns, towering portico, double gables, decorative iron railings, and red tiled roof. It wasn't as huge as a lot of the mansions of its ilk, in fact it fit perfectly on the neat town-sized block, but given the neighborhood, it was a little on the…ostentatious side. The kind of thing she expected to see in a two-dollar snow globe, not on the streets of rural Colorado.

"You're shitting me?"

He shook his head and gazed at the monstrosity like he'd laid every brick himself. "She's a beauty, isn't she?"

CC's normal objection to feminizing objects died on her lips. She was *something* all right. "Oh my God." She turned to him with raised brows. "You own Tara?" She'd had no idea Wade's house in Credence was pure *Gone With The Wind* antebellum.

He rolled his eyes. "Very funny."

It *was*, actually, and she laughed. Wade's taste was generally impeccable, but this was out there. "Well…" She fluttered her hand theatrically in front of her face and dredged up a Southern accent. "I do declare."

"Okay, it's a little over the top," he admitted. "But I've wanted this house since I was five years old."

CC blinked. She was glad little Wade had grown up to become a quarterback and not an architect. Still, it was sweet, in a childhood wish-fulfillment kinda way. And if anyone understood the power of a childhood dream, it was her. "Aww. Bless your heart."

Ignoring her amusement, he swung the wrought-iron gate open. "After you."

She shook her head and refused to budge. "We're not seriously going to live here in this…this…" There were no words.

"This classic, reproduction piece of fine antebellum architecture? Absolutely."

CC had been thinking mausoleum. White elephant for sure. She supposed they could go with his version. "But…what will we do when Atlanta burns?"

"Okay, wiseass." Wade picked up their bags to the sound of her laughter. "Get your butt in the house."

Laughing, she followed him in, shutting the gate behind her and mounting the wide sweep of stairs that led to the portico and the grand front entrance. She'd arranged for a housekeeper—Sally Tait, who'd been recommended by Wade's mom—to air things out and get the house ready for habitation.

She was about to tell him the door might be locked when he turned the handle and it opened. CC rolled her eyes. Things gave way far too easily for Wade Carter.

They entered and, once again, CC found herself stopped in her tracks. The inside was dimmer than the outside but just as startling, and she stared open-mouthed. A large reception area was dominated by a massive chandelier and a grand staircase. It curved to the upper gallery, around which, she assumed, were the bedrooms.

The parquetry floor beneath their feet was covered in elegant, if a little worn, rugs, and, against one wall, a grandfather clock chimed the hour. *Forget Tara.* This place was Downton freaking Abbey.

She half expected to see Lady Mary sweeping regally down the staircase.

"Did you say Sally was going to be here?"

CC nodded, desperately trying to correlate the Wade she knew with this house. His apartment in Denver was the ultimate in style and sophistication. Sleek lines. Glass and space. All the high-tech gadgetry.

This place seemed about as low-tech as was possible in the age of Netflix.

"She's probably out back sipping a mint julep," CC murmured.

He grimaced. "Are you going to do this for three months?"

Recovering a little from her culture shock, CC smiled. "Probably."

He could consider it his penance for insisting she reside with him while in Credence.

"I look forward to that, then," he said drily and picked up the cases again. "Do you know which rooms she's prepared for us?"

"Not sure." All she knew for certain was that her room was to be as far away from Wade's as possible.

The sound of a door opening somewhere interrupted them, and a woman whom CC presumed to be Sally bustled into the large open reception area. She was a pretty blonde in her early thirties and about twelve months pregnant, gauging by the size of her belly.

She smiled with apple pie and sunshine in her eyes, rushing forward to shake CC's hand like she wasn't about to give birth to a hippo. "Hi. You must be CC? I'm Sally."

CC shook hands, staring apprehensively at that swollen belly like an alien might erupt from it at any moment. Holy Moses, how many labor laws had she broken by employing someone who should rightly be sitting at home with her feet up awaiting the impending birth of her baby zoo animal?

What had Ronnie been thinking?

"Wade." Sally's voice lowered in delight, and her gaze changed to one of pleasure as she glanced at the big quarterback taking up space beside her. "How lovely to see you again. Your momma is thrilled to have you back home for a bit."

She lifted on tippy-toe and kissed his cheek.

"Hey Sal, how's Benji? How's business?"

"Same old, same old," Sally confirmed with a shrug. "Calls me every minute to check I'm not overdoin' things."

CC couldn't blame him. Sally's ankles looked like they were going to snap under the strain of her belly, even if she seemed fresh as a daisy.

"I keep telling him, I've got a whole month to go, but he's as antsy as a turkey at Thanksgiving."

A month? Was the woman giving birth to *twin* hippos?

"Well come on, I'll show you where I put you." She went to reach for one of the bags, and CC almost had a heart attack. But Wade very smoothly grabbed both handles.

"After you," he said.

Sally laughed and rolled her eyes at CC. "Men, huh?"

CC rolled her eyes back and laughed along to hide her alarm that Sally would even contemplate dragging a suitcase up those stairs in her condition. Hell, if she was that big she'd find a nice, comfy couch somewhere and just loll. Maybe insist her baby daddy fan her with palm fronds and feed her grapes.

Sally, who wasn't even panting a little after the climb to the second floor, turned right at the top, then traversed a short gallery before turning right again into a longer gallery bordered by an elegant wooden balustrade. She stopped about halfway along.

"I put you here, CC." She opened the door to reveal a large room with big windows, beautiful parquetry floors, and a massive four-poster bed. "I thought you might appreciate a little grandeur."

It was grand, all right. CC was starting to feel like Scarlett O'Hara.

"Thank you."

The doorbell rang. "Oh, that'll be the electrician. One of the outlets in the kitchen needs fixing, and he's had to come from the next county, so I better not keep him waiting. I've put you in the same room in the opposite gallery, Wade." Sally tipped her head in the direction of the room. "I'll just get that, if you don't need anything else for the moment?"

"No, all good, thanks, Sal."

Sally smiled and dashed off as if she wasn't lugging around a gigantic belly. "Wade," CC whispered as they watched Sally go. "I don't think she should be working.

She looks like she's about to pop."

He shrugged. "She's got another month. And mom said Benji's construction company's been struggling the past couple of years, so Sally's been taking on work where she can get it."

"I guess." Still, CC couldn't help but worry.

"Don't worry, Sally grew up on a corn farm, she's not afraid of a little hard work. They breed 'em tough out here."

They bred them huge, too, by the looks of things.

"Okay." He returned his attention to her. "Unpack, freshen up, then meet me downstairs. I'll take you out to the farm and show you around the town."

"You go on ahead. I want to get your computer set up and all the research laid out. I can have a look around tomorrow while you're working on the book."

She wanted to get to know Credence on her own terms, not as some extension of Wade, and they'd brought two cars for a reason.

He hesitated. "The town can be a little...hinky with strangers."

"I'll win them over with my sparkling personality."

He snorted. "Do me a favor, CC, and humor me."

"You should know by now I'm not so good at that."

He grinned, unperturbed by her resistance. "Frankly, my dear, I don't give a damn."

Yeah. She deserved that.

CC listened to the running commentary from Wade with half an ear as he drove slowly along the main street. Country music played on the radio, but all she could hear was the picking of banjo strings. He pointed out the library and the police station and a bar called The Lumberjack, which an old school friend ran. There was a gas station and the municipal offices of the local council, where his mother went to her meetings.

It wasn't at all like she'd imagined it would be.

The street was wide, lined with storefronts on either side, and cars had parked angled to the curb. The storefronts had all been painted different colors, but most of them were faded and peeling, and a lot of shops were empty, some even boarded up. The fronts were flush with the sidewalk, no fancy boardwalk with overhanging eaves, which somehow made it seem even more stark and bare.

There were trees every twenty feet or so, providing some shade for cars, but even they seemed scraggy and disinterested in life.

It was the middle of the day on a weekday, and there was barely any traffic. In fact, CC half expected to see tumbleweeds. Credence wasn't a town bustling with energy.

It looked like a town in decline.

The diner—apparently run by an old woman named Annie since Jesus was a baby—was the only business that appeared to be doing okay. CC could see people sitting inside, and the street parking outside was popular.

"And that's where I had my first kiss."

CC tuned back in and focused on where Wade was pointing. It was the football field, a lush bright green amidst the faded wooden bleachers and the peeling goalposts.

"Right there under those bleachers." He smiled and sighed. "Kathy Williams. I became a man that day."

"It was that good, huh?"

He laughed. "I suspect it was terrible at first."

He shook his head, and a tiny little hitch near CC's heart snuck up and surprised the hell out of her. Her gaze was drawn to his profile, to the tilt of his lips. Usually those lips just exasperated the hell out of her, articulating his ridiculous demands, but, she had to admit, he had a great mouth. Kinda made a girl wonder what other demands lips like those could make.

Not that she'd *ever* wondered. Nor was she about to start. Crushing on her emotionally unavailable boss would be dumb. Especially when she was only a few months away from never having to see him again.

"I fumbled it badly, went like a bull at a gate. She pulled away and said, 'softly, Wade,' and then…"

It was hard to believe Wade had ever fumbled anything. His had been the safest hands in the NFL. And he'd obviously improved beyond kissing, if that thing he did with his tongue was as good as Annabel had said.

"Well…" He smiled, obviously still caught up in the memory. "Let's just say she was patient, and I'm a fast learner."

"How old were you?"

"I was fifteen. She was seventeen. The head cheerleader."

CC rolled her eyes. "How very *Riverdale* of you."

"What about you? Where was your first kiss? How old were you?"

She cocked an eyebrow. "Really?"

This is why she shouldn't have come to Credence. He never would have asked her this in Denver. He'd be too busy actually kissing women there to be worried about her game.

"Oh, come on, what? Sweet thirty-two and never been kissed?" he teased. "Give me something, CC."

CC's stomach tightened. She'd given him her life for the past five and something years—wasn't that enough? But he was looking at her with those flirty blue eyes. She was immune to them, but she liked that he tried.

"On my school trip to California. A guy in my learn-to-surf class. He was from Ohio. I was thirteen, he was fifteen. He kissed me under the pier."

It was CC's turn to smile. She remembered everything about that day, that moment. The breeze lifting her hair, the way the sun shone on the beads of water on his chest, the sand between her toes, the slap of the water against the wooden pylons of the pier.

He'd been wearing one of those wet suits, which he'd peeled off to his waist, and, even at fifteen, he had this fascinating trail of hair that led down from his belly button. Wade had one of those, too. She'd seen it a little more than was good for her sanity.

Unfortunately for her, professional athletes had no issues with nudity.

"How was it?"

Pulling back from the memory, she glanced at him. "*I* was spectacular."

He grinned. "Never doubted it."

A tightening across her middle made CC squirm in the seat a little. "So was he."

Wade grabbed his chest. "Go easy. Not all fifteen-year-old boys are made equal."

"No, Danny was exceptional."

"Danny?" His deep laughter filled the cabin until he was slapping his knee he was laughing so hard. Yeah…CC knew where this was going.

"Was his last name Zuko?"

She guessed she deserved that for the *Riverdale* crack, but still. "You can be a real asshole sometimes, you know that, right?"

He broke out into a rendition of "Tell me more, tell me more," and despite her dislike of country music, she pumped up the radio volume to drown him, and *visions of him* in a half-pulled-down wetsuit, out.

CHAPTER FOUR

CC had always been curious about the farm where Wade had grown up. It was hard to reconcile the wealthy jock with his humble Midwestern farm boy beginnings. Yeah, yeah, she knew, Colorado was *not* technically part of the Midwest. But hell, they were so close to Nebraska and Kansas right now, she could spit and it'd probably land in both states.

The landscape swung from flat to gently undulating. From pastures to crops to miles of what looked like open grassland. Animals and agricultural machinery dotted fields. Grain silos rose from the earth. Everything seemed yellow, from the sun glinting off barn roofs to the color of the fields.

Unlike the Tara nightmare she was calling home for the next three months, the Carter family's farmhouse *was* what CC had imagined. Low-set, ranch style, stone walls, covered porch, and a chimney. It might have been a warm eighty today, but she bet it'd be bitterly cold here in the winter.

No sooner had they pulled up under a large willow tree than Ronnie was rushing out to greet him. Wade's mother was deceptively agile. She may be in her sixties, but she was strong and fit and she hugged with her entire body.

"I can't believe we've got him for three whole months, Cecilia," she said as she squeezed CC extra tight. Ronnie always called her by her full name, and CC kinda liked it. Reminded her of her own mom.

"Whatever you said to him, I owe you one."

"I can't claim responsibility for that, Ronnie. It was all Wade."

"And here I thought you were the brains behind the operation," she teased.

"Hey," Wade protested in a voice that didn't sound particularly offended as he pulled his mother in for a hug. "How's Dad?"

Ronnie's smile seemed a little strained as she shooed away his worries with a flick of her hand like they were annoying little gnats. "You know Cal. Wanting to do more than he can. Complaining about it, generally."

"That sounds about right."

"It's taken a lot out of him though, you know? He won't admit it, but he didn't object to sitting down with the runts and giving them their bottles."

CC's ears pricked up. "You have piglets in there?"

Wade laughed. "There's always a piglet in there."

"Come on," Ronnie said. "Let's go introduce you."

CC stepped inside eagerly. She'd always liked Wade's parents, so it wasn't any hardship to spend some time with them. Baby animals were a bonus. When she got her place at the beach, she was getting a dog.

The front door opened into a large living room area dominated by a massive stone fireplace and filled with plump, cozy couches. The entire house smelled like sugar and vanilla.

"Mmm." Wade sniffed the air. "I smell chocolate chip cookies?" He smiled at his mother. "You baked me some, didn't you?"

"Are they or are they not your favorite?"

"They are."

"Then of course I baked them."

"I'm going to get fat," he said, kissing her cheek.

CC snorted. *Right.* Like Wade had to watch his waistline. She'd seen the man eat three family-sized pizzas without breaking a sweat or a single fat cell sticking to his ass.

"Why don't y'all come on through?" Ronnie ushered them into a large kitchen with a flagstone floor, pots hanging from a rack above the sink, and old-fashioned AGA stove. Windows overlooked the fields in one direction and the barn in the other, and a big wooden table took up all the space in the center of the room. Racks of cooling cookies sat on one end.

It was exactly what CC imagined the perfect ranch house kitchen would look like, right down to Kenny Rogers singing "The Gambler" from a battered-looking radio set back on the countertop.

"Hey, Dad."

"Wade! CC!"

Cal, sitting at the opposite end to the cookies, stood. He was nursing a small, pink piglet wrapped up in some kind of fabric covered with sunflowers. It grunted a little in protest but did not relinquish the teat of the bottle, a milk moustache formed all around the eager suckling snout.

"Oh my God." CC thought she might *die* from all the cuteness. "I don't think I've seen anything this cute since that teacup pig video on YouTube a couple of years ago."

"Plenty more where they came from." He tipped his chin at the bottles lined up on the counter near the fridge. "Grab one, then pull up a chair. Wade, get this woman a piglet, would you?"

"Putting me to work already," Wade grumbled good-naturedly.

He walked into the mudroom as CC swiped up a bottle and sat next to Cal. Wade returned with a squirming piglet, hushing it as it fussed and carried on. "It's okay," he crooned to it, lifting it to rub his cheek against its cheek. *Do piglets have cheeks?* "Dinner's coming."

CC blinked at the picture. She was used to Wade's good looks. Hell, after witnessing the swinging door of his love life, she was *immune* to them. Or so she'd thought. Watching him croon and calm a fussing piglet was about the damn sexiest thing she'd ever seen. It was like…farm porn.

Farmer porn.

Wait. Was there such a *thing* as farmer porn?

He wrapped the baby pig in something that looked like a shawl, trussing it so its flailing trotters were tucked in tight, and passed it down to CC like it was an *actual* newborn. She took the squirming package awkwardly.

"Get that bottle in fast," Cal said. "It'll quit fussing real quick."

Cal was right—as soon as the teat brushed the piglet's mouth, it latched on and sucked fiercely, all the squirm gone.

"There you are, now." CC smiled down at the precious little pink thing in her arms, her heart swelling. "It's okay. I got you."

"You're a natural, darlin'," Ronnie said.

CC beamed at her. She could see herself coming out here a few times a week just to help out with the feeding. "You're a gorgeous one, aren't you?" CC smiled and nodded at the completely disinterested pig. "Oh yes, you are. I'm going to call you Wilbur."

Wade laughed, so did Cal, and CC glared at them.

"What? It might be a little clichéd, but this face is definitely a Wilbur."

They laughed harder. It was Ronnie who explained the joke. "That little one is a girl."

Miffed at her rookie error, CC decided to stick to her guns. She tended to do that. A girl growing up with five brothers knew how to stand and fight in her corner when she had her back pushed against the wall. "Well, I don't care. Why can't Wilbur be a girl's name, too?"

Ronnie nodded. "Don't you listen to them. You can call the animal whatever you want."

CC blasted a superior look in Wade's direction. He was eating cookies, and crumbs had stuck to his lips. The sudden urge to lick those crumbs off those lips hit her out of the blue. Who knew farmer porn got more interesting with the addition of cookie crumbs? She knew they made ice cream better, but…

Oh, for crying out loud—what in hell was *with* her today?

Was she delirious? Or did every woman who entered the Credence town limits suddenly develop a thing for the town's number one son? Like he needed any more adoration.

Welcome to Credence, Colorado, population 2,134. Birthplace of Wade "The Catapult" Carter.

That's what the welcome sign had said on the way in today. She'd thought it kinda funny and had given him some shit about it, but maybe it had been some kind of portent? A warning to poor, unsuspecting females.

Beware, all ye who enter here, estrogen hazard ahead.

"We don't name them, anyway," Wade said, breaking into her analysis.

Cal nodded. "That's right, darlin'. Mighty hard to eat something that's going to end up in burgers and sausages when it has a name."

CC gasped, horrified, looking down into Wilburta's— she'd already feminized the name, despite her earlier insistence—pretty face. "What, *all* of them? Don't you..." She glanced between Wade and his father. "Keep some? Like for...kids' parties and...petting zoos and stuff?"

Wade laughed again. "Hell no. But dibs on suggesting it to Wyatt."

His mother shot him a look. "Hush your mouth, both of you. It wouldn't be the first one we've kept as a pet, don't suppose it'll be the last. I seem to remember you at six years old crying your eyes out over that cute little runt with the gimpy leg, Marigold."

"I was *six*, Mom." He reached for another cookie.

"Cried every night for a week, he did," Ronnie said, turning to CC, ignoring her son completely. "It was the *sweetest* thing."

Wade rolled his eyes, but CC's heart gave a funny wobble. Her boss had always been this big uber-alpha jock, and everyone knew there was no crying in football. A lot of women got off on that. But seeing him in his parents' kitchen eating cookies and cuddling piglets, hearing stories about a broken-hearted little boy, was *her* kind of catnip.

And then there were the cookie crumbs.

Just then, a dog bounded into the house—not much older than a puppy, really—tongue lolling, mischief in its eyes. It stumbled and fell over a boot and landed in a potted plant before rolling off and skidding to a halt at CC's feet, tail swishing against the flagstones, an adoring gaze melting her heart. He looked like some kind of Border collie, his black-and-white face dominated by unexpectedly blue eyes.

Eyes that reminded her of Wade.

CC's heart flopped over in her chest as she stroked his soft head with her spare hand. "Well hello there, gorgeous, look at you."

Wade shook his head at CC. "She's like some kind of magnet. Shut the door, we'll have little woodland animals in here next."

CC ignored him as Cal sighed at the dog. "That's George. All feet and energy. Dumb as a box of nails."

George angled his head from side to side, his freaky blue eyes curious. "I'm sure that's not true," CC told the dog.

"He gets distracted by butterflies. *Butterflies*."

Wade chuckled. "He's from Lou Lou's last litter?"

"Yes," Ronnie confirmed. "We've managed to sell all the others, but…"

"You can't give this dog away," Cal finished. "Nor can you train the blasted thing, either."

"Oh, now, I don't believe that," CC murmured, rubbing the soft tips of the dog's ears before she grabbed his face and smooshed it a little. "You're just a curious George, aren't you, boy? And butterflies are very pretty, who can blame you?"

"Oh sweet Jesus." Wade shook his head. "Never

marry a farmer, CC."

She opened her mouth to tell him she didn't think there were too many farmers in Malibu or Redondo or San Clemente, but his mother cut in.

"There'll be no cussing or taking the Lord's name in vain in this house, thank you Wade William Rhett Carter."

Rhett?

CC glanced away from the dog and laughed. "*That* explains the whole *Gone with the Wind* house."

Cal shook his head. "Nothing but vanity explains that monstrosity."

CC laughed some more. Undeterred by the criticism, Wade picked up a handful of cookies and stood. "Think I'll catch up with the bro."

His mother nodded. "You do that. I'll take Cecilia and show her all your trophies."

Wade groaned. "Mom, no, I'm sure—" He stopped abruptly when she laughed, and he realized she was only goading him. He bugged his eyes. "You know people stop me on the street and ask for my autograph, right?"

He said it with feigned exasperation and complete self-deprecation, mischief lighting his features.

"Yes, darlin'." His mother nodded. "Don't forget to take a pitchfork from the barn. Wyatt's spreading new hay."

CC liked that Wade's family didn't fawn over him like so many other people did when they came in his sphere. She'd seen too many sycophants kissing his ass in her years by his side. Sure, his parents were obviously proud, but they were obviously just as proud of Wyatt, even if he didn't have his name on the welcome sign.

"Yes, ma'am." He whistled to the dog. "C'mon, George."

George slid to his belly and practically lay on top of CC's feet. She swooned a little, but she was pretty sure she heard another cuss word being muttered under Cal's breath.

"You might as well just go on, son. I think George just found him another butterfly."

Wade snorted, but CC preened. She'd never been called a butterfly before, nor had the unwavering attention of a male as cute as George. She'd take it.

• • •

Wade breathed in deep as he flew down the farm track on the ATV, the wind in his hair. The sun glinted off the roofs of the convex hog shelters. The pungent smell of animals mixed with the earthy aromas of grass and hay, filling his nostrils. There was something about coming home to the farm that grabbed at his gut. Something visceral.

Something encoded into his DNA.

He'd had a great career and a great life away from Credence. And being back in a small town after the luxuries of life in the city always drove him batshit crazy. Life moved too slowly, and everyone drove like they were ninety, and a man couldn't get a decent cup of coffee for love or money. Not even at Annie's, who'd been serving drip-filter coffee from the same pot for four decades.

But, despite all that, Credence was in his genes.

He spotted his brother three fields over and

waved when Wyatt lifted his head as the noise of the motor reached him. Wade put on a spurt of speed and pulled into a field where a few dozen Chester Whites and Berkshires, including several litters of piglets, all rooted around the green grass, foraging for goodies.

Several more were getting relief from the warm day by wallowing in some muddy water that had pooled in a depression in the ground.

"Hey, man." Wade dismounted from the ATV as his brother took his thick gloves off, and they exchanged the half handshake, half hug thing they did.

Wyatt may have been his older brother, but they were only fifteen months apart and had always been close. Sure, they'd squabbled growing up and been fiercely competitive, but they'd have fought to the death for each other, too. Wade just plain *admired* his brother. Those big Carter hands could turn to anything broken and fix it. A fence, an irrigator, an engine. It was incredible.

He'd never met anyone who could come up with a solution to a problem with whatever materials were at hand like Wyatt. His brother could have been a mechanic or an engineer. Hell, he could have played ball—his arm was almost as good as Wade's. But he'd lacked those kinds of ambitions. Wyatt had only ever wanted to be a farmer. To work the land their great-grandfather had bought all those years ago.

"I'm surprised your multi-million dollar ass can take such a bumpy ride."

"Fuck you." Wyatt grinned, and Wade grinned back. "You still seeing that woman from Burlington?"

"Nah." Wyatt shook his head. "We only went out the once."

"Man. You suck even more than I do at dating."

"Not a lot of opportunity out this way." Wyatt feigned interest in his boots. "No practice. I never know what to say. Besides, I leave the smooth up to you."

Wade laughed. "Yeah, yeah." A large sow wandered nearby, grunting as she rooted, a dozen or so piglets meandering behind her. "The place is looking sweet, bro."

"Yeah." Wyatt looked around the field as if trying to see it through different eyes. "Lotta happy hogs."

"It's a credit to you."

Wyatt shrugged it off. "I'm not doing it on my own, here. Dad works just as hard."

"Yeah, I know. But you're the one who talked him into going free-range all those years ago when the industry shift was toward large-scale confinement farming. You set up the partnerships with specialty brands to establish markets and distribution. You modernized the process every step of the way."

Wyatt shook his head. "Couldn't have done it without your backing, Wade."

"That's just money," Wade dismissed. "It's what you do with it that counts. Plenty of farms have gone under despite having backing behind them."

It was true. Wyatt and his father had busted their asses to keep the farm a going concern. It was hard physical labor. Long hours. Lots of interrupted sleep. And what had Wade been doing?

Throwing a ball two nights a week.

"Well, look at us," Wyatt said, smiling as he exaggerated his accent. "Shall we call this the first meeting of the Carter brothers fan club? Could you rustle us up some cheerleaders?"

Wade laughed. "I know one or two."

"You planning on using that dang thing?" Waytt tipped his chin at the pitchfork secured to the back of the quad. "Or you gone soft and forgotten how?"

Wade slapped his abs. He may have been retired for three years, but he kept himself in shape. "I helped you with the hay at Christmas, asshole."

"Just checking. Wouldn't want you to break a nail or anything."

He ignored his brother as he reached for the pitchfork. This was what they did, they talked smack to each other. It wasn't that different from the locker room. Except Wyatt knew really personal stuff about him. But that was okay. He had a ton of shit on his brother, too.

Wade hoisted the pitchfork over his shoulder, tines in the air, as they walked to where Wyatt had been working when Wade had interrupted. "Mom says Dad's testy."

Wyatt snorted. "That's being polite. I doubt I'll be able to hold him off for six weeks."

"Reckon you'll be lucky to get two."

"Probably."

"You don't think he should…retire?"

Wyatt laughed. "Of course he should. It's not like the man's got anything to prove. But you and I both know he won't."

"Yeah." Wade sighed. The whole pacemaker thing had shaken him. For the first time in his life, Wade could see his father was getting older.

"I've been thinking, though…"

Wade glanced at his brother. The last time he'd used those words, he decided to introduce electronic stock control. "That sounds expensive," Wade said and laughed.

"Oh yeah, it won't be cheap. Take a while to start seeing a profit, too."

"Okay…go on." It wasn't like money was a problem.

"Been thinking for a while how cool it'd be to produce our own gourmet pork products. Small-scale, heritage breeds, boutique market. Salami and prosciutto, stuff like that for artisan restaurants and farmers markets. Dad could take the reins. Big project to keep him occupied for a good five or so years while I keep on with the more physically demanding side of the farm."

Wade whistled. He was impressed. His brother never stopped thinking of ways to expand and grow.

"This just spitballing, or have you started some planning?"

"I've done a lot of preliminary stuff. A cost analysis. A business plan. Even before Dad's heart thing. But it makes even more sense now. I just wanted to be sure it was the right thing for us, for the farm and the family, that I wasn't biting off more than I can chew."

"I think you have great instincts." Wade was a big believer in instincts. He'd relied on his on the field, just like he knew his brother relied on his for all things farm-related. "If anyone can make a go of it, you can."

"Yeah." Wyatt nodded as they stopped in front of three massive round bales of hay.

Wade grounded the tines of the pitchfork into the soft earth and pulled out the pair of gloves he'd shoved into his back pocket before he'd jumped on the ATV in the barn. "Where are you up to?"

"I'm on this row."

Wade followed the direction of his brother's pointed finger as he pulled on the gloves. He'd learned a long time ago that gloves were essential for this kind of work, and blisters sucked. "Cool." He pulled the pitchfork out of the dirt. "What's on the agenda for tomorrow?"

"The usual morning routine, then some maintenance."

"Awesome." Wade stabbed the hay bale with the pitchfork. "Count me in."

Wyatt was quiet, and Wade looked over his shoulder as he loosened a forkful of hay. His brother was regarding him with serious eyes. "Look, I appreciate it and all, but I *can* do it myself, dude. Ain't you got a dang book to write?"

"Yeah. I know you can." Wade nodded. "And yes, I do have a book to write. But…I want to help."

Wyatt's gaze narrowed. "Trouble?"

"Nah." He'd left his distractions behind him in Denver. "The physical labor will do me good. Might help shake a few ideas loose, too, you know. Writing a book isn't as easy as it looks."

"That's what I always say."

Wade laughed. "Are we spreading hay or not?"

Wyatt grinned as he drove his pitchfork into the haystack. "Race ya."

The Carter boys—competitive as ever.

CHAPTER FIVE

They were just about done—Wyatt was whooping his ass—when Wade heard the engine in the distance. It was going really slowly, so he figured it was probably CC. He doubted she'd ever driven anything but that butt-ugly Prius hybrid her entire life.

A new car had been part of her employment package, but she'd stubbornly refused to take the zippy Jeep he'd bought her, citing her concerns about pollution and the ozone layer. Yeah, CC might have been Nebraskan born and bred, but she was a California chick, right down to her toes.

Although she had looked rather good at the big old wooden table earlier. He smiled at the image of CC bottle-feeding a piglet with a crazy dog flopped over her feet. She might not have been impressed with his house in town, but she'd been right at home in his mother's kitchen.

His ribs suddenly felt tight. He should have brought her to Credence earlier. Maybe seeing him in his home environment would have shown her a different side to him, made it harder for her to just suddenly decide she was going to leave.

He wiped the sweat off his brow with his forearm as the engine noise drew closer. She'd be here soon, but he probably still had time to finish spreading the hay in this shelter if he put his back into it. He leaned over the pitchfork and got to work, grateful for it being cooler in here out of the sun.

It didn't take long to work up a sweat in the summer. Hell, he'd taken his shirt off after the first fifteen minutes, which had earned a laugh and a shake of the head from Wyatt, who still looked cool as a cucumber.

Wade wasn't farm-ready these days at all, but he fully intended to correct that, keeping strong and fit with good, hard, manual labor rather than an elliptical or pounding the streets of Denver.

The engine cut out, and Wade stopped what he was doing to listen to the low chatter of his father and CC as he gave her the usual farm tour spiel. Mom must have caved and let him out of the house.

Wade wasn't paying any attention to the sow snuffling around the hay as he strained his ears to listen, stepping forward to get a little closer. He didn't know the animal was right there until he tripped over it and toppled. The hog squealed in protest as it scooted away, clearing the shelter remarkably quickly for an ungainly two-hundred-and-twenty-pound beast. But it was too late for the two-hundred-and-twenty-pound man.

Wade fell square on his ass.

It was a soft enough landing with the hay cushioning his fall, despite the tines of the pitchfork being a little too close to his junk for comfort. Jesus Christ, was everything on the farm determined to upstage him today?

"Wade, that you?"

"Yeah, Dad." Wade sprang to his feet. Hay clung to his hair and his jeans and the film of sweat on his chest. It poked and scratched as he brushed it off.

CC and his father appeared at the entrance. His

father took one look at Wade and said, "Hog knocked you on your ass, didn't it?"

"Well, to be fair, I kinda tripped over it."

His father laughed. Actually he *guffawed*, because that was the way he laughed, the way he'd always laughed. Big and wide, with his whole body, holding his ribs and slapping his thigh.

"Hey, Wyatt," he called. "Your brother landed on his ass."

Wyatt's hoot of laughter rang around the field.

"I'm okay, thank you for being so concerned," Wade muttered, wiping his hands on the butt of his jeans as he headed toward them.

CC was staring at him like she'd never seen him before. She'd certainly never seen *this* version of him before. In fact, he doubted whether she'd ever seen him this disheveled. Sure, he'd been put on his ass on the *field,* plenty, but that had been a badge of honor.

Today he'd been bested by his brother and a goddamn hog.

Wyatt joined them as Wade strode out into the sunshine. His father was practically crying now he was laughing so hard.

"Are there some drugs left in his system, do you think?" Wade asked his brother.

Wyatt shrugged. "Hey, I'm still laughing on the inside."

"Thanks, dude." He turned to his father, who was turning red in the face. "Didn't they say you shouldn't exert yourself for six weeks?"

It only made his father laugh harder.

"Hi." CC stopped looking weird, turned to Wyatt, and smiled as she extended her hand. "I'm CC, your brother's PA. We've never met."

She had a nice smile. It went all the way to her eyes. The kind of smile that told a person they had her full attention. Wyatt, who'd always gotten kinda quiet around women, sure seemed dazzled by it. "Hey," he said, shaking her hand and releasing it quickly. "Pleased to meet you."

It was mumbled, though, coming out more like *pleastameetya.*

"That's a lot of hogs you got here," she said, making polite conversation while his father pulled himself together.

"Yes, ma'am."

"Oh please." She waved his formal address away. "CC's fine."

Wyatt shifted from one foot to the other, glancing at Wade before he said, "Yes, ma'am."

CC laughed. "Okay, we'll work on it." She filled her lungs with air, her nose sniffing. "I thought it'd smell more than this."

"Intensive hog farms stink to high heaven," Wyatt confirmed, clearly in his comfort zone now. "Free-range farms less so."

His father finally quit guffawing and cleared his throat. Wade shot him a stern look. "If you think you have your shit under control, why don't you and Wyatt finish off the tour? I've got four more shelters."

Cal nodded, pressing his lips together, obviously trying to suppress his smile.

"I can do them," Wyatt said. "You go with Dad and…CC."

Wade got the impression Wyatt was about to say

and the girl for a moment. It'd been a long time since he'd seen Wyatt around a woman. He hadn't realized they still made his brother so nervous.

"Nope. I'm doing my fair share, and I'm not stopping till they're done." Wade was not going to let this fairly simple, bread-and-butter farm chore get the better of him.

"Well you heard the man, CC. Come on over here to the wallow, and we'll see if we can't find you some more piglets to gush over while we're at it."

CC beamed at Cal. "That would be awesome."

Wade was relieved when they walked away, his father forging on with CC, Wyatt dragging a little behind. At least he'd have some peace now.

His father looked over his shoulder and grinned like he wasn't a man approaching seventy with a bum ticker. "Mind your step, son."

Wade laughed and shook his head. "Bite me."

• • •

Wyatt Carter had never been envious of his younger brother. Wade had excelled at what he loved and had worked hard to reach the dizzying heights of the NFL. He deserved all the success that came with it. It was weird having a celebrity brother, but none of that hoopla had ever interested Wyatt. *He* was doing what *he* loved, and the rest was bunkum.

But he envied Wade today.

Watching his brother and CC as they all ate lunch around the kitchen table stirred a bunch of feelings he'd tried mighty hard not to think about over the years.

They'd been back from the lower fields for an hour, but they'd only just started lunch because CC wouldn't relinquish Wilburta. His mother had insisted they wouldn't be eating with a hog at the table, not even if every spider on the farm started weaving webs singing the animal's praises, so the animal was reluctantly returned to its makeshift home in the mudroom.

CC was asking their father about the birthing practices of hogs, and Wyatt liked that she seemed genuinely interested in the answers. He glanced at Wade. His brother hadn't brought a woman home since Jasmine—over thirteen years ago. For what it was worth now, Wyatt had liked Jasmine, but she'd been overpoweringly pretty, and his tongue had tied into a dozen knots every time she'd spoken to him.

He was certain Jasmine had thought he had some kind of condition. Like a stutter. Or a head injury. More often than not, Wyatt felt like he had both. His track record with women was such that it was just easier not to say anything than blush and stammer his way through a conversation.

He must have been hiding behind the barn door when the smooth-talking gene was handed out, and God had given both their shares to Wade instead.

CC wasn't as stunningly pretty as Jasmine, which, in theory, should have made it easier for Wyatt, but, in practice, not so much. Nearly forty years on this earth and he still felt like a big ol' country bumpkin whenever a woman looked at him.

"Don't you think so, Wyatt?

Wyatt blinked, his heart practically stopping in his chest as he realized that not only was CC talking to him, but everyone was looking at him expectantly. His vocal chords went into spasm just as CC reached for the nearby ketchup bottle which, thankfully, gave his frantic brain some seconds to catch up.

"Oh…ah." He cleared his throat and prayed like hell he didn't look as clueless as he felt. Wyatt flicked his gaze to Wade, who was sitting beside CC. Wade cocked an eyebrow, a slow grin spreading across his dumb face.

So much for brotherly solidarity.

Wyatt returned his gaze to CC. "Y…yes ma'am," he said, taking a guess at the right response, ignoring Wade's low, amused chuckle.

CC smiled. "Wyatt, I'm going to be hanging around here with Wilburta a lot."

She grimaced a little as she twisted the ketchup top, which was obviously not playing ball. Wyatt half wished he could disappear into the ketchup as her eyes fixed on his face. Without turning to look at Wade, she passed him the bottle, which he took automatically, like a surgeon accepting an instrument.

"You should just call me CC."

The very thought gave Wyatt an itch up his spine. He was a formal kind of guy. Between his Southern momma's upbringing and his chronic shyness around women, it was hard to be anything but formal.

"Nah," Wade said as he passed the opened bottle back to CC, who took it as automatically as Wade had accepted it. He winked at Wyatt. "Our momma raised us right, didn't she, bro?"

CC drowned his mom's hand-cut fries in ketchup. Wade snatched one and popped it into his mouth. "Hey," she protested, slapping at his hand as he came back for another. "You already had a mountain."

"But they're my favorites," Wade complained.

"There's plenty more, Wade," his mother said.

"Nah, they taste better off CC's plate."

CC rolled her eyes and pushed the plate between them so Wade could share her fries before asking his mother about her recipe.

Wyatt dropped his gaze back to his plate, a hot spike of envy lancing him clear through the middle. He knew his brother and CC weren't in a relationship, despite what it seemed right now, but he'd like just a bit of whatever the hell it was they *did* have, because there was a familiarity between them that Wyatt yearned to have with a woman.

As a younger man, he'd dreamed about how his life would pan out. By now, he'd have thought he'd be married with a couple of little ankle biters riding around on the back of his ATV, bringing up another generation on this land he loved so much.

But his chronic, crippling shyness around women had made that little more than a fantasy. And the fact that there weren't too many eligible women around these parts, anyway, had compounded his isolation.

Depressingly, he didn't see it changing any time soon. It was something he'd been too busy to dwell on over the years, but watching Wade and CC together had brought it into sharp focus.

He was lonely, he realized. So damn *lonely*.

• • •

CC hadn't been too keen on hitting The Lumberjack

tonight, although apparently everyone around these parts called the saloon Jack's. Again, she wanted to be a separate entity to Wade, and that wasn't going to happen when she walked into the bar with the town's number one son.

But mostly, she was still recovering from seeing Wade stripped to his jeans, hay in his hair and sticking to his chest. Her appreciation for farmer porn trebled on the spot this afternoon, and she'd been able to think of little else.

Sure, she'd seen Wade in various forms of undress before—shirtless, in Speedos and underwear during a commercial shoot, both of which left very little to the imagination, and in nothing but a low-slung towel. She'd also seen him sweaty during and after games, as well as after a morning run or a brutally hard workout session.

Hell, a few years back she'd even seen those infamous online pictures of him buck naked except for a fuzzy grayed-out area. The ones an ex had taken and sold to a tabloid back when he'd been a rookie.

The ones *he did not talk about.*

But seeing him shirtless and sweaty in that hog shelter?

Ooh la *freaking* la. It was like her ovaries, which had been lying dormant—almost extinct from years of little to no action—had suddenly roared to life. That fine sheen of sweat on his chest and abs and arms? The way his jeans had hugged low on his hips and that trail of hair had led her gaze *down, down, down*? His tussled mess of hair, complete with hay, and the smell of grass and animals and *man* flaring her nostrils?

That was why ladies loved country boys. And she'd definitely had a lady moment. Hell if she hadn't wanted to trade her environmentally friendly Prius for a pickup truck.

Which was extra confusing, considering she didn't even like Wade that much about 50 percent of the time. And oh, that's right…he was her *boss*.

That was the line right there.

She'd left the employ of two CEOs prior to Wade who'd thought her services should extend beyond work hours. She'd be a complete hypocrite if she compromised her ethics for Wade. And a fool as well to choose a man who preferred a carousel of women to eternal monogamy.

Because that's what CC demanded.

Her father had left her mother and the family home when CC had been three years old to live with another woman and her kids in the next town. Her mother had never fully recovered from his betrayal, and the long-term repercussions on her family and CC's own relationship with men had been far-reaching.

No way could CC be with a guy who wouldn't know monogamy if it knocked him on his ass.

But seeing Wade in farmer mode—all sweat and muscle and hay—had tripped some kind of switch. It was like a portal had opened to a whole other world and was sucking her in.

And that just wouldn't do.

"Wade!"

About half a dozen people called to Wade as they entered the bar, and CC felt as if she'd been thrust into a scene from *Cheers*.

But it was different to the usual public adoration she'd seen in other places. Wherever Wade went, people came up to him, asked him for his autograph, wanted to shoot the breeze about a game or criticize a play. And it didn't seem to matter to them if he was on a date or at a private party or in a meeting. It always got CC hot under the collar, but Wade took it all in his stride. She knew he considered it one of the pitfalls of celebrity.

But here, in his hometown, after an initial greeting, people turned back to their drinks and resumed their conversations. They didn't get up or approach him. Nobody asked him to sign anything.

In Credence, apparently, his presence didn't raise an eyebrow. He was just part of the fabric of the town—one of them. But more than that, it seemed as if they knew he needed to not be a celebrity every now and then. No wonder he wanted to come here to write, to get away from everyone always demanding a piece of him.

"Well, look who the cat dragged in."

CC took in the grinning man behind the bar. A very *sexy* guy, maybe a bit younger than Wade. Tall and built, with sandy-blond hair, a little long and shaggy at the back, a spectacular mouth, and a pair of cute dimples.

On another man, it might have all looked girly. But on this guy, it worked.

"Hey, man." Wade grinned back, extending his hand. "Still ugly as ever, I see."

The other guy laughed, his dimples perfectly symmetrical, his lips a wide, neat bow. Wade was certainly as handsome, but he had darker hair and more brooding features, his face looked more lived-in, like it'd been ground into the dirt a few dozen times. This guy looked like he could have sat for Botticelli.

His gaze cut to CC, and even she felt a little dazzled by it. Man, that smile should have been illegal in all fifty states. He needed to be careful what he did with that thing, especially to a woman who was suffering from farmer porn/estrogen overload.

"And who do we have here?"

"This is my PA. Cecilia Morgan. CC, meet Tucker Daniels. We played on the school football team together, he was a freshman my junior year."

"Yeah," Tucker said, putting out his hand. "So I know all his dirty little locker room secrets."

CC shook Tucker's hand. "I know one or two as well. Maybe we should compare notes?"

Tucker chuckled—even his laugh was spectacular—as he turned his gaze on Wade. "I like this one. You should keep her."

CC laughed at the outrageous statement—she wasn't anyone's to keep. But his eyes danced, and his smile dazzled, and she didn't take it any other way than the tease he'd obviously intended.

She was going to like Tucker, she could just tell.

"He making you live in that god-awful mausoleum?"

CC sighed. "He is."

"Hey." Wade's fingers drummed on the bar. "It's a classic piece of antebellum architecture, dickwad."

"Whatever you say, *Rhett*." Tucker grinned, and CC could totally see how it'd work on women. The man was an utter charmer. Smooth as cream. But apart from her initial dazzled reaction, it did nothing for her.

Not now that she'd developed a hankering for farmers.

"I think—" Tucker planted his elbow on the bar and leaned across a little, dropping his voice an octave. "Deep down, he's one of those people who go around reenacting the Civil War."

CC laughed at the picture that created in her head. She didn't know how bored Wade would have to get to consider lying around pretending to be dead on a field somewhere all day.

"Can't a man get a drink around here, or does he have to pour his own?"

Tucker laughed. "The usual?"

"Yep."

"Can I get you something to drink, CC?"

"Thanks."

"You want what he's having?"

CC's mind wandered to a shirtless Wade with hay stuck to a very fine-looking pectoral—she wanted some of *that*—before she pulled it back. "As long as it's tequila."

He glanced at Wade. "A keeper, I tell you."

"Tequila?" Wade cocked an eyebrow.

Yep, *tequila*. Just because she didn't drink very much didn't mean she didn't drink *ever*. Or didn't know how to cut loose. And today she'd not only moved to small-town America, but had experienced a hot flash *for her boss* in the middle of a *hog* field.

It was a tequila kinda night.

Tucker was putting their drinks in front of them on the bar when somebody thumped Wade on the shoulder. "Who gave this dirtbag permission to enter Credence?"

CC turned along with Wade, who was smiling. It wasn't a dazzler like Tucker's, but it still tickled between her ribs. "My name's on the welcome sign, dude. That's all the permission I need."

"Hey, man." The newcomer shook Wade's hand and yanked him forward into a manly hug with much back-smacking. "I hear you're going to be in town for a few months."

"For the summer. Writing a book."

The other guy laughed and shook his head at Tucker. "Can you believe this horseshit? I didn't even know he could read, did you?"

Wade laughed. "You're such an asshole. No wonder you're a cop."

New guy laughed before turning his attention on CC. "Hey there. I'm Arlo Pike. You must be CC."

CC blinked as yet another Credence hottie addressed her. Tall, lean, his hair jet-black, a five o'clock shadow that made you want to reach out and touch. About the same age as Tucker, at a guess.

What the hell was in their drinking water around here?

She looked around the bar and realized she was the only apparently single woman in it. There were three other women, but they all appeared to be attached to someone and about twenty years older.

It suddenly occurred to CC that she was in an awesome position—had she been interested in living in a small town with supernatural powers over estrogen cycles. For the rest of her life.

Which she was not.

The male/female ratio may have sucked for the men of Credence, but for the women? Hell, it was raining men. *Good*-looking men not wearing wedding bands.

And Jack's was like the Jell-O pit.

"How in hell do you know who she is?" Wade demanded.

Arlo shrugged like he was the fount of all Credence knowledge, gossip, and hearsay. "It's my job to have my finger on the pulse."

"My mother told you, didn't she?"

That was the problem with having the police station next door to the municipal county building.

Arlo smiled at CC. "He always this moody?"

"Only at certain times of the month."

Arlo looked stunned for a second or two, like he hadn't quite heard such a thing come from the mouth of a chick before, then he threw back his head and laughed out loud.

He looked at Tucker and pointed at CC. "She is awesome."

Tucker nodded. "I know, right?"

Wade sighed. "Can I get you a drink, Arlo?"

He nodded. "The usual." Then he noticed the shot glass in front of CC. "No. Wait. I'll have what she's having."

Tucker knocked on the bar. "One tequila coming right up."

Arlo took the barstool on the other side of CC and looked at Wade. "You coming to the meeting tomorrow night?"

"What meeting?"

"The special town meeting."

"There's a special town meeting?"

"Yes, there is," CC said, quickly knocking back her shot, shutting her eyes as it burned all the way down. She opened her eyes and pushed her shot glass at Tucker. "Hit me again."

Wade blinked. "How do *you* know?"

"Your mother told me."

"What in hell requires a special town meeting?" Wade asked Arlo. "They're not trying to put another wind turbine in, are they?"

"Nah." Arlo knocked his shot back and shoved his toward Tucker for a refill, too. "It's the women problem."

"We have a women problem?"

"Yeah," Tucker said in a voice that dripped with sarcasm. "We don't have any."

Wade shrugged. "Suits me."

"Says the man who gets laid more often than all of One Direction put together," Arlo scoffed.

CC laughed as Wade rolled his eyes. She could tell she was going to like Arlo, too.

"What are they going to propose? You can't force anyone to come and live here."

"Don't know." Arlo shrugged. "But I sure as hell want to find out."

"Yeah, well, have fun with that. I'd rather watch grass grow than listen to whatever harebrained scheme my mother and her cronies are cooking up."

"Oh, but…" CC frowned. "I told your mother you'd be there. That we'd both be there."

Wade shook his head. "Hell no."

"I promised her, Wade." Ronnie had been excited that Wade would be around long enough to participate in the civic life of Credence. And CC had figured it wasn't going to kill him.

"Why?"

"It's a town meeting. Are you part of this town or not?"

"Yeah, Wade." Tucker grinned at him. "You in or out, dude?"

"It's your *mom*," CC pressed. "She's doing her civic duty, the least we can do is go and support her."

For a moment, CC thought Wade was going to be recalcitrant, but he sighed and muttered "For fuck's sake" under his breath as he pointed at the shot glass and said, "Give me one of those."

CHAPTER SIX

Wade had never been to a Credence town meeting before, and it was nothing like he expected. He'd thought maybe a couple dozen people on fold-out chairs in one of the elementary school classrooms. But no. It seemed like most of the town had gathered at the municipal offices, which were quite plush, considering the aging feel to the building.

This was the first time Wade had seen the inside of the offices. His mom had been elected ten years ago, but he hadn't been in town long enough to take the tour he'd kept promising her. There was bright green carpet on the floors and rows of padded seating. The town councilors sat at a long table on a slightly elevated stage-type area at the front of the room. And to one side there were tables groaning with food.

It was a bake sale wet dream. Cookies, cupcakes, and a dozen of Annie's pies all lined up in rows.

He wouldn't mind betting most of the town had actually turned out for those pies. The woman had been a baking ninja for forty years, and she wasn't losing any of her skills with age. He'd headed straight for her legendary Key lime pie—not something often seen in rural Colorado—and was contemplating another piece.

But Arlo was getting a little too friendly with CC for his liking, and it was really bothering him. The guy sure hadn't let a missing leg dampen his

flirting reflex. Of course, they were both entitled to
flirt with whomever the hell they wanted, but they
just weren't…right for each other. Arlo would never
leave Credence and, given the way she'd fought even
moving here for three months, CC wouldn't abandon
her dreams of moving to California. And if she did,
he wanted it to be for him, damn it.

Plus, she *was* still his PA. For another three lousy
months. He didn't want her attention divided while
Arlo played the wounded cop hero he already
played to good effect whenever the opportunity
arose. The thought didn't sit well. He'd always
guarded her place as his number one employee with
fervor. But he didn't think this sudden disquiet had
much to do with their professional relationship.

Thankfully, the meeting was coming to order,
which gave him a much-needed distraction. His
mother, in some kind of sweater set and pearls, looked
impressively official in a genteel Southern lady way.
She was sitting next to Don Randall, the mayor, who
looked like an idiot, wearing his robes of office and
the mayoral chains around his bullfrog neck.

Don had been born officious.

Wade snagged a second piece of Key lime.
Annie's pies made everything better—even Don. He
made his way back to the chairs. His mom waved,
and he waved back as he sat next to CC, his thigh
muscles protesting slightly after his morning helping
Wyatt around the farm.

Arlo was on her other side, and Tucker and Wyatt
were in the row behind. Drew Carmichael, the local
funeral director, also sat beside Wyatt. Drew, who'd
been on the football team with Arlo and Tucker and

in the same freshman year as them, looked nothing like one imagined an undertaker to look. He was more Indiana Jones than Harry from *My Girl*.

"Better watch your waistline, dude. Nothing sadder than a porky ex-jock," Tucker said, leaning forward.

His brother snickered. Possibly because of the hog reference, possibly because he enjoyed anyone giving Wade shit. *Great*. The peanut gallery.

"You wish you had this body, pretty boy."

Tucker laughed, and they all started to laugh, but then Don stood and cleared his throat and asked everyone to come to order—and Wade bit into his pie and prayed for a sugar coma.

"You think he hides a permanent hard-on beneath those robes and that's why he wears them?" Arlo whispered.

"I think the only time he can get a hard-on is when he's wearing them," Wade said, his voice low. "He probably wears them to bed with Mrs. Randall, that poor long-suffering woman."

"Oh God." Drew winced. "Man, why'd you go put that picture in my head. You think I don't have enough macabre shit going on in there already?"

"I like to share." Wade smiled as he licked whipped cream off his lips.

"Shut up, all of you," CC whispered with unconcealed annoyance. "Quit being rude."

The guys all suppressed smiles but, suitably chastised, turned their attention to the proceedings.

Don went through an incredibly long preamble, outlining the problem of young women from Credence drifting to the cities to pursue college and careers, and the issues that arose for the town because of the low female population in the child-bearing age bracket.

Everything from decreasing birth rates and business profits to school closures and declining community spirit. Wade was pretty sure he was working his way up to plagues of boils and locusts.

"He hasn't mentioned mass breakouts of blue balls yet," Tucker whispered from behind, which led to another round of stifled schoolboy laughter and more eye rolling from CC.

As if Don had heard Tucker's point, he went on to cite the increased levels of male frustration resulting in higher-than-normal levels of public drunkenness and aggressive behavior.

"Oh Jesus... Is this guy for real?" CC whispered out the side of her mouth.

"Yup."

"So a bunch of horny men get drunk and then get angry and carry on like rutting bulls, and he wonders why women prefer college and careers?"

Wade chuckled. That pretty much summed it up. "I don't think Don quite sees it that way."

It was another few minutes before Don got to the point. Minutes during which Wade contemplated a third piece of pie.

"So it is our proposal that Credence advertises nationally through our website and sites such as Facebook and YouTube for single women to come visit with a view to staying in Credence."

Wade blinked and sat up straighter in his chair. A low murmur buzzed through the assembled citizens as they all looked at one another and started to talk at once.

"What the heck?" CC said.

Arlo leaned forward in his chair. "Son of a—" He glanced at CC. "Biscuit."

"There is a precedent for this," Don continued over the din. "A few other places have tried it in the past with good results."

Yeah. Those towns had been the butt of jokes all over the country. Not to mention being overrun by women more keen on hooking up than settling down. How many stayed once the novelty wore off?

"We're thinking two invitational events. The details are yet to be ironed out, and it will depend on interest, but we could bus them in from Denver to Credence on Friday and bus them back on Sunday. That'll give us a couple of days to showcase the charms of the town."

Charms of the town? As far as Wade was concerned, lack of women *was* the charm of the town.

Christ. Busloads of women. Coming to Credence? The national press rocking up if the whole thing went viral, which it probably would, because wacky shit always did. News vans staked out down the main street. And how long would it take for them to discover he was in town? There'd be reporters standing outside his house, trying to look through his windows. Going through his garbage.

How was he supposed to write with all that going on? Wade shook his head. This *could not* be happening.

"We'll open up to comments now before we take a vote."

About two dozen people sprang to their feet.

"Yes, Arlene, you first."

Arlene Cox was a middle-aged corn farmer's

wife with three children. All daughters. All had left Credence for city life. "Where are these women going to work?" she asked. "I mean, I like the idea in principle. But what if some women choose to stay on and settle here? We don't really have employment for them, do we? And unless they get hitched to someone real quick, they're going to want to support themselves."

Wade almost stood up and cheered. Arlene was making good economic sense.

Wade's mom pulled her desk mic forward and said, "I can answer that."

"Yes… I'll pass the discussion over to Ronnie for the details. I'm just the ideas man." Don laughed at his own joke.

Yeah, you old lech. Wade could see exactly where this harebrained scheme had evolved—Don Randall's dick.

Ronnie smiled at the audience. Beside her sat Chuck Rimes, his bald spot the only thing showing as he sat, head down, hunched over the table, madly scribbling down the minutes.

"There's the odd job around town," Ronnie said. "We have an admin position here, and Brett's always looking for staff at the old folks' home. Annie hires from time to time, as does Tucker. Also Drew at the funeral parlor. And there's the feed store and co-op and sometimes the school. But we're actually really looking for women who'd be keen to start businesses. The state gives out grants to rural start-up businesses, and we think this would be a golden opportunity for any young woman and for the life of the town. We have plenty of empty buildings along the main drag begging to be occupied."

Another murmur went through the audience. New business. New people. New life. Community.

"What kind of businesses are ya thinkin'?" a voice called from the back.

"Well, I guess that'll be up to the young woman, to an extent, and whether there's a population base to support that particular type of business," Ronnie said. "But I for one would love to see a place where I can get my hair and nails done without having to drive an hour. Somewhere local where I can drop my computer to be fixed, or see an accountant or a lawyer? Maybe some bright young thing will come up with an idea to attract tourists back to the town, like a shop that sells gourmet chocolate and free-range eggs and specialty produce from farms in the district? A coffee shop, maybe."

Wade's mouth watered at the thought of having a place where he could get a decent coffee around here. It was almost enough to make a man forget his objections to this ridiculous idea.

"We don't want to put Annie out of business," somebody else called, from off to the side this time.

Annie, as inscrutable as ever, piped up in her crackly pack-a-day voice. "Nobody comes to my place for the coffee, doll."

People laughed, but it was true. Annie's coffee was basic at best, the kind that cowboys used to drink on the range about a hundred years ago. Before Starbucks and Keurig. People went to Annie's for her homespun food. Grits, beans, peach cobbler.

Going to Annie's for coffee was like going to McDonald's for salad.

"We can use our barn for some kind of cookout one of the nights."

Wade wasn't sure who said that, but there followed a bunch of other called-out offers, too. "The details are yet to be worked out," Ronnie said. "But we'll be forming a committee if the vote goes our way tonight, so y'all are most welcome to be part of that."

Of course they'd form a fucking committee. Credence had more committees than there were hogs on the farm. And his mother was on every last one of them.

There were a few more questions, but mostly about logistics, not about a town basically advocating some modern-day mass mail-order bride scheme. Was it really appropriate in a new century to be luring women for their marriage and child-rearing qualities?

He glanced at CC for a barometer reading. She didn't seem to be taking particular offense.

For fuck's sake. Was the whole town dropped on their heads overnight? Wade stood. "Permission to speak."

People turned to look at him in surprise, a ripple of interest murmuring through the audience. Don acknowledged Wade with a nod of his head. "Granted, Wade. And can I just say what a pleasure it is to have Credence's own hometown quarterback hero in town for the summer."

Wade smiled awkwardly at Don. No one fawned over him in Credence—it was what he liked about it. If someone thought he was being a dumbass or a dick, they told him. There was no pussyfooting around *the celebrity* in his hometown.

"Thank you, Don, but I gotta say this idea, with all due respect, is horseshit."

Half the audience laughed, half gasped, and CC almost choked on her own tongue. His mother frowned as she openly chastised him. "Wade!"

"Sorry, Mom, and my apologies to the council for the cussing, but I really don't think we need busloads of women overrunning the town. Not to mention the media attention this might get. Trust me, that can be really intrusive."

He glanced around the room at the familiar faces. Faces he'd known most of his life. They'd had media interest in the town over the years because of Wade, but nothing too invasive. They had no clue how persistent television and tabloid reporters could be. Of what they might be getting themselves in for.

"The charm of Credence," he continued, "*is* its small town feel, that sense of community. The way we stick together and have one another's backs. We all know one another and we've always been a little wary of outsiders. Having a…free-for-all might seem like a solution to a problem, but you gotta ask yourself, why would a woman pick up her life and move to a small, isolated part of Colorado where she doesn't know anybody? I think we run the risk of attracting women who are coming for all the wrong reasons, maybe. Coming here to escape their lives, not make a whole new one."

Another murmur ran around the room as Wade finished, and Annie stood and turned to face him. "All due respect, Wade, but *that's* horseshit."

A lot more people laughed at Annie's horseshit quip than they had at his. His mother didn't dare chastise the older woman.

"You don't get to swagger into town twice a year, no matter how cute your tight end is, and pretend like you give a rat's ass when we all know it's just self-interest speaking."

"You go, girl," Drew encouraged under his breath.

"We love it when you're home, and we know you like it here because no one's trying to stick a camera in your face or ask for your autograph—but our town is *dying*, Wade, and we're trying to revive it, and your need for privacy don't mean squat next to that. So hush up and listen."

People started applauding, but Annie wasn't done yet. "And who says Credence can't be a haven, a place to escape, to rebuild your life? This town took me in when I ran from a man who used to beat me up for entertainment. I had three little kids clinging to my skirts. Your grandfather gave me the money to start the diner. Who says we can't be that for other women?"

Wade blinked. He hadn't known any of those details. And despite the public smackdown, his admiration for Annie grew.

She sat to raucous applause, and there wasn't much for Wade to do but sit as well. Annie had just told him he was being a dumbass *and* a dick, and the town had agreed.

"Way to go, bro." Wyatt clasped his shoulder from behind.

"I like Annie," CC said, barely suppressed glee in her voice.

Wade ignored them both, patting his pocket for his box of Nerds, and realized he didn't have any. He cussed in his head—a word significantly worse than horseshit—but it was short-lived as a box appeared in front of him.

He took them, so used to CC's weird Wonka-related ESP by now it didn't even occur to him to question it. He opened the box, poured a small, colorful pile into the palm of his hand, then threw them all into his mouth in one hit. Without looking at her, he nudged the box toward CC. She stuck out her hand, and he poured her a pile, too. But she'd eat them slowly, a couple at a time.

It was the most infuriating way to eat Nerds he'd ever had the misfortune to witness. But CC had never gotten the Nerds-eating memo.

"If there are no further questions, perhaps we can vote on the motion to put an online advertising campaign in place to attract single women to Credence?" Don said.

Wade sighed as a murmur of agreement spread through the gathering, resigning himself to this madcap scheme. He didn't need to be a genius to figure out the way sentiment was running tonight. But it didn't stop the feeling of doom. This was going to be nothing but trouble, he just knew it.

He consoled himself with another handful of Nerds from the box and the comforting thought that maybe it *wouldn't* go viral. Maybe they'd get interest from only a handful of women. That wouldn't be so calamitous.

"All those in favor?"

Everyone in the room except Wade put up their hands. Even CC. He frowned at her. "You don't get a vote."

"Sure she does," Arlo said.

"Sure I do," CC agreed, not putting her hand down.

Wade cocked an eyebrow, ignoring CC. "She's not a resident of Credence."

"Neither are you."

"I was *born* here."

"She's living here temporarily. She gets a vote."

"Who says?"

"I do."

CC nodded. "He does."

"And who put you in charge of town residency?"

Arlo grinned and tapped his police chief badge. "The county did."

Wade half laughed, half snorted. "For the love of—"

"All those against."

Wade's hand shot up straight as an arrow. Everyone turned in their seat, staring at his hand. Annie narrowed her eyes at him, a look that would have caused him to crap his pants as a teenager, but now only gave him a slightly uncomfortable feeling in his bowels.

Annie didn't need that look anymore. Not with him. She could just threaten to withhold pie, and he'd do anything the old biddy wanted.

But if they had to go through this farce, he wanted Chuck to note in the minutes that he'd objected. Then, when everything went pear-shaped and Credence was overrun by desperado bachelorettes with criminal records *and* the town became the laughing stock of the United States, he could say *I told you so*.

"The overwhelming majority has spoken," Don said. "The motion is passed." He banged his gavel.

Yep. Nothing but trouble.

CHAPTER SEVEN

CC whimpered at the pleasurable sensation building deep inside the muscles behind her belly button. God, it had been so long since she'd had an orgasm that involved a man she'd forgotten how much more intense they were.

"Wade."

The name on her lips sounded wrong, and she shook her head from side to side, confused as to why she was saying her boss's name. She tried to open her eyes, to figure it out, but her lids were too leaden, refusing to open, too damn caught up in the pleasure swirling through her abdomen and her inner thighs.

"Shhh, baby, I know," he whispered back, his breath hot against her puckered nipple.

Still Wade. CC fought against the voice as silken tentacles wrapped around her middle and squeezed, tension building alongside the pleasure. But his fingers—those big, long fingers that could pluck a ball from the air with pinpoint precision—pushed deep inside her and found her G-spot with equal pinpoint precision.

A cry rising in her throat cut off just before her vocal chords, becoming a low sonorous moan as his mouth closed over her nipple. Her hand pushed into his hair, cradling his head.

It was unbelievably good, her climax edging closer

with each suck of his mouth, each hard rub as a finger stimulated her G-spot. But also bad—so, *so* bad. Why was Wade doing this to her? Why was she naked?

Why was *he* naked?

His big, hard body lying alongside hers? Why did the thick intrusion of his fingers and the hot, wet pull at her nipple feel so good? He was her boss, it was *wrong*. She squirmed, her brain fighting slumber and an ever-devolving haze of lust, her head rolling from side to side. "*Wade.*"

"What do you need, Cecilia?" Her name whispered from his lips on a soft sigh like it was some kind of benediction as his mouth hovered over hers, their lips almost touching.

"You can tell me," he said.

To stop. She needed him to stop because he was calling her Cecilia and it was confusing and *waaaa*y too good.

Which was doubly confusing.

"Fuck me," she whispered. Wait. *What?* She didn't mean to say that—did she?

But Wade was going there anyway. With those clever, ball-plucking, G-spot-rubbing fingers, pulling them out and shoving them in as his thumb found her clit and his lips lowered to hers, kissing her like he'd *never* been her boss. He tasted like Nerds and sugar rushed to her head and her heart raced and she came, gasping and mewling against his mouth with breathtaking speed. Shuddering and crying out and sobbing as the orgasm touched down like a tornado.

CC rocked her head faster and faster from side to side as it ravaged her, murmuring, "*No, no, no,*" even as her body and her breath and her pulse pounded *yes*, *yes*, *yes* and her back and hips bowed off the bed, bucking against Wade, reaching for every second of pleasure until the tornado spun away again and she collapsed against the mattress.

CC's eyes flew open.

She lay in the dark, her heart pounding, her breath sawing in and out, an overriding sense of confusion swamping her body.

Where was she? What had happened?

She was in her bed. And it was night. And she was sleeping. And…

One last tiny little shudder rippled through the internal muscles buried deep between her legs. Oh God… She knew that sensation.

She'd just had an orgasm.

Then it all came rushing back to her. In full Technicolor detail.

No. Sweet mother of pearl. *No.*

Wade. Kissing her. Touching her. *Calling her baby.*

Calling her *Cecilia.* He *never* called her Cecilia. Or baby, for that matter.

But it'd just been a dream. A stupid dream. A woman couldn't actually *orgasm* from something she was dreaming, could she? Except she had, *most definitely*, just come. Which meant she must have… been touching herself…masturbating…in her sleep? But both her hands were firmly entwined in the sheet to either side of her.

CC shook her head. This could not be happening.

Good God, not only had she just had a *sex dream* about *Wade* but, to add insult to injury, he'd made her come without actually laying a finger on her.

Without even being in the same freaking room.

Was there anything the damn man couldn't do?

• • •

CC was grateful that Wade was gone when she got up the next morning. The thought of facing him after… Well, she didn't know how she was ever going to look him in the eye again, let alone work for him for the next three months.

God. She'd had a *sex dream* about her boss.

She didn't know how to unpack that. She didn't even have a friend she could call. Her friends had given up on her years ago after one too many canceled plans and forgotten birthdays because Wade had sucked up her entire existence. CC had always figured she'd have time to make and cultivate friendships once she was in SoCal, but that wasn't helping her now.

She certainly couldn't talk to her mother about it. Being abandoned by a husband had given her some strident views about the perils of sex, including absolute faith in the old adage about masturbation leading to blindness. And her brothers would rather *be* blinded than listen to CC talk about the perils of sex dreams starring her boss.

All five of them preferred to think of her as some kind of infantile version of herself, a girl who didn't drink, cuss, or indulge in any kind of sexual activity whatsoever.

They were such morons. Lucky she loved them.

The only other people CC was in a relationship with were the people she regularly played online Scrabble with. But they weren't friends. Just random strangers…anonymous people somewhere out there in cyberspace.

Hell, they could be bots for all she knew.

Not anyone she could message and say *wanna talk about my sex dream?*

So she was left to her own devices, which was never good. The dream kept playing on repeat in her head, and the echoes of that orgasm still hovered in muscles that didn't usually get that kind of workout. Considering how few truly good orgasms she'd had in recent years, the muscle memory was bound to linger for days, if not weeks.

Just lying there, dormant.

Ready to leap to life again when she least expected it. Launching stealth attacks on her in the car, or feeding Wilburta in the Carter family kitchen, or in deep REM.

Her phone rang, and she snatched it up gratefully. It rang all day, usually. Being Wade's PA was a busy job. Between his NFL mentoring responsibilities, his endorsement schedules, and the speaking circuit, he was in huge demand. And juggling all that was her job. As was maintaining his brand, which meant she managed everything from his website to his social media profiles.

And it hadn't really slowed down since clearing his schedule for three months. The calls just kept coming.

This call, however, was from Ronnie.

A spurt of guilt hit CC's system as the name flashed up on the screen. What on earth would Wade's mother think if she knew CC had been having sex dreams about her son?

Wait. God…what if she *already* knew? Somehow?

In that weird way that mothers just *knew* shit.

CC's mother always said she knew when her kids were up to no good. Did Ronnie have some kind of radar about women who were having risqué dreams about her son? He'd been the target of women looking for a meal ticket in the past, maybe she'd developed some kind of sixth sense about it over the years?

Or maybe she'd just detect it in CC's voice as soon as she answered the phone. Heart pounding, CC sent the call to voicemail, then stalked to the fridge and grabbed an icy cold can of Red Bull. She popped the top and knocked back half of it in one swallow.

It was going to be a six-can kinda day. She could just tell.

Her phone beeped to let her know a message had been left, and she took another big mouthful before heading back to the bench and playing the message.

"Cecilia? Honey. No pressure at all, but I was wondering if you'd like to join the committee for organizing that thing we discussed at the town meetin' last night."

There was a muffled noise and a clunk as if Ronnie had dropped the phone, and CC stifled a smile as a very unladylike expletive slipped from Ronnie's genteel Southern mouth.

"Sorry, honey, the damn dog tripped me up, and I dropped the phone. What was I sayin' again?"

CC loved how Ronnie hadn't lost any of her Southern drawl, even in a flap. If anything, it became more pronounced.

"Oh yes. I know you'll be at a bit of a loose end

with Wade out here most mornings, and we thought you might appreciate something to do."

A snort-laugh escaped CC's mouth. There was always plenty to do in managing Wade's life. In fact, it was easier to get stuff done when he wasn't around.

"Anyways…give me a call and let me know."

The message ended, and CC replayed it, smiling again at the cuss word. It wasn't an offer she'd been expecting, but it was a damn fine one and hell if she wasn't interested. Particularly with Wade so opposed to the scheme.

CC was up for anything that would drive an axe through the images in her head, and a pissed-off Wade was far preferable to naked Wade.

. . .

"CC?"

"In the parlor."

Now there were three words CC never thought she'd ever say in her lifetime. Like chamber pot and water closet. But Wade's house had an honest-to-God parlor, and it was where they'd set up his office.

Normally, he had his space and she had hers, but this room was big enough for two of them, had a big old window overlooking the street, and the best internet connectivity.

They appeared to only have twentieth-century internet speed to go with the nineteenth-century architecture.

Sounds of Wade's whistling—since when did he start *whistling?*—drew closer, and CC skulled the remainder of her Red Bull, needing that extra little charge. This was it. The first time she'd faced him since *the dream*. She could do this. He didn't know about the dream, and he *couldn't* see inside her head.

She had this. *Think of the endgame, CC. Only three months.*

"Hey."

Her stupid stomach clenched at his standard casual greeting. She drew in a slow breath and exhaled before turning in her swivel chair to face him.

"Hey."

He was lounging in the doorway, his shoulder shoved against the jamb as casual as his greeting, and CC had to work overtime to keep her smile in place even though she was almost swallowing her tongue behind her closed lips.

Dear Lord. He was all farmer porn again.

Sure, his shirt was on this time, but it was damp with sweat, clinging to his abs. His hair was all tousled, and there was dirt on his jeans.

Since when had *dirt* been so damn sexy?

CC blinked. For the love of Pete, this town was turning her into some kind of farmer groupie/sex maniac. If she started having sex dreams with him in dirty jeans, he could sue her all the way to Timbuktu and back—she was out of here.

He tipped his chin at her computer screen. "What's going down?"

She swallowed at his choice of words. Now all she could think about was that sweaty tousled head going down on her and his apparently talented tongue getting busy between her thighs.

He frowned. "CC?"

"Sorry." She gave herself a mental shake. "Just…

doing some website updates."

He nodded slowly, then frowned again, looking at her strangely. "What?" he demanded.

What? CC swallowed. "Nothing."

"You're looking at me funny."

CC shook her head. "No, I'm not."

"You're all...tweaky." He glanced at the empty can on her desk and sighed. "How many of those god-awful drinks have you had today?"

"This is my third."

"Jesus. It's a wonder your heart hasn't exploded from all that stimulant."

CC swallowed. God...why would he use *that* word? Now she was back to how she'd exploded around his fingers in the dream.

California. California. California.

"Says the man who should have been in a sugar coma a decade ago from his Nerds consumption."

He grinned at her and, even though he was a good distance away, it brushed against her body like feathers. "Enablers anonymous unite."

CC laughed at his easy comeback. It felt good to do something natural with her mouth, and she liked being reminded that at least 50 percent of the time she *didn't* want to stab him with the fancy letter opener he'd bought her for Christmas a few years back.

"Anyway..." Wade crossed his arms. "We're going out. Give me time to grab a shower, and I'll be down."

CC's brain battled between resentment at his casual disregard for her timetable—the urge to use that letter opener returned—and a frenzy of sensations all centered on a naked Wade with soap bubbles running down his body.

"Where are we off to?"

"The old folks' home," he said as he pushed off the doorway.

CC couldn't figure out why he wanted to go there. "Are you visiting someone?" In which case, why the hell did he need her?

Take notes for his book? Grease the wheels of conversation? Hand-feed him Nerds?

"No. I'm going to do a little meddling."

And with that he was gone, the smudge of dirt on his ass horrifyingly fascinating.

• • •

"What do you mean you *joined* the committee?!"

CC looked out the car window as Wade drove. "Your mom called and asked me, and I said yes."

"Why?"

"Why did she ask me, or why did I say yes?" CC was feeling pretty damn annoyed at the moment, and his exasperation wasn't helping. She had a bunch of stuff she needed to get done, not to mention Wade needed to sit his ass in the chair and write, but instead they were going on this fool's errand, hoping to enlist the town elders in a campaign against the single-women scheme.

"Both."

"Because I'm the demographic they're hoping to attract. Single and of child-bearing age. I also run your social media, so I know a thing or two about it. They thought I'd have some good ideas about how to attract and entertain the women who decide to come to Credence while they're here. I do have ideas outside of the Wade Carter brand, you know that, right?"

His fingers tightened around the steering wheel. "You're supposed to be on my side with this."

"Says who?" CC snorted. "You might very well have bought and or manipulated every single second of my time for the last five and a half years, but you don't get to buy my opinions. I still get to make up my own mind about which side of things I come down on. That's not for sale."

He flicked her a quick raised eyebrow. "Is there a particular reason why your panties are in a twist today? Did I do something to piss you off?"

Yeah. Being naked in her dreams had really pissed her off. Her dreams were the one place Wade hadn't been able to dominate her life. Also, the crack about her panties hadn't helped.

"I have work to do, work you *pay* me for. I don't see why you can't go to the old folks' home by yourself."

"'Cause I'm paying you to do that as well," he said, clearly annoyed at her recalcitrance. "Look... I'm hoping I can get some kind of petition organized, maybe some kind of joint letter of objection to present to Don. You know how to do all that stuff."

Oh yeah, because putting pen to paper was *real* hard.

CC sighed. "Fine." How the man thought he could write a whole damn book, she had no idea.

Whatever. She was out of here in three months. A pinch under her diaphragm made itself known. She ignored it. "What makes you think the old people are going to care about this?"

"Oh, trust me," Wade said, "they'll care. Two years ago, a wind generation company wanted to put up a turbine. A *single* turbine. *Five* miles outside of Credence. Bob Downey—he used to be the mayor about forty years ago—and his gang at the old folks' home ran that company out of town with their tails between their legs."

CC frowned. That was just plain dumb. Wind power was cleaner and greener and would have meant some money flowing into the town coffers, as well as some initial employment opportunities. "What on earth for?"

"I know this might be hard for a SoCal soul to understand, but they don't like change, CC. They like their quiet backwater existence. They especially won't like the idea of their little corner of the earth being some kind of chick magnet or curiosity or media drawcard. Bob Downey is a stickler for rules and formality, and I just can't see him getting his head around a bunch of screaming city chicks looking to get hitched. And when Bob Downey ain't happy, trust me, ain't nobody happy."

He sounded like a real tyrant. CC was even less sure about going there now.

"Come on, CC, you *must* be able to see the downside of something like this?"

"Sure." CC understood his concerns, even if they were, largely, as Annie had so rightly pointed out, coming from a place of self-interest. The media could be your best friend or your worst enemy. She'd dealt with a lot of media outlets as PA to CEOs and even more so since working for Wade. The trouble was, a person never quite knew which way the wind was going to blow.

"So why agree to help my mother?"

"Well for a start, she's your mom and she asked me. And hey, if I have to be single in Credence, I might as well have company, right?"

And God knew there were enough hotties to go around.

But also, she had to admit, there was a tiny bit of revenge involved. For dragging her here in the first place. *And* the sex dream. Yeah...that wasn't his fault, but she wasn't in a particularly charitable mood at the moment.

"Okay...fine. How much of a time commitment is this committee crap?"

"Don't worry, Wade, I'll do it while you're at the farm so I can be back here to help you *type*."

"You do have your panties in a wad."

CC shot him a bland smile, disguising the fact her panties had been in a freaking *uproar* all day. "Are we there yet?"

"One minute."

It couldn't come fast enough.

· · ·

The Credence Retirement Home for the Aged was a nice little set up. Quite large, considering the town population.

"I didn't think it'd be this big," CC whispered to Wade as they waited in a large sunken sitting room overlooking a lush garden area. They'd been told to wait there while the staff gathered the residents.

He nodded. "Credence has an aging population. That's half the problem, everyone growing old and passing on with no families and babies to replace them."

Which is what Annie had meant last night when she'd said Credence was dying.

A woman who looked to be in her early twenties wandered by.

"Hey, Della, are they coming?"

She glanced in their direction, but her gaze almost immediately skittered away from Wade's to meet CC's instead, her cheeks pinking up. "The first one should be here any tick of the clock."

CC did an internal eye roll as the woman scuttled away. Wade's ability to fluster the female sex was damn near universal. Even in rural Colorado, young women were swooning over him just as much as the rest of the female population in the New Adult demographic.

"I thought you said there weren't any younger women in Credence."

"There's the odd one," Wade said. "Not many. That's Arlo's sister...half sister, actually. He didn't know he had one until a couple of years ago. She's had a bit of a tough life. She's shy and wary and not really in the market for a relationship just yet."

Interesting. CC had assumed Della's shyness was due to Wade's dazzling celebrity, but maybe it was deeper than that.

"She needs TLC, and Arlo is very protective of her, so..."

Yeah. Definition—men didn't dare approach her anyway, with the chief of police hovering. Part of CC admired that—a brother looking out for a sister— but having five brothers herself, she knew how overbearing it could be as well.

Snowy-haired residents trickled in over the next ten minutes. Some weren't as agile as others, but they generally seemed quite mobile and happy, chatting amongst themselves and greeting Wade with surprise, pleasure, and affection. They asked about his career and what he was up to now and reminisced about his high school football days. But they also asked about his parents and Wyatt and the farm, talking about hog prices as if they watched it as closely as the Dow Jones.

"Wade, that you?" A spritely-looking man in what CC judged to be his late seventies, early eighties, squinted at Wade from across the room, then bounded over enthusiastically. Bushy white eyebrows moved expressively as he pumped Wade's hand. "Heard you were in town for the summer."

He bashed Wade on the back a couple of times, and CC bit her lip to suppress the smile as Wade fought against coughing. He may be getting on, but the old guy still packed a bit of a punch.

"It's good to know our number one son still appreciates where he was brought up."

"Hey, Mr. Downey."

Bob Downey? So this was the guy who'd led the charge against the wind company? The old man turned his attention to CC. He smiled at her as he extended his hand, and Wade said, "CC, this is Mr. Downey."

"Bob, please," he said with a twinkle in his eye. "No need to stand on formality."

CC suppressed another smile as Wade almost choked on Bob's statement. "Thank you, Bob." She shook his hand. "It's *so* nice to meet you."

"Oh no... The pleasure is all mine." And he performed a little bow over her hand.

Aww. CC almost sighed over the old-fashioned gentility. What a pussycat. Wade rolled his eyes.

"So...this your girlfriend?" Bob asked, piercing Wade with inquisitive eyes.

"No." Wade's response was blunt.

CC's was equally as blunt. "Absolutely not."

"She's my PA."

Bob glanced at CC, his white caterpillar eyebrows extraordinarily mobile. "PA?"

"Personal assistant," CC explained.

Bob hooted out a laugh. "He needs someone to wipe his ass and tie his shoelaces, does he?"

CC laughed at Bob's frankness. "Something like that."

"*Nothing* like that," Wade insisted, giving CC a *don't encourage the old coot* look. "CC takes care of all aspects of my schedule. She keeps me on track and on time and keeps away the time-wasters."

"So she's like...a girl Friday."

"Well, yes, except women take exception to being called girls these days."

Two fat, hairy eyebrows lifted high on his forehead as he turned to CC for confirmation. "What on earth for?"

CC suppressed a smile. "Um...because they haven't been girls since they were twelve?"

"Well...yes...I guess," Bob said gruffly. "If you want to get all technical."

CC supposed Bob's old-man bluster and confusion should annoy her. But it didn't. He was a guy of a certain era, when things had been different. She preferred a bit of misguided, old-fashioned paternalism about the way things were now than the more frank displays of sexism she'd been subjected to as a PA over the years.

And a girl growing up in the shadow of her father's desertion tended to yearn for old-fashioned values.

"I still think PA sounds more like a nurse."

Wade grimaced. "Then think of her as my left tackle, Mr. Downey."

Bob perked up at that, narrowing his eyes slightly as he thought it through. "Left tackle, huh?"

"Yep."

CC had heard Wade describe her as his left tackle about a million times. In fact, they were the words he'd used that day in Denver to convince her to come and work for him. *Come be my left tackle, CC.* That's what he'd said after he'd whisked her away from her ex-boss, who was still rolling on the floor clutching his testicles.

It didn't sound as romantic as girl Friday, but CC hadn't been looking for romance. In fact, Wade had sworn that day that he'd never do anything necessitating his balls being mashed against CC's knee and, apart from her sudden penchant for farmer porn and an embarrassing sex dream she was trying to forget, their relationship had remained strictly business.

"She stops anyone who isn't supposed to be close from getting close."

Hell yeah she did. She worked her *ass* off at that. As far as she was concerned, she should have a dozen MVP awards all of her own. She should be on the TV ads selling Disney World.

"You want me?" Wade tapped his chest. "You gotta go through her"—he pointed at CC—"first."

Yep. Apart from a select group of family and close friends, nobody got to Wade unless she allowed it.

Bob nodded. "I had one of those. She was so good at it, I married her." He cracked up then and slapped Wade on the back a couple more times before turning twinkling eyes on CC. "You better watch out, little lady."

CHAPTER EIGHT

CC couldn't decide if she was amused or horrified. The last person on earth she would marry was Wade. Hell, she wouldn't even *date* him. And one sex dream did not alter that conviction one little bit. The man went through women like he was trying to be with every single female on the surface of the planet before he died. But Bob cracking himself up was funny as hell.

"Okay then." Wade rolled his eyes. "How about you take a seat, Mr. Downey, and we'll get started."

Bob nodded, still laughing as he sat his ass down in the circle of chairs that CC had quickly thrown together.

"He's a sweetie," CC murmured in an effort to quash the awkwardness Bob's warning had produced.

Wade snorted. "Don't be taken in by the silly-old-fool act he's got going on. He's a bloody shark, he owns half of the buildings and businesses in this town."

CC's admiration for Bob grew. "Why's he in an old folks' home, then?" she asked. "He's pretty spritely still."

He shrugged. "Mom says he got lonely after his wife died. Likes the company, apparently. So now he terrorizes the town from behind these walls instead."

"Oh, don't say that." CC half laughed at the image. "He looks like he wouldn't hurt a fly." She remembered his potent backslap and mentally revised it to *horse-fly*.

Another snort told CC exactly what Wade thought of that statement. "I do like his description of you, though," Wade added, a smile playing on his mouth. A distracting enough mouth without the addition of that smile.

CC shot him a stern look, folding her arms. "You ever call me your girl Friday, I'll kill you and bury your body where no one will find it." It was one thing for an eighty-year-old to say it, something entirely different for a *thirty-eight*-year-old to say it.

He chuckled, and all the hairs on CC's arms prickled. "How are you going to get paid if I'm dead?"

"I know the combination to your safe, as well as all the passwords to your bank accounts."

He opened his mouth to respond, but Bob, still in fine form, jumped in ahead of him. "Well come on then, Wade, don't keep us in suspense. None of us are getting any younger around here, you know."

Another gale of laughter, this time added to by a dozen other seniors.

"Thank you, Mr. Downey," Wade cut into the laughter, and everyone hushed. "And thanks to everyone for coming and listening to what I have to say."

There were general murmurs of "Of course" and "Anything for you, Wade." Clearly, they'd have turned up to listen to Wade read the dictionary.

"This is CC. She's my PA."

CC gave a little wave, and the assembled oldies murmured their greetings, except for an old guy at the far side of the circle with wild hair and coke-bottle glasses. "His what?" He cupped his ear and turned to the woman beside him. "What did he say?"

"His PA," the woman said. She was wearing a cardigan and a Broncos cap perched on top of her springy permed hair.

"What in tarnation is a PA?" Glasses asked.

"It's a girl Friday," she clarified, and CC pressed her lips together to stop from laughing.

"Ah." He nodded sagely and turned his attention back to Wade.

Wade waited until everyone's attention was back on him. Not a process he was used to, given his celebrity, but one that seemed fairly typical of Credence.

"I don't know if any of you heard what happened at the town meeting last night, but—"

"The mayor wants to bring in some women," somebody called out.

"Did he say we're getting women?" Glasses asked the woman beside him again.

"That's right, Harry. For Pete's sake, turn up your damn hearing aid."

Harry fiddled with the external controls, grinning the whole time. "Women," he beamed as he sat forward in his seat. "Now we're cooking with gas."

Wade recapped the essence of last night's meeting, stopping every now and then as people asked questions or decided to throw in a comment or two.

"Now, I'm sure you'll all agree this would be a terrible thing to happen to Credence."

Nobody in the circle said anything. They all just sat blinking owllike back at Wade as if waiting for him to explain *why* it was a bad idea. CC rubbed her hand over her mouth, covering her smile.

Finally Harry spoke again. "Why?"

"Yeah," Bob repeated. "Why?"

"Think how disruptive it'd be to have busloads of women, invading all our peace and quiet, Bob."

A slight murmur rippled around the circle as people looked at one another. "Been too damn quiet around here lately, anyway," the woman with the Broncos cap said.

"But there'll also be a problem with media. It'll add to the big red target already on Credence."

He didn't say it, but everyone in the room, including CC, knew what he meant. Credence was already a huge media draw because of it being Wade's hometown. There had been incidents in the past.

"This kind of thing goes viral, and suddenly everyone in the country will be talking about Credence," Wade continued. "And not in the usual way. It won't just be sports journalists. Tabloids will come here. And they won't stick to the sidewalks and be polite. They'll be running all over town trying to find the *human interest* stories. They'll be trampling over flower beds to stick a microphone and camera in people's faces."

Quite a few members of the circle perked up at the thought. Hair was patted, outfits were straightened. Even Bob ran a finger over each of his eyebrows.

Wade could obviously also sense the sudden flush of vanity in the circle. "I gotta tell you, some of those media outlets won't care much about the truth if they have an angle they want to prosecute. They might not be so flattering to Credence and its residents."

"I remember when the town was jumpin'," Harry said, a wistful note shrouding his voice. "When we used to have dances every week and once every two months we'd shut down the main street to have a big ol' hoedown and everyone in the county came. Old Ed Jones played his fiddle, and there'd be babies everywhere and little kids running in and out between legs."

"I remember that, too," said a man with a bad dye job.

"Yes. But don't you think the peace and quiet around here is part of the charm of the town?" Wade pushed. "I don't know about any of you, but I like being able to come home and know that I could walk down the street naked and nobody's going to mind or take a picture of me."

A flash of Wade hard and naked between her thighs sucker punched CC out of the blue, and she spluttered and half choked on the water she'd been sipping. She desperately tried to drag in air that felt as if it had bones in it.

Everyone's attention turned to her, their eyebrows raised, including Wade's. "Oh come on, Wade," she said to cover for her weirdness. "I'm sure these ladies here would mind if you walked down the street in the buff."

Just because the man had a beautiful body didn't mean everybody in the damn world wanted to get a look.

75 percent of the women in the circle clearly disagreed, shaking their heads. The other 25 percent were either deaf or asleep. "Oh hush now," one said, "none of us mind at all if Wade wants to get about in

his altogether."

There were general nods and a lot of very frank eyeing up, which was making CC uncomfortable even as it caused Wade to grin in triumph. "This is what I mean," Wade said, seeing an opportunity to press his point. "I can't do that kind of thing with cameras around everywhere."

"So maybe keep your clothes on while the women are in town," Broncos cap suggested.

CC bit back a snort. Wade keeping his clothes on while women were around seemed highly unlikely.

Harry laughed, slapping his thigh. "She got you there, sonny."

"Thanks," Wade said, smiling despite the exasperation in his voice. "I'll be sure to do that."

"I reckon…" Bob spoke slowly, tapping his lips with his index finger as he paused. Every head in the circle turned to face him. Bob was, after all, their unofficial leader. "I reckon we could put up with the inconvenience of a few trampled flower beds if it meant we were going to get some new blood injected into the town."

There were general noises of consensus. "Haven't been to a wedding here in about a decade," said a short, stout woman whose feet didn't quite touch the floor.

"The kids leave and they don't come back," said the woman beside her.

"I can offer up the old boardinghouse," Bob said, his finger still in place against his mouth. "There are six rooms in there that can provide temporary accommodation to any woman who wants to make the move permanently. Lick of paint and some community donations of beds and sheets, maybe some curtains and kitchen stuff, and it'll be good as new." His finger tap, tap, tapped against his lips. "Ray here used to work for the electric company, he can check on all that."

Ray Carmody was sitting next to Bob. He was a tall, elegant black man with snowy white hair who looked like he'd be more at home playing classical piano than tinkering with electrics. He seemed about the same age as Bob, and CC would bet any electrical license he may have possessed had expired a long time ago.

"Sure can."

"It'll be basic, but…" Bob shrugged. "Reckon we could make it a bit homey as well."

"Got all those quilts I made years ago still tucked up in a trunk," Broncos cap said. She sniffed. "Too old-fashioned for the grandkids, apparently."

There were a dozen suggestions all tossed around then as Wade looked on in dismay. "That went well," CC said out the side of her mouth. Poor Wade, he came from a world where everyone said yes to him and all the doors opened.

Not so in Credence.

"I'm not sure you fully understand how intrusive it'll be to—"

"Wade," Bob interrupted. "We're old, not stupid. We get it."

CC stifled laughter as Wade threw up his hands in surrender. He'd fought the good fight, but every career sportsman knew to quit while you were ahead.

"I don't want 'em too skinny," Bob said, returning his attention to his fellow inmates, who all nodded in assent. "Women these days are all bones and fancy fingernails."

Harry nodded. "Whatever happened to buxom?"

"And freckles," Ray threw in. "Freckles are cute."

"Oh for the love of…" Wade muttered under his breath. "They'll be specifying measurements next."

CC laughed this time, she couldn't stop herself.

"You think we can put that in the advert, Wade?" Bob asked, consulting Wade suddenly.

Wade sighed. "You're going to have to speak to my mother about the content of the ad, but I can tell you now, you're not allowed to specify physical attributes like that."

"Well, why not?" Bob frowned.

"Because—" Wade rubbed a hand over his face. "It's discrimination, Bob."

Bob's bushy eyebrows beetled together. "No such thing in my day."

Harry shook his head in solidarity with Bob. "World's gone crazy."

"Man can't even appreciate a woman with freckles anymore," Ray added.

CC laughed some more. She knew that probably made her a lousy feminist, but these guys were the living end. They were like the Rat Pack of the old folks' home—Sammy, Dean, and Frank all sitting around reminiscing about the good old days in Vegas.

"You say your mother is in charge?" Bob clarified.

"Yep." Wade nodded and narrowed his eyes a little at CC, who was trying to stifle her laughter behind her hand. "And CC's helping her."

CC stopped laughing pretty damn quick as the old-timers zeroed their attention in on her. She

glanced at Wade with a raised eyebrow. He just
smiled at her and said, "Why don't you guys talk
over your ideas for the ad with CC, and she can take
them to Mom."

The Rat Pack greeted the idea with enthusiasm,
and Wade grinned at her, flashing his white teeth,
laughter dancing in his eyes, and damn if it didn't
make her a little swoony.

"How about we all adjourn to the dining room
with CC?" Bob suggested.

Wade grinned harder, and CC swooned a little
more. Three months could not come soon enough!

Ten minutes later, Wade was strolling into Jack's, still
grinning over the look on CC's face as he left her
surrounded by a bunch of old men, all ear-bashing
her with their ideas.

"I need a beer," he said to Tucker. "A big one."

Drinking before five o'clock was something Wade
wouldn't normally countenance, but Credence and
its intransigence was enough to drive anyone to
drink.

"Went that well at the old folks' home, huh?"
Drew asked, a half-full glass of beer in hand.

Wade snorted as he sat on the stool next to Drew.
"I swear Bob Downey exists just to drive me nuts."

Tucker placed Wade's beer on the bar in front of
him. "I told you, you were wasting your time."

"I can't believe they're behind this crazy idea."
Wade hadn't, for a single minute, thought they'd be
so open-minded. "Bob's getting a helper together

from the home to prepare the old boardinghouse as *free* temporary accommodation."

Drew laughed. "He must be getting mellow in his old age."

Wade snorted. Bob wouldn't know mellow if it bit him on the ass. "The whole town's gone mad."

Tucker folded his arms across his chest. "It's a good idea, man. Worth a try at least."

"Yeah." Drew drained his beer. "You're just worried that a bunch of NFL groupies are going to come to Credence looking to bag a celebrity husband. Which is kinda shortsighted *and* self-centered. Plus, and I hate to be the one to mention this, but not every woman is a Jasmine."

Wade scowled. "Don't you have to polish the hubcaps on the hearse or something?"

Jasmine, his first and last serious girlfriend, had done a number on his head, but this wasn't just about him being able to walk around without groupies and cameras everywhere. He actually feared for Credence at the hands of the national media. He feared the town's quirkiness would be exploited and their way of life held up to ridicule.

Because as much as this place and these people drove him nutty, Credence was *his* place and they were *hi*s people, and he would defend them with his dying breath.

"*Plus*," Tucker added with a grin, "I hate to break it to you, dude, but you're not that much of a catch anymore."

"Oh, bite me."

Tucker and Drew cracked up as Wade drank half his beer, the cold ale going down well after a morning of labor in the sunshine and an hour of futility with the Credence elders.

A big hand landed on his shoulder from behind. "Is this guy being a nuisance, barkeep?" Wade didn't have to turn around to know it was Arlo.

"Nah." Tucker shook his head. "I think he needs a hand having the stick removed from his ass, though."

Arlo glanced at Drew. "I believe that's your territory."

"Not if he's alive, it isn't," Drew said, and Arlo laughed as he took the seat on the other side of Wade.

"Beer?"

Arlo nodded. "Please. It's hot as a three-dollar pistol out there."

"Should you be drinking on the job? Don't you have bad guys to arrest?"

"I knocked off ten minutes ago. And we don't have bad guys in Credence because people fear me."

Wade snorted at his friend's attempt at a joke. "You will when a bunch of strangers start running around all over town."

Drew groaned, and Tucker shook his head. "Jesus, Wade, turn the record over."

"Della said Bob Downey overruled you at the old folks' home," Arlo said just before lifting his beer and taking a swig.

Wade would have liked to have heard a lot less glee in Arlo's voice. "Aren't you worried about how a sudden influx of people is going to impact the police resources of the town?"

"Hell, Wade. They're coming for a look-see, not a rave."

"Yeah, but nobody's going to do criminal checks

or anything, are they? We'll have no idea what kind of undesirables might be sneaking into town under the cover of single women looking for love."

"You're right, Wade, maybe we should just build a wall?" Drew drawled.

Wade glowered at Drew before addressing Arlo again. "What if things get unruly?"

Arlo smiled. "I'm sure I can handle a few unruly women."

"I'll help if you need backup," Drew volunteered.

Tucker nodded. "Hell yeah, me too."

Wade shook his head. "You're all perverts."

"Dude, you got any idea how hard it is for a one-legged cop to get laid in Credence?"

"Ha!" Drew stared morosely into his beer. "You should try being a terminal specialist."

Wade cocked an eyebrow. "A terminal specialist?"

"I'm working on euphemisms for undertaker."

Tucker laughed. "Keep working, buddy."

"So go out of town," Wade said, getting the conversation back on track.

"What do you think we do?" Tucker demanded. "And that's okay if you're after something casual. But what about if we want more, Wade? If we want someone in our lives for good? Marriage and children, the whole shebang. Women from outside Credence aren't so thrilled at the idea of moving to a small town, and who can blame them? It's not like there are huge career prospects here for them. Which means we either leave to be with them, or we choose Credence over the chance at a different kind of life."

Wade blinked. He wouldn't have thought Tucker

Daniels had that many words in him. Arlo nodded. "I'm thirty-five, Wade. So's he." He pointed at Tucker. "So's Drew. Your brother is almost forty. None of us have wives or girlfriends or anything really past a casual hookup somewhere outside the town limits or when the fair comes to town."

"Right." Drew nodded his head vigorously. "So the town council identified a problem and has come up with a solution, and I think we should at least give it a whirl and see if it works before we start listening to horseshit about public law and order from probably the most frequently laid guy in Colorado. If you're worried about the goddamn women, stay inside that mausoleum of a house of yours and batten down the hatches."

Wade was going to protest the mausoleum dig, but hell, if anyone knew about mausoleums, it was a *terminal specialist*.

And it wasn't the relevant part of Drew's spiel anyway. His broader point was they weren't getting any, and Wade could hardly tell three guys in their prime to tie a knot in it while he was the grateful recipient of very regular action.

"There's Della," Wade said.

Arlo almost choked on his beer. "No there is *not* Della." He banged his beer down on the bar, causing a wave of liquid to wash over the edge. "She's only *twenty-four*—that's way too young for any of you, and she'd still working through her issues from her crappy childhood and shitty ex. She's off-limits to all you perverts, so don't even think it."

Wade held his hands up. "Whoa, sorry."

"Jesus, dude." Tucker frowned as he wiped up the

puddle of beer on his bar. "You gotta let out some of that rope, or she'll come to resent you."

"I'm protecting her. I couldn't do that for the first two decades of her life, but I sure as hell can now."

"A gilded cage is still a goddamn cage, Arlo."

Arlo didn't say anything, just drank his beer, his forehead scrunched into a frown, as if Tucker's assessment had bothered him. When the glass was almost drained, he put it down and turned to Wade. "Speaking of women *other* than my sister... Where's that pretty PA of yours?"

It was Wade's turn to frown as Tucker and Drew also turned their attention on him. "Yes." Drew nodded. "Where is the lovely CC today?"

Pretty. Lovely. Wade had used many words to describe CC over the years. Neither of those fit.

Smart. Efficient. Professional. Resourceful. Competent.

Infuriating. Neat freak. Opinionated.

As a man, he recognized that she was an attractive woman. Not his type, but attractive nonetheless, with her petite athletic figure and that cute little pixie cut. Every now and then he surprised himself and noticed she had boobs.

But that was the Y chromosome for you.

More than anything, CC *blended*. He was surrounded by people a lot of the time. Not as much as he was during his NFL career, but still enough. Friends and colleagues as well as the hangers-on and people who either wanted to give him stuff or wanted something from him.

A lot of egos.

So, to have someone on his team that was there

for him when needed, but happy to fade into the background when not, was a godsend. In fact, CC had become so much part of the furniture of his life that no one really noticed her.

Until she spoke. And then people listened. Because she just didn't speak unless it was necessary. And, petite or not, she was as immovable as a brick wall when it came to his schedule.

Her borderline OCD had come in real handy for that.

And the thought she would be gone in three months beat like hummingbird wings inside his brain. In his arrogance, he'd just assumed she'd always be around. That she wouldn't *actually* leave when her time was up. The knowledge that she *was* going to leave sat like a burr beneath his skin, and Wade knew he had to use this time in Credence to try and convince her to stay.

Wade shook his head as he stared at Arlo. "Leave my PA alone."

That goddamn uniform made women stupid. He'd seen it firsthand. Probably not CC who, thanks to five brothers, failed to be impressed by anything overtly male. But he wasn't taking any chances. Wade didn't want that kind of attention on his PA. That kind of *male* attention. She was here to work, not hook up.

"Oh…" Arlo frowned. "Sorry, are you two…?"

"Nope." Hell no. No way, no how, no siree.

"So she's single?"

"Yep."

"So then…you wouldn't mind if I…"

Wade did not like the way Arlo had let his

sentence drift off like that. Full of possibilities. "Hell yes, I would."

"But..." Drew was frowning now as well. "You just said there's nothing between you?"

"She's my PA. It's strictly business between us— that's it. That's all it's ever been. But she's here to work, not play."

"To be fair, dude," Tucker interrupted, "I don't really think you get a say in what she does in her free time or who she does it with."

Wade snorted. "That's nice that you think she has free time."

The three guys looked at each other and started to smile. "What?" he demanded.

"So you don't want her," Arlo clarified, "but you don't want anyone else to want her, either."

Wade sighed. It was like explaining stuff to a two-year-old. Times three. "At the end of the summer, she's leaving my employ for good and going to SoCal to live. I don't give a rat's ass how many dudes she sleeps with on her own dime." An unfortunate little stab in his chest confused the hell out of him, but Wade plowed on. "I do care when it's on mine."

"So, that's a no to me asking her out?" Arlo said, an expression of faux disappointment fixed to his stupid face.

The sudden thought of Arlo, of any of them touching CC, *any man* touching her, was extremely discomforting. Like ants marching under Wade's skin. "Touch her and I'll break your fingers."

Arlo chuckled. "I'm the chief of police, dude."

"Then you can arrest me afterwards."

All three of them laughed again in a smugly

superior way, which was starting to piss Wade off. Tucker placed another beer in front of him. "Here you go, man. Shall we drink to denial?"

"Screw you all," Wade said. But he drank anyway.

CHAPTER NINE

A week later, CC was sitting at Ronnie's farmhouse table, surrounded by neat stacks of paper, color-coordinated pens, and Post-it Notes, an open can of Red Bull at her elbow. This had been ground zero for the GCC—Grow Credence Committee—for the past seven days. CC spent her mornings here with Ronnie, Wilburta, and George, plotting and planning, while Wade helped out around the farm. In the afternoon, they traveled back to Tara together to work on the book.

"It's had over six hundred and fifty thousand views on Facebook," Ronnie said, blinking at CC over the top of her laptop screen. "Fifty-two thousand shares. Almost two hundred thousand likes. And the comments."

"Oh no." CC reached across the table and pushed the screen with a firm click. "Do not read the comments." That shit could be toxic, and she wasn't sure if Ronnie's Southern sensibilities were ready for the less-than-subtle art of trolling. "All that matters is the video has gone viral, we're fielding calls from interested women and the media, and we've thus far had over a hundred confirmed as coming."

Ronnie grinned. "Success."

"Yeah." CC grinned back, her foot absently stroking George's fur. The animal had parked himself at her feet about five seconds after CC had sat down and stayed. "Success."

It was a relief. CC had managed to talk the

council into doing something quick and simple, using just an iPhone and some editing to present Credence's case to the country. Something slicker would have cost more money and taken too long. This had taken half a day of CC's time and about half an hour of editing. The video may have been a little on the hokey side, but it was full of heart, with everyone from Don to Bob and Ray and Annie plus a bunch of Credence bachelors throwing out the welcome mat.

And it'd been a hit.

Which meant forward plans were well underway. Buses were leaving central Denver at midday next Friday, and so far they'd managed to place all the confirmed single women in Credence households, including surrounding farms. Even Ronnie and Cal were taking in two. Bob's helper almost had the boardinghouse to rights, and the whole town had pitched in to furnish it. Just as they'd pitched in to help with the welcome party planned on Friday night and for the cookout by the lake the next evening.

They'd set themselves an impossibly tight schedule, but the town had risen to the occasion, and the buzz it had created was tangible. *Everyone* was talking about it.

"A paper from New York called this morning," Ronnie said as she reopened the lid of her laptop, clicking to the FB video again.

CC glanced up from the spreadsheet she was working on. "An interview?"

She shook her head. "They wanted to know if we could book them into the local hotel for three nights."

CC snorted. Of course they did. The media were

pretty much all the same—we want to do a story on you but you're going to have to pay for it by putting us up and letting us have an all-access pass.

Blah. Blah. Blah.

"I hope you told them to take a hike."

The truth was, Credence didn't need the publicity. The video had gone viral, and they had enough eager women willing to come and check the town out without being plastered all over the news as some kind of weird curiosity.

"Told them the same thing I told the others. They're welcome to come, but they're going to have to sleep in their vans."

CC laughed. "Good."

Ronnie grinned. "Wade'd be proud."

Which focused CC's brain firmly back on the man in question. Thankfully, she'd had no more dreams about the guy, and she was just about over her embarrassment and dwelling on it a hundred times a day. But reading through Wade's pages yesterday afternoon had caused a different kind of consternation she hadn't been able to stop thinking about.

Wade had reached the point in his memoir—which he was telling chronologically—about Jasmine. He'd written precisely half a page and moved on. His brevity spoke volumes, and it had been niggling at her. She'd never asked Wade about it before—she didn't talk about her private stuff, he didn't talk about his—but she'd Google-fued the bejesus out of it when she'd first started in his employ and knew the basics.

Nude pictures of a sleeping Wade early in his NFL career had been sold to a tabloid by his then-girlfriend. His first Super Bowl ring, all new and shiny and prominent, had been obvious and perilously close to a part of his anatomy that some online media outlets had chosen *not* to pixelate.

Wade had taken the tabloid to court over it and won, but...removing pictures from the internet was like trying to chop the head off the Hydra.

His silence on the subject, the way she had to brief any media even fifteen years down the track that the topic was off-limits, was understandable. But surely his memoir would be the perfect place to explore the incident? Not only for catharsis, but to give his side of the story? Tell all and put the whole sleazy tale to bed for good.

Not to mention how the inclusion of this incident might make the book more attractive to readers. Especially for someone like her, who wasn't a diehard NFL fan. Readers bought memoirs for intimate details of the subjects' lives, and CC thought something like this was fair game. In her opinion, women would go nuts for the full story.

And that was, after all, what Wade had wanted her here for. To help and *advise* him as he wrote the book.

CC flicked a glance at Ronnie. Maybe if CC understood more detail about what had gone down, she'd know whether to push it or not with Wade. But was it appropriate to ask his mother about it?

In the end, she decided it was.

"Ronnie..."

"Yes, darlin'." Ronnie looked up from the screen absently.

"I know this isn't any of my business, but...do you know what happened with Jasmine?"

"Oh." Ronnie sat back in her chair, her hand fluttering at her neck a little, obviously surprised by the question.

"It's just that…Wade only wrote a half page about the whole incident yesterday, and I kinda think he should go deeper. I think people reading his memoir will be expecting some more in-depth reflection."

Ronnie shrugged. "He doesn't talk about it to anyone, Cecilia. Certainly not me or his father. I can't see him opening up about it to potentially hundreds of thousands of readers."

"So you don't think I should push him on it?"

"You can try, but…"

CC nodded. "It's been fifteen years. You don't think he should have dealt with it by now?"

"She hurt him deeply. He loved her, and she betrayed him." Ronnie's lips flattened. "He was going to ask her to marry him, you know? He'd shown me the ring."

Oh. Well. *Fuck*. CC hadn't known that. Obviously it had been serious with Jasmine if he'd been all set to marry her.

A spurt of something hot and dark bubbled through CC's veins. Why would a woman squander that kind of commitment from a man she supposedly loved?

"I was thrilled," Ronnie continued. "Wade had been sowing his wild oats a little too much for this Texan momma. Made it a little hard for me to hold up my head in church, he did. But then Jasmine came along, and she was a lovely young thing. A little immature, but Cal and I really liked her."

CC asked the question that had always bugged her. "Why'd she do it?"

"I don't know, Cecilia." Ronnie shook her head. "I think she had some student debt and she thought Wade would see it as a bit of a lark."

A lark? To have his junk spread all over the internet? Could anyone be that naive?

"Why didn't he take her to court? Not just the tabloid?"

"The court case was a bit of a circus. I don't think he wanted to repeat the experience."

CC nodded. Which was probably the same reason he didn't want to write about it. "So you don't think I should push him?"

Ronnie leaned forward on her elbows, regarding CC seriously for a moment. "I think...it might be good for him, mentally, you know, to at least get it all down. Even if it doesn't make it in the final cut? I've always fretted that he bottled too much up during that time."

Yeah. CC was starting to think that might be true. And maybe the best way to sell it to Wade? Write it, all of it, and then decide whether to include it at the end.

George, hearing a distant drone of an engine, lifted his head and cocked it to the side and barked.

"That'll be the men." Ronnie stood. "Land sakes... time got away from me. They'll be wantin' their lunch."

It was on the tip of CC's tongue to suggest that the men were perfectly capable of making their own lunch, but that wasn't the way things were done in Ronnie's household. She might be on the city council, but on the farm it was all home and hearth.

"I'm fixing some hoagies, you want one, darlin'?"

"Sure." CC stood. "I'll help."

Ronnie waved her down. "No, darlin', you keep going with that spreadsheet. It won't take me long."

The dog barked in agreement, and CC sat again as the rumble of motors pulled up outside and switched off. The sound of water running in the mudroom came next, then Cal and Wyatt entered moments later. Cal had struck up a compromise with his sons, because being inside was making him as restless as a caged lion. They'd agreed he could come out with them, get some air, but he wasn't allowed to do any work. So far he was sticking to the agreement, but apparently only because the brothers were playing hardball.

Wade entered a couple of seconds later, and her heart gave a funny little leap.

It hadn't stopped leaping in her chest at the sight of him playing farmer. She wished it would, because frankly, it was really freaking inconvenient. It wasn't like she hadn't seen him hot and sweaty and accomplished-looking hundreds of times. It was exactly how he looked each time he'd run off a field after a game. But there was just something so damn *male* about *this* kind of hot and sweaty.

In jeans and a T-shirt, the smell of hay and sunshine clinging to his skin and hair, dirt on his jeans, a ten-gallon hat hanging from his fingers. He looked less athletic, less polished.

Less *jock*. More…rough and raw and ready. More me Tarzan, you Jane. More…Cro-Magnon.

Like he could toss her over his shoulder, throw

her down in a haystack, and—*Whoa!* Jesus. She was turning into a sexual deviant. Or at the very least a sexual *idiot*.

That's what too much farmer porn did for you. If she wasn't careful, she'd start salivating wildly every time Wade pointed the car in the direction of the farm.

Cal kissed his wife on the cheek, his hand sliding onto Ronnie's butt as he did so. She laughed and batted it away. "The children, Cal."

"Yeah, Cal," Wade said, "the children."

Wyatt rolled his eyes at his brother, and CC laughed as Cal ignored all of them and continued to snuggle Ronnie from behind as she made the hoagies.

A pang of something that felt very much like jealousy slammed into CC's chest. What she would have given to have had parents like this growing up. Openly affectionate, plainly still in love after all these years. Instead of a father who hadn't wanted *any* of them and a mother who'd never quite gotten over his dessertion. Who's grief had manifested itself in a severe case of female helplessness with a side of emotional manipulation.

Seriously, if they'd owned a fainting couch, her mom would have spent most of her life draped upon it.

"Let me just make some space at the table," CC said, springing up to quell the swell of emotion rising in her chest.

"I'll help."

CC glanced up, surprised that Wyatt had spoken. She knew he was capable, she'd heard him joking around with Cal and Wade, giving as good as he got. But he'd barely said boo to her this past week.

In fact, he'd barely looked at her and radiated awkwardness whenever she said hi or smiled at him. Wade had told her his brother had always been shy around women, but this was DEFCON-level awkwardness. This was socially crippling.

This was Raj from *The Big Bang Theory*. Without the magic bullet of alcohol.

"Thanks."

He nodded before quickly looking away, but CC took him speaking directly to her as a win, as Wyatt finally relaxing around her enough to communicate.

It was a shame, really, because Wyatt was a decent-looking man. He was probably a touch taller than Wade, but not quite as broad through the shoulders. His legs and arms were more lanky than sculpted, and his face was…homey, his features plainer than Wade's and weathered from years of outdoor work. It was like Wyatt had been the prototype and Wade was the polished product.

He reached for the nearest pile of papers, stacking them on the ones next door, then stacking both of them on top of the next.

"Careful, bro," Wade *tsked*. "You're a braver man than I am, messing with CC's system. If you get the colors out of order, she gets all twitchy."

"Oh, jeez, sorry…" Wyatt looked at the papers in his hands as horrified as if he'd dropped them in the middle of a hog wallow.

CC *was* getting twitchy watching Wyatt mess up her beautifully ordered piles, but she quelled the irritation. "It's fine." She smiled at Wyatt. "Your brother likes to exaggerate."

He still looked stricken but relaxed a little and

said, "That's what all the girls at high school said."

CC let out a burst of surprised laughter. So did Cal. Ronnie chided Wyatt and Cal for their lack of decorum.

Wade grinned, completely unconcerned by his brother's dig. "Change the subject all you want, but I can see CC's eye twitching from here. Admit it, woman, you're a neat freak."

"I like things to be tidy and ordered, that's all," she said as she absently tapped the pile of paper against the table to line up all the edges.

Jeez, there were worse things a person could be.

Wade quirked an eyebrow, looking pointedly at the papers in her hand. "You're Monica Geller." He turned to his brother. "You should see her desk, you could take an appendix out on that thing."

"Unlike yours, which is buried under sports magazines, hundreds of bits of random paper, half of them scrunched into balls, all types of sporting paraphernalia, several coffee mugs leaving dirty rings everywhere, and two hundred empty Nerds boxes."

"A man's gotta eat, darlin'."

CC rolled her eyes, ignoring the way her nipples perked up at the very Southern and deliberate way he'd said darlin'. Just like his momma.

Only sexy.

"For a man who saw a professional sports nutritionist for years, you have a terrible diet."

"Maybe." He shrugged. "It doesn't change the fact that you, Cecilia Morgan, are just a tiny bit obsessive."

CC faltered at him calling her Cecilia. The only other time he'd done that had been in *the dream*, and that was the last thing she needed to be reminded of right now. Her cheeks grew warm, and she busied herself some more.

"Am not."

Jesus. How old was she? She might as well just stamp her foot and get it over with.

"You floss your teeth three times a day."

"Flossing is important." She'd learned that from *Pretty Woman*.

"Okay you two, quit bellyaching at each other." Ronnie placed a plate loaded with hoagies in front of them. "You sound like an old married couple."

CC blinked at Ronnie, who was staring at the two of them, a speculative gleam in her eyes CC didn't like at all. She snuck a look at Wade, who was staring at his mother as if she'd lost her mind.

The sad thing to admit was they'd probably spent more time together in the last almost-six years than most married couples did. There were few things she didn't know about Wade.

Although she doubted the same could be said for him.

Wyatt laughed into the sudden silence in the room and reached for a sandwich. "Yep, that did it."

CHAPTER TEN

CC glanced at Wade as they drove back to the house. Neither of them spoke. It hadn't been what his mother had said, as far as she was concerned, rather that calculating expression of Ronnie's that had been the most worrying. Between that and the way Wade had called her Cecilia, she had a lot on her mind.

So maybe now was the perfect time to think about something else entirely. To broach the subject of Jasmine? Ronnie had, after all, indicated that she thought it would be a good idea for Wade to at least get it all down on paper, even if it did end up on the cutting room floor.

"I have a suggestion," she said into the silence. "About the book."

He glanced at her briefly, frowning slightly as if he'd been deep in thought as well and she'd dragged him right out. "Okay."

"You might not like it."

He sighed. "I'm not getting someone else to write it, CC."

CC. Phew. Yes, that was better. Back to normal. No Cecilia. Back to employer and employee. Back to him being a bossy, demanding jerk.

It gave her the courage to plow on.

"You wrote half a page about the Jasmine thing," she said, her gaze glued to his profile, his strong jaw, the blade of his cheekbone.

A stillness came over his frame. Others might

have missed it, but CC had been reading Wade's body language for a lot of years now. Even doing something as passive as driving, Wade always vibrated with energy, so yeah, she noticed. The angle of his jaw tightened, and in her peripheral vision his knuckles whitened around the steering wheel.

"The *Jasmine thing* is private."

He was using his haughty don't-you-know-who-I-am voice she'd heard him use to good effect on several occasions over the years. But it didn't scare CC. And the more he objected, the more certain she was that it should go in the book.

"I think that's a mistake."

"Your objection is noted."

His voice had gone from haughty to frigid. But, again, CC wasn't perturbed. "It's your memoir, Wade, people will be reading it *for* the private stuff. That's what a memoir is."

"Not this one."

"People want to read about you. They want to know stuff they can't already find out by Googling you, and I know for damn sure the publisher, who, by the way, paid you a shitload of money to write it, is expecting the Jasmine thing to be in there, too."

He unwrapped and wrapped his fingers around the steering wheel several times before he answered. "She's in there."

"She's practically a footnote, Wade." He didn't reply, just stared resolutely forward. "Your mother said—"

"What?" His head turned with raptor-like precision as he speared her with thunderous eyes. "You talked to my mother about it?"

"It came up."

His gaze flicked back to the road. "I didn't realize you two had time to gossip while plotting a mass street orgy for Credence."

CC ignored his sarcasm. "She worries about you. About how the whole incident affected you. She feels it might be therapeutic to at least write about it. In full. You don't have to use it in the final edit. And, I gotta say, I agree with her."

"Goddamn it, CC. My mother doesn't know the half of it."

CC blinked. *There was more?* More than taking nude pictures and selling them to a tabloid? CC wasn't sure she wanted to know. But backing off wasn't her role here. She was supposed to be pushing him to dig deeper. "So tell *me*, then."

"No."

CC had lost count of the number of times she'd wanted to brain Wade Carter over the years. The urge hadn't diminished in these penultimate months. "Look…Wade… You asked me to stay and help you with this book, you wanted my editing skills *and* my advice. So let me advise you, damn it. Otherwise I'm not really sure why I'm here. I might as well just pack my bags and leave now."

He didn't say anything for the longest time, his knuckles whitening again. The sound of the car wheels against the road the only noise in the cab. CC sighed and returned her attention to the fields of drying yellowed grass.

"She came back. A couple of months after the tabloid stuff. Said she was pregnant."

CC shut her eyes briefly at the devastation in his

voice. Ronnie had been right, he really had loved her.

"My lawyer demanded a paternity test. She came back two days later, said she'd miscarried... She looked awful. It was...awful. I mean, a baby would have been..." He shook his head. "I didn't want a baby, but..."

But he'd have done the honorable thing.

"It was still my baby." His knuckles looked like they were about to burst through his skin now. "My mother would have been over the moon."

CC smiled. "I imagine she would have been."

"Anyway, I found out a couple of months later, from one of her friends, she hadn't been pregnant at all. She'd...faked it. I'd spent two months wondering what that baby would have looked like and feeling shitty and like I'd let her down even though *she'd* violated my right to privacy, and...it hadn't ever existed."

"Oh, Wade." CC reached out and slid a hand onto his forearm without even thinking about it. She'd have done the same for anyone, but this felt a lot more personal. More intimate. She hadn't known, until just now, that this man, who could exasperate her beyond distraction, could also tug on her heart strings. "I'm so sorry."

"Yeah. Well." He shrugged, and her hand slipped from his arm. "I don't think it all needs to be dragged up again, okay?"

"You're still in love with her?"

The realization cut deeper than CC would have thought possible. Maybe that was why Wade treated women so casually, because he was still in love with a woman who had destroyed his trust and broken his heart and he was never going *there* again.

"*Hell no.*" He shook his head vehemently, his voice laced heavily with conviction. "But she was twenty-three years old. She's thirty-eight now and very sorry for what she did."

CC shrugged. "So say that."

"No. She's married with two teenage daughters. She's a public school teacher. None of the people in her life need the kind of shit storm that me *revealing all* will bring down on them."

CC had to admit that was a real possibility, and his generosity of spirit was humbling. A lot of people might not have been so forgiving. "Fine…" She sighed. "No Jasmine."

He shot her a triumphant grin, and just like that she wanted to brain him again.

• • •

"Hey, what you watching?"

Wade stood in the doorway of the red sitting room—yup, he owned a *red sitting room*—eyeing CC, who was lounging in one of the old-fashioned wingback chairs, her legs tucked up under her, deeply engrossed in the television as she absently wound something in her hands.

It was close to midnight, and he'd assumed she'd gone to bed when she'd left her desk a few hours ago.

She glanced up as if his presence had startled her, that little v drawing her brows together, her hands stilling in their task. "*Escape to the Country.*" She returned her eyes to the screen. "My favorite show."

He'd never heard of it. "Looks English," Wade

remarked as he moved into the room, coming to a halt behind the elegant vintage Chesterfield sofa, placing his hands on the rolled leather top.

"It is. BBC. Netflix streams older seasons."

"What's it about?"

Her hands resumed what they'd been doing as she continued to watch the screen. Bandages, she was rolling bandages. Obviously his mother had enlisted CC's help in her latest project, which was rolling up strips of old bedsheets into bandages for shipment to third-world countries for struggling health clinics.

There was already a neat stack of rolled bandages lined up on the chair beside her.

"It's a property show that helps prospective buyers find their dream homes."

Wade laughed. Of course that would be her television choice. No *The Real Housewives of New York City* or *Game of Thrones* for CC. "Sounds like your kind of crack?"

A small smile brushed her lips, but she didn't bother to respond as Wade traversed the sofa and sat his ass down on the end seat closest to CC's chair, which wasn't far from the Chesterfield. If he wanted, he could reach across the small gap and lay his hand on the arm of her chair.

He wouldn't. But he was surprised by how much he wanted to.

Telling her about Jasmine today had been cathartic. Difficult, but cathartic. She wasn't a subject he usually discussed with anyone, and nobody but he and Jasmine knew the full story.

And now CC...

He didn't know how he felt about that. About

exposing his underbelly to her view. He wasn't used to being...*vulnerable*...to anyone. But her soft empathy had been comforting. They didn't really have that kind of relationship. Not before Credence, anyway. Not before cohabiting so closely and having the town welcome CC so warmly.

His heart kicked in his chest. Their relationship was shifting. It was subtle but undeniable. Right now it felt...*cozy*. And *domestic*. And he liked it. Liked sitting next to CC watching TV late at night.

Made it even harder to contemplate her leaving, though...

Her question about whether he still loved his ex had taken him by surprise. His vehement response maybe even more so. Prior to her asking, he'd have thought it would be a question he'd grapple with. But the answer had been clear and unequivocal. He'd been clinging to this idea that because he'd loved her once, he was destined to love her always— he was a Carter, and they loved for life—and that's what kept him from committing to anyone else. But when forced to look closer, he'd realized he'd fallen out of love with Jasmine a very long time ago.

He watched the show for a minute or two before saying, "You know there'll be sports on ESPN, right?"

Without looking at him, CC said, "You know there are two other TVs in this house, right?"

Wade laughed. "Okay then." He held out his hand. "Pass over some of those damn bandages."

CC passed him a large unopened bag of clean, laundered strips and a wooden tongue depressor to wrap them around.

Wade opened them and plucked the first one out

and started winding. "So who's the presenter chick?"

Her hands stoped mid-wind, and she shot him an impatient glare. "Are you going to talk the whole way through?"

He laughed again. "No, ma'am."

They settled in, watching as they companionably wound bandages. They did talk, commenting on bits and pieces throughout the episode. The things they did and didn't like about each house. The price. The unrealistic expectations. They even hotly debated which house was better. But mostly Wade just watched CC's face, the mix of emotions as she went on the journey with Reg and Shelagh. Her smile when the couple fell in love with the mystery house was big and dazzling only to fall, her teeth digging into her bottom lip, when it was just a titch above what they could pay.

She really went on the roller coaster ride with the couple, and it was so damn cute. *She* was so damn cute.

"You reckon they'll work out a way to get the mystery house?" Wade asked, the chipper orchestral music playing as the credits rolled.

"I hope so. They obviously fell in love with it."

"But they can't afford it." Wade kept his tone matter-of-fact, hoping to rile her a little.

She turned a frustrated gaze on him. "But it's obviously their *dream home*."

Wade laughed at her adamant response, and she rolled her eyes at him, realizing he'd been hoping she'd react. "So…do you have a dream house?"

CC glanced down at the bandage she was rolling. "Just anywhere I can see the ocean will do."

Wade shook his head. "Nope." No way did someone who'd been saving for almost six years to buy her own place and claimed *Escape to the Country* as her favorite television show *not* have a house she aspired to. Especially not CC. She was methodical and organized and obsessively stalked real estate websites. "Don't believe you."

For a moment, she looked like she was going to blow him off again, but then she sighed. "There's this place... It's not for sale anymore, I saw it online years ago. It's a quaint little beach cottage just out of San Clemente. It's more Cape Cod than California, but it's cute and kitschy with this little white picket fence that goes all the way around and flower beds lining the front path, and it's perched on a headland, and the views...ocean for miles."

Her expression had turned dreamy and her gaze distant, and Wade sucked in a breath, his lungs suddenly tight. Man, she *really* loved that house.

"I have a picture." She grabbed her phone and did some swiping. "I can't afford it, not even with the money I earned recently from that investment, but yeah, it's a definite dream home." She handed her phone over. "There are three different pics, keep swiping."

Wade took it and looked at the images. He vaguely recognized the area, and she was right, the views were incredible. But it was teeth-achingly cute, not something he'd pictured CC in at all.

"I didn't take you as the white-picket-fence type."

She made a little noise in the back of her throat, which was either emotion or dismissal. "It's all I wanted as a little girl. There were a lot of white picket fenced houses in my town, with flowers peeking through the slats and children who laughed and families who smiled. Our fence was all ramshackle, and my mother used it as some kind of weapon between her and my father, constantly calling him about fixing it because he was the man and it was his job to take care of her, and why wasn't he taking care of her, they'd made vows and how was she supposed to do this stuff without a man around."

Wade was surprised at the admission. It seemed like today was the day for opening up to each other. In five and a half years, it was the most they'd ever talked about their pasts. Their wounds. "Could your brothers not have fixed the fence?"

"Of course." CC laughed, but it wasn't a happy sound. "But it wasn't about the fence. It was about Mom being so old-school she didn't even know how to access their bank account when Dad left. I was little when he walked out, but Mom laments about it often enough to know the whole sorry story. They had a very traditional marriage, where he was the breadwinner and she was the homemaker. He dished her out an allowance at the beginning of the week for groceries and the like, and he dealt with everything else. If she needed something outside the household budget, he bought it for her. She'd relied on him for everything, had been happy to be the little woman and to be taken care of. It *did not* equip her to be alone."

CC's bangs had fallen forward on one side, and she tucked them behind her ear as she took a breath. Wade followed the motion, one he'd seen her do thousands of times, wondering when it had gotten this distracting.

"Look… I know my mom wouldn't have been the first woman of her generation to be like that, but she made no effort to change either, to learn. She almost…*thrived* on her helplessness, she *definitely* played on it, instead of doing something about it."

Wade would have described his parents' marriage as reasonably traditional, but he couldn't imagine what his mother would do to his father if he even suggested he give her an *allowance*. He'd have needed more than a pacemaker, that was for sure.

And Veronica Carter would have had that fence fixed lickety-split.

"That must have been difficult," he said tentatively, not wanting to pry, afraid she might realize she was giving away too much and pull back if he pushed too hard, too soon.

Getting to know *this* CC was fascinating.

"Yeah." Her shoulders sagged. "It could be, but… it also made me really determined. To *never* make myself so reliant on a man that I couldn't do a damn thing for myself. Determined to have a job and my own money and my own dreams and ambitions. To buy my own stuff, to *fix* my own stuff, to be independent."

Wade nodded at the truth in her words. CC was fiercely independent. "I guess that's the silver lining in all those dark clouds?"

A grudging smile touched her mouth. "Definitely."

"Well…for what it's worth, I'm…sorry you went through all that. "

An apology wasn't much, and what was done was done, but he *could* acknowledge what she'd been through and its impact. He could be sorry that she hadn't had the white picket fence upbringing she deserved. That hundreds of thousands of kids growing up in broken homes in this country deserved.

Tonight, more than ever, he was grateful for his upbringing, for parents who loved each other and a community that took care of one another.

He handed over her phone, and she took it, her cheeks pinking up as if suddenly embarrassed by her spiel, by what she'd given away. "Other kids have it much worse."

Sure. But one did not negate the other. Sensing she was closing off, he changed the subject. "So... why the ocean? You can get white picket fences all over the country."

She perked up a little at the change of subject. "It's the first place I remember being happy, you know? That school trip I went on to California. It was so wild and beautiful and...*free*. There's something so free about the ocean. And...everybody was just so damn...*happy* around me. Of course, the fact it was far, far away from Nebraska also helped. I don't—" She shook her head. "It's hard to explain. It's like you and this place."

She looked around at the heavy brocade curtains covering the tall windows, at the embossed wallpaper and the high ceilings.

"You remember how much you wanted this house as a child? It wasn't rational or even possible at that stage, but it was there, in your gut."

"Yeah..." Wade nodded. He understood irrational pulls, he was feeling one now, feeling a warmness in his gut and a skip in his pulse as CC's lashes made shadows on her cheekbones whenever they closed.

"That's how I felt after I'd been to California. So I headed there as soon as I was finished with school. Got my first job at a reception desk of a Rodondo Beach hotel. And, until you, I hadn't moved from California."

And, too soon, she was going to be moving back. *Christ.* What would he do without her? He'd spent years building their working relationship, and she knew all his *stuff.* The way he liked things on his desk and what was his favorite takeout and which auto shop he used and which bow tie he liked best and… and when *not* to talk to him and who he went to for particular career issues and…who he confided in, who he trusted.

It would take forever for someone else to learn it all. And who else would put up with his crap? "About that."

His heart beat double-time as his brain crowded with the words to say next, the dozen ways he could open a dialogue about extending her contract. But the next episode started, and she was returning her attention to the screen, shushing him quiet. So he shushed. Because sitting companionably with CC was preferable to her getting cranky.

And he was a big, fat coward.

CHAPTER ELEVEN

Wade could not believe he was sitting in the bleachers at the Credence High School football field a week later, watching four buses loaded to the gills with women disgorge their cargo.

But his mother had made him promise he'd be here, and CC had guilted him into keeping it.

"Well *hello*, ladies," Drew said, grinning as the sound of female voices and laughter drifted to them on the breeze. Even from this distance, the women of all shapes and sizes sparkled in the summer sunshine.

Most of the town had turned out to witness the spectacle, as evidenced by the parked cars ringing the perimeter of the field. It made Wade feel less pervy sitting up here with his friends when the entire town appeared to also be staring.

Sure, most of them were actually there to pick up one of the temporary arrivals as their hosts for the weekend, but they were still agog at so many women. Wade doubted Credence had *ever* had this many women, even in its heyday.

One hundred and eighty, according to CC.

"Who said all your Christmases can't come at once?" Drew mused.

Wade snorted. "Bah humbug," he muttered, then threw back a fistful of Nerds.

He was sure his face was somehow going to end up on the front of a tabloid, either from one of the women snapping a sneaky pic on her phone or one of the many telephoto lenses strung around the necks of so-called journalists currently fluttering around the women in the middle of the field.

And no one could convince him any different.

"Who brought the Grinch?" Arlo asked. "Or whoever the hell you're supposed to be," he added as he took in the baseball cap pulled low on Wade's forehead and the dark sunglasses.

The guys laughed, and Wade rolled his eyes. "I'm incognito, dickwad."

"You really need to work on your attitude toward law enforcement there, buddy."

"Bite me."

More laughter as Wyatt sat forward, twirling his hat between his legs. "They sure do look pretty."

Which, for Wyatt, was profuse praise. Wade would have thought this was the kind of place his brother would have run a hundred miles from, but his mother had tasked Wyatt with picking up the two women they were hosting for the weekend, and what his mother wanted, his mother usually got.

She might have been little, but she was fierce.

God knew what Wyatt was going to say to them, given how tongue-tied he was around the opposite sex, but maybe they'd be gaga for the strong, silent type. Wade didn't know how long it had been since his brother had last gotten laid, but the guy clearly needed a bit of *somethin' somethin'*.

"Yeah, they do," Tucker agreed. He'd shut the bar for an hour so he could also be here to check out the newcomers. "Sure hope they like to drink."

It was Wade's experience that when women flocked together, they were all about the drinking. He expected it to be kinda wild at Jack's the next couple of nights. "Been brushing up on your fruity cocktails?" Wade asked.

"Just because you yokels only drink beer doesn't mean I can't mix a mean daiquiri. I even bought little umbrellas."

Wade laughed. He'd never thought he'd see drinks with umbrellas being served at Jack's.

A megaphone crackled to life and carried across the field. "Okay ladies, gather around." It was his mother doing what she did best—corralling. "We have our mayor, Don Randall, to say a few words of welcome, then we'll get you all situated with your hosts."

About half of the women followed the no-nonsense authority in Ronnie's voice to a small raised dais supporting a mic stand and a preening Don. Several trestle tables had been set up next to the dais. CC and Cal were one of a half-dozen people sitting behind the tables, manned with clipboards, ready to let the visitors know where they were being hosted. Bob and Ray were there, as was Arlo's sister.

The other half were too busy chatting or hugging or squealing excitedly to follow his mother's instructions. They were braver people than he. Clearly, these were the ones who were here to have fun. Something to tell their city friends about when they got home.

Wade shifted uncomfortably in his seat at the thought.

"If you would please, ladies?" His mother's voice again, this time in *that* tone he knew so well. "We want to get you settled in with your hosts as soon as possible."

Arlo stood and pulled his hat low on his fore-head. "That's my cue. Looks like there's some crowd control needed."

"Shit, man," Drew lamented. "Some days your job just sucks, right?"

"Well…it's tough, I can't deny, but someone's got to do it."

Tucker laughed. "What a prince. Taking one for the team like that."

"I think the word you're after is upstanding citizen," Arlo said as he turned away and tramped down the bleachers like he had springs in his boots. As soon as he hit the grass, though, his limp, usually so subtle most people weren't even aware he had a prosthetic leg, suddenly became more pronounced.

Upstanding citizen *bullshit*. Arlo was really working it.

"He's so getting laid tonight," Drew said.

All the guys nodded.

• • •

CC was thrilled with the turnout. It was warm in the sun, and she was grateful for her baseball cap and her icy cold Red Bull. Not that she needed it; the buzz from the crowd in the middle of the field was energizing. The chatter had risen tenfold as the host families had descended to claim their charges. It seemed like everyone was already getting on like a house on fire.

There was only about a dozen women left to allocate, and then they could move on to the next part of the proceedings—checking all was going according to plan for the street party tonight.

CC smiled at the next woman in the line. She had a small battered-looking carry-on sized case at her feet, which were shod in scuffed-looking sneakers. She looked about thirty, average height, average size, and was wearing jeans that were faded in the kind of way that spoke of multiple washes rather than designer labels. Her T-shirt was plain blue, and her hair, which might have been red once, was now a faded kind of chestnut and pulled back into a ponytail.

"Come on over," she said, waving her closer.

Rather than dragging the case by its handle, she picked it up, and CC could see that it was missing a wheel.

"Hi," she said. "I'm CC, welcome to Credence."

The woman smiled, and it was warm and lovely, but CC was hit by how *tired* she looked. "I'm Jenny. Jennifer. Jennifer Charles."

CC consulted the printouts she'd painstakingly prepared for everyone helping with the check-in procedure. They were all arranged alphabetically according to surname, and every page had details of each visitor as well as which family was hosting them, including which family representative would be picking them up from the field.

"Oh yes, Jennifer. Here you are." CC was surprised to read that the woman in front of her was twenty-five, not thirty. She must have been *really* tired. "Oh, how lucky, you're with the Carters." CC nudged Wade's father in the ribs. "Cal, meet Jennifer, your second guest."

She couldn't have been any more different from the bouncy twenty-two-year-old blonde CC had checked in about twenty minutes ago. Roxy had been in tiny shorts and an even tinier T-shirt that was more boob tube than anything else. She'd been sporting two large suitcases—one apparently for her accessories, although, if they were as tiny as the rest of her clothes, CC wasn't entirely sure why she needed such big bags. Wyatt had practically retreated inside his shell at the sight of her as he'd come forward to collect his charge.

Cal looked up from his papers and smiled at Jennifer, reaching out his hand. "Pleased to meet you." They shook hands. "Wyatt's going to take you back to the farm." Cal moved his body back and forward, craning his neck to see around the milling groups for his son. "He should be around somewhere. And Ronnie, that's the mad woman with the megaphone—but don't tell her I said that." He chuckled deeply at his own daring. "She's my wife. We'll be along in a little while. Gotta check on some last-minute things for tonight."

"Thank you. I appreciate it."

CC handed over the welcome pack, something they'd prepared to help their guests become acquainted with the town, and a copy of the program that had been organized for them over the course of the weekend.

"Just a little something to help you navigate the weekend." She spotted Wyatt's hatted head a little ways off. Roxy was chatting away madly, and he looked like he wanted to be *anywhere* else.

"Oh, thank you."

Jenny scanned through the pages as CC waved her hand at Wyatt to get his attention. She didn't know where Wade was, but she knew he was here.

She could feel his eyes on her, which she'd been too busy to dwell on, thankfully. Because something had shifted between them since the night they'd folded bandages and she'd opened up a little about her childhood and why California was so important. It wasn't something she'd ever done with Wade and, had he not shared the Jasmine story earlier that day, she probably never would have.

It wasn't that she'd felt she *owed* him. It wasn't quid pro quo. But it had felt…right…in that moment. She'd *wanted* to tell him.

And there'd been a sense of *ease* between them ever since.

Ronnie approached with her megaphone, and CC performed the introductions. "So lovely to meet you," Ronnie said, smiling pleasantly before picking up the megaphone and calling, "Wyatt to the registration desk, please."

CC clamped down on a smile as Wyatt reacted immediately. Any other time, she suspected he might take exception to his mother embarrassing him like this, but Wyatt looked relieved for any excuse to leave Little Miss Chatty. He strode over in long lanky strides in his usual efficient manner.

"This is Jenny, darlin'," Ronnie said as he approached. "She'll be staying with us for the next two nights."

Jenny turned to face Wyatt just as he was pulling up, and what happened next was like something out of a cartoon. Wyatt performed a double-take at the first sight of Jenny, and neither of them did or said anything for a beat or two, they just stared.

Ronnie nudged CC in the ribs and glanced at Cal,

who was also watching the interplay between his son and their guest.

Finally, Jenny stuck out her hand and said, "Nice to meet you, Wyatt." She didn't look so tired anymore.

Wyatt, to his credit, had the wherewithal to remove his hat before sliding his hand into hers. CC was sure she saw his Adam's apple bob—twice. "Likewise, ma'am."

Neither broke the handshake, they just looked at each other like neither had seen a member of the opposite sex before. Ronnie was beaming at the exchange.

"It's just Jenny," she finally said.

"Yes, ma'am."

Jenny laughed then, and so did Wyatt and it was warm and sincere, and then Jenny was beaming and it was like being dropped into the middle of a headlight factory.

"Maybe you should be getting this young lady home, Wyatt?"

Ronnie's interruption brought the two of them out of their trance, and Wyatt dropped her hand and quickly glanced away from Jenny, cramming his hat on his head. "Sure," he said, picking up her bag.

"I can get that," she said, reaching for it.

He looked at her again. "I got it."

She dropped her hand. "Thank you."

Wyatt just nodded and said, "Let's go."

Jenny smiled at them and said, "See you later, Cal, Ronnie," and turned to follow Wyatt, who was three paces ahead.

"Well…I'll be…" Ronnie's hand fluttered around her throat as she and Cal and CC watched Jenny and

Wyatt depart.

"Chemistry," Cal said, nodding.

And CC had to admit he was right. The air had bristled between Jenny and Wyatt. She was happy for Wyatt. The guy might be quiet and not quite the dazzler that was Wade, but he was a good, kind, decent man and, in a world full of jerks, that wasn't to be sneezed at.

Maybe this crazy idea hadn't been so crazy after all.

· · ·

Wyatt barely dared to breathe as he steered the ATV to the bottom field where the hogs were grazing. On the seat behind him sat Jennifer, her thighs warm and soft along the outside of his, her arms around his waist.

"You can go faster, you know?" Her voice was low and throaty, like she had a cold, and it tickled his ear and, if possible, his pulse picked up even more. Could she feel his heart pounding through his abdomen?

Go faster? And have this end quicker? No way.

He couldn't get his head around what had just happened. Thinking about it had his hands trembling around the handlebars. He'd been ready to head for the Rockies when Roxy had landed on him with her bags and her fancy nails and her incessant chatter about the heat and the lack of wifi and Instagram.

She was very pretty, with a cute nose and a smattering of freckles. But way too outgoing for him—not that she was in Credence for *him*, but he'd known if they were all like this he'd be staying home tonight. His own shyness was magnified tenfold by such extroversion, and he didn't need to feel any more awkward than he already did around women.

Roxy thought everything was *cute* and wanted to take a picture of it for her Instagram followers, of which there were apparently many. In twenty minutes, while he'd politely listened, she'd told him all about her best friend's recent operation for bigger boobs and showed him the pics on *Insta*, how her boss was having an affair with one of the customer's wives, and recounted the disasters of her last date with a guy she just should have swiped left on.

These also all seemed to be hysterically funny, if her constant giggle was any gauge. He hoped it was just because she was nervous, otherwise her lack of filter was staggering. He couldn't imagine confiding any of his secrets to her. And he wondered how hilarious she'd find him still being a virgin *at his age*.

For him, it was no laughing matter. Just thinking about it made his ears hot and his chest tight. It was embarrassing and...*weird*.

Roxy would probably want to take a snap of his cute virginal dick and put it on *Insta*.

Hashtag *fortyyearoldvirgin*.

Then his mother was hollering at him through that dang megaphone he'd been wishing someone would take off her, and he'd met Jenny, and everything he'd always known was missing was suddenly right in front of him. It was such a ridiculous thing to feel in one instant, one tick of time, but he'd never been more certain of anything. Maybe she didn't flash and sparkle like Roxy, who had preferred some alone time with the house wifi than a tour of the farm, but it felt like he'd been made for Jenny, that he was put on this earth for her.

Maybe she didn't feel the same way. His experience with reading women was, after all, pretty much zero. But he thought he'd felt a connection.

The shyness he always felt around females didn't seem to be as acute around her, either. He was never going to be as slick as Wade, but he felt like he could actually talk to Jenny instead of stammer like a fool and kick the ground.

"We're here," he announced, turning his head slightly so his words wouldn't be whipped away. Even the curve of her cheek made him lightheaded.

Wyatt slowed the ATV even further and brought it to a gentle halt next to a gate. A few of the hogs grazing in the paddock looked up, but most just went about their business.

She didn't move, even after he cut the engine, just sat there, gazing at the field, her arms around him. With the wind gone, her scent enveloped him, which was no mean feat when hogs were nearby. She smelled like coconut, and his mouth watered as he inhaled and wondered if he'd totally lost his mind.

The urge to slide his hand onto her arm rode him hard, and Wyatt's heart beat faster trying to summon the courage. Wasn't it a little forward? He'd known her for two hours.

His hesitation cost him as she loosened her arms, her hand sliding away. It galvanized Wyatt into moving, offering her his hand as she dismounted, letting her go as soon as she was on her feet.

"So…" She pressed her forearms to the gate and

stared out over the field. "These are the hogs, huh?"

Wyatt nodded and smiled, his gaze resting on her profile, on the way her lips pressed together in pensive thought. "Sorry about the stink."

Her nose wrinkled as she sniffed the air. "It's not too bad." She turned her head to face him, and Wyatt's breath caught in his throat. "They look happy."

If his hogs were a fraction of the happy that he was right now, they'd be the happiest damn pigs on the planet. "We like to think they are."

"Could I go in? Are they…violent or something? Will they charge me?"

Wyatt gave a half laugh. The only thing in the field that was likely to charge her was him, and given his lack of experience in that department, he'd probably trip over his feet and end up facedown in a wallow.

The fact that she wanted to go in, that she hadn't shuddered the way Roxy had when he'd suggested the tour, squeezed fingers around his heart. "Sure."

He opened the gate and indicated she should precede him, her coconut aroma drifting to him as she passed, dizzying him further. She entered tentatively but didn't hang back, looking around her as she walked. Not down at her feet, worried about stepping in manure, but at the field and the animals and their shelters.

"Oh…piglets," she said, looking over her shoulder at him as she pointed at some bouncy pink babies happily following their mother.

Wyatt's breath hitched. Jenny was smiling, and the sun was shining and the whole landscape suddenly felt like a Dalí painting—utterly surreal. Was it possible to fall for someone so quickly?

He nodded. "You want to hold one?"

Her eyes lit up, her mouth curved bigger again. "Could I?"

This woman could do whatever the hell she wanted. He was 100 percent gone on her. She could ask him to leave and go back with her to Pittsburgh— she'd told Roxy where she was from in the car—and he'd turn his back on this farm and these hogs and Credence, all of which he loved with a ferocity as deep as the dark, black soil, and do it happily.

He hoped like hell she felt the same, because when she smiled at him like that, he felt like he was the only man on the planet.

They spent half an hour puttering around the field, during which time Jenny nursed several piglets. He'd been concerned that she'd get dirty, and she'd dismissed his concerns quickly. *What's a bit of dirt?* That was what she'd said. And Wyatt had fallen a little deeper.

They'd talked as they puttered. She'd asked him about the hogs and the running of the farm and the town and his parents and hadn't mentioned Wade once. It wouldn't be the first time he'd scored some female attention because of who his brother was, which had been monumentally wasted on a guy who clammed up whenever a woman got near.

Except for Jennifer. Wyatt didn't think he'd ever talked to a woman so much in his life.

"So what do you do?" he asked as they wandered back to the quad bike. "Back home in Pittsburgh?"

Wyatt blinked at the words tumbling from his

mouth. He was initiating conversation? He could spend all day talking about the farm ad nauseam to anyone who would listen—even a woman—the farm was his safe zone. But he couldn't quite believe that he was venturing into the land of small talk.

Jennifer was so easy to talk to, though. Normally just being with a woman, even showing her around the farm, would have his adrenaline flowing. The fear that he'd do something or say something stupid, almost paralyzing.

It *was* flowing, but not because he was anxious.

"Minimum-wage stuff, mostly."

Wyatt was so aware of her—the brush of her arm, the rasp of her breathing, the husky timbre of her voice like sandpaper against his skin.

"I didn't finish school, so it's mainly just waiting tables and working a cash register."

"Do you like it there? In Pittsburgh."

"I like it better here."

She glanced at him, and Wyatt's gut clenched. He *knew* she was feeling the same things. But…

His heart raced at the mere thought of asking the next question, but he had to know. "There's no…" He was going to say boyfriend, but couldn't even bring himself to say the word. Couldn't bear the thought that there might be someone else, even though this whole weekend was supposed to be for single women. "No one special back in Pittsburgh?"

She looked away and stumbled a little, and Wyatt's hand slid onto her elbow to steady her, his palm tingling from the contact even after he removed it. "No. There's no man in my life."

Wyatt grinned then, and she smiled back, and

the sun was behind her, gilding her faded red hair to spun gold, and it seemed like the most natural thing in the world to slip his hand into hers.

Christ. When had touching a woman ever felt anything other than excruciatingly fraught?

"So, you'd seriously think about moving here?"

She nodded. "So far, so good."

Wyatt squeezed her hand as his heart just about leapt out of his chest. "And you could just pick up and leave? From Pittsburgh?"

She looked away again. "Sure."

"There's a talk tomorrow at the civic center about how Credence can help any of the women who want to move to town."

"Yes. I saw that. I'm very interested in learning more."

They got to the gate and paused at the barrier. Wyatt knew it'd be the perfect spot to dip his head and kiss her, even though he'd only known her for a few hours. The sun was shining, and the air was sweet with grass and coconut, and she was looking up at him again like maybe she was expecting it, and he didn't think he'd read the signals wrong, and he wanted to kiss her so fucking bad.

A jungle drum beat inside his head and his chest as he stared at her mouth, but a spurt of the old anxiety jettisoned into his system and he lost his nerve. He'd kissed only four women in his life. The last had been over three years ago.

What if he screwed it up?

"Ladies first," he said, his hand slipping from hers as he reached for the gate and unlatched it, silently castigating himself for his hesitation. He felt like an idiot and awkward as all fuck again, the guy who couldn't get laid in two decades because he let his nerves get in the way of getting close to a woman.

But she smiled so sweetly at him as she brushed past, like it didn't matter, like they had all the time in the world, like he hadn't just committed the biggest fucking faux pas of his life, and the voices of reprimand inside his head settled.

Wyatt held out his hand, and she took it, swinging her leg over to mount the ATV. He slid in front of her, and this time when she put her arms around him, he slid his hands on top of hers. She responded by settling her cheek against his back and sighing, and Wyatt knew, as long as he lived, he'd never forget this afternoon in the field with Jenny.

CHAPTER TWELVE

Wade was impressed with how well the street party organizers had transformed the main street. He'd been tucked away writing all afternoon and had joined the festivities a short time ago. CC had been in the thick of it, which was annoying because he missed having her in the same room to bounce things off on a whim. But she'd been swept up in one of his mother's mad missions, and no one got in the way of Veronica Carter on a mission.

A section of the street had been closed off using bales of hay as dividers. They also doubled for seating. Party lights had been strung from one side of the street to the other, criss-crossing to form a colorful canopy currently filtering the gilded pink clouds and purple haze of dusk.

Trestle tables were set up within the perimeter, laden with food and depressingly non-alcoholic drinks. One of the county's finest country bands was set up in a corner, punching out tunes to which a mass of people were all dancing.

It seemed like just about everyone in the town had turned up in their finery to meet and greet and dance to the lively fiddle beat.

The party, as they say, was going off.

"Now, you boys all have something to drink, right?"

Drew, Arlo, and Tucker, seated on hay bales, nodded dutifully, raised their red Solo cups of lemonade, and said, "Yes, Mrs. Carter."

Wade smiled. No matter how many times she insisted they call her Ronnie these days, the three of them resisted.

"I hope you're dancing, there are a lot of women here tonight wantin' to dance with our hottie Credence bachelors."

Hottie? Wade winced a little at the word coming from his mother's mouth.

But she needn't have worried. The guys had rarely been on their asses. Except for Wade. As far as Wade was concerned, he was here to show his mother support and that was it. An hour tops. He was wearing his old Stetson pulled low on his forehead and putting out *stay the hell away* vibes. His plan this weekend was to lay low—the last thing he wanted was to be recognized.

Before they could confirm or deny, Wade's mother had switched track. "Wade, don't forget to ask Cecilia to dance, will you?"

Her request startled Wade. He and CC didn't *dance*. "Why?"

His mother looked scandalized at the question. "Wade William Rhett Carter, that girl has worked her patootie off these past two weeks, the least you can do is show off some of those good Southern manners I know I taught you and not leave her sittin' around like a wallflower."

Wade blinked. *A wallflower?* If CC danced any more, she'd wear out the heels on those very distracting red cowgirl boots she was sporting. Every damn time he'd looked up, she'd been jigging away with some guy or other. It was making him pretty fucking *tense*, actually.

But he knew better than to get into it with his mother when Southern manners were at stake. He just nodded and said, "Yes ma'am."

"Thank you, darlin'," Ronnie said, smiling indulgently before fluttering away to the next thing. She hadn't sat still all night, between all the schmoozing and introducing and generally doing her thing. She'd even managed a dance or two with her husband.

"There is something mighty rewarding about seeing a rich-ass, six-foot-two quarterback being put in his place by a little old five-two Texan lady," Tucker said.

Arlo started to laugh, Drew did too, and Tucker followed. Wade shook his head at them. "I'm going to tell my mother you called her little and old."

Tucker's laughter cut off as if he'd been garroted, and Wade grinned with a certain satisfaction.

"I can't believe your momma just called us hotties," Drew said, which caused more laughter.

"Yes, thank you. I'm trying not to think about that." Wade downed his current drink, wishing it was whiskey. "Christ, can't you go and grab us a bottle of something a little stronger from that bar of yours?" he griped. "I think I'm turning into a goddamn lemon."

"Public drinking is against the law," Arlo said mildly, his gaze glued to the dance floor. "I'd have to arrest you."

Wade snorted. He could try.

"Hey, is that—" Arlo leaned forward at the hips. "Is that Wyatt?"

Another snort from Wade. "Wyatt doesn't dance." But they all looked in the direction of Arlo's finger, the crowd parting enough at the right time to identify Wade's brother.

"Well," Drew said. "I'd call that more ass-grabbing and feet shuffling but yeah, I think you're right."

"Since when does Wyatt dance?" Tucker asked.

"Since when does Wyatt ever get that close to a woman he doesn't know without breaking out in hives?" Drew clarified.

They *were* close. Wade could just make out a sliver of light between the two bodies.

"They seem kinda into each other," Tucker said.

Wade nodded. "They do, don't they?"

Good for Wyatt. If anyone deserved a bit of recreation in his life, it was his brother. He just hoped he didn't get his heart broken come Sunday.

The crowd moved then, obscuring Wyatt and his dance partner from view but revealing someone Wade wished wasn't getting quite as much recreation.

CC.

She was currently dancing with Don Randall, whose fashion choice of mayoral chains was as idiotic as usual, but Wade barely noticed, distracted as he was by her fringed skirt playing around her knees and those red cowgirl boots. Honest-to-God *boots* that came to mid-calf and looked, even at a distance, the real, hand-tooled, deal. She had on a blouse that sat wide on her neckline, almost falling off her shoulders, and she had some kind of flower in her hair.

No jeans. No baseball cap. No stripy shirt. It was about as far from Where's Waldo as was possible.

Also hot as fuck. Christ…he'd never had *indecent* thoughts about his PA, but hell if he wasn't tonight.

"CC looks good in a skirt," Arlo mused.

CC looked *incredible* in a skirt. It was something else Wade was trying not to think about. A little bit of hard liquor would really go down well about now.

"She'll want to watch Don," Tucker said. "He's been known to get grabby."

Wade snorted. "Don't worry about CC. She can hold her own."

"Yeah." Drew nodded. "Guess a girl with five brothers knows how to look after herself."

Wade raised an eyebrow at Drew. "How in hell do you know that?"

Drew shrugged. "She told me."

"See, this is your problem, Drew," Tucker said, clapping him on the back. "Chicks see you as a big brother and tell you their life story."

Drew sighed as he watched the movement on the dance floor. "This is true."

Arlo nodded. "You're a good-looking guy, but women bench you because they can't see past the whole dead-people thing."

"I prefer the term mortally challenged."

Arlo and Tucker laughed. Wade rolled his eyes. "*When* did she tell you?" He clung precariously to his patience as he tried to bring the subject back to CC. And her skirt.

Actually no, *fuck*, not her skirt. Her brothers.

"At Annie's last week."

Wade shook his head. "She'd been working for me for months before she said anything about her brothers."

Drew shot him a pitying look. "It's called conversation, dude, you should try it sometime."

The criticism stung even though Wade knew Drew was just yanking his chain. CC had wanted things kept strictly business, and that was the way he'd kept them. Until recently, anyway.

"I wasn't aware she was hanging out at Annie's *conversating*." Wade was pretty sure that wasn't a word, but it worked for him at the moment.

"You think she stays in that ridiculous meringue of a house you live in all morning while you're at the farm? She gets around. You don't keep her under lock and key."

No. But he was beginning to think he should, with this many *hottie bachelors* around.

"Speaking of which." Arlo rose and tossed his cup in a nearby trash can. "I promised her a dance."

Oh no. No, no, *hell no*. "Don't even think about it." Wade stood, scowling at his friend. Watching Don dance with CC had put his guts in a tangle. Watching Arlo limp around heroically was about more than he could stand now.

"Yeah, Arlo," Drew said. "Wade's gotta dance with her. His momma told him to."

Wade flipped Drew the bird. "Bite me."

The guys laughed some more. Their amusement at his expense tonight was becoming irritating.

Peachy. *Fucking peachy.*

"Thought you were keeping a low profile," Arlo said, taking his seat again, not remotely concerned by being usurped.

Most of the media had snapped their pictures and taken off for the night, but there were a couple still hanging around. Wade pulled his Stetson lower on his forehead. ·

"Oh yeah," Tucker said drily, "now you look *completely* different."

Wade ignored them, a strange itch in his blood obliterating his normal sense of caution as the fringe of CC's skirt flared and showed off her knees. Christ, since when were *knees* sexy? Was this how dudes back in the dark ages had felt? When a glimpse of ankle was enough to give them a hard-on?

"Good luck, honey," Arlo called after him as he strode away. "Remember, no spaghetti arms."

And one of his jackass, so-called friends whistled the *Love Boat* theme song.

The itch in Wade's blood intensified as his legs shortened the distance between them. It wasn't a feeling he was used to, this feeling of…uncertainty. Normally, he approached women with absolute certainty of the outcome. He knew how this went down. He was practiced and pretty damn perfect at it, even if he did say so himself.

But then, CC wasn't a woman. She was his *PA*. And they didn't *dance*.

The fiddles were belting out a jaunty polka-style dance as Wade took the last couple of steps. CC spotted him honing in over Don's shoulder and frowned.

Wade stopped and tapped Don on the shoulder. "Can I cut in?"

CC blinked, her mouth parting slightly in surprise. Well, she could take a number. She wasn't the only one surprised here tonight. He had no idea why he was doing this other than his mother's insistence. And cock-blocking Arlo.

Nothing to do with that fucking skirt and those cowgirl boots. Nothing at all.

Don puffed himself up and patted Wade on the back enthusiastically. "Of course you can, son. Pretty little thing like this doesn't want to be dancing with an old fogey like me."

He chuckled in a fake kind of self-deprecation and, when neither of them jumped into refute his description, he coughed and muttered something about mayoral duties and departed.

Wade was excruciatingly aware of their stillness as couples all around them jigged along to the upbeat tempo of the music. He held out his hand. "Shall we?"

She eyed him suspiciously. "*You* dance?"

"I can dance."

"*This* kind of dancing?"

Wade grinned, the itch dissipating at her incredulous expression. "Yes, *this* kind of dancing. I grew up here, remember? With a Texan mother whose sworn duty it was to raise sons who could do-si-do. I can even line dance, but I will deny that under pain of death if you tell anyone." He reached for her hand again, but she leaned away slightly.

"Why?"

"Why not?"

She narrowed her eyes at him, and Wade could see she had some kind of dark liner where her eyelashes met her eyelids. She wasn't the first woman to kohl up her eyes, but he was pretty sure it was the first time she had. That he'd noticed, anyway.

"We don't dance, you and I."

Yeah. No shit. "Well I guess there's a first time for

everything." He waggled his hand at her. "Cut me some slack. My mother seems to think it's an affront to *Texas* if I don't ask you, so…here I am, asking you to dance."

"Fine." She sighed, but a small smile twitched at the corners of her mouth as she took his hand. "I wouldn't want to insult Texas."

Wade's hand buzzed as CC's slid into his. He ignored it by holding her at a decent distance and quickly picking up the steps, going through the familiar motions, looking anywhere but down.

Too soon, though, the song came to an end, and the band struck up a slower, more intimate ballad, and they were left standing awkwardly in the middle of the dance floor as couples melted into each other.

The guests and the locals seemed to be getting on very well indeed!

Wade wasn't sure if this weekend would be a success in regards to the long-term prospects of Credence, but in the short term, he wouldn't mind betting on a population explosion in nine months' time.

He felt a tug on his hand as CC tried to pull away, but for some reason he resisted. "Where are you going?"

Her gaze didn't quite meet his eyes. "Song's over."

Her cheeks were flushed, he noted. Maybe it was just from the exertion of the polka and the previous dancing she'd done, but her face looked pretty, all warm and pink, and got him to thinking about other ways he could put color in her cheeks, which led to a startling stirring behind the zipper of his jeans.

That alone should have warned him to unhand

her, but the devil was riding him tonight.

"One more. For my mother's sake?" He tipped his chin, and she followed the direction of his gaze. His mother—God bless her—beamed and waved at both of them, and he could have kissed her for her timing because for some reason he couldn't explain, Wade wanted to pull CC closer, not let her go.

Something had a hold of him tonight. Maybe it was the music, maybe it was the stars, maybe it was nostalgia for Credence, which filled him everywhere he looked.

Whatever it was, he was finding it impossible to resist. Finding her impossible to resist.

"Okay, fine," she murmured. "One more."

Wade grinned and stepped in closer, sliding a hand around CC's waist, careful to still keep a little distance between them. Her body was warm and pliant beneath his palm, but she shivered. "Cold?" he murmured, his voice suddenly raspy.

She shook her head, but unconsciously he stepped a little closer, adding some of his body warmth to the heated space between them. All around them people swayed to the music, and they followed suit, not talking for a beat or two, not even looking at each other.

A strange kind of silence settled over them. The music, the chatter of the crowd around the edges, the movement of the other couples around them faded to black until it felt as if they were dancing alone on the street.

"So…" She cleared her throat and glanced at him, her chin stuck out in that determined way he knew so well. "Line dancing, huh?"

His breath caught at the dance of red and yellow
and blue in her eyes from the colored lights overhead and the way they bathed the exposed skin of
her neck and chest in a muted rainbow of soft light.

"Yup. I even won a trophy for best junior line
dancing boy at the county fair one year."

She laughed. "So you've always been competitive,
then?"

Wade laughed, too. "That and naturally light on
my feet."

Someone bumped them from behind, pushing
CC against him, and Wade's hands tightened around
her waist to steady her before returning her to her
previous position. Or maybe a touch closer. She
shivered again, and he realized his fingers were
absently stroking her waist, and he swore he heard
the rough intake of her breath.

Or maybe it was his. Did her lungs feel as
ineffectual as his all of a sudden?

It'd been three years since Wade had been so
attuned to the internal workings of his body. As
an athlete it'd been his *job* to listen to internal
feedback. In retirement that skill had gone by the
wayside. But he was listening now. Listening as it
hummed with an awareness that was terribly familiar
yet utterly foreign.

Different to the sharpened focus demanded by
football. Different, too, to the familiar stir of sexual
interest.

This was much more intense. This was an awareness of his pulse bounding at his wrists, his temple,
his abdomen, and his groin. And it wasn't fast and
hectic like it was when he was chasing a touchdown,

but slow and thick. Wade was aware of the scorch of air, hot and ragged, in his lungs, the electric tingle in the pads of his fingers where they touched her body, the vibrations along nerve endings that cranked taut every muscle he owned.

Aware, too, on some level, that she was feeling the same.

He glanced at the top of her head. The flower in her hair was fake, he realized, glued to a clip, but it was quirky and playful. So *not* the efficient PA he'd known for five and a half years. But a woman. A sexy, vibrant, flesh-and-blood woman.

"You're looking very nice tonight."

Wade wasn't entirely sure where the words had come from. They'd just slipped out of his mouth unfiltered and unchecked.

She glanced up at him, startled, her lips parted, that slight v between her brows. "Oh…thank you."

"I didn't know you *owned* a skirt."

Wade blinked as more stupid fell from his mouth. Why in hell would he say that? *Why?* If anything, her v deepened and her mouth closed, her lips pressing together. "Guess there's a lot of things you don't know about me, Wade Carter."

She dropped her gaze, and Wade frowned at the top of her head. What the hell did that mean? Was she trying to distance herself from their conversation in front of the television last week? Yeah, they hadn't talked much prior to Credence, but he still knew her, and he'd bet his last cent she didn't have some closet somewhere full of girly shit. He opened his mouth to say as much, but she got in before him.

"So today's been a roaring success."

Her voice was tinged with triumph, but Wade let it slide, concentrating instead on the warm fan of her breath where his open neckline met the first button of his shirt. It was as distracting as her fucking knees, making the air in his lungs hotter.

"Yes."

She gave a half laugh that huffed more air across his skin, drifting to his throat and caressing him there. Sensations prickled at his scalp and his groin, and his hand tightened a little more at her waist.

"And you thought the sky was going to fall in."

Wade gave a soft snort. The way his body was reacting to the tickle of her breath felt pretty fucking apocalyptic. "The weekend's not over yet."

"You haven't been recognized, have you?"

"No."

She glanced around. "Everybody seems to be enjoying themselves."

"Yeah." Wade's body, for example, was enjoying itself way too much. He forced himself to look around too, take his mind off every sway of her hips. "It's nice, actually. Seeing Credence like this." And it was; it'd been a long time since he'd felt part of the town. "It takes me back to the fourth of July parties when I was a kid. Mom and Dad would bring us into the parade, and then they closed off the street like this, and we'd eat hot dogs and cotton candy and drink soda until we puked."

She laughed, and goose bumps feathered up his throat. "That sounds nice."

He glanced down at the wistful note in her voice, understanding the origin much better now, but found himself staring at the top of her head again. "Yeah, it was." He gazed at the criss-cross of lights above him. "You've all done a great job with the decorations. The street looks real pretty."

She glanced up at him the same time he looked down at her, and their gazes meshed. "Yeah?"

Her voice was husky and hopeful and burrowed under his ribs quicker than if she'd taken his compliment as a matter of course or shrugged it off. Wade nodded and smiled as his gaze drifted briefly to her mouth before returning. "Yeah."

Just like you.

Why hadn't he noticed how damn feminine she was before tonight? That under those jeans and ball caps, she was delicate, her features almost feline.

They were still staring at each other, barely even swaying, when somebody cleared their throat behind him a beat or two later and Wade felt a quick tap on his shoulder.

Arlo. Wade didn't even have to turn to know that.

"Okay, okay, hotshot, unhand that woman. You get to see her every day, and she promised me a dance."

Wade didn't want Arlo to dance with CC, but his brain, suddenly back in control, was telling him to step away. They may be getting friendlier, but CC was still his PA, *his employee*, and the things he was thinking and feeling were putting him in dangerous territory.

Arlo taking over was probably for the best.

"It's true," she said, her gaze still holding his. "I did promise him."

And then she stepped back, breaking their eye contact, their physical contact. Wade's hands slipped from her waist, his palms still hot and buzzing from their contact. Arlo nudged him aside, taking his place, and Wade was almost overwhelmed with the urge to tear him away, the pulses at his temples throbbing with a surge of primal testosterone.

What the fuck was wrong with him tonight?

CHAPTER THIRTEEN

The night air was cool on her flushed skin as CC made her escape along the deserted Credence main street an hour later. She'd been working hard for a week and had worked like a junkyard dog today. When Ronnie had ordered a yawning CC home to bed, she'd mumbled a vague protest about helping with the cleanup but hadn't insisted when Ronnie had shaken her head.

"We have a whole cleanup team, darlin'. You organized them."

And CC thanked God she had. Her feet ached from all that dancing in a pair of boots that had arrived special delivery only yesterday. It had seemed like a good idea to get her country on a few days ago when she'd seen them and the skirt on Amazon, but maybe not so much now. Dressing up for a change had been nice, but she was probably going to suffer over it for a few days.

That'd teach her to be vain.

And it had been vanity, she realized as she sucked in a lungful of sweet, clean Colorado air. Something about an influx of almost two hundred women had goaded her into it. She wasn't used to being around a lot of women—she'd grown up with brothers and worked in the hotel industry before becoming a personal assistant.

All her bosses had been men working in male-oriented industries.

Hell, the last five years she'd been *drowning* in men. From Wade's NFL teammates to executives and agents and advertising people, not to mention the professional hangers-on. And, as Wade's PA, she'd essentially been an intimate part of that world. Accepted as one of them. Marinating in an ocean of testosterone.

It was a wonder she hadn't started to grow hair on her chest.

So, suddenly being thrust into a bull pen with all those other women had freaked her out a little. But not as freaked out as she was now about Wade.

About dancing with Wade.

About how dancing with Wade had made her *feel*.

Her cheeks grew hot again just thinking about it. They'd never been that close before. Sure, they had in that impersonal way of people who work together, who passed by each other or handed each other things. Just yesterday she'd stood behind Wade's chair and leaned over his shoulder as he'd Googled something on his computer. She was pretty sure her chest had probably unintentionally brushed his shoulder blade once or twice.

Whatever. That wasn't this. That wasn't *dancing*.

Dancing was intimate. Or it had certainly fucking felt that way.

Hell, she'd barely been able to breathe as his hand had slid onto her waist and he'd stepped in closer. Her whole body had come alive, aware of Wade as a *man*. Not her boss. Not Ronnie and Cal's son. Or Wyatt's brother. Not a famous Broncos quarterback.

A man.

Her heart beat triple time just remembering his touch. Remembering how her skin had felt energized and her nipples had tightened to painful peaks and the band of muscles slung between her hips had heated and liquefied as his fingers had stroked at her waist. And when his gaze had dropped to her mouth, she'd wanted to push up onto her tippy-toes and kiss him—hard.

Which was all kinds of crazy.

Maybe if she hadn't had that dream, if her body hadn't already made a seismic shift in the way it regarded him, she'd have been oblivious to any undercurrents while they danced. But the dream *had* happened, and a portal had been opened to another world, and she was very afraid she'd never be able to go back.

It hadn't helped that he'd cleaned up well. His sweaty, down-around-the-farm look had been switched up for country-boy-on-the-town casual. His soft jeans clinging to his quads and ass, his checked flannel shirt open at the neck and rolled up to the elbows. And that Stetson, pulled low.

If she hadn't known he was a quarterback, she'd have pegged him for some cowboy just ridden into town on his horse. CC had taken one look at him tonight and her ovaries had burst into a rendition of *home, home on the range.*

She'd moved on from farmer porn to cowboy porn.

CC drew in a shaky breath, which seemed loud in the relative quiet broken only by the drift of music fading away behind her. This was a bad time to be getting a case of the hots for her boss. Especially when she knew what he was like with women.

And why.

How deeply rooted his mistrust of women was because of Jasmine's betrayal. How he made the dating rules because he could never truly trust that a woman wanted *Wade* and not *The Catapult*.

She supposed it would have been worse had she developed this exceedingly inconvenient…fascination with him years ago. It would have been untenable for her to continue in her position, and that would have put her California dream out of reach.

As it was, she should probably pack her bags and go now. But it was only another couple of months until she left his employ for good anyway and, as she had absolutely *no* intention of acting on any of her unwanted feelings—that was too weird to even contemplate—it seemed a little extreme.

Plus she'd told Wade she'd stay. So she'd stay. Professional integrity was important.

"*CC!*"

Wade's hiss from behind her scared the crap out of CC. She startled and stumbled backward, sprawling into the hedge she'd been passing. She clutched at her chest as her pulse hammered madly at her temples.

Wade's low chuckle reached her just before he jogged to her aid. "You're in the hedge there, CC."

The foliage prickled at her arms. "Are you trying to give me a heart attack?" she hissed as he offered his hand. She refused, too pissed at him to take his help as she disentangled herself from the scratchy, green embrace of the hedge.

But she'd take anger over the tumult of sensations he'd caused when they'd danced earlier. In fact, anger was a good antidote to those annoyingly unwanted sexy feelings!

"Sorry, I didn't want to startle you by suddenly appearing by your side."

"How'd that work out for you?" she said waspishly.

He had the good grace to at least look like he was *mostly* sorry for alarming her, although she suspected that if they'd been under a streetlamp, she'd also see humor lurking on his features.

CC straightened her clothes and brushed at some twigs in her hair. The fact he looked so damn well put together when she literally looked liked she'd been fighting with a hedge needled CC even further. *His hair*, which had been crammed in a hat all night, didn't appear to have suffered at all, looking gloriously finger-tousled.

"What do you want?" Surges of adrenaline made most people edgy. They made CC bitchy.

"Nothing. I just thought I'd walk you home. You shouldn't be out on the streets at night by yourself."

A bubble of laughter rose in CC's chest as she looked around the deserted town. Past his shoulder she could just see the rainbow flare of lights criss-crossing the street in the distance. "In Credence? At nine-thirty?"

The entire town *not* at the street party would have been tucked up in bed an hour ago. CC had a feeling she could strip off her clothes and walk naked down the middle of the road right now and Credence wouldn't be any the wiser.

He shrugged. "It never hurts to be careful."

CC ignored him as she started on her way again. If he thought any woman with five brothers needed a lecture on personal safety, he was crackers: Wade fell into step beside her, and her pulse, which had started to settle, picked up again.

"You don't have to walk with me." It was difficult to concentrate on putting one foot in front of the other when a large portion of her brain was deep into the logistics of pushing *him* into the hedge and showing him just how adept she was at taking care of herself. And her needs. "Go back to your friends."

"Nah." He shook his head. "I'm done now."

CC went to object again but decided to keep her mouth shut. They were less than five minutes away from Casa Del Tara. She was sure she could make it home without succumbing to the urge to jump him.

The hedges of Credence were safe.

So they walked, turning right onto their street, leaving the lights and music behind, the quiet of a sleeping Credence surrounding them. Whether it was the silence or the man beside her, CC was hyperaware of her surroudings. The pool of light below the streetlamp up ahead, the trill of insects, the hooting of an owl, and the rustlings of little things in the undergrowth.

Unfortunately, she was also aware of Wade, too, and how her body was reacting to his nearness. She kept her gaze trained firmly on the path ahead, but it didn't seem to make any difference. She was attuned to the sound of his boots on the sidewalk and the occasional brush of his arm and how it made her aware of *herself*. Of the cool play of air around her knees between the fringes of her skirt and the steady thump of her heartbeat as it pressed against all her pulse points. Her temples, her wrists, her abdomen.

The thick pound right between her legs.

How had this unwanted physical awareness of him started? Had farmer porn been the inciting incident? Or had it been less overt? Like him opening up to her about Jasmine? Maybe her opening up to him? Or had it just been the closeness of their dance?

"Do you know who that woman was dancing with Wyatt?"

His voice startled her as it broke the silence and fractured her thoughts. She wasn't usually the jumpy type, but Wade was making her jumpier than a june bug.

Tonight she just had *jumping* on the brain.

"Yes." CC cleared her voice. It sounded too wobbly in the stillness of the night for her liking. "Her name is Jenny. She's one of the two women your mom and dad are hosting at the farm. She seems really nice, quiet but nice. She's from Pittsburgh."

"They seem to have hit it off?"

CC laughed at the understatement. "You could say that."

"That's good, I guess."

CC risked a glance at him. "You guess?"

Wyatt looked happy as a clam. Surely Wade wanted that for his brother? His gaze met hers, and even in the night she could feel the power of it.

"What if she doesn't want to stay? Liking Wyatt's only the half of it, right? There's a big difference between Pittsburgh and Credence, CC. What if she stays for a while and my brother falls in love with her, and she decides one day that she just can't stand not being able to walk into Macy's on a whim or hit the nearest Starbucks? Or that being in a relationship with a guy who's going to spend a lot of his life smelling like hog shit isn't quite as *gosh darn awesome* as she thought? What if she's just setting him up for a whole bunch of heartache?"

CC wasn't sure if Wade was talking about a potential situation for his brother or the *actual* heartache that Jasmine had caused him, but the flash of worry she caught in his eyes as they passed under the streetlamp was genuine. He may have been projecting, but he was definitely coming from a place of concern for Wyatt.

"All those things could happen, that's true. But what if she loves it here?" The night blanketed them again as they stepped out of the pool of light. "What if she starts up a business that's successful and willingly becomes an integral part of the town? What if Wyatt and Credence and the farm fill her up and give her joy and purpose?"

CC could see Jenny was smitten. This afternoon, just stepped off the bus, Jenny had looked tired and five years older. Tonight, she'd practically *glowed*.

"None of us are guaranteed a happily ever after, Wade." She knew that better than anyone. "It doesn't mean we still shouldn't strive for it. Or take a risk on it."

CC wasn't sure if *she* was talking about Wyatt now, either. Wade certainly hadn't let any woman close, taken any risks since Jasmine.

He huffed out a sigh. "Yeah...yeah, I know. I hope for his sake it does work out."

"Me, too."

"It'd be good to see Wyatt settled. I think Mom and Dad would love to see it, too. Maybe they might even finally get those grandchildren Mom keeps bellyaching about."

CC laughed. "Your mother would be an awesome granny." She'd only had one grandparent growing up, her maternal grandmother, who had died when CC had been about six years old. She didn't remember much of her, just a little gray-haired old lady, hunched in a chair.

Wade grinned. "*Memaw*, please. In great Southern tradition, she will be called Memaw. As my grandmother was and her mother was and her mother before her." He rolled his eyes dramatically. "And on it goes."

CC laughed harder, but there was a strange hollowness in the pit of her stomach. She'd always figured she'd have kids one day, but at thirty-two she guessed time was running out. Had Wade ever thought about kids? She could just imagine a mini Wade with a cute little lisp calling Ronnie Memaw.

She blinked at her sudden train of thought. She was thinking about Wade's kid? *She'd given Wade's kid a lisp?*

What. The. Actual. Fuck.

Snap out of it!

"It's hard to imagine your mom being a Memaw. She seems so young."

There. That was better. Normal. Sane. No imaginary kids with imaginary lisps.

"Yeah, Dad's heart thing notwithstanding, I think they're pretty good for their age."

A sigh slipped from CC's lips. "It was nice to see them dancing. You're lucky to have parents that love each other."

CC wasn't sure why she'd added that little extra observation. She certainly hadn't planned to. It had just slipped out. They passed under another streetlamp, illuminating their faces, and Wade's expression was searching as he looked at her before the dark swallowed them up again. It was warm with empathy, which caused a stupid lump in her throat.

"Yeah," he agreed. "I know."

Seeing a couple still so happily married after forty years, seeing them express that love and closeness in public, was a novelty for CC. One she couldn't get enough of. How she'd *yearned* as a kid to have parents like Ronnie and Cal—loving and affectionate. Parents who went to things, who turned up together, who laughed and touched and enjoyed each other's company.

CC still remembered the ball of anxiety that had blazed in her gut whenever her parents had been in the same room. Her father politely indifferent, her mother weepy and fanning herself like some delicate Southern belle.

He didn't say anything else for a beat or two, and CC's nerves stretched in the silence. Was he gathering himself to ask more about her family? She hoped not. Her emotions were a little too raw right now.

"I'm surprised Mom let him dance at all," he said eventually, as if sensing, like he had the other night, her desperate need of a subject change. "He'd dance all night if it was up to him, but she's still trying to get him to take it easy."

"He's been given the all-clear though, right?" she asked, her brain returning to the conversation.

"Yeah. Cardiologist is happy."

Another circle of light illuminated the white wrought iron fence of Wade's house. "Home sweet home," he said with a flourish and bowed as he opened the gate for her, indicating for CC to precede him.

CC laughed at his use of the word *home*. She was getting used to living in the monstrosity of a house, but she wasn't sure it'd ever feel like home. Had it felt like home to the woman for whom it had been built?

He crammed his hat back on his head as she brushed past him and started down the path. The faint squeak of the gate shutting indicated he was following. She walked under the giant portico, the sensor light detecting her movement and flooding the vast area in white light. She'd traversed the four steps and was inserting her key in the front door when Wade joined her.

"Listen," he said as she coaxed the old lock, which needed a bit of a jiggle and a certain tongue position before it would admit anyone. "Thanks for helping my mom with this whole thing."

The lock gave, and the door opened, but CC wasn't paying it any attention as she quirked an eyebrow at Wade.

"I thought you were annoyed that I was spending all that time on your mother's *crazy-ass scheme to pimp out strange women to the bachelors of Credence*. Or words to that effect."

He chuckled, unperturbed by having his sentiments thrown back at him. "I may have been exaggerating for dramatic effect."

CC gave a soft snort. "Ya think?"

"I was wrong."

She shook her head. Wade's ability to apologize had always been his redeeming grace. He was man enough to own his mistakes.

"Who knows…" He shrugged. "It might just work."

"Could I have that in writing?" she asked sweetly.

He grinned down at her, the deep grooves bracketing his mouth adding an extra layer of sexy, and CC's breath hitched. Just as suddenly, though, his smile faded, and his gaze grew serious as it trekked north and zeroed in on her bangs.

"CC…" He put up a hand in a stopping motion. "Stay. Very. Still."

CC froze. "What? Why?" Adrenaline surged into her system as Wade's hand slowly moved toward her hair. Keeping her head still, she looked up, trying to see what he was seeing even though part of her *did not want to know.*

"*Wade,*" she hissed. "What?"

"I think you collected a spider when you were parlaying with that hedge."

A wild surge of fear cramped through her diaphragm. *Spider.* Jesus, she *hated* spiders.

"Don't move."

Despite wanting to jump up and down, shake her head, and brush wildly at her hair like a mad woman, screaming, "*Get it off, get if off,*" she doubted she was capable of moving.

She turned her eyeballs upward again, suddenly seeing in her peripheral vision what Wade was seeing. The creep of skinny legs traversing her bangs like the spider was already setting up house.

"Oh God, *get it off*!"

He chuckled as he stepped closer, his fingers at face level and descending unhurriedly. Heat poured off his body, but CC was oblivious to everything but the frantic beat of her pulse rushing like a waterfall through her ears.

"Is it big?"

"Nah. It's only a baby. It's quite cute, actually."

Cute? She glared at him. Or as much as she could with her head straight and her eyes practically rolled back in their sockets, trying to monitor the progress of her unwanted arachnid visitor.

CC clamped her teeth together. "Get. It. Off. Me."

He chuckled. "Yeah, yeah."

He slid a hand onto her nape. Probably to stop her from taking matters into her own hands and doing the wild, hand-flapping spider jig, which every primal instinct she possessed was urging her to do.

CC shut her eyes tight as he reached for the uninvited creature with his other hand, not wanting to watch as a live spider was plucked from her hair. The thought of having to touch it herself gave her the heebie-jeebies, and she was grateful Wade was volunteering.

Even if it was his fault she'd ended up in the damn hedge.

She felt a light brush against her forehead and squeezed her eyes even harder, tensing everything so tight she doubted she'd have been able to squeeze a credit card between her butt cheeks.

"Is it gone?"

Another chuckle, the warm fan of his breath on her face. "It's gone."

CC slowly opened her eyes and unclenched,

Wade coming into hazy focus, looking at her with amusement sparking in his gaze.

"I didn't know you were an arachnophobe."

She'd already told him tonight he didn't know everything about her, and she wasn't going there again. Besides, his closeness, his intense gaze, the way his thumb was stroking at her nape was more than enough to deal with at the moment.

Her heart was beating entirely differently now. He was so big. She was so used to seeing him, to being around him, she sometimes forgot how big he was. Hard to ignore the span of his chest from this close, though.

She should be moving away. She knew that. In fact, somewhere her wiser angels were telling her just that—screaming it at her, actually. But his stubble and the sexy indents around his mouth and the softness of his lips were dangerously fascinating.

Their gazes meshed for a beat or two, and she couldn't look away as his dropped, drifting to her mouth. As if he was going to kiss her. The stroking of his thumb halted, and they just stared at each other. They stayed so still for so long the sensor light went out, plunging them into darkness again. CC's breath grew thick as the night surrounded them, her body throbbing with awareness and need.

"Cecilia," he whispered.

And that was enough. In a blinding flash, CC threw out caution and almost six years of professional boundaries, rose on her tip-toes—and kissed him.

He met her halfway, their lips clashing in a frantic mash, opening wide, tasting and searching and demanding everything from the other. It was no tentative starter, no teaser, no slow and steady. It was on fire from the first touch of mouth on mouth, and it was far sexier than anything he had done to her in her dream life.

He tasted better, his body against hers felt better, he smelled better and he *sounded* better, groaning deep in his throat. She felt that groan all the way to her toes and every hot spot in between. His spider-catching hand slid onto her hip, hitching her closer as the hand at her nape held her fast.

The movement must have tripped the sensor, because the portico flooded with light again, and it was like a bolt of lightning had hit them, repelling them from each other, forcing them apart, forcing them two steps back.

CC gasped in horror. Holding her hands up in front of her, she contemplated what the hell had just happened as her heart beat a wild tango in her chest. It was no consolation that Wade looked just as stunned.

What had she done? She'd kissed Wade. And he'd kissed her back. This was not good.

Not. Good.

Wade recovered first, taking a step toward her. "CC—"

"No." She shook her head, taking a step back, her hands up higher now, almost level with her ears. Whatever he was going to say, she couldn't deal with right now. Her cheeks were flushed, and she was hot all over.

Sweet baby Jesus! He was her boss! And she wanted to *die.*

"I'm so, *so* sorry…"

CC desperately tried to come up with some justification for her actions to follow her apology. Like being in post-arachnid shock or temporary possession by the devil. But nothing—not even the clear and present need for exorcism—justified crossing the line she'd just crossed. The line that *she* had drawn all those years ago.

"It's okay," he said, his voice calm and placating, as if she was some kind of incendiary device primed to go off at any second.

CC shook her head vehemently. How could he be so damn composed? How was *kissing him* ever okay? God…she just wanted to hit the erase button.

Yes. That was it. The erase button. Or the next best thing.

"Do you think," she asked, locking her gaze with his, "it might be possible to *never* speak of this again?"

If they couldn't erase it, they could at least pretend it had never happened, right?

"Sure." He nodded, his voice still placatory. "Whatever you need."

What she needed was a time machine, but this would have to do. "Thank you."

Then she turned on her heel, shoulder checking the door open as she hurried inside, her shaky legs carrying her up the stairs and into her bedroom, where she burrowed under the covers and curled into a ball.

Sweet mother of pearl. What had she done?

What. Had. She. Done?

CHAPTER FOURTEEN

Wade was still kicking his ass as he sat it down on a stool at the bar. He hadn't planned on coming to Jack's, but staying home hadn't appealed after what had happened. The semi-dark and the smell of hops were far preferable.

The bar was jumping tonight, with many of the street party-goers obviously deciding to keep the night going. The booths were full, and what looked like an impromptu line dancing lesson was going on over by the jukebox. He couldn't recall the last time he'd seen this many women—single or otherwise—at the bar, and he was pleased he'd switched out his Stetson for a ball cap.

Everywhere he looked, there were women with pink drinks decorated with little umbrellas. *City chicks.* If they thought this blur of noise and color was Credence, Colorado, they were going to be left bitterly disappointed when the dust settled.

His anxiety kicked up another notch. As if he didn't have enough to worry about, what with losing his mind and kissing CC.

God knew how many workplace laws he'd broken. How many sexual harassment suits he'd opened himself up to. Not to mention how badly this might screw up his chances of getting CC to stay on as his PA now he'd done the one thing he'd promised he'd never do.

Actually, to be precise, *she'd* kissed him, *she'd*

made the first move. But he'd followed her willingly into it, clocking her first move, maybe even subconsciously waiting for her to make it, then seizing it. *Running with it.*

He didn't know what in the hell had come over him. He'd never even thought about kissing CC prior to moving to Credence. He might have noticed she was a woman from time to time, but that was as far as it had ever gone.

But they'd become…friendlier this last little while, and dancing with her tonight? That'd been a game changer. Hearing her so wistful about his parents' close relationship had been gut-wrenching. Making him realize anew the impact of her parents' broken marriage.

You're lucky. That's what she'd told him, and he knew it for a fact. He knew having a stable home life had set him on the path to success. He didn't doubt that he had the talent to get to the top without all that, but it had kept a good head on his shoulders while he'd gotten there. Having seen too many ball players throw away their chances by allowing themselves to get distracted, he was grateful for a solid upbringing.

"Beer," he said to Tucker as he approached. "Keep 'em coming."

Tucker took one look at him, reached for a bottle, cracked the lid, and set it in front of him.

"What? No umbrella?"

Tucker cocked an eyebrow but reached under the bar, extracted an umbrella, and shoved it in the neck of the bottle.

"Satisfied?"

Wade snorted. Tucker had no clue just how *un*satisfied he was. With what had happened. With his part in it. With how horrified CC had looked. With how he'd wanted to sweep her up in his arms like Rhett fucking Butler, take those stairs two at a time, and toss her on his bed. Or hers.

Or hell, the door, the nearest wall, or that god-damn staircase, if she'd been amenable.

Yeah…they could *not* speak about the kiss as much as she wanted, but it wasn't going to stop him from thinking about it every waking moment of the day.

"What bug crawled up your ass?" Tucker asked.

"I'm fine."

Tucker looked pointedly at the umbrella. "Whatever you say."

"I'll have another one of those piña coladas, please."

The quiet female voice came from Wade's right, and he glanced over to find Della, Arlo's sister, sitting two stools down. He'd been so steamed at himself, he hadn't seen her when he'd plonked his ass down.

"You've had three," Tucker said.

"In two hours."

"Arlo's not going to be happy."

"The woman has to wrangle Bob Downey all day, get her a goddamn piña colada," Wade grouched.

Della seemed momentarily surprised before shooting him a smile. "Thank you, Wade."

Tucker sighed but headed down to the cocktail end of the bar. "How you doin', Della?" Wade asked. "You been at the street party?"

"Sure have. It was wonderful." Her eyes sparkled, and Wade smiled. Della may have arrived here a couple of years ago as a frightened little mouse, but she'd clearly come out of her shell quite a bit since then. "Your mom's such a powerhouse, isn't she?"

Wade half laughed, half grimaced. "That she is."

"I haven't seen Credence this alive the whole two years I've been here."

"Yeah." Wade nodded. It'd been a long time since he'd seen it like this, too.

Tucker came back with a piña colada, setting it down in front of Della. "Drink it slowly."

Della drew a cross over her heart, and Wade grinned. "Where are the others?" he asked.

"Arlo got called out. Drew's over at the booths."

He tipped his chin in the direction of the semicircular booths. Drew was there, surrounded by three women who seemed intent on his every word.

"He's telling them his life story, isn't he?" Wade said.

"That's the way to bet."

Wade squinted as he realized two of the women looked remarkably alike. "Am I seeing double?"

"Nope. Molly and Marley, twins. From New York."

Tucker waggled his eyebrows, and Wade laughed. He had no desire to court double trouble, but he was all for some distracting conversation.

Wade slipped off the stool, glancing at Della. "I'm heading over. You want to get away from this bozo?"

Tucker flipped him the bird. Della just shook her head. "I'm good here, thanks."

"Alrighty." He touched the brim of his cap. "See you later."

Drew grinned up at him like a Cheshire Cat as Wade approached the booth. "Wade!" He lifted his beer glass. "Join us."

"Don't mind if I do." Anything to keep his mind off the slow-motion reruns of the hottest kiss he'd had since he couldn't remember when. Probably his first one under the high school bleachers. His gut was still heated from the afterglow. Unfortunately he could also still see CC's mortified face and hear her horrified gasp.

"Sit here."

The woman to his right scooched over, and he slid in beside her. Drew performed the introductions, careful, as usual, not to make a fuss over Wade's identity. Just, *this is my friend Wade*.

Simple.

The twins appeared to be in their late twenties and were clearly identical, with long, lean builds and cute chipmunk cheeks. The only hope of telling them instantly apart was their hair. Molly's was brown with no bangs and all one length, brushing her shoulders, where the ends kicked up a little. Marley's, although a similar color and length, was a lot less conservative. The cut was more choppy and layered, and her bangs, which were almost down to her chin and carelessly flipped back, were dyed a vibrant purple.

They both had truly magnificent eyebrows, thick and perfectly arched. Wade absently wondered whether they were tattooed. A recent date had told him it was the latest fashion *thing*.

The other woman, sitting opposite Wade, was Winona. She seemed a lot closer to his age than Molly and Marley, bigger, though, stronger, with muscular arms and an angular face that was more *interesting* than pretty. Tall, statuesque.

Great rack.

In total contrast to her muscular physique, her hair was a riot of honey-blond curls. She was like Xena the Goldilocks Princess. She wore an anti-nuclear pendant on a leather thong around her neck and similar leather cords around her wrists, strung with beads and shells. All she needed was a garland of flowers and she'd be the full hippy.

Xena the Hippy Goldilocks Princess.

Arlo was just going to love that. He was professionally bound to think all hippies were up to no good.

She peered at him through narrowed eyes. "So, you're The Catapult, huh?" Her voice was a husky vibrato, reminding Wade of smoky speakeasies.

Wade shifted uncomfortably—so much for the ball cap.

"Yes."

He put on his game face and tensed for the usual questions and requests for selfies from the women. They didn't eventuate. The twins confessed to not being avid football fans—they were never going to survive here in Bronco country—and Winona said she only ever watched the Super Bowl, but mostly because of the ads as she'd worked in advertising for a while.

Which suited Wade just fine. He wasn't short on adoring fans and didn't need his ego constantly stroked, unlike other players he knew. As CC would say, his ego was big enough.

And if his brain could just stop thinking about her every five seconds, his body would be sincerely fucking grateful.

"You should ask Winona what she does, Wade," Drew said, still grinning. Marley and Molly nodded enthusiastically, their smiles almost as big as Drew's.

Wade played along. He'd been going to ask anyway. "It sounds intriguing, whatever it is," he said, smiling at Winona encouragingly.

Her answering smile softened her features. "I'm a writer."

"She writes *romance* novels," Molly supplied.

"*Erotic* romance novels," Marley added.

Wade didn't think it would be appropriate to laugh right now, but thinking about how that news would be welcomed by the town populace made his lips twitch. Forty years ago, a teacher who had taught at the elementary school had penned a raunchy novel about a *fictitious* small town, which had caused much consternation and scandal in Credence as everyone had tried to work out who was who.

It didn't matter how many times she maintained the characters weren't based on anyone in Credence, suspicions ran high and she eventually left town.

Winona's eyes narrowed again, clocking his twitch. "You don't approve."

"Not at all. Erotica for everyone."

"Cheers to that," Drew said, lifting his glass.

"Are you planning on moving here to write?"

Winona nodded. "Yes…I am, actually. I'm looking for something quieter, more secluded after Chicago. And I can write anywhere, really."

Wade didn't blame her. He'd never gotten the

fuss about the Windy City.

"Wade's writing a book at the moment," Drew said.

"Oh really?"

Wade shrugged it off. "It's just a memoir."

Winona nodded. "You're doing it yourself?"

"Yes."

"My condolences. Writing's hard, isn't it?"

"Yes." Wade laughed. "I had no idea. My PA nagged me to get a ghost writer, but I figured how hard could it be, right?"

Aaaaand he was back to CC. That kiss. That mouth—sweet and hot and urgent under his. The press of her breasts against his chest, the hard pebbles of her nipples.

Cali-*fucking*-fornia.

Wade chugged half his beer bottle and turned to Marley. "What do you do?"

"I'm a hairdresser." Which explained the vividness of her bangs. "I work in a salon in Queens. Mol and I work together. But she does all the beauty stuff."

Molly nodded. "Pedicures, manicures, facials. Makeup. Waxing."

Waxing.

The urge to smile again intensified, but Wade did a better job of suppressing it this time. He knew his mother would love having a hairdresser in town, but he couldn't wait to hear the gossip if these two set up a business offering bikini lines and Brazilians on the main street.

"Manscaping too," Marley added.

Drew almost choked on his beer, and Wade laughed as he gaped at Marley before turning his attention to Molly. "Is that what I think it is?"

Molly nodded shyly. She was definitely the more reserved sister. For someone who was taking money to rip hair off cracks, backs, and sacks, she certainly blushed easily.

"It's anything from facials and pedicures to tanning and…waxing."

"Wax?" Drew blinked. "Near my…" He trailed off, but his expression said it all. Drew looked like he'd rather have his eyeballs waxed than let anyone near his junk with a boiling-hot substance designed to rip hair out by the roots.

"I think the word you're after is penis," Winona provided in her husky voice, all matter-of-fact and anatomical.

"Don't you mean love club?"

The question came from behind his shoulder, and Wade glanced up to find Arlo, his arms crossed, an eyebrow cocked at Winona. "Isn't that what you erotic writers call it?"

Clearly Arlo and Winona had already met.

Wade was surprised at the edge in Arlo's voice, but on closer inspection of his friend's face Wade could see a red mark and a slight swelling to Arlo's cheek bone. They weren't there earlier, so he could only assume that whatever he'd been called out to had gotten nasty.

Maybe Arlo was still running on adrenaline.

"Only the bad ones."

Wade laughed. Adrenaline or not, Arlo deserved that, and watching him get smacked down by a woman never got old. Arlo often came to Denver on police business, and Wade was always amazed at how gaga women went for that uniform and the prosthesis. The number of offers Arlo had had from women wanting to help ease the pain of losing his leg was impressive.

Winona, on the other hand, looked like she'd wanted to whip off his prosthesis and beat him with it.

"And you're one of the good ones, I suppose?"

Winona quirked an eyebrow, folding her arms. "I'm very, very good."

Obviously annoyed at the response, Arlo pierced Drew with the look they all liked to call his *bad cop* face. With the shiner on his cheek, it looked pretty damn fierce. "Where's Della?"

Drew had known Arlo too long to be fazed by *bad cop*. He just grinned, and Wade pressed his lips together so he wouldn't laugh again. "She's at the bar."

Arlo frowned and looked over his shoulder. "What in hell is she doing at the bar?"

"Lion taming?" Winona suggested, her voice full of sarcasm.

Arlo ignored Winona, glaring instead at Drew, then at Wade in turn. "She shouldn't be drinking."

"Why?" Winona demanded. "Is she underage?"

Arlo, not used to being questioned, blinked. "No."

"An alcoholic?"

Wade could hear Arlo grinding his teeth from across the booth. If he was a betting man, he'd say whatever job Arlo had just attended had put a real itch up his spine.

"*No.*" Although Della had relied a little too heavily on a glass or two to smooth out the edges when she first arrived, and Wade knew that Arlo worried it was an easy crutch for her.

Knowing what his sister had been through, even when he hadn't known she was his sister, had been a hard thing for Arlo to come to terms with. Arlo was a rescuer—that was what he did. It was how he'd lost his leg. It killed him to think he hadn't been able to do the same for his own flesh and blood.

"Does she turn into a gremlin?"

Drew laughed and raised his glass to Winona. "I think you're going to fit in around here real well."

Arlo snorted, obviously unimpressed. "Thanks for keeping an eye on her," Arlo snapped, turning his wrath on Drew.

"She's right there," Drew said, a little exasperated now, pointing at Della oblivious to the interchange at the booth.

Drew glanced at Wade, who lifted a shoulder. Arlo obviously needed to blow off a little steam, and they were copping the brunt. That was the way it happened sometimes.

Arlo didn't say any more, just turned on his heel and strode away.

"Who shoved the stick up his ass?" Winona asked.

Wade laughed. He very much suspected that the job had, tonight. But *Winona* had very definitely given it a twist.

• • •

CC woke, disoriented, a few hours later. She was hot from still being fully dressed and buried under the covers, and there was a buzzing in her head that wouldn't go away.

Maybe she was hungover? But she hadn't had

anything to drink. Maybe it was one of those silent migraines. Or a stroke? That might explain her demented behavior with Wade tonight.

If whatever the hell it was could just result in some kind of associated amnesia so she never had to relive that embarrassment—or the passion—again, it mightn't be so bad.

The buzzing stopped suddenly, and CC turned her head and squinted at the luminous dials of her kinetic digital clock, so out of place next to the art deco lamp under the canopy of her original four-poster bed it was laughable.

Three-thirty.

The buzzing started again, and CC realized it was coming from her phone, which she'd dragged under the covers with her to Google how to induce memory loss until she fell asleep.

Who on earth was calling at this hour? She snatched it up. It was her oldest brother, Joey.

Mom.

Heart suddenly fibrillating in her chest, she hit the answer button, vaulting upright. "Joey? What's wrong? Is Mom okay?"

"Mom's fine. It's Dad."

CC's pulse settled quickly at her brother's assurance, but the ominous note in his voice didn't bode well. Whatever it was, it couldn't be good. No one called at this hour in the morning with good news. Good news could wait until a decent hour.

She knew, even before she asked "What happened," what her brother was going to say.

"He had a heart attack. He was revived, and they took him to the OR, but his heart stopped again and they couldn't restart it."

CC had a complicated relationship with her father. She'd spent most of her life torn between yearning for him and hating him. Her brothers had been older at the time of his leaving, so they'd actually had a relationship with him. One they could remember, they could hold on to.

She'd had nothing.

She knew from overhearing family gossip that she'd been her parents' last-ditch effort at staying together. At rekindling their love. It had failed.

She had failed.

And, rightly or wrongly, she felt responsible for her father's desertion.

But she'd always thought that one day, they'd work things out and she'd have the kind of relationship she'd always fantasized about. Or at least a less acrimonious one.

"CC?"

Joey's voice was laced with concern. It was probably wrong to have a favorite brother, but Joey was hers. Because he was the oldest, she knew he felt as betrayed as she did over their father leaving, and the solidarity had been comforting.

"Yeah."

"Are you okay?"

CC didn't know how to feel. Between what had happened with Wade and her dad, her brain bulged with too much *stuff*. "No."

"Will you—"

"Yeah." CC didn't think her father deserved her prayers or her presence, but her mother did, and this was a time for family. "I'm leaving now."

CHAPTER FIFTEEN

The sun was warm on Wade's back, and it wasn't even ten in the morning yet. But it felt good to be out in the field with Wyatt, stringing a fence. Good to have hard physical labor take his mind off CC. Off the kiss. Off her overnight disappearing act. Off the note she'd left him.

When he'd discovered she wasn't home and spotted the note on the kitchen counter, he'd been filled with dread, expecting it to be a resignation letter. His hand had shaken as he'd opened the folded paper.

Wade,

I'm heading home to Nebraska. There's a family situation I need to deal with. I apologize for any inconvenience, I should be back in four or five days. I'll keep you up to date.

CC.

Concern for the muck their kiss had landed them in was quickly replaced with concern for CC. What did a *family situation* mean? For the Carters, it usually meant his second cousin Raymond had gone off his meds again or a shotgun wedding was imminent. But he knew CC's family dynamics weren't that straightforward.

He assumed it wasn't anything too drastic, otherwise surely she'd just have said? He'd called and texted a couple of times but had no response. His mom had said CC had left a similar message on her voicemail, apologizing for leaving her in the lurch this weekend. So all he could do was wait for CC to call with an update.

Wade sucked at waiting.

It was slightly cheering to know she was planning on coming back to Credence. But what frame of mind would she be in when she did? Would she spend her time away psychoanalyzing to death what had happened between them? He didn't want to lose CC as his PA and he was sure he could still change her mind. Yes, the kiss had thrown a wrench into the works, but he was fine with *never speaking of it again*. Just as she'd asked. He might *think* about it obsessively, but she didn't have to know that. He'd agree to whatever she needed as long as she stayed in his life.

Wyatt approached, peeling his gloves off, wiping sweat from his brow with his forearm. Grabbing a frosty bottle of water from the cooler, he tossed one to his brother.

"Thanks."

Wade pulled his gloves off and drank half, removed his hat, splashed some cold water over his hair and face, and crammed the hat back on.

"Jenny and Roxy at the information meeting?" Wade asked.

Wyatt deliberately avoided his gaze. "Yep. They left with Mom."

"Are they interested in staying? In starting up a

business?"

"I don't think Roxy could handle living here, but Jenny's interested."

"She told you that?"

Wyatt splashed his face, too, then looked directly at Wade. "She told me."

"Does she have a business idea?"

"She's thinking about selling coffee. The real stuff. She knows how to work one of those fancy city machines."

Wade laughed. There was no such fancy machine anywhere in Credence. "I like her already."

His brother's gaze skittered away again, but he was smiling. In fact, Wade would go as far to say that Wyatt was *glowing*.

Wade leaned his elbow on the nearest post and rested his foot on the bottom strand of wire. "So she's just going to pick up and leave Pittsburgh. Just like that? No job or…other things keeping her there. Family and…friends?"

Wade didn't want to push, but he could see that Wyatt was clearly smitten, and he hated to think his brother might end up with a broken heart if things didn't work out because Jenny started to miss her mother or her bestie or an ex…

"Yeah, Wade. *Just like that*."

Wade contemplated shutting up. His brother's tone had turned testy, and he really didn't want to rain on his parade. But…

"I don't want to be some kind of downer, Wyatt, really I don't. But I saw you dancing with her last night, and you're practically blushing right now, and I just don't want to see your heart broken if she's not as committed to this as you are, that's all. I mean… it's been less than twenty-four hours. What do you really know about her, bro?"

"She comes from a broken home and left high school before she graduated. She's working minimum wage bussing tables at the moment, busting her ass every day and just can't get ahead. But she can here. She only has a great aunt in Pittsburgh and no other family. And she said the minute the bus drove into Credence she knew it was the place for her, and I gotta say, it looks real pretty on her."

Wade held up both of his hands as his brother threw his water bottle on the ground. "Okay."

"I know, to a guy who has a revolving door on his apartment, settling for one woman isn't your jam. But all I ever wanted, Wade, is to find someone to love and who loved me and live happily ever after. Maybe have a couple of kids if we're lucky. Like Mom and Dad. What the hell is wrong with that?"

Wade wanted to dispute his brother's summation about what was and wasn't his jam, but it was hard to refute. He had found *the one* with Jasmine, had been happy to *settle down*. But that had gone pear-shaped, and he'd been so badly burned that going back there again wasn't an option.

But the yearning in Wyatt's voice had taken him back to those days. To the promise of what was to come and, unbidden, an image of CC rose in his mind.

"Nothing." He smiled at his brother as he shook the image away. "Nothing's wrong with it at all." He downed the last of his drink.

"You don't think she's too young for me?"

"How old is she?"

"Twenty-five."

Wade whistled. "She looks older than that."

"She hasn't had an easy life."

"No. I mean…she looks like an old soul, you know? Like she's been around once already."

"Yeah." Wyatt nodded. "You're right. She does." He retrieved his water bottle and took a swig. "So, you think the age gap is okay?"

"What does she think?"

Wyatt shrugged. "She knows how old I am. But I haven't specifically raised the issue."

"Well, if the way she was dancing with you last night was any indication, I'd say she doesn't have a problem with it."

Wyatt smiled a goofball smile, and Wade couldn't help but return it. It was ridiculously hopeful. Which made Wade happy and wary all at once.

"So, what…you're in love with her?"

His brother looked at his feet for a beat or two before raising his gaze to meet Wade's. "Yeah. I know it sounds crazy, but I think I am."

Wade laughed. "A little. Are you sure it's not your dick talking? I mean…how long *has* it been since you got laid?"

Wyatt looked away again, busied himself putting his gloves back on.

Wade laughed. "That long?"

Still no answer or eye contact from Wyatt. Just a "Let's get back to work."

"Oh no," Wade joked. "It's worse than I thought."

There was a snort and a muttered "You have no idea" as Wyatt turned away, grabbing the roll of wire behind him.

Wade frowned. "Wyatt?"

"Fuck's sake, Wade. The fence won't string itself."

Wade's frown deepened as he inspected his brother's back. He reached across and put a stilling hand on his brother's arm. One moment he'd been all goofball and now he was shutting down. "Talk to me, Wyatt."

Another snort as Wyatt bent over and unraveled a length of wire like the planet's well-being depended on it right at this second. "I'm not talking to *you* about this."

"What. Sex?"

They always smack-talked about sex. Joked around about it. It was like 50 percent of their relationship, since they'd fought over the Victoria's Secret catalogue as teenagers. But now his brother could barely look at him, and Wade wondered if it was because it had been so long or maybe because Wyatt hadn't had a lot of opportunity to practice.

Unlike quarterbacks with three Super Bowl rings.

"It's okay to be inexperienced, Wyatt. It's not like you forget how to do it, it'll all come back to you, trust me."

Wyatt stood and looked at Wade for the first time, a mix of frustration and exasperation in his gaze. "It's not…look, I…haven't, okay? Enough already."

Defiance and resignation burned in Wyatt's gaze, and Wade's confusion grew. Enough already? No fucking way. "Haven't…what?"

"Done it."

Done it? "Sex?"

His brother nodded quickly, averting his gaze again before admitting "Yes" in a soft voice.

Wade blinked. *Oh.* "Like…at all."

Wyatt glared at him. "Yes, Wade. *At all.* I'm still a virgin, okay? You can laugh now."

Wade blinked. Holy Toledo. *That* he hadn't expected. "Shit, man. I'm not going to laugh at you."

Wyatt may have been glaring and defiant, but he was also clearly embarrassed, and the fact that he'd confided in his younger, much more sexually experienced brother was a *big deal.* Wyatt wasn't a touchy-feely kinda guy, he wasn't a talker. He didn't poke his nose into anyone else's business and expected the same courtesy in return. He deserved Wade's respect and admiration, not his flippant jokes.

"Actually, it's kinda—"

"If you say sweet, I'm going to punch you in your pretty quarterback face."

Wade laughed. "I was going to say amazing, actually. It also explains the calluses on your hands."

Wyatt, despite his embarrassment, hooted out a laugh as he pulled a glove off and inspected his hand. It was hard and lumpy from years of fencing and myriad other physical labors involved in farm work. His smile faded quickly, and he shot Wade a quick, pained look.

"It's embarrassing is what it is. I'm a forty-year-old virgin, for fuck's sake. I've only ever been to second base, and to be honest, I've only been there twice. I'm the full yokel cliché. It's… *I'm* pathetic."

"No, man." Wade shook his head emphatically. Just because his brother didn't go for deep and meaningfuls didn't mean he didn't feel deeply about things, and his virginity was obviously something of which he was ashamed.

Fuck that shit.

"Don't do that. You're the most decent, honorable guy I know, and that's the true measure of a man. Not how many chicks he's bagged. That's just horseshit guys spout off to save ourselves from the agony of actually talking to each other."

"You must be full of shit, then."

Wade laughed at his brother's dig. "It's not all it's cracked up to be."

A manly snort huffed from Wyatt's mouth. "My heart bleeds for you."

Wade laughed again. "Seriously, though, do you mind me asking *how*? I know you've dated from time to time, so I assumed you'd…"

Wyatt looked down at his hands and shook his head. "Honestly, man, I don't know. I keep asking myself the same question. I just… I'm not good around women, you know that. They're so pretty and smart and sophisticated, and they smell so good, and…I'm not like you. I never really got how to talk to them, and I get tongue-tied so I clam up, and it's not like we're spoiled for choice around here, right? I haven't had a lot of chance to practice, and just screwing up the courage to ask a woman out brings me out in a cold sweat, and I never know what to say when we are out, so dates are usually a disaster, and…I don't know, suddenly I'm nearly fucking forty and I've never done the deed."

"And it's different with Jenny?"

A goofy look lit Wyatt's face as he glanced at Wade. "Yeah, man. Right from the beginning, I felt like I can talk to her."

"Have you kissed her?"

"Hell no." Wyatt shook his head.

"But you want to."

"Jesus, Wade." A dull flush stained Wyatt's cheek-bones. "I like it better when we talk about hogs."

Wade knew this conversation must be excruciating for his brother; it wasn't exactly a walk in the park for him, either. They just didn't talk about this stuff. Not in any kind of plain, honest way. But Wyatt had opened the door. And damn if getting Wyatt laid wasn't something he could occupy his mind with to forget about his idiotic behavior with CC.

"C'mon, man, it's just me. Would you rather talk to Dad?"

Wyatt gaped at his brother. "I'd rather stick a rattlesnake down my boxers."

"So talk to me."

Wyatt did a good impression of squirming while standing but took a deep breath and continued. "Yes, I'd like to kiss her. Like to do more than that. But I've known her for less than a day. I just don't have those kind of moves, Wade."

"Don't worry about your moves. Do you think she wants the same thing?"

"Yeah." Wyatt nodded slowly. "I'm not exactly tuned in to what women want, but when I look at her, I swear I *know* she feels the same way."

Wade chewed over that for a moment. He might be cynical about love and relationships, but he remembered a time when he'd been sure of a woman, too.

"And if the opportunity arose...to sleep with her...you'd be up for it?"

Wade laughed at his joke as Wyatt rolled his eyes.

"Of course."

"Okay…" Wade nodded as an idea formed in his head. "Here's what I think. You should tell her. About being a virgin."

Wyatt blinked, then his face screwed into an expression of absolute horror. "*What?* Did you take a stupid pill this morning? Hell no."

"Tell her. Trust me, she'll love it. She'll admire your honesty and—" Wade grinned. "She'll be gentle with you."

A low growl rumbling in the back of his brother's throat widened Wade's grin.

"I think you're getting way too much enjoyment out of this."

"Sorry, I couldn't resist." Wade made an effort to pull himself together. "I still think it's the right way to go."

"I'm not telling a twenty-five-year-old woman who's pretty enough to have had a dozen lovers by now that I'm a virgin."

"You'd rather her wonder about your technique as you fumble through it instead?" Wade remembered how bad he'd been at it the night he'd lost his virginity and how nerves had made it even worse. "Or have her think you've got a trigger thing going on down there when you're done in approximately ten seconds, which is about how long I lasted the first time?"

Of course, he had been seventeen, not nearly forty…

"Oh God." Wyatt cradled his face in his palms for a couple of beats before dropping his hands and looking at his brother. "What if she…I don't know…

thinks I'm some kind of freak? What if she *laughs*?"

"If she laughs?" Wade turned suddenly serious at the thought. "Run away, man. She's not the woman for you."

Anyone who didn't have the sensitivity to intuit that revealing such an intimate detail about his life was excruciating for Wyatt wasn't worth his time. She wasn't the woman that his stalwart brother needed.

"Christ, Wade." Wyatt took off his hat, raked his hand through his hair, and placed it back on his head again. "I don't know."

"Look…it's an option." Wade shrugged. "Just think about it, okay?"

"Like I'm going to be thinking about anything else," Wyatt muttered.

Wade smiled to himself as he picked up his gloves. "We done now? Or you want the birds and bees talk as well. I give a good one. Complete with diagrams."

Wyatt snorted. "I will feed you to the hogs if you even try." He shoved his hand into his glove and stalked away.

• • •

Three days later, Wade and Wyatt came in from their chores to find their mother pacing the kitchen, George watching her with worried eyes, whining softly.

"Oh boys, there you are."

Dread, thick and hot, surged into Wade's chest. "What's wrong? Is it Dad?" His father had an appointment to see Credence's only doctor this morning.

"No, no." She shook her head.

"Is it Jenny?"

Jenny had insisted on moving into the board-inghouse Bob and his merry helpers had done up when the other women had left Credence en masse on Sunday. Ronnie had been happy for her to stay, and Wyatt had asked her not to leave, but she hadn't wanted to impose any longer. She'd insisted she needed to stand on her own two feet, and Wade had admired the hell out of her for that.

"No, darlin'." Ronnie smiled at her eldest son as she reached up and briefly cupped her hand to the side of his face. It fell away as she turned to face Wade. "I've just been talking to CC. Her father died, she's just been to the funeral."

If his mother had punched him in the chest, Wade couldn't have been any more shocked. The news hit him square in the solar plexus. "What?"

Why hadn't she told him? Why wouldn't she say something?

"When?"

"On Friday evening, apparently."

That news was probably even more shocking. She'd known when she left that her father was dead, and she hadn't said anything?

Just *a family situation*.

A funny pain, like a stitch or a cramp, grabbed Wade around his ribs. Yes, things had been up in the air between them on Friday evening after the kiss, and yes, CC had always been very private about her family, but hell, she'd *opened up to him* about her childhood, her parents, and hell, they'd been practically inseparable for almost six years. He'd have thought she'd confide something this big, this shocking, this *earth-shattering*.

George, as if sensing Wade's disquiet, padded over and sat at his feet, leaning his body into Wade's leg. He whined softly again, and Wade absently reached down and petted his head.

"She called you?" *Why* would CC tell his mother and not him?

"No. I called her about something to do with the next singles event in three weeks and, well, just to check on her really, because I don't know…I've been worried and she sounded terrible, and I asked her if everything was all right, and she didn't say anything for the longest time…" Tears glittered in his mother's eyes. "I thought she might have hung up for a moment, and then she just said, 'No, my father died.' Oh Wade." Ronnie pressed a hand to her stomach. "She sounded so…hollow and awful."

Wade felt pretty fucking hollow and awful, too. *Christ*…why hadn't she said something? He turned to Wyatt. "Will you be okay here for a bit if I go for a couple of days?"

Wyatt nodded. "Of course."

"Oh yes, darling." Ronnie nodded. "Please go to her. She needs you."

Wade suppressed the snort. He wasn't as confident as his mother. In fact, given CC's history, he wouldn't put it past her not to deliver a delayed knee to his testicles. He knew she had that maneuver down perfectly. But he couldn't *not* go, either.

He couldn't explain the compulsion bubbling inside him, he just knew that CC might need somebody outside the family, and he wanted it to be him.

"I'll go home and get cleaned up."

His mother crossed the kitchen and embraced him. "You're a good man, Wade Carter." She pulled away. "You drive safe now, you hear? CC doesn't need your death on her conscience, and black is not my color."

Wade smiled. "Yes, ma'am."

He nodded at his brother and turned to go. George whined and thumped his tail, staring at Wade with those freaky blue eyes. The dog might be as dumb as a box of rocks, but he had clearly picked up on the emotion in the room, and CC loved the damn animal. George never failed to make her smile, and she'd even managed, despite everyone else failing, to train him a little.

He shook his head at the dog. "You pee in my Mustang and I will leave you on the side of the road."

George gave an excited little yip, and Wade rolled his eyes. "C'mon then, let's go get CC."

He didn't have to be asked twice. He was up and out the door before anyone could blink. Wade followed him with grim determination.

CHAPTER SIXTEEN

CC didn't know how many tequilas she'd drunk when the knock came on her hotel door. But the bottle had been full a few hours ago and now it was half empty.

For damn sure she was drunk.

Ignoring the knock, she poured another one. She could still feel all her fingers and toes and the brick sitting against her chest, so she wasn't drunk enough for her liking.

She wanted to be numb all over.

The knock came again. "Go away, Joey," she yelled in the general direction of the door. Her brother had been knocking every twenty minutes or so for the last few hours. "I told you I'm fine."

And she threw back the shot, squinting as the fiery liquid hit the back of her throat.

"CC?" Another knock. "It's me. Wade. Open up."

Wade? CC's stupid heart leapt in her chest. Wade had come? Then she frowned. *Wade* had come?

Why?

Damn it, she shouldn't have said anything to Ronnie. But her motherly concern had thrown light into the well of grief and darkness, and it had felt good to tell someone oblivious to her family history. Who could console without careful choice of words.

"Go away, Wade." She wasn't numb enough to face him.

A dog barked. "I brought George with me. He's missing you."

CC frowned. *George?* Wade had brought George? Tears blurred CC's vision, and she blinked them away as she leapt up from the couch. Or as nearer an approximation of leaping as a woman who'd consumed a half bottle of tequila could make. Concentrating on her footsteps, she crossed to the door in a reasonably straight line.

It wouldn't pass a sobriety test, but it got her there.

Grabbing the door handle, she yanked it open. It stopped dead as the chain pulled taut and jarred through her arm. Swearing under her breath, she fumbled with the chain and fingers that were number than she'd realized, maneuvering it off, encouraged by the soft whining of George from the other side.

Finally, the chain slipped free, and she pulled the door the rest of the way open. George entered enthusiastically, wagging his tail, barking and turning around and around, gazing up at her adoringly.

"Georgie porgie." CC was so damn happy to see him she dropped to a knee to give the dog some love, petting him and telling him he was a good boy, kissing his snout and scratching behind his ears as he nuzzled her neck.

But all the time she was excruciatingly aware of the man standing patiently in the doorway, and it was inevitable that she turn her attention to him eventually.

He looked her up and down as she straightened, George leaning against her leg, staying by her side. It was only then she remembered that she wasn't exactly dressed for company. She'd stripped down to her tank top and underwear as she'd settled in for a little oblivion in the safe hands of Jose Cuervo.

Sure, she was wearing more clothes than most women wore on the beach these days, but way fewer clothes than he'd ever seen her in. Way fewer clothes than Wade, who was looking like the answer to every sad, desperate, drinking-in-a-motel-room-alone woman's problems. Those soft jeans cupped *everything*, and his T-shirt stretched across a chest her nipples still remembered in intimate detail.

Yep—definitely wasn't numb enough to forget that.

Heat suffused her face both at her state of undress and the memory, but she was a little too drunk to care, and in her current state of inebriation it only made her snippy.

"How'd you know I was here?"

He held up his phone, showing a little dot with her face in it over their location. "The app."

Yes of course, *that stupid app*. "I meant which room."

"I ran into Joey in the bar."

Wade had met all of her brothers at one time or other. She'd gotten them tickets to Broncos games over the years, and Wade had always invited them back into the locker room and introduced them around. As far as the Morgan men were concerned, Wade was a freaking superhero.

CC made a mental note to rip Joey a new one.

"Can I come in?"

"Why?" CC may not have been thinking very straight, but even three sheets to the wind, she could still hear her better angels screaming *danger, Will Robinson*.

Not even Señor Cuervo drowned those bitches out.

"Because your brothers are worried about you, and so am I."

CC scrubbed a hand over her face, her eyes were gritty from the crying—so much crying—and God alone knew what state her hair was in, given all the finger-twisting she'd done. It probably looked like rats were nesting in it, while Wade's looked as perfectly messy as always.

"Brothers *schmothers*," she said belligerently.

He narrowed his eyes at her. "Are you drunk?"

CC tried to coordinate her thumb and forefinger apart an inch to indicate just a little, but gave up instead. "Not nearly enough, no."

She turned on her heel—George sticking close—back to the couch to continue her journey into oblivion. She vaguely heard the door click shut and lock behind her as George made himself at home on the couch, resting his chin on CC's leg.

CC felt Wade's gaze on the back of her head and then its slow sweep as he took in the coffee table, the half-drunk bottle, a trash can full of wadded-up tissues, the printed order of service from the funeral, complete with a picture of her father on the front.

She reached for the bottle.

"Maybe you've had enough."

Maybe she was going to have to drink the whole damn thing if he kept standing there judging her. "Nope." A little tequila sloshed over the side of the shot glass as she poured.

"How about I make some coffee?"

He looked around for a kitchen as CC picked up

the glass and saluted him. "You can drink whatever you want. George and I—" George thumped his tail. "We're sticking with the hard liquor."

She giggled then, thinking about the other kind of *hard liquor*, which took her to Wade going down on her, which took her to the kiss, which stopped the giggles abruptly, and she threw the shot back.

Wade rolled his eyes. "I'll get us some food."

"No." CC's stomach turned as she shook her head vehemently.

Food reminded her of the wake she'd had to endure while a bunch of people she didn't know talked about her father as this warm, loving family man, and the children *who weren't even his* grieved about the great man that had raised them.

Dainty sandwiches had stuck like glue in the back of her throat, and she'd wanted to leave, but her mother, bitter to the end, had insisted they all stay. She'd wanted every person in that room to know that the man they were all lauding wasn't so great after all. That he'd abandoned a family—a wife and six children—and CC had been too empty to fight about it.

"Fine." He sat beside her then, and CC's equilibrium, already hinky from a half bottle of tequila, lurched.

The couch was only a two-seater and hardly a generous one at that, especially with George also taking up room. The entire side of Wade was smooshed against the entire side of her. Given that most of those parts involved her bare skin, everything from shoulder to knee flared with heat.

Levering his hips off the couch slightly, Wade

reached into his jeans pocket and pulled out a packet of Nerds. CC automatically held out her hand as he gave them his usual comforting shake and flipped the lid.

A small pile of Nerds was poured into the palm of her hand, and for the first time ever CC threw them all back, desperate for a sugar hit. She shut her eyes and let the rush take her as she chewed and swallowed, absently petting George's head as some of the candy dissolved on her tongue.

"Wiburta's missing you."

CC's eyes flew open. "Your mom said she'd feed her for me."

"She is, but the damn pig fusses like a sack full of cats, takes her forever to drink her bottle."

"She likes having her left ear stroked while she suckles."

George thumped his tail as if he knew they were talking about his nemesis in CC's affections, but the truth was, she loved her new babies equally and was going to have to find a way to get them both to California. The silence stretched as she considered the logistics—no easy feat with a pickled brain.

But then Wade broke the silence with the verbal equivalent of a sledgehammer.

"I'm sorry about your dad."

It was soft and gentle but struck like a blow, and CC swallowed hard before opening her mouth to say she wasn't sorry but closed it again. So many of her feelings toward the man who had given her life revolved around years of her mother's bitterness, and that was so hard to separate out, she didn't know how *she* felt about him anymore.

230 NOTHING BUT TROUBLE

It had been a shock to feel as devastated as she had. And whether she liked it or not, there were two stepsiblings who, through no fault of their own, were grieving the loss of the only father they'd ever known tonight, too.

"You could have told me, you know."

CC's eyes flicked open. "Yeah." She didn't know why she hadn't. She could easily have put it in the note. Or returned any of his dozen calls or texts these last few days.

But it was…complicated.

"I was going to tell you when I got back."

He nodded. "Okay."

Maybe it was the booze, but that okay sounded judgey. "You wouldn't understand, Wade. You have two parents who've been together forever. That still love each other, that nurture and champion and look out for each other. That's not my experience."

"I know. And I'm sorry for that. I know how lucky I've been. You deserved better than that. Every kid does."

Hot tears scalded the backs of CC's eyes, but she refused to let them fall.

Damn straight she deserved it.

She held out her hand again, and Wade poured in more Nerds. Once she'd thrown them back, she leaned forward and poured herself another shot. "I don't have another glass," she said, peering over her shoulder at him, "but you're welcome to the bottle if you want to join me?" She held it up and raised an eyebrow at him.

His lips lifted in a ghost of a smile as he shook his head. "I couldn't possibly deprive you."

CC shrugged. "Suit yourself." She knocked the shot back, wincing as the fire hit her esophagus and spread heat through her chest. She slammed the glass back down on the glass top of the coffee table. George, who'd drifted off to sleep under the rhythmic stroke of CC's hand, startled.

Wade didn't say anything, just offered her more Nerds, which she refused. The mix in her stomach was not sitting well.

He bent his knee and anchored his foot on the coffee table. It was exceedingly distracting. Denim pulled taut across his quad, and CC followed it all the way up to his knee. She didn't know why it should be so damn sexy. She'd seen those quads bare more times than had been good for her sanity.

But there was just something about Wade in denim that was hitting her in all her lady parts since moving to Credence.

She blamed farmer porn.

"Is that a good likeness?"

CC dragged her gaze off his leg to find him pointing at the order of service with his booted toes. It was a recent picture of her father. She knew that because he looked older than she'd remembered. Grayer. His face more lined than the last time she'd seen him, which had been just before she'd started working for Wade.

But that wasn't what Wade was referring to. She'd defaced the image with a sharpie a few hours ago. Back when she'd still been sober enough to coordinate her fine motor control. It had felt good drawing a moustache and beard and devil's horns, but now it just seemed petty and sad.

Great. She was the full pissy cliché.

"I hate him."

It wasn't the question he'd asked her, but the emotion welled in her chest as she looked at her father again and the words just fell out, her heart aching with the heaviness of their truth.

CC was pretty sure it wasn't some kind of mortal sin to hate your father. But to admit it out loud on the day he was buried in the ground seemed especially sinful.

"That's understandable." He picked up her hand and intertwined their fingers, plonking their joined hands on his thigh. It was such a simple thing, but her heart felt a little lighter just looking at them, and its warmth was an instant comfort.

"He never told me he loved me. Not once. Not ever."

Wade nodded. "But you loved him anyway, right?"

Tears welled in CC's eyes again, and she didn't try to quell them this time. "Yes," she whispered. "I don't understand how I can hate him and love him at the same time."

"Because love isn't rational, CC. Hate can be quantified and reasoned out. Love, particularly for family, just…is. Whether we like it or not." He squeezed her hand. "But, for what it's worth, I'm sure he loved you, too. He probably just wasn't very good at saying it."

"No." CC shook her head, sniffling as her nose started to run again. "He didn't. I was supposed to be the baby that saved their marriage." She turned anguished eyes on him. "I had one job, Wade."

He smiled at her so gently her heart cracked a

little. "You were three years old, CC."

She glanced away. He was right, of course, but it still hurt, like a big, purple bruise right in the center of her chest. "I was a reminder of his failure."

Tears slipped down her face. Christ, she was thirty-two years old, and this was ancient history, and yet still it cut like a knife. Her brothers, at least, had memories of a man who had played with them, laughed and hugged and kissed their boo-boos better. All she had was memories of a distant man who could barely look at her.

No wonder she'd shied away from a relationship with a man when the most important male role model in her life had left her. Her father had taught her that men leave. Taught her it was better all round not to give them the chance. And working for Wade in this very demanding job had provided her with the opportunity to stay unavailable.

She dashed the falling tears from her face, sniffling some more. Wade squeezed her hand, and George roused to give her leg a lick.

"Everyone knows having a baby to save a marriage is a truly stupid idea and never works. The breakdown of your parents' relationship is not your fault, CC. That's on them. They were the adults. Your only job was to be adored."

CC had no idea why those words should be the ones to make her break, but they did. *Adored?* She'd felt a lot of things where her parents were concerned—blamed, scapegoated, and fought over. How amazing would it have been to be adored? Like he and Wyatt had been.

Her face crumpled. If she'd been sober and in

her right mind, she'd have been mortified, but she was neither. So she fell apart instead, sobbing deep, wrenching sobs, her nose streaming, her face red and blotchy, her expression twisted into an ugly mask of grief.

And Wade was wonderful, letting her hand go and lifting his arm to put around her, tucking her into his side. He didn't try to worm away or placate her or pass the buck like he usually did with crying women. Although it was probably difficult to do that, given she was usually the one he passed the buck to.

Her and a downtown Denver florist.

She didn't know how long she cried for, but she was aware the whole time of the press of his chin against the crown of her head and the warmth of his arm around her shoulder. It was hard to believe it was Wade, but he felt solid and real.

And safe.

Crying on her boss's shoulder—literally—was risky. Also occupationally stupid. Just like the kiss had been. But he didn't feel like her boss right now. Like Wade "The Catapult" Carter, famous ex-quarterback with Super Bowl rings in his safe and abs on billboards all around Denver.

He was just Wade. The man who'd been by her side for almost every day of the last five and a half years. It felt…natural, even if it wouldn't have a few weeks ago.

He didn't say anything as she silently shed her last tears, sniffling to bring her emotions under control, breathing in and out to clear the thickening at the back of her throat. Unfortunately, she didn't feel any more sober, despite the loss of what felt like a pint of tears. Her head spun, her tongue felt thick, and a lethal mix of booze and Nerds churned in her stomach.

Wade leaned forward, lifting his arm from around her and grabbing a tissue from the box. "Here," he said as he handed it over.

"Thank you." Her voice was raw from crying as she dabbed at her eyes. She probably looked a fright. "Sorry."

"It's fine."

"No, I—"

"Really," he interrupted, his voice brooking no argument, his face serious. "It's fine, Cecilia."

"Oh God." CC groaned as her arms prickled with goose bumps and her nipples stiffened beneath her tank top. He was looking at her with his sexy blue eyes, and the way he said Cecilia, kinda stern, kinda husky… *Sweet baby Jesus.* "It's bad enough you called me Cecilia in the sex dream. Must you do it to my face, too?"

He stared for a moment and then half laughed as his eyes widened. "What?"

Every muscle CC owned snapped frozen. Except for her heart—it was beating fit to explode. "Crap." She swallowed as he continued to look at her incredulously. "Did I say that out loud?"

He chuckled. "Oh yeah."

Mental note—never drink tequila around Wade Carter. "Well…fuck."

"You had a *sex* dream about me?"

CC shook her head. All she had left was denial. "No."

He laughed, the kind of laugh that called bullshit. "Oh yes you did."

CC's cheeks were so hot she worried they might burst into flames. It certainly didn't help prove her innocence. Although being drunk made it slightly less mortifying. And her slightly more candid.

Who needed truth serum when there was tequila?

"Okay, okay fine, I did. But it was only once. And ages ago. I barely remember it."

CC prayed that God was done with smiting people this week as she lied through her teeth.

"And what did we do in this sex dream?"

Hell no. If she could have stood without falling over she would have. She settled for wriggling as far away from him as she could on the small couch. "I told you I barely remember." She'd take that shit to the grave with her. "But you weren't very good."

It was a desperate attempt to deflect, to throw a dart at his overinflated ego. It failed.

He chuckled. "Oh honey, I think we both know that's not true."

CC shut her mind to just how good he had been and lurched to her feet despite the uncoordinated state of her legs. George's tail thumped as she glared down at Wade. He was looking so full of himself. Like he knew that even in *her* dreams he was a total sex god. Arrogant damn jock. She should have never opened the door to him.

Standing, however, had not been the best move at this point in her tequila journey. Too much alcohol and Nerds were finally making themselves felt. A sudden roll of nausea cramped through her gut.

"I'm going to be sick."

CHAPTER SEVENTEEN

Wade was impressed with both the vivid rainbow effect of Nerds on stomach contents and how much one woman could vomit. He was no stranger to hugging the porcelain bus, but, hell, CC could have puked for America.

There wasn't much he could do but rub between her shoulder blades and make soothing noises. At least it kept his mind off the tiny palm tree tattoo in the small of her back and the fact she'd confessed to having a sex dream about him. Both of which he was pretty fucking sure she'd have gladly taken to her grave.

Thank you, Jose!

"Oh God..." CC groaned as she came up for some air. "Why did you let me drink so much?"

Wade let the rhetorical question slide. There was no time to answer it, anyway, as she groaned again and hurled one more time.

He rubbed her neck absently as his mind drifted to the sex dream. *CC had had a sex dream about him.* He supposed he should be alarmed about it—she worked for him, for fuck's sake. But he was too damn *male* not to be intrigued by it.

Just what had they gotten up to in this dream?

Her blush, her quick denial, told him it was probably pretty damn explicit, which filled his head with images he'd been trying not to think about since they'd kissed. Up until now, he'd thought that kiss had been an aberration, a one-off thing that had come from nowhere.

Now he wasn't so sure…

Had it been a moment of unexplained madness, or the result of a deeper craving CC had been masking for who knew how long?

And why the hell wasn't that thought scaring the crap out of him?

The sudden cessation of CC's retching brought Wade back to the here and now. He noticed the shake of her hand as she reached for the roll of paper and tore some off, wiping her mouth before grabbing the toilet lid and shutting it, resting her forehead against the plastic.

George whined from outside the door. Wade had shut him out when he'd tried to get his snout in next to CC and lick her face mid-retching.

Wade's hand rested on her nape. "Okay now?"

She shook her head. "No. I want to die."

Wade chuckled. "Yeah. Cuervo's got a kick like a mule."

Giving her neck one last squeeze, he pushed to his feet and, leaning over her, flushed the toilet. He took two paces to the vanity. Her toothpaste, tooth-brush, and floss were lined up like soldiers on the hand towel beside the sink. Even in her grief she was obsessively neat and ordered.

He picked up her toothbrush and loaded it with a generous dollop of toothpaste, noticing with surprise the Broncos T-shirt neatly halved and hanging over the side rail.

Did she wear it to bed? *Christ.* That was way more titillating than it should have been.

Determinedly dragging his head out of her night-wear, he held the toothbrush toward her. "You wanna brush?"

She nodded, her eyes still closed, her forehead still attached to the lid, but it took her a moment or two to move, and when she finally pushed to her feet, the muscles in her thighs trembled visibly. Wade reached out to grab her arm, suddenly worried her legs might not support her and she'd end up on her ass on the cold, hard tiles.

He knew how weak she must be feeling when she didn't even bother to shrug his hand away. She glanced at him through her bangs, and, silently, he passed her the toothbrush. She took it, getting it almost to her mouth before her nostrils flared and she thrust it back at him, said "One moment," and threw herself down on the floor again, whipping the toilet lid open and throwing up some more Technicolor stomach contents.

Her stomach muscles were going to ache like a bitch in the morning. And God knew what her head would feel like.

She was less shaky on the second try of standing, although she did lean heavily against the vanity. She managed her teeth without any further throwing up, however, which was progress, but she looked like hell. Her hair was a disheveled mess, her face was blotchy, and her eyes were bloodshot with dark smudges beneath, and he wondered just how much sleep she'd had these past few days. And how much tequila she'd consumed.

Despite her general scariness, something shifted deep inside Wade's chest. This was CC, and she was hurting.

She swayed a little as she straightened from rinsing. He handed her a towel, and she wiped her mouth. "Bed?"

It was only eight o'clock, but she was clearly wiped out.

"Yes," she said, wincing at her face in the mirror before turning away from the sight.

George was thrilled to see her as Wade opened the door, and she gave him a wan smile and patted his head as she made a beeline—a little crookedly, but hardly surprising considering how much booze she had on board—for the neatly made bed.

She didn't bother with pulling back the sheets, just threw herself on top, rolled on her side, grabbed the spare pillow, hugged it to her chest, and shut her eyes.

She was out before Wade reached the bed.

He sighed as he looked down at her sleeping form, the bedside lamp throwing her pale features into stark relief. She looked exhausted, the skin of her face stretched taut across her cheekbones.

He told himself not to let his gaze drift any lower. Not to check out the way her underwear had ridden up high on one ass cheek or how that palm tree tat played peek-a-boo with the band of her panties. He told himself not to return to the fascinating issue of what she'd been wearing in the sex dream.

He failed spectacularly at all of them.

George whined, and Wade started guiltily. She was drunk *and* asleep.

Look away, doofus.

Wade glanced at the dog. George stared back at him, turning his head slightly to one side then the other like he was reading every inappropriate thought circulating through Wade's head.

The dog obviously wasn't that dumb.

"What?" he said testily. "Someone who can lick his own balls has no right to judge."

Not deigning to answer, George took a couple of paces and launched himself onto the bed, settling in beside CC.

Yeah. Not stupid at all.

"No, George." Wade shook his head. "You're not even supposed to be in the room." It may not have been a luxury hotel, but even shitty ones had rules about animals. "You can lie at the bottom."

Wade pointed to the spot where a wide strip of worn, faded fabric was draped over the end of the bed in some attempt at being fancy. For a few seconds he and George stared each other down. The dog lost, picking himself up and padding to the end of the bed and stretching himself out at CC's feet, his nose resting against her ankle.

"Good boy." Wade patted him on the head. George's tail thumped a couple of times before he shut his eyes.

He glanced back at CC, at all her exposed flesh, and prayed like hell there was a spare blanket in the closet. He almost whooped when there was—a little small and thin, but perfect for his purpose. Hastily he crossed to the bed and covered her, George thumping his tail in approval and his sanity thanking him for the reprieve. His body, however, was not impressed.

That sorted, Wade looked around the room. The only place he could sleep was the couch. It was a foot too small for him, and he knew he'd probably ache like he'd just come off the field in the morning, but he wasn't going to leave CC.

For a start, he wasn't sure if Jose was quite finished with her yet, and that was a safety issue. A pro baller he'd known once had been so drunk he'd thrown up in his sleep and asphyxiated on his own vomit and died.

But mostly, she was just too damn sad to leave her.

He'd never seen CC undone by *anything*. She took everything in her stride. For the first three years of her time with him, she'd been in the middle of the zoo that was the NFL, and *nothing* had fazed her. It was hard to see her so…lost.

Tonight, he instinctively knew *she* needed *him* to be her left tackle.

Wade glanced at his watch—still only just past eight p.m. But it had been a long day, up early to work on the farm then a six-hour drive. He stretched, his back already protesting the couch as he contemplated its ineptness. Sighing, he resigned himself to his fate, sitting on the poor excuse for furniture to toe off his boots, then swinging his legs around.

It took him several minutes to find a position that was halfway comfortable. He doubted he'd get much sleep, but it was probably marginally better than the floor. At least the back of the couch blocked CC's bed from his view, and with that and the discomfort factor, he might not think about the woman lying a few yards away. Who'd admitted to having a sex dream about him.

Yeah. *Probably not...* He doubted even electric therapy to his junk would ever erase that from his brain.

He shifted uncomfortably and lifted his back to unbunch his T-shirt. Normally he'd have shucked his clothes off. He usually slept naked, and he stupidly hadn't brought an extra pair of clothes with him—just showered, changed, and jumped in his car. Removing them was the easy solution both for comfort and not looking like he'd slept in his clothes tomorrow.

But one barely dressed person in this room was more than enough. *Fuck.* He was never going to sleep.

Surprisingly, though, Wade did. He'd been sleeping well since working on the farm, and the combo of that with the long drive had helped ease him into a slumber he hadn't thought he'd find.

He woke to a noise some time later. Or rather a wet tongue licking his hand and a whine in his ear, and then the more distant noise of retching coming from the bathroom. Wade vaulted into an upright position, petting George as he squinted at his Smartwatch. Just after midnight.

George whined again. "She's okay, buddy," Wade murmured, stroking the dog's head a couple more times before striding to the bathroom. The door was closed.

"CC?"

There was silence for a beat or two, then a rather cranky, "Go away."

Wade touched his fingers to the door, torn between leaving her be, like she'd requested, and the urge to take charge. Another round of violent retching had him pushing open the door on a spike of concern.

She was on her haunches, her tattoo on full display. A nerve ticked in Wade's jaw. "CC?"

"God...Wade...I'm *fine*," she said testily, still hugging the toilet as she waved him away with her hand. She didn't look at him, but her voice sounded thick with emotion. Was she crying? "I don't want you seeing me like this. Just *leave*."

It was a little late for that, but Wade backed away anyway at her firm rebuff. If she was sober enough to crankily order him out and be embarrassed by her state, she didn't need him. But the emotion in her voice clawed at his gut. If she thought him seeing her crying and throwing up in a bathroom would somehow matter to him, she didn't know him very well at all.

Was it vanity or some kind of misplaced professionalism? Either way, it was misguided. They weren't boss and employee right now, no matter how much he was trying to keep her in a box.

She was grieving, and he'd be whoever she needed him to be.

He went back to the lounge, where George was waiting patiently. "She'll be fine," he told the dog.

And she would be, but he didn't think it was going to be tonight.

He sat and ran his hand over George's head a couple of times before forcing himself to get horizontal again. He didn't go back to sleep, though.

Noises coming from the bathroom seemed magnified in the dark quiet of the room, and he lay there listening. So did George, who was obviously unsettled by CC's grief. Wade was relieved when he heard the faucet turn on and run for what seemed like forever.

Maybe she was taking a shower?

Fifteen minutes later, the door opened and George deserted him. He heard her footsteps pad over to the bed, listened to the rustling of the bedclothes as she settled. He thought about saying something, asking her how she was, or *something*, but ultimately decided to keep his mouth shut. She'd been annoyed at his interference earlier, perhaps even a little embarrassed. Maybe not saying anything at all would be easier for her to stand.

But it took only a few minutes of her quiet crying to break his resolve. At first, he didn't know what it was. She was obviously trying to muffle the sound. But as he lay there straining to interpret the noises, it dawned on him. George's low sympathetic whines helped.

Wade clenched his fists by his sides, the urge to go to her, to check on her, almost overwhelming. He resisted for another few minutes, but when her very palpable grief showed no signs of abating, he gave in to his instinct to go to her.

George, who'd inched up the bed, his nose on her thigh, thumped his tail as Wade approached. CC had placed a pillow over her head, anchoring it with an arm, her shoulders shaking as she cried muffled tears. She'd changed into the Broncos T-shirt he'd seen in the bathroom earlier. It covered a lot more than what she'd been previously wearing, reaching mid-thigh, which was good.

But the number nine was plastered over the back—*his number*—and that *was not* good. It called to every possessive instinct Wade owned, and there were a fuck ton of them right now.

Did she sleep in his number every night? Had she been sleeping in his number the night she'd had the sex dream?

Fuck. He shut his eyes and reached for sanity. Hell, he almost turned his ass around. But another muffled sob sealed his fate.

"CC."

She groaned, and her shoulders shook some more as she choked out another, "Go away."

Wade shook his head as he crossed to the other side of the bed. "No."

He reached over and whipped the pillow off her head.

She made a low rumble of protest at the back of her throat and covered her face with her hands. "Just leave me alone," she said, her voice thick and hoarse.

Wade shook his head. "No."

"Wade…Jesus." She took her hands away and glared at him. His eyes had adjusted enough to the darkened room to see she was all puffy around the eyes. "This isn't appropriate."

Wade figured it was a good thing she was obviously sobering up enough to recognize the un-orthodox situation and worry about the propriety of it all. "I'm not your boss tonight, CC. And you're not my employee. Tonight you're just someone who's lost her dad, and I'm a friend who's offering comfort. That's all. No big deal."

But that was a lie. It was actually a big, fucking hairy deal. It was a revelation to realize he and CC had moved beyond their contractual relationship without him even realizing. CC had become so much more than his left tackle. She was his confidant, his sounding board, his go-to girl.

He ran everything past her, from his speaking circuit speeches to advertising scripts to press statements and which suit to wear on the red carpet. She'd become his touchstone.

And, yes, since moving to Credence, they had become *friends*. His heart pinched and his breath hitched at the thought.

"And right now I'm going to do what friends do for each other, which is get on this bed with you, put my arms around you, and hold you while you cry."

He didn't give her a chance to rebuff his suggestion. Just crawled onto the bed.

"Couch, George."

Wade was used to a plush king bed, and this rock-like double ensemble was definitely *not* big enough for the three of them. The dog whined but, recognizing the authority in Wade's voice, shifted away and jumped off the bed, padding over to the couch.

Wade lay back and held out his arm to CC. "Come here."

She shook her head, wiping at her eyes as she insisted, "I'm really f…fine." But her voice wobbled and her face crumpled.

"You're really not," Wade whispered, shifting closer to slip his arm under her neck and scoop her close.

She didn't resist, but she didn't submit, either. Not

for a beat or two, anyway, holding herself stiffly at his side, but then she stopped. "I don't understand why I can't stop crying," she said, her voice plaintive and tremulous in the dark.

Wade squeezed her shoulder. "Because he was your father and the rest doesn't matter."

The tears came then—again—and she melted into his side, her face turning into his shoulder, her hand landing on his chest, twisting in his T-shirt as, for the second time tonight, she let it all out.

Wade just lay there, staring at the ceiling, letting CC cry, holding her close, his fingers gently stroking her arm as the storm raged inside her. He held her until she'd cried herself out. Held her until she grew heavy against him and her breathing evened out. Held her until his own breathing evened out, and he too drifted into sleep.

CHAPTER EIGHTEEN

CC's eyes drifted open some time later. They were gritty, as if they'd been rolled in gravel and shoved in backward, but at least they still opened. She had no idea what time it was, but it felt like hours had elapsed. It was still dark in the room, no light peeked in around the edges of the terrible motel curtains, so it had to be before four in the morning.

Way too early, even for her.

Her lids fluttered closed again, a relief to her aching eyeballs, and she sighed and sunk a little further into the delicious heat surrounding her in the air-conditioned room. There was warmth at her back and a cushiony heat hugging her ass, spreading along the backs of her thighs. It was almost as good as the warm tickle at her nape and the heavy band of heat pressing low against her abdomen.

She sighed and pushed back against it, her ass cheeks finding hardness as well as heat as the band across her stomach shifted slightly, and she vaguely realized it was a hand and fingers.

Not her own.

Wade!

CC's eyes flew open as the whole evening came crashing back to her in the kind of downer that people took drugs to avoid.

Holy shit.

Wade was in bed with her. Wade was holding her. And, if she wasn't very much mistaken, Wade was *hard.* It may have been a while since she'd been this close to a male erection, but it wasn't something a woman ever forgot the shape of—or the feel.

Sweet mother of pearl.

It felt just like it had in the dream. *The dream she'd told him about.* CC almost groaned aloud as that particular realization dawned. She'd asked him to never speak of their kiss again, yet she'd just gone and blurted out about the dream.

What the hell had been wrong with her?

Oh…yeah, that's right—Señor Cuervo had been wrong with her.

She shut her eyes and wished she was still drunk, wished that this awful moment of self-awareness could be put off for just a little bit longer.

Sobriety sucked.

Almost six years of an unblemished record (notwithstanding the kiss they weren't speaking about) with Wade, and she'd blown it. And not in a small way, either. Oh no, not only had she gotten drunk, puked everywhere, then cried all over him, but she'd told him about the dream.

About the *sex* dream.

This was bad. *Very bad.* Although her current situation was probably the baddest of all. Her back squashed into his front, Wade's…biological reaction to the situation making itself well and truly felt.

Because that was what it had to be, right? He was a man, and she was a woman, and they *were* spooned together rather intimately. Intimately enough to feel every freaking contour of what felt like a very large package.

She shut her eyes, trying to hold back a tide of

need. His erection wasn't *about* her, it wasn't *for* her, it was just…male biology. Her body didn't seem to care, though, as the urge to touch the hardness currently cradled between her butt cheeks, to wrap her hand around it, to suck it into her mouth, to feel it buried deep inside her drove her to distraction.

Her stomach muscles contracted. A slow burn kicked to life between her legs. Sweet Lord—she was going to hell.

Her father had just been buried, and Wade, *who was her boss*, was being very sweet loaning her the comfort of his body. And she was lying here with a gigantic lady boner—far bigger than anything he was currently boasting—getting all hot and bothered over his completely subconscious erection.

Bad. *Bad, bad, bad.*

But damn it, this was Wade's fault, too. If she'd managed to get laid some time in the last few years, maybe all that sexual frustration wouldn't be choosing now to rear its ugly head. Nor would flashes of the sex dream. Like the scrape of his stubble against her breasts and the hot pull of his mouth.

CC's nipples hardened in Pavlovian response, and she squeezed her thighs together—tight. It didn't help. If anything, it intensified the tingle growing between her legs, and she shifted a little—a tiny flex of her hips—to try and ease it.

That didn't help, either. Not with the hard length of him dragging against her in a scandalously erotic way. It felt good. *Too damn good.* Even through two sets of clothing.

And she wanted to do it again.

CC's heart thrummed in her chest and battered frantically against all her pulse points as she tried to deny the roar of sexual demand. It surged through her ears, loud and insistent, and flowed thick and heavy through her breasts and thighs and groin.

Stop it, Cecilia!

She ordered herself to cease and desist, to go to sleep. That she was grieving and sad and this wasn't the answer. Not with this man, anyway. *Never this man.* But he was big and strong around her, holding her safe and close, his meat cleaver hand possessive on her stomach, and it was making her crazy and it was *Wade* and her body was not listening to her head.

Her hips flexed again of their own volition, a little more this time. Her stomach contracted at the hard press of him, a ripple of pleasure detonating low and deep, zig-zagging a path to her inner thighs. She bit back a moan, shut her eyes, fought to control her breath which sounded loud and ragged in the night.

Stop! She needed to stop.

It would be all kinds of wrong to rub herself to orgasm against him, even though she was already alarmingly close. Wade was her boss, her *sleeping* boss. It broke God knew how many workplace laws.

Not to mention her messy emotional state.

Frankly, everything about this was *wrong*.

She should get up, move away. Go take another cold shower. Stop this before it went any further. Salvage what she could of her pride and her integrity. Her professionalism.

This wouldn't bring her father back. It wouldn't make him love her, either. Oh God, the irony. If her father had only loved her, she wouldn't be making such a fool of herself tonight.

A spike of anger joined the squall of emotions battering her insides, and she pressed back into Wade again before she could think better of it. Just briefly. Just seeking an antidote for the anger in the soothing intensity of pleasure.

Just one more time.

The hand low on her abdomen tightened as a low, ragged groan brushed against her nape. "Christ… *Cecilia*…"

CC's heart practically fibrillated at the ragged utterance. If Wade had said anything else, it would have broken the spell. She would have frozen. Or, more likely, have fled. But her name from his mouth, all hot and gravelly on her neck, was right out of her dream, and before she could check herself, she was turning in his arms.

That was it, just her name uttered like that, and every molecule of common sense fled. In two seconds, her front was plastered to his front and her lips were seeking the heat and press of his lips. She found them in the dark, a low moan escaping as her mouth clashed with his, hot and hard and needy.

Greedy. For more. For all.

He met her with the same level of greed. With a long, deep groan and a thigh, hard and hot and insistent, pushing between her legs just exactly where she needed it, hiking her higher.

CC rubbed herself against the thick intrusion shamelessly, both easing and stoking the burn that she'd ignited when she'd so recklessly started this thing.

For five and a half years, she'd *deliberately* never thought about kissing Wade. Since moving to Credence, she'd thought of it too damn much.

This was better than anything she'd ever conjured.

He was a master, and she was desperate for more, greeting the sweep of his tongue with the sweep of her own, ceding control and taking it back with each twist and turn of their heads. A low groan rumbled through his chest, and she reveled in it, reveled in the way he rolled on top of her, slipping her arms around his neck and opening her legs.

CC gasped as he settled in the cradle of her pelvis, his erection pressing fully against the roaring ache between her thighs. Their kiss broken, he levered himself onto his forearms placed either side of her head. He was breathing hard. So was she. The intensity of his gaze stripped her bare as his eyes searched hers.

Even in the dark, they pierced her right down to her toes.

"On a scale of one to ten, how drunk are you still?"

CC gave a half laugh. Most of the tequila she'd consumed had been flushed down the toilet. "Negative ten. I am depressingly sober."

He nodded. But if she thought that would be enough for him, she was wrong. He continued to stare at her with grim intensity. "We shouldn't be doing this."

CC's heart thudded like a gong. "I know." *And she did know.* Her brain knew it full well, but her body had the con.

She sensed the same kind of battle going on inside him. The thick erection pressed into the juncture of her thighs was telling her one thing, the tension in every line of his body, another. He was drawn so taut, CC was amazed his body hadn't bowed.

"I'm your boss."

She nodded. Yes, he was. But she wanted this. Hell, she *needed* this. "I quit."

She was leaving soon anyway, and she needed this more than her job, more than her professional integrity, more than her pride. Suddenly, she needed Wade more than her next breath. He searched her gaze for a beat or two, and CC sensed that the outcome hung in the balance for excruciating seconds.

He growled low in this throat. "I accept."

A surge of sexual triumph jettisoned into her system, and CC didn't wait for him to come to her. She lifted her head off the bed and met him halfway, her tongue storming into his mouth, her hands sliding beneath the waistband of his jeans and his underwear to the hot, taut globes of his ass, pulling him in tighter, pressing him more intimately against her, grinding into him.

"Fuck," he muttered, the cuss word vibrating against her mouth and filling her head with its promise.

Yes. That was exactly what she wanted. Wade. Inside her. Wade, *fucking* her.

It may have been a long time for CC, but instinct took over as her hands slipped off his ass cheeks to the hem of his T-shirt, burrowing underneath to the hard planes of his back, lifting the shirt with her, up, up, up until she could pull it off his head. They broke lip contact only briefly as Wade ducked out of the fabric, but his mouth was back on hers, hot and hard, in the next second.

He kissed her like no other man had ever kissed her. Like it was Armageddon eve and they were both about to perish. And perhaps they were, because for damn sure, this incredibly stupid deed would *not* go unpunished.

But hell if it wasn't going to be worth her while.

Wade's big hand was suddenly hot on her thigh as he grabbed the hem of her Broncos shirt and pulled, gathering the material bit by bit, lifting himself off her a little to pull it all the way off. His fingers brushed her belly as he exposed it and then her ribs and then her breasts before he was yanking it over her head and off her arms, tossing it over his shoulder.

"Oh yesssss," he whispered, all hushed and reverent as his gaze drifted to her breasts. Breasts that were tight and achy and screaming for his touch. "Sweet baby Jesus."

CC's nipples tightened at the gleam of pure lust in his gaze before he dipped his head and claimed one of them in a lightning-swift maneuver that stole all the air from her lungs.

She gasped at the hot suction and the flick of Wade's tongue, grabbing the back of his head, twisting her fingers in his hair. She'd barely had time to catch a breath when he switched to the other, stealing it again, a hot dart of pleasure tunneling beneath her skin straight to the throbbing center between her legs.

Instinct took over then as he drove her mindless with his tongue, her hands feeling between their jammed bodies for his fly, finding it, fumbling the buttons and the zipper as his tongue lashed over the tip of a nipple, finally getting it down, reaching inside his underwear with one hand as the other pushed the denim off his hips.

Her fingers wrapped around his girth, and Wade reared back with a cry as if he'd been whipped. The air conditioning hit her nipples, and they scrunched into engorged buds.

"Fuck." He shut his eyes and panted as CC ran her palm from root to tip. "That feels good."

He wasn't wrong. Wade was long and hard and thick in her hand. It should have frightened the hell out of her, considering her vagina had been a penis-free zone for years now, but she was too damn greedy for it. For him.

And what a way to break a dry spell. With Wade Carter's very impressive cock.

"I need you in me now."

He groaned and muttered, "Fuck yes."

His eyes were glazed as he plundered her mouth, one hand busy between them with her underwear, working them lower. She was busy, too, her hand still firmly wrapped around Wade's erection as she worked his jeans down farther.

There wasn't much finesse in their disrobing. CC was sure they looked like two drunken seals as they undulated and twisted, unwilling to stop touching each other for the sake of efficiency. But they got the job done, and then Wade was notching himself at her entrance and she was wrapping her legs around the backs of his thighs and he was bending his head to kiss her as he pushed inside, and then he was filling her and it was everything CC hadn't known she was missing in her life.

She moaned as he slid in to the hilt, stretching her to capacity, so hard and high inside her CC almost orgasmed from that alone. She was so damn close, and she doubted she'd ever been this thoroughly possessed in her life.

What the hell had she been doing wrong all these years?

He withdrew and slid in again, and she cried out at the intensity of it, and the answering contraction low and deep inside her belly threatened to trigger another and another.

Wade eased away a little, peering down at her, panting hard. "Are you okay?"

Okay? She was the freaking *Queen* of okay. "Yes… *God yes*. Don't stop." She'd *die* if he stopped now.

Lucky for her, he didn't. He just lowered his head and kissed her—*hard*—his tongue thrusting into her mouth with every thrust of his hips, driving her quickly, so quickly, to nirvana.

This was what she wanted, what she needed. Him and her like this. His body giving her what she'd been craving since she'd woken shocked and frustrated from that dream. His body taking her away to another place, to another plane, far away from the grief and torment of earthly worries.

CC came lightning fast. She *never* came this fast. She'd definitely never come from penetration alone. But this was no ordinary night, and Wade was no ordinary lover.

She clutched the cheeks of his ass as hot ripple after hot ripple shredded through her abdomen, her inner thighs, her butt, and the muscles deep inside her that clamped tight around him. She cried out as the ripples swamped her, drowning her in pleasure, breaking their kiss.

Wade buried his face in her neck, hunched himself over her, and fucked her harder. CC wouldn't have thought it could have gotten any better, but Wade clearly knew what he was doing as she spun higher and higher with every slam of his hips, every pant and grunt and groan from his mouth, until she swore she saw the face of God.

Or whoever the hell it was out there that dished out spectacular orgasms.

And just when she thought it couldn't get any better and that the fall would soon be upon her, Wade came too. He came with a muttered curse into her neck, his hips snapped to a halt, his glutes like rocks beneath her palms, his biceps bulging and trembling, his face twisted in a paroxysm of pleasure so intense CC's orgasm surged again as Wade's hips jerked back into motion and they flew together into the night.

CHAPTER NINETEEN

CC was out of her body so long it seemed like time stood still. It wasn't until Wade slid from her and rolled onto his back, scooping her against his side, that all her scattered atoms came together.

That was when reality intruded.

She may have been half joking when she told him she quit, but it was time to pay the piper. What they'd done was serious. He had to see she couldn't keep working for him now.

"Wade, I—"

"It's okay, CC." The deep slurring of his voice as he cut in was more effective than his usual authoritative confidence. "Just go to sleep."

His lips pressed lightly against her forehead, and his big hand on her shoulder was achingly reassuring. Sleep would be so easy. It had mostly eluded her for the last four days, and the prospect of it was so damn seductive. Her limbs were heavy as lead, her blood flowed thick and sluggish through her veins, and her eyelids were losing the fight to stay open.

But surely they needed to talk about this?

She forced her drifting eyelids open and tried again. "I don't think—"

"Good," he interrupted again, his hand squeezing her shoulder this time. "Don't think."

"We probably should."

He sighed. "I know we screwed up here, CC. But there's time enough in the morning for recriminations.

Right now, I've got a nice buzz on, and I sure as hell hope you do too. Let's not kill it just yet, huh? I'm sure the cold light of day will do that for us soon enough."

CC *had* been fighting the buzz as she tried to do the responsible thing and own what had happened—get the inevitable talk out of the way. But she liked Wade's suggestion better.

"Yeah, I guess," she murmured, allowing the buzz free rein, sighing as it sunk into her bones.

"Go to sleep, CC."

His sleepy voice poured over her like honey, his gentle entreaty like sweet music to her ears. She sighed and snuggled closer to him. He was right. Morning was only a few hours away, and there would be time enough then to fully realize what they'd done.

She suspected it was going to make her even more miserable than the last few days, but she knew with absolute certainty she'd never *ever* regret it.

• • •

"Hey, sleepyhead."

CC cracked an eye open. Sunlight blazed into the hotel room and stabbed straight into eyeballs that now felt like peeled grapes. She squeezed her lids shut.

"Up and at 'em."

She winced. Both at the cheerfulness of Wade's voice and the low, dull throb behind her eyes. She silently thanked God she'd taken a couple of painkillers after her midnight shower last night. She had enough to contend with this morning without a blinding hangover.

If only there were pills for sexual remorse…

Why couldn't she be the kind of drunk that got amnesia with a bender? But no…it had all come back in vivid detail. From how much she'd had to drink and other more unfortunate decisions she'd made.

Like her and Wade doing the wild thing.

Coffee tickled her nose, and something soft and light landed on her chest. She felt it with her hand and realized it was her shirt. Oh yes…of course…she was also naked under the sheet.

God. How was she ever going to face Wade? Maybe if she just lay here with her eyes closed he'd get the hint.

The mattress depressed beside her. "I got you some Red Bull."

Of course he got her Red Bull—exactly the kind of sugary caffeine charge she needed right now, and he knew it, damn it.

Why was he being so kind? Why wasn't he being the self-centered asshole he could so often be, insisting she talk to his weepy women, setting a pack of determined Credence seniors on her, making her buy his condoms?

Condoms. The ache between her legs and the slipperiness at the juncture of her thighs reminded her that not only had she and Wade done the wild thing last night, but they'd been reckless with it, too.

Which not only made her a fool, but an idiot as well.

"C'mon, CC, ignoring me isn't going to make it go away."

CC opened her eyes and glared at him. He looked disgustingly chipper, considering. He held out a can of Red Bull and cracked the lid. She took it automatically but didn't sit up. "Turn around."

His mouth quirked like he was about to make some quip about having seen it all already, but just as quickly it was gone and he was turning away and standing up, calling to George, who was draped over her feet. "Come on, dog. Let's give your mistress some privacy."

If CC hadn't been in such a dither, she'd have let the tiny little trill in her chest at being George's mistress bloom into a deeper pleasure. But now wasn't the time.

George looked at her for a beat or two, thumped his tail, then reluctantly jumped off the bed, ambling after Wade.

And Cal had said he couldn't be trained.

Wade stopped near the couch, his back to her, hands shoved on hips, his fingers drumming in an impatient gesture she knew too well. Considering how much she'd already screwed up the last few days, it got her moving pretty damn quick.

Placing the open can on the bedside table, CC threw the shirt over her head while still lying horizontal, pulling it down over the sheet at the front before easing herself upright. Her stomach muscles protested the move, reminding her just how much time she'd spent throwing up last night.

And how Wade had been there rubbing her neck…

Annoyed at the memory, she yanked the T-shirt down at the back and pulled the sheet out from under her. She reached for the Red Bull and guzzled half the can down as she swiveled her legs out of bed.

She stood and strode to her bag, grabbing some other clothes. No way was she going to have a conversation with him in her Broncos T-shirt looking like some kind of Wade "The Catapult" Carter groupie. "I'll be out in a moment," she said as she headed for the bathroom.

CC resisted the urge to take another shower, shucking the shirt as soon as the door closed and climbing into her usual cotton underwear. She pulled on some capris and a green striped T-shirt. She resisted looking in the mirror, too afraid of what she might see. And not just her general red-eyed, hungover appearance, but what was beyond that.

The primal expression of a woman who'd had the best sex of her life. With her boss... There wasn't enough Red Bull in the world to face that.

For a beat or two, she contemplated hiding in the bathroom and never coming out. But Wade was right, this had to be dealt with—better to just rip the Band-Aid off in one quick movement. Just get out there and tell him it was a mistake, a one-off, a combination of grief and comfort, and she had to resign. Not like she'd done last night, in the heat of passion. But calmly and soberly in the cold light of day.

There really wasn't a choice.

Taking a steadying breath, she opened the door to find Wade sitting on the couch, disposable coffee cup in one hand, patting George's head with the other. He stood as she approached, and George slipped off the couch, padding over to sit at her feet.

His warm body leaned into her shin, bolstering CC a little for the excruciating conversation ahead.

"Are you okay?"

CC blinked. She hadn't expected him to get right to it. She nodded. "I feel foolish, but—"

His quick "Not about that" cut her off. "I meant about your father."

"Oh." CC scrubbed a hand over her face. She was as okay as could be expected, she guessed. Crying an ocean of tequila-flavored tears last night had helped. "Yes. I guess." She shrugged. "I'm sorry. About last night. About being drunk. And the vomiting." *And rubbing myself against you like a human scratching pole while you slept.* "You were sweet to stay with me."

CC suspected nobody had ever called Wade sweet in his life, but he took it in his stride, waving away her words as if what he'd done was of no consequence. "It's fine." He shoved his hands in his pockets. "Maybe you should…talk to someone, though? About your dad. About what you went through?"

"Yeah. Probably."

She probably should have seen someone years ago, if the repressed shit from last night was anything to go by, but the fact that Wade cared, that he was worried about her mental state, was surprisingly touching. It was the kind of thing a *friend* would worry about. He'd said those words last night, and she guessed, given all they'd been through, their relationship was more than boss and employee.

"I hear seeing a shrink is very popular in California," she murmured. "I'll fit right in."

Wade laughed, a short, sharp noise before it

petered out and he filled his lungs with air. "So...
you're leaving, then?"

"Yeah."

His shoulders hunched as he burrowed his hands
deeper in his pockets. "It doesn't have to be this
way. We could just pretend this didn't happen. What
happens in Nebraska and all that?"

CC blinked. *What?* There was no way she could
wipe last night from her memory bank. Could *he*?
"You think that's possible?"

He stared at her for long moments, his lips rolled
tight together, before shaking his head. "No."

"Right." Relief flushed through her system. It
would have been a blow to think he could just put
what they'd shared behind him. Their kiss, sure. But
sex? Really freaking great sex? "So...I'm leaving."

"If that's what you want."

CC had wanted nothing more for over five years.
Hell, she'd been counting the days this past year.
But now it was upon her, she didn't want to go.
Not like this. Even though she didn't see how they
could have the same kind of working relationship
anymore. They hadn't just overstepped their normal
professional boundaries by doing the horizontal
rumba, they'd blowtorched them to a pile of burning
rubble.

"I'll stay for another couple of weeks. I told
your mother I'd help her out with the next group of
bachelorettes, and I don't want to leave her in the
lurch. Plus it'll give me time to start looking for a
replacement PA for you."

If anything, his mouth turned grimmer. "Who else
is going to put up with my crap, CC?"

"There'll be someone." There was always *someone*. He'd found her, hadn't he? "WWW dot Saints dot com?"

He laughed, but it was short-lived. "I realized this morning that I…" Wade shifted a little and folded his arms across his chest. He cleared his throat. "I didn't wear a condom."

"Yeah. But I haven't had sex in a very long time and have a contraceptive implant which finally gets to do its job." Unless those suckers somehow detected celibacy and switched off—then she was screwed. "And having bought your condoms for five and a half years, I know how many of them you go through, so I assume you use them diligently and I have nothing to worry about in relation to STDs."

He nodded. "I always use a condom. *Always.*"

It was on the tip of CC's tongue to ask why he hadn't last night. Why had last night been so different? Had he been as swept up as she had? So desperate to be inside her, as desperate as she had been to *have* him inside her, that nothing else had mattered?

Even hours later, the driving need for his possession still hummed through her cells.

"Okay. Well…good." CC stared at her hands. "Nothing for either of us to worry about, then. We're free and clear."

"Yes. Free and clear."

And just like that, it was dispensed with. They could wash their hands of the whole regrettable incident.

"Are you coming home today?"

CC's heart hitched in her chest at his choice of

words. *Home*. She assumed he meant Credence. That quirky little town, his crazy *Gone with the Wind* house she'd come to love in such a short space of time. Except it wasn't her home. Hell, even her apartment in Denver wasn't really home—it belonged to Wade.

God...*home* had been connected to Wade for so long now, she couldn't think about it outside the context of him, and that probably scared her the most.

Definitely time to move to California. To put down roots. To make a home of her own. Make friends. Find a community. Hell, find a *guy*, a chill kinda beach guy who liked dogs and pigs and wasn't allergic to commitment. Make some little beach babies with him before all her eggs died.

"No. Tomorrow. Should be in Credence by five."

He smiled. "Just in time for Happy Hour at Jack's."

CC smiled, too, but it was tight and fake. For some stupid reason, she felt like crying. "You?"

"I'll head off now." George whined at that piece of news, and Wade glanced at the dog for long moments before raising his gaze to CC. "Unless you want me to stay?"

"No." Her pulse skipped a beat. The last thing she wanted was for Wade to stick around, reminding her of what they'd done. Some distance now would be good.

All of Nebraska should just about do it.

"I can stay. I don't mind."

His gaze was earnest, and CC had no doubt he was genuine, but she shook her head, suppressing a well of emotion rising in her chest. God...she'd jump him again for sure. She was too fragile to be strong.

"I'm fine, really. But you could leave George." George hovered his ass off the floor and gave an excited little yip at the mention of his name.

"You know there are no pets allowed, right? I had to sneak him in last night."

"And I thank you for it." Seeing the puppy again had given CC a real lift.

"You'll have to keep him locked in your room."

CC nodded. It was a more sensible option than keeping Wade locked in her room. "Yep. I'm good with that." She patted George's head. "What do you think, Georgie porgie?" Another excited yip sealed the deal.

"Alrighty," Wade said. "Be careful."

"Will do."

He stood awkwardly for long moments. Prior to last night, he'd have just walked out and tossed a goodbye over his shoulder. Probably asked her to pick up some more Nerds on the way home because walking into a store and getting his own was not something he'd *ever* had to do. But now he was standing there, clearly debating how to navigate this strange new world. A world where they'd seen each other naked.

This was why she had to leave.

Two more months of moments like this would be excruciating, their relationship growing more and more stilted.

"See you tomorrow," she said, breaking into the awkward silence. "Drive carefully."

He nodded. "You too."

He turned away then, strode to the door without a backward glance, but CC didn't breathe until he was on the other side of it.

It was going to be a long couple of weeks.

• • •

Wade beat himself up the entire journey back to Credence. He couldn't remember ever feeling this low in his life. And he'd been through some major downers. Jasmine. Injuries that had taken him out for months. His father needing a pacemaker. But falling from the high of having the most spectacular sex of his life to *knowing* that it had signed CC's resignation letter in indelible ink had been the worst.

He'd *known* when she'd faced him that she was going to leave. And he'd *known* he couldn't stop her, even though he had tried. They'd stepped so irrevocably over the line he couldn't even see the damn thing.

Wade had been so sure that with three months together in Credence he'd be able to convince her to stay on as his PA, even if it meant some kind of reduced capacity. *So sure.* But even if he *had* managed prior to last night to convince her to stick with him, what they'd done had well and truly ensured she could no longer be in his employ. The sex, the crazy, uncertain, mixed-up *feelings* that were between them now, would make a professional relationship difficult.

How could he ever concentrate on work when he was thinking about the sounds she made when she came? Thinking about how soft she was and how her nipples tasted and how soon they could do it again.

And again.

Their kiss, as amazing as it had been, was something they *could* have gotten past. He'd been absolutely convinced of that. But sex? Even he knew it was impossible to get past something so profound, and no amount of finagling was going to change the fact.

Wade Carter didn't like losing. He'd come to Credence with a game plan where CC was concerned. But he had to face facts, he'd lost her, he'd lost CC and he had nobody to blame but himself.

Slamming his hand against the steering wheel several times, Wade roared out his frustration.

Stupid, stupid, so-*fucking*-stupid.

But in his heart of hearts, he knew he'd do the same thing over again. He could no more have stopped himself last night than stopped the tide. She'd needed him. And he'd needed to be the man she'd turned to.

Now he just had to live with the consequences.

CHAPTER TWENTY

If Wyatt hadn't been sure his mother was match-making before, he knew it the second she suggested he take Jenny up to the hayloft to watch the sunset through the big window in the gable that looked out over the eastern Colorado landscape.

"Supper's still an hour away, and it's so pretty up there."

His mother used to take Wade and him up there as kids to watch the sun sink below the horizon. All three of them would sit close to the edge and dangle their legs free and watch in awe at the ritual as old as the earth itself.

And Wade, of course, had made out with many a girl up there.

"Ladies first." Wyatt stood back to let Jenny precede him on the ladder. His mother would expect nothing less of the good Southern gentleman she'd raised.

Jenny laughed. "Are you trying to look up my skirt, Wyatt Carter?"

A surge of heat swamped Wyatt's face as he took in Jenny's skirt. He'd been admiring the way it flared around her knees since she'd arrived on the farm a couple of hours ago. That and the tiny row of pearl buttons holding her blouse together. But he hadn't really thought through the logistics of ladder climbs and skirts.

Maybe if he'd had more girls up here he might have.

"Oh, no, sorry, *God* I didn't—"

Her soft laugh broke into his panic. "Relax, Wyatt." She nudged him gently with her shoulder. "I'm only teasing."

Wyatt blinked and then laughed as a wash of cool relief flowed through his hot face. "Right. Sorry." He was pleased for the shadows in the barn hiding his blushes, not that she seemed to mind. "I'll go first, shall I?"

"That's probably best."

Wyatt scrambled up the ladder with practiced ease, quickly turning back for her when he reached the top, holding out his hand as she stepped on the last rung. She smiled at him as she placed her hand in his, and he helped her onto the loft platform. For a few seconds she leaned into him. Coconut filled his nostrils, and Wyatt got a little dizzy.

How could just the smell of her make his dick harder than the wooden boards beneath his feet?

She pulled away and looked up at him, her gaze drifting to his mouth, and Wyatt's heart beat so fast it was fit to explode out of his chest. He wanted to kiss her—badly. And the way she was looking at his lips, he thought maybe she did, too. But was it too soon? Too forthright? What if he went for it and he'd misinterpreted her look? It had only been one week.

He didn't want to rush things and frighten her away. He wanted Jenny to stay in Credence. He wanted her to come and live with him on the farm. He wanted to put a ring on her finger and babies in her belly.

He wanted the whole nine yards.

Fuck…it was scary how much he wanted.

A knot of confusion and indecision had him stepping back. "So…" He cleared his voice. "This is the hayloft."

"Yes." She smiled at him. If he'd blown it just now, she didn't seem to mind. "So I see."

She glanced around her, taking in the bales of hay stacked in neat piles almost to the rafters on either side and the pitchfork tossed on top of the nearby mound of loose hay on the floor.

"Just a sec." Wyatt strode to the window.

The loft was deep with afternoon shadows as he rolled back first one large wooden shutter and then the other. Sunlight poured into the space, capturing the dust motes in its path.

"Oh, Wyatt…"

Jenny's breathy gasp filled Wyatt with delight. "It's pretty as a picture, isn't it?" But he wasn't talking about the flaming sky and the golden burnish of the landscape.

She crossed to his side, coming to a stop close to the edge. "It sure is." She gazed out at the vista. "Is this all Carter land?"

Wyatt pointed out the boundaries, pride in the farm swelling in his chest. Hogs took advantage of the last rays of sunlight to graze on the flower-speckled fields, and the tin roofs of the hog shelters glowed in the setting sun. The late summer afternoon still had some warmth to it, but a light breeze blew in from the fields, making the loft a very pleasant place to sit a while.

"You want to watch the sunset?"

"Yeah." Jenny nodded. "I'd like that."

He held out his hand, helping her down, and

when he shoved his legs out the window and dangled them over the edge she followed suit. They sat close—not touching, but almost. Wyatt was aware of her every breath, though, and the way the breeze fluttered the hem of her skirt, lifting it periodically, flashing glimpses of her knees and higher.

"It so beautiful up here," she said as she swung her legs back and forth. "You're so lucky, Wyatt."

"Yeah. I know." The breeze blew her hair back, the sun picking out the golden highlights amidst the faded red tresses. Right now, he was the luckiest sonofabitch in the world.

They talked about the farm for a bit. About the hogs and Wyatt's plans for expansion. "I like an ambitious man," she teased, and Wyatt blushed, dismissing himself as merely practical before asking her about the grant application his mother had helped her with for the coffee place she wanted to open.

"All done. I should know in a month. Bob has offered one of the shopfronts in main street he owns rent-free until the business is making money. There's even a small apartment above it where I can live."

Wyatt's breath hitched to hear Jenny talking long-term. He hadn't wanted to hope too much. "So…you're really staying? Really putting down roots here in Credence."

"Yes." She pulled her gaze away from the sunset and captured his. "Would you like that?"

"I would. Very much. I…" Wyatt swallowed and fought against the rising pressure in his chest as the words he'd never said to a woman before tumbled out. "I like you. Very much."

Wyatt already knew, in his heart of hearts, it was more than that, but he'd have probably needed Xanax to use the capital L word. And even he knew you didn't tell a woman you'd not long met that you loved her.

Not if you wanted to keep seeing her.

She smiled and held out her hand. "I like you, too."

Wyatt almost passed out at the rush of blood to his head. He returned her smile and took her hand, sliding his fingers into hers, entwining them. "And our age difference…?" The fact he was almost fifteen years older than Jenny had been a cause of anxiety.

She shook her head. "It has never entered my mind."

Maybe he should press her more. Insist she seriously think about it. But she seemed so dang certain, holding his gaze without wavering, wrapping him up in her conviction, and he believed her.

"You still planning on staying at the boarding-house until you can move in over the shop?"

Wyatt wanted to ask her to move in here with him, but that was also way too fast. A ridiculous thing to do after only one week, and if she said no, it might gut his confidence with women for life.

"Ummm…no, actually. I was thinking I might go back to Pittsburgh for a month or so."

A hot slug punched Wyatt right in the center of his chest. A *month*? But…she'd been so gung ho about staying.

He should have known it was too good to be true.

"Oh. Right." Just the *thought* of her leaving, even temporarily, made him sick to his stomach.

She broke eye contact, turning back to the rapidly setting sun. "I need to pack and stuff."

"It takes a month to pack?"

Wyatt blinked at the words that tumbled unchecked from his mouth. They'd been knee-jerk but rude nonetheless, and he opened his mouth to apologize, but Jenny's hand wriggled out of his as she faced him again and she was so damn serious the words got stuck in his throat.

"I have a confession to make."

Wyatt swallowed. *Crap.* Here it came.

"I'm telling you this because I *do* like you *a lot*, but I haven't been entirely honest and I think… I hope you and I might be starting something here, and I don't want to lie to you anymore. You deserve the truth, and if we can't be honest from the start, then what hope do we have? I understand perfectly if it changes the way you feel about me, though. If you want nothing to do with me."

The edges of Wyatt's vision darkened a little, and he realized he hadn't taken a breath. "Oh God." He sucked in some air. "You're married, aren't you?"

It was Jenny's turn to blink then. "What?" She shook her head. "No. *God no*." She put both her hands over the top of his and squeezed, saying "No" another time, more firmly. "But…"

She removed her hands. "I did lie when I said I didn't have a man in my life. I do. His name is Henry, he's my son, and he's five years old."

Wyatt stared at Jenny as the news sunk in on a wave of relief that finally filled his lungs with sweet, sweet oxygen. His vision cleared. Jenny had a son.

Not a husband, not a boyfriend, not a lover.

2278NOTHING BUT TROUBLE

A son.

"I'm sorry I wasn't upfront with you about it. In my experience, men tend to run when they find out about him, and I really like you and didn't want to scare you off, but I should have told you that first day."

Wyatt couldn't believe men could be such assholes. Sure, a child was a big responsibility, another man's child even more so. But he'd take Jenny even if she'd had a tribe of kids.

"And that's why I have to go back to Pittsburgh. I thought I could leave him with my great aunt for a few months, while I got settled here, but...I was wrong. I miss him so much, Wyatt, and he cries on the phone when I call him every night, and it's killing me to be away from him."

Tears shimmered in her eyes, and Wyatt could see how much it was breaking her heart to be away from her son. He could only imagine how tough that had been. Just the thought of Jenny leaving him was torture, and he wasn't a five-year-old child.

"Oh God, Wyatt..." She turned imploring eyes on him. "*Please* say something."

Wyatt didn't say anything. Instead he pulled her into a hug. "I'm sorry," she whispered and melted against him, and Wyatt knew he'd do anything for this woman.

"Of course you have to go to him," he said, his voice gruff as he pulled back, his hands sliding to her upper arms. "Go to him tomorrow. But don't wait a month in Pittsburgh. Go and get Henry and bring him back to Credence straightaway. Bring him back here, to the farm, there's plenty of things around this place for a little boy to be getting into, and I can't wait to meet him."

Her eyes got shiny. "Wyatt...you need to be sure about this. I come as a package deal, and taking on another man's child is big."

Wyatt smiled. "He's yours, that's all that matters."

"I..." Jenny shook her head. "I don't know what I did to deserve you." And she melted into him again.

Wyatt eased back after a beat or two. "Can I ask? Henry's father...?"

If he had to deal with another man he would, but he needed to be prepared.

"Is not on the scene. Never has been. He never wanted Henry and split when he found out I was pregnant."

Surprisingly, there was no heat to her words. No anger or even contempt in her voice. Had there been, Wyatt would have worried about the depth of Jenny's feelings. But there was just acceptance, as if she'd moved on from it a long time ago.

"I'm sorry."

She shrugged. "We've done okay by ourselves."

Sure, but Jenny had had it tough, he'd known that from the first day. "You don't have to do it alone anymore."

He smiled at her then, slipping his arm around her shoulder, tucking her into his side, and they sat in silence, watching the sun slowly slip behind the horizon, casting a golden halo over the landscape. She sighed, her hand sliding onto his thigh as the sun disappeared completely.

Wyatt was conscious of that hand, of their legs so close. Of her body warm against his and the press of her breast into his ribs. Of the coconut in her hair and the play of fading light on her skin. He was conscious of everything about this woman, and that was when he knew that he had to fess up also.

He hated that Wade was right, but Jenny's bravery had shamed him. His biggest secret seemed like small fries compared to what she'd been holding back, and she was right, if they couldn't be honest with each other from the start, then what kind of a relationship would they build?

"I have a confession, too."

Wyatt was conscious of her body going very still in his, and he winced at the tremulous sound of his voice. Just when the touch of her hand had caused enough testosterone to kill a dinosaur, he had to go all squeaky.

"Okay." She eased away from him, her gaze hot on his profile. But he couldn't look at her. Hell, he wished he could retract what he'd said. "Tell me."

Her voice had the grim determination of someone who was used to preparing for the worst. Wyatt swallowed as the familiar sensation of panic spread through his chest. He forced himself to breathe. A minute ago this had seemed like a good idea. Damn Wade to Hell. He *was* going to feed him to the hogs the second he stepped foot back on the farm.

"Wyatt?"

He forced himself to breathe. In. Out. In. Out.

"Wyatt?" Jenny's voice had risen a little at the end. She placed her hand on his arm. "Look at me."

There was just the right level of command in her voice to cut through Wyatt's panic. He turned his face, and their gazes locked.

"You don't have a secret child, do you?"

Her humor, even in this awkward moment, was

refreshing, and he smiled despite the jangling bells inside his head. "No."

"You're not married or gay or a vegan, are you?"

Wyatt laughed this time. "No."

"So you can tell me. Anything." She squeezed his arm. "Trust me, I won't—"

"I'm a virgin."

There. He'd said it. The words had risen in his throat like a tidal wave, and it was blurt them out or swallow them down and never say them until it became obvious at the worst possible time. His heart was beating like a drum and his face was burning, but the feeling he was going to drop dead receded quickly.

She stared for a moment or two, her hand sliding off his arm to press against the center of her chest. "God…is that all?"

Wyatt blinked. *Is that all?* He was almost forty and had never been with a woman. That was a big deal. Wasn't it?

"You were looking so serious, I started to think you were going to tell me you were a serial killer and there were a hundred bodies buried out there among all those pretty flowers."

Wyatt laughed, feeling less embarrassed the more relief he saw in her eyes. "No, not a serial killer."

"Good. Virgin I can handle, serial killer not so much."

"Really?"

"Of course." She slipped her hand on his leg and squeezed. Sensation shot straight to his groin, hot as buckshot.

"I'm just…surprised more than anything. A good-looking guy like you? I'd have thought you wouldn't have made it out of high school with your virginity." She smiled at him then. "I'd have done you for sure."

Wyatt laughed. "I'd have let you." They smiled at each other, and it felt like his heart doubled in size. "So...it doesn't freak you out? Because it's been freaking me out for about twenty years."

"Wyatt, I just told you I had a kid, which you took completely in stride. What kind of a person would I be if I cared about how many women you've been with?"

"Or *haven't* been with. As the case may be."

"You do know how to kiss a girl, right?"

"Sure." But it'd been a while. Wyatt swallowed at the way her gaze was lingering on his mouth again. "I'm probably a little rusty, though."

"Well now." She moved a little closer, her gaze still locked on his lips, and Wyatt's breath caught in his throat. "Why don't you let me be the judge of that?"

Her lips pressed against his then and stole his breath. He'd dreamed of this moment since he'd first laid eyes on her, and it didn't disappoint. She sighed against his mouth and leaned into him, and she tasted sweet and felt soft, and his pulse raced as a groan rumbled from deep in his throat at the perfection of it all.

She pulled away on another little sigh. "Nope." Jenny shook her head and smiled up at him, her eyes a little unfocused. "Not even a little bit rusty," she whispered, and she kissed him once more.

He groaned again as she leaned into him, harder this time, one of his hands sinking into the hair at the nape of her neck, the other sliding around her waist, pulling her nearer still, reveling in the feel of her breasts squashed against his chest, the brush of her knees against his.

She was right, this didn't feel rusty. It felt like—for the first time in his life—he knew what he was doing with a woman. That he was made to do exactly *this* with *this* woman. That he'd been born with the blueprints to their joining.

She pulled away again, and it was gratifying to see two fat, dilated pupils, to hear the roughness to her voice. "I have a suggestion."

Her words poured cold water over his ardor, and Wyatt's heart skipped a beat. God…was she about to give him pointers?

Only slightly mortifying…

"I think we should get this virginity thing out of the way, huh?"

Okay. *That* he hadn't been expecting. Wyatt swallowed. "Uh…sure?" His heart boomed in his chest and hammered at his neck. Hell, if it beat any harder he'd die on the spot.

He'd die a fucking virgin.

She quirked an eyebrow. "Now?"

"Now?" Wyatt repeated like an idiot.

"Yes. Now." She smiled at him. "I don't know about you, but I've been wanting this since the minute I saw you, and your virginity is obviously a *thing* for you, so let's take care of it so it's not a thing any longer."

She clambered to her feet and held out her hand. "Care to join me?" She tipped her chin toward the mound of loose hay.

Wyatt looked up, following the line of her body, gilded by the last glow of sun reaching across the sky, and his heart just about flowed over. He didn't need to be asked twice, scrambling to his feet, reaching for her, pulling her in for a long, deep, drugging kiss until she backed away, grabbing his hand as she did, a smile on her face as she led him to the hay.

CHAPTER TWENTY-ONE

"So, that's it then." Ronnie closed her notebook. They'd chosen to meet at Annie's for their last planning meeting before the next—and last—arrivals. "Looks like everything's on track."

CC nodded. It was hard to believe it had been two weeks since she'd returned from Nebraska. In some ways, it was like she'd never left. Credence had embraced her return, and she'd fallen back in the same routine—working on the Grow Credence project during the morning with Wade's mother, and helping Wade in the afternoon with his book and trying to find him a new PA.

Which, of course, he was being picky as hell about.

She hadn't wanted to advertise, preferring to work her contacts, which were extensive after a decade in this field of employment. Wade's lifestyle took a lot of getting used to, and being his PA wasn't like any other job she'd had. It was a full on twenty-four seven caper and required a particular type of person. She'd brought him several prospects, but he was being a difficult asshole about all of them.

Which only made things more awkward.

Well…apparently not for Wade, who, despite what he'd said in the motel room, *was* carrying on like nothing had happened, which was pretty much his MO with women he'd slept with and another reason to get the hell out because *she* couldn't be so damn unaffected. CC hadn't been able to stop thinking about her and Wade burning up the sheets.

Or dreaming about it, for that matter.

She should just move into the motel out on the interstate, but for one, she didn't want Wade to think, *even for a second*, that what happened between them was some kind of *thing* she was having a hard time getting over.

Even if it was.

And secondly, it'd just remind her too much of what had happened in another motel room in Nebraska. At least in Tara, they were on neutral, if somewhat surreal, ground.

"CC?"

CC realized she was staring at the window and Ronnie was trying to get her attention.

"Sorry, what?"

Annie held up the coffeepot. "More coffee?"

"No thanks." What she really craved was icy cold caffeine delivered in a can of Red Bull. First order of business when she arrived in California was to kick the habit, but for now, she hadn't been sleeping so well and a can of that sugary shit gave her a real pick-me-up.

"Something wrong with my pie?"

CC glanced guiltily at her untouched slice of cherry pie, then back at Annie, who was clearly not used to people neglecting her food. "Sorry, no." She smiled at the older woman. "Just distracted."

Annie gave her an inscrutable look. "There ain't nothin' a good piece of pie can't help you get over, girlie."

CC would normally have agreed wholeheartedly and, if all she was getting over was her father's death, she had no doubt pie would help considerably. But she didn't think there was enough pie in the world to get over her *oops, slept with Wade* faux pas.

Not that she was about to admit that to Annie. *Or Ronnie.* Instead she picked up her fork and dutifully shoveled pie into her mouth.

Annie nodded approvingly. "There you go." She glanced at Ronnie and said "Girls today are too skinny" before pushing off.

Ronnie grinned as she watched Annie pour coffee at the next table, but when her gaze returned to CC it was more sober.

"You sure you're okay, honey? You know, if you need to go and spend some time at home with your momma, you should."

"Thanks, I'm good." CC would be gone next Monday anyway. Not that anyone knew that—except Wade.

She planned on heading home for a week before setting out for California. Her yearning for the ocean had grown exponentially these past couple of weeks, although CC suspected that anywhere other than Colorado would work for her right now.

"I hope Wade hasn't been working you too hard. He's been in a helluva mood these past couple of weeks. I don't know what's up with that man. Things not going well with the book?"

CC couldn't even look at Ronnie. "Something like that."

"Why didn't he just get one of those ghost writers the publishing house offered?"

CC laughed despite the turmoil inside. "I did try to talk him into it, but…he's too damn stubborn."

"Always been the same, even as a little boy. Once

he got an idea in his head, he'd hang on to it like a dog with a bone. Gets it from his father."

CC laughed some more. If Wade got his stubbornness from anyone, he got it from Ronnie, her scheme to bring more single women to Credence being a very good example. But CC wisely changed the subject.

"Jenny's back tomorrow?"

Ronnie smiled, her face becoming animated again. "Yes. Wyatt's like a kid on Christmas Eve. He's missed her so much these past couple of weeks."

"The first of many success stories from these weekends, hopefully."

"Fingers crossed." Ronnie sighed. "Oh, he's just so happy, Cecilia. I heard him whistling in the barn the other day. Whistling! He used to do that as a kid all the time, drove Cal nuts because he was really bad at it. But I haven't heard it for years. It's like he's got a whole new lease on life."

CC was happy for Wyatt and Jenny. They were plainly made for each other. "But she's going to be staying on at the boardinghouse for now, yes? With Henry."

"Yes." Ronnie nodded. "Until the coffee shop is ready, then they'll move in above there for a while. Jenny wants Henry to get to know Wyatt and us and feel comfortable in Credence first before making their relationship official, which is very sensible."

"There's good company there for her, too, with Molly and Marley awaiting their salon application."

The New York sisters were setting up a beauty salon. Just a small one to start with. Hair, makeup, nails, and facials. One pedicure chair. But they had room to expand if business was good. Ronnie, along with half the town—the female half—were thrilled they'd finally be able to have their hair done locally.

"And I hear Winona's bunking there until she finds a house to buy." CC had even heard that Winona might be building, which would be fantastic for Benji's business, especially now that Sally had finally popped and they had another mouth to feed.

"Yes." Ronnie nodded. "And if we're lucky, there could be some more joining them after this weekend."

Ronnie grinned. "Not bad, huh?"

CC laughed. "I would call it an outstanding success."

"Now all we do is put on a bunch of different social functions throughout the year and let booze and nature take its course."

Ronnie waggled her eyebrows, and CC laughed again at Wade's mother reveling in her role of Cupid. Maybe Wade was right, maybe his mother was some kind of closet pimp.

"How do you feel about being a Memaw?"

"I am over the moon!" Ronnie's smile shone so big and bright CC almost reached for her sunglasses. "I didn't imagine it'd happen this way but, honestly, I'd started to think it'd never happen, so I'm ecstatic. Wyatt loves Jenny, we love Jenny, and Jenny comes with Henry, and you can bet your last nickel Cal and I are going to love and spoil that sweet child from here to Timbuktu and back again. It'll be good having a little one around my skirts that isn't four-legged."

CC had no doubt that Ronnie and Cal would make great grandparents. Henry was a lucky little boy.

Ronnie sighed. "I only wish Wade would find someone and settle down, too. Do you think it'll ever happen, Cecilia? You probably know him better than anyone these days."

If it looked like CC was some kind of small, furry animal caught in the headlights of a car, it was because that was exactly how she felt. She knew Wade *way* better than she had a couple of weeks ago. She knew what his mouth felt like on hers and the feel of him hard in her hands and what he sounded like when he came. But if his mother thought that gave her some kind of insight or understanding into his psyche, then she was wrong, because she had no idea how he could be so intimate with someone and pretend like it never happened.

It was what he did. It was what he'd always done. But she wasn't one of his disposable dates, and CC was beginning to wonder if she ever really knew him at all.

"I wouldn't be going out and buying two mother-of-the-groom dresses if I were you."

"Yeah." Ronnie put her coffee cup down on its saucer. "I liked Jasmine, I really did, and I know she's older now and sorry for what she did, but that girl." She shook her head. "She has a lot to answer for."

The entire time she'd known Ronnie, CC hadn't heard an angry word pass her lips about *anything*. She'd been nothing but cool, calm, and collected. But right now there was a glint in her eye that was pure momma bear, and CC was just a tiny little bit afraid.

It was on the tip of her tongue to tell his mother that it'd been fifteen years and Wade was a grown-ass man who should have moved on. But she was just a little bit pissed at Jasmine, too, right now. "Amen." She picked up her coffee mug, and she and Ronnie clinked.

• • •

Even at five in the afternoon, it was still warm out at the lake for the cookout. The sun sparkled off the water, and plenty of people were swimming and diving off the end of the pier. The sounds of laughter and splashing and people having a good time mingled with the aroma of wood fires and cooking meat. Steaks and sausages sizzled on BBQs being manned by eager bachelors trying to impress the eighty-two single women who'd made the trip this weekend.

And had all brought their bikinis…

CC watched it all from under one of the many shady trees that lined the narrow rocky beach fringing the perimeter of the lake with the satisfaction of a job well done. She hadn't been to the last cookout because she'd taken off for Nebraska, but Ronnie had claimed it to be a huge success, and if today was like the last, CC could see why.

She might have only been destined to stay in Credence for half the summer—half the time Wade had originally decreed—but CC was pleased to have played a part in what promised to be the social revolution of the town. How many here today might make a connection like Wyatt and Jenny?

Her gaze tracked to the lovebirds standing at the edge of the water. Henry was standing between them, and they each held one of his little hands, jumping him over every gentle curl of water against the shore. He squealed as they lifted him in the air and giggled as they swung him a little before putting him back on his feet. Henry's boyish laughter carried to her on the breeze, and she smiled.

She was so happy for Wyatt. And Jenny and Henry. And Ronnie and Cal. And Credence. The population had grown by five, and CC would be amazed if it didn't grow by at least a couple more over the next few years as some little Carters came into the world.

Looking out over the men and women mingling all around her, CC wouldn't mind betting that if she came back in a year or two or five, the population may well have exploded.

"Mind if I join you?"

CC smiled at Winona, who was looking very boho in her loose, lace-trimmed dress and big floppy hat. She was more dressed than 75 percent of the women here, but the way the dress flowed in the breeze, blowing against her body and flirting with her curves, made it practically indecent.

Wriggling over to make room on the rug, CC patted the space beside her. "Don't mind at all."

Winona settled in the spot indicated, mimicking CC's pose by reclining back onto her bent elbows, scanning the activity. Neither of them spoke for a while, but eventually she said, "I feel old. And overdressed."

CC laughed. She knew exactly how Winona felt. "Yes."

"It's lovely out here though, isn't it?"

"Yes. Such a gorgeous day."

"You know, when I saw the Facebook video, I

thought this was the craziest idea I'd ever heard and, to be honest, I really only came here on a whim. An artistic whim. I thought I might get some story fodder. But…" She shook her head. "I think it actually might work."

CC laughed. "I know what you mean. It does seem crazy, but Credence was pretty desperate so…why not?"

"Why not indeed."

"So…" CC flicked a glance at Winona's profile. "You think you can live here?"

"Yeah. I think I can." She rolled her head to the side and met CC's eyes. "I can write anywhere, and I was getting tired of the rat race. There's land for sale around the lake, big blocks, cheap land, much cheaper than anything I can afford in the city. And I've been talking to Benji Tait. I can build cheaper here, too. My own place, built the way I want, near all of this."

She glanced back over the lake and sighed. "No rent, no city noise, no neighbors yelling at each other. Space and quiet and sunshine and water. There's something about water that's good for the muse, you know?"

CC didn't know anything about muses—her brain was far too OCD to be creative—but she understood the pull of water. Was she not heading to California for her own water view?

"I have friends who'd love it here, too. Painters and potters and other writers. Successful ones. *Female* ones. Single ones." She smiled at CC. "They're always looking for places to be at their creative best, that inspire them every day. And they can't beat this."

The idea of a flourishing artist's colony in Credence

was intriguing, one CC was sure Ronnie had never envisioned. But still a different avenue to bring new blood to Credence. That could grow the population and contribute to the community.

"Unless, of course, Chief Uptight has a problem with it."

CC smothered a smile as a uniformed Arlo wandered among the crowd.

"You know, that man has a mighty fine ass. Shame about the stick up it." CC laughed this time. "Speaking of asses, there's one I wouldn't kick out of bed," Winona said. "What's in the water around this place?"

CC glanced in the direction of Winona's gaze. *Wade.* Looking *mighty fine* in tan chinos and a dark T-shirt, a ball cap pulled low on his head. He'd stopped down the beach a little to skip stones into the water, the pure physicality of him bending and twisting, stretching his clothes over hard packed muscles, making her legs weak. Thank heavens she was already supine.

"You don't agree?"

CC felt the heat of Winona's scrutiny on her profile. She shrugged. "I've worked for the man for almost six years. He's like a brother to me."

Which was possibly the biggest lie she'd ever told in her life, but CC supposed if she was going to be struck down by lightning, there could be worse places.

He'd *never* been like a brother to her. For five and a half years he'd been her boss and a freaking exasperating one at that, and, as of two weeks ago, he'd been something else entirely, the nature of which was a total mystery.

But it wasn't brotherly.

She had five of those suckers, and whatever she felt for Wade was *not* that.

"Oh come on." Winona's voice was laced with amusement. "Even sisters can be objective about how good-looking their brothers are."

"Do you have brothers?" CC cocked an eyebrow at Winona.

"No."

"Yeah, well I have five, and trust me, I try very hard not to think of them in that context at all."

Winona laughed as she returned to ogling Wade. "Careful there, CC, some people might think you protest too much."

CC blinked at the statement, her insides twisting in knots at the implication as she tried to come up with a zingy rejoinder. But Winona had moved on, shaking her head and sighing. "He never knows when to turn it off, does he?"

Before she could check the impulse, CC's head was swinging back, seeking out Wade. A tall, leggy blonde was talking to him now. Just like the many tall, leggy blondes CC had dealt with over the years in his employ.

He was nothing if not predictable.

She was smiling up at him, leaning toward him a little, her head cocked to the side. He said something, and she laughed, and he laughed, too. She touched his arm, and her hand lingered for a second or two before sliding away. She flicked her hair a little and laughed again. He handed her a stone he already had in his hand and demonstrated how to stand and how to throw one.

Blondie mimicked his stance and the action, failing miserably at the skipping part. CC almost rolled her eyes. She'd been a champion stone-skipper by the time she was in elementary school. But then Wade was shaking his head and touching her arm, manipulating it to a better angle, demonstrating how to throw by pulling her arm back and showing her how to follow through.

"Oh man, really?" Winona shook her head, clearly disgusted. "He's not going to fall for the oldest trick in the book, is he?"

CC barely heard her. The wash of her pulse flooded like a torrent between her ears. White-hot pain lanced her straight through her center. Her chest tightened, crushing the ability of her lungs to move.

The blonde turned to look at him, and there was more laughing and smiling. Wade stepped away so his companion could make the throw. The stone arced and skipped once, and the blonde jumped up and down, clapping her hands.

Wade laughed and handed her another stone.

CC had always felt a little sorry for Wade's blondes. But not right now. Right now, she wanted a bolt of electricity to fry this one to a pulp. It wasn't fair to her, she was probably a really nice woman, and Wade was equally culpable in their little exchange, but there wasn't a lot of rationality floating around inside CC right now.

There was rage and panic. Both so visceral she knew she had to leave. Get out of Credence and never come back. Not Monday.

Now.

"Men can be such idiots," Winona murmured.

CC nodded. So could women.

CHAPTER TWENTY-TWO

It was ten the next morning when CC finally made it down the sweeping staircase for the last time. She'd have never thought it, but she was going to miss the daily exercise. And this ridiculous wedding cake of a house.

She'd planned on getting away earlier, but she hadn't slept last night until close to dawn and had, subsequently, not long woken. Fortunately, it hadn't taken long to pack.

Now that it was here, she couldn't believe this was the way it was going to end. Slinking out of *Credence* with her tail between her legs. She'd always thought she'd be heading to California in a buoyant mood with fond memories and an eye to the future. Maybe a couple of ritzy farewell functions in *Denver* to see her off.

She certainly hadn't pictured an early departure, professional disgrace and personal disarray nipping at her heels.

The overwhelming urge to just open the front door and leave and not look back swamped her. But she'd done that once before, the night she'd received the news about her father, and this was different. She was leaving *for good*, and Wade at least deserved a face-to-face explanation.

A face-to-face goodbye.

After wheeling her bag to the front door, she backtracked across the voluminous vaulted foyer and headed for the kitchen, where she could hear the low pulse of Wade's voice and the higher one of Sally's. Normally at this hour, Wade would have been at the farm, but it was Sunday and everyone would be at church.

Taking a quick breath, she entered. The sight that greeted her stopped her dead in the doorway and deflated her lungs just as quickly. Wade looked up from where he was lounging against the central bench, cooing at Sally's daughter, Mable. He was cradling her, and he looked so damn good with a baby in her arms CC could have sworn her fallopian tubes twanged a little.

Wade smiled at her. "Have you seen how much this little one has grown in two weeks?" He glanced at the baby. "She's a honey just like her mother. But don't let Benji know I said so," he said, grinning at Sally.

CC's heart thrummed in her chest. "She's a cutie," she acknowledged, each word feeling as if it had been surgically extracted from her vocal chords.

Sally glanced at her. "How good does Wade look with a baby?"

He looked good enough to spray with whipped cream and lick all over. But when didn't he? "It suits him." The words felt thick and jagged at the back of CC's throat, but she must have sounded normal because neither Wade nor Sally looked at her funnily.

"It's good to get in some practice," Sally said. "Henry might be five, but if Wyatt and Jenny haven't had a baby by the end of next year I'll eat my hat. And uncle duties are very important."

Wade nodded. "I'm going to kick uncle ass."

He would, too. Wade kicked ass at everything he did.

Sally laughed and glanced at CC, no doubt expecting her to also be laughing. But CC's face was frozen into some horrid kind of mask, and Sally's change in expression was all the confirmation she needed. Or maybe it was the shine of tears that had to be there as her vision went glassy. The other woman frowned slightly, and, for a horrible moment, CC thought Sally was going to ask her what was wrong.

Thankfully, she didn't.

"Well, anyway. I should get going. She'll be kicking up a fuss soon, wanting to be nursed."

Efficiently, the way Sally did everything, she scooped the baby out of Wade's arms and bustled out of the kitchen, shooting CC a sympathetic smile as she brushed past. Wade watched her go, laughing and shaking his head. "I hope that kid has a crash helmet, Sally's always been a whirlwind."

His smile faded as his gaze settled on CC, and Wade straightened from his casual slouch. "What's wrong?"

Shaking on the inside, CC blinked away the threatening tears and took a breath. "I'm leaving."

He was silent for the longest time, and CC couldn't read a damn thing on his inscrutable face. His *game* face. "I thought you were staying until tomorrow?"

CC shrugged. "What's a day? Everything's set to go for the last day of activities, and there's a team in place to help your mother with the bus departures."

He folded his arms, his usually relaxed features

tight. "And what about me?"

CC's heart skipped a beat. "What about you, Wade?"

"You haven't found me a PA yet."

She hadn't meant to snort, it just kinda slipped out. It was that or cry. She couldn't believe she was never going to see him again. His face, anyway. She was pretty sure his ass would be all over billboards in California, too.

"Maybe if you hadn't rejected the four candidates I've already found you?"

"They weren't right."

"They were all perfectly capable, Wade."

"It's not about capable. You know that. I need an X factor."

CC rolled her eyes. "Like what? An ability to read minds? A bullshit detector?"

His gaze didn't leave her face. "The kind of person that'd knee their boss in the nads without caring about the ramifications."

CC shut her eyes. How dare he take her back to that day. Now. When she was trying to leave. "Yeah, well…she's no longer available. But don't worry, I won't leave you in the lurch. I said I'd find you a PA, and I will."

"And what do I do in the meantime?"

CC grabbed a breath and prayed for patience. Maybe the man should find his own damn PA. It was her fault, she'd catered to his every whim for years and now he couldn't even pick up a damn telephone.

"Write the book, Wade. You're almost done." He was up to the last few years of his career. They'd achieved a lot these past six weeks, and CC had to admit it had been a good idea to come to Credence, back to his roots. He'd actually made huge inroads to the manuscript and been more focused here. Maybe it had just been being away from the distractions of Denver, but CC felt like it was more than that.

It was as if Credence was his muse. Wasn't that how Winona had put it?

A ghost of a smile flitted across his mouth. "That might be hard with my research assistant quitting on me."

"You don't need me to finish it, Wade."

"Maybe I don't need it, but your help with the book is invaluable, CC. Your input, your notes, your editing."

"You can hire someone to do that."

"Yeah, but you're on top of what's already been completed, and it's hard to buy that kind of continuity. Hell, CC, you've pushed this book to be better with every word and every page, and I guess I stupidly thought you were as invested in this as I was."

If he meant to make her feel guilty, then he succeeded. And he was right. Despite her opinions on a ghost writer, she *was* invested in the book. It felt as much hers as his.

"Fine. I can keep doing the research and beta reading on it if you want, but I can do that from anywhere, Wade. The same with managing your schedule."

Which was what she'd suggested when he'd originally insisted she join him in Credence. She should have stuck to her guns. Hell, she should have just left then and not let him smooth talk her into another three months.

"And I can also do interviews and get someone up to speed for you. All you need to do is finish the book."

As soon as that was done, she could officially sever all ties with him. Because having him in her inbox all the time would be just another way to keep her on the hook. And that was just plain cruel.

But, probably more importantly, he *needed* to do it. To finish it. For himself as well as the publisher. To prove he was someone else outside of being The Catapult. That he could make it outside of the NFL.

"Did something happen? Between yesterday when your plans were to leave tomorrow morning and now?"

"No."

CC shook her head even as the leggy blonde from yesterday floated into her head. The anonymous woman had kept her company all night, no matter how hard CC had tried to shake her image. Because, as CC had finally realized in the wee small hours, the blonde was the personification of all the reasons why CC couldn't entertain the thoughts she'd been having.

Thoughts that had been heading decidedly in the direction of her and Wade becoming something *more*.

Becoming a couple.

For a start, she wasn't a tall, leggy blonde with a body like one of those curvy Rocky Mountain back roads. She was short and dark-haired and petite. She *wasn't his type*. But for damn sure, there was *always* going to be some blonde or other hanging around.

CC was *always* going to have to contend with women who thought that because Wade was a celebrity the normal rules of relationships—fidelity and monogamy—didn't apply to him.

That they could flirt with impunity.

And she couldn't do that. Couldn't sit by and watch it unfold. Or be amused by it like so many celebrity wives. After her father's affair had thrown a bomb into their family life, fidelity was her line in the sand. And even if Wade never cheated, she wasn't sure she had the emotional fortitude to watch their bond come under constant attack.

CC didn't want to have to fight off women from here to eternity, but she'd be naive to think that wasn't going to be her lot.

And even if she could get past the blonde thing, the man hadn't had a relationship the entire time she'd known him. He didn't do longevity. He was a serial dater. That was just the way he worked.

CC, on the other hand, didn't go out with guys who only wanted some laughs and some sexy fun times between the sheets. She was totally up for sexy fun times between the sheets, and she already knew that Wade was pretty damn gifted in that department, but she didn't hit the mattress with any guy who wasn't interested in starting something serious.

That was just the way *she* worked.

"Nothing happened, Wade. It's just…time. I think we both know that."

He sighed and shoved his hands in his pockets. "Are you sure I can't change your mind? I don't want it to end like this. After all we've been through together. My career and then my retirement and building a brand outside football. And…Nebraska. It shouldn't be like this."

CC almost laughed. It was because of Nebraska it was like this. Or maybe it wasn't, maybe Nebraska had just been the physical manifestation of the things she'd started to feel about him since coming to Credence.

"Maybe not." She hadn't wanted it to end like this, either. "But this is the way it is."

"Hell, CC, I didn't even get you a going away gift."

A going away gift? Considering she was the one who bought all that stuff *for him*, she'd have liked to see him try. What would he consider an appropriate token of his appreciation?

A gold watch? A fountain pen? Like they were just…*colleagues*.

She bit down on her lip. The only thing she wanted from him she was pretty sure he didn't know how to give, and she dared not even articulate it out loud— not even to herself. "It's okay. I got one for you." She fished in her pocket, searching for the packet of Nerds she'd found at the bottom of her bag. "Here." She pulled them out and tossed them to him. The last packet of Nerds she'd ever give him. "There's more in your desk drawers to tide you over."

He caught them perfectly with his big, safe quarterback hand. She wouldn't have expected anything else.

"I'm going to see my mom for a week, and then I'm heading to California. I'll get someone to pack up the apartment in Denver as soon as I can arrange it."

He took a step toward her. "There's no rush, CC."

CC shook her head and held up her hand to keep him back. She wasn't sure why. Whether it was a rejection of his words or a warning to stop where he was. But he heeded both. The faster this was severed, the better. Agreeing to continue helping him with his book was going to drag it out enough without leaving all her crap in a place he was going to need for his new PA.

"I'll let you know when I make arrangements. I'll also sort out something for George and Wilburta, because I want them with me."

He frowned. "I'm not sure you can keep a pig in a domestic situation in California."

CC shot him a *don't fuck with me on this* look. No way was Wilburta ending up on a Christmas platter somewhere. "I'll work it out."

"Okay." He held his hands up in surrender. "Sure."

She pushed off the doorway. This was her big exit and, unlike Scarlett O'Hara, she wasn't going to give Wade a single hint of how much emotion she had bubbling under the surface.

She was really doing it. She was really leaving.

"Goodbye, Wade," she said, and, before he could reply, she turned and walked away, her legs as wobbly as dental floss.

• • •

By Monday the whole town knew that CC had left for good, and Wade was utterly sick of being asked about her. It was a relief to get away from the gossip and curiosity as well as the afternoon heat in Annie's for a bit. There were only one or two patrons, and Wade was pleased to be able to hide himself away in one of her old booths. She approached him with her standard coffee pot, and he held up his empty cup.

"Annie, you are a sight for sore eyes. I could kill for coffee."

Even her deadly black tar.

It was a far cry from the subtlety of a city espresso, but right now it suited his mood—strong and bitter.

"And I'll have a slice of your peach pie, please. Actually, make that two."

Annie didn't pour him coffee. Nor did she greet him with her usual curmudgeonly affection. She simply said, "No."

Wade blinked. "What?"

"Wade Carter, what on earth did you do to that sweet child?"

He sighed and put the cup back on the saucer. It was bad enough his mother had been on his case. "Annie…"

"Don't you *Annie* me. She was supposed to be here all summer. She was going to help me set up a Facebook page for the diner."

"A Facebook page?" Surely if Annie wanted to go all new century on them, her first stop should have been a proper coffee machine? Thank God there was soon going to be one of those in Credence.

Finally.

Wade laughed but sobered quickly as Annie's lips thinned. "It's a free country, Annie. I can't lock her up and keep her prisoner in the house."

Though *dear God*, he'd been tempted.

Wade had worked his ass off to keep things normal between them because he'd thought she'd want it that way, but every time he saw her he was right back in bed with her, those desperate breathy pants falling from her lips, stroking his ear. And parts significantly lower.

Erections? Hundreds. Productivity? Zero.

He'd known even as he was doing it that sleeping with CC would be different to the other women he'd taken to his bed. That he couldn't just be one and done with her because they worked closely together. But he hadn't expected to be consumed with what they'd shared. The last time a woman had ruined his focus so badly, it had been Jasmine, and he had *no* desire to ever repeat that train wreck.

"No. But you could pay her more, right?" Annie demanded. "Did you offer her a big fat bonus check?"

"I did indeed," he said morosely.

"Well it obviously wasn't enough. Good Lord, Wade, you're richer than God. What's the matter with you?"

Wade suspected Annie would be shocked to know how much he'd paid CC over the last almost-six years. And that was without the car he'd bought her and her rent-free apartment. But it wasn't actually any of her business how much he paid his PA.

Or whether he was, or was not, richer than God.

"Come on, Annie," Wade coaxed with one of his winning smiles. His momma always said you caught more flies with honey. "Cut me a break, here. I wish she was still here, too, but it's *my* name on the welcome sign." He held up his cup.

"Yeah, but I like her better than you."

If Wade had been drinking his nonexistent coffee from his cup right now, he'd have probably choked on it. It seemed like everybody in town had suddenly adopted his PA as their long-lost daughter. "I was *born* here. I had to practically *drag* CC here."

Annie humphed. Annie humphed better than anyone he knew. With her entire body. "Maybe. But at least she embraced us all while she was here. Unlike you, who lives less than two hours up the road in your fancy Denver apartment but only graces us with your presence twice a year, *if your momma is lucky*, and spends your whole time bellyaching about redneck drivers and"—she lifted the pot a little higher, the line of liquid sloshing around—"no decent coffee."

Wade was embarrassed to meet Annie's eye over the coffee thing and embarrassed to be called on his cavalier attitude toward his hometown. It was true, coming back to Credence in recent years had been done more out of duty than anything else.

"Oh yeah, I hear that. I see and hear *everything*, Wade Carter."

Annie said it in such a way that, for one horrible moment, he wondered if she somehow knew about Nebraska in some kind of weird, witchy female way.

Wade certainly knew when he was beat. He placed his cup on the chipped tabletop. "So, I'm not getting coffee?"

Annie shot him a sardonic smile. "Pretty smart for a city slicker." And she walked on.

CHAPTER TWENTY-THREE

A week later, Wade had written the sum total of three pages and deleted them about a dozen times a day. He was up to the CC years now, and he didn't know how to start. He couldn't even ask her because she wasn't here, and he didn't want to email and ask because he felt like he *should know* how to start, and he didn't want her to think her departure had affected him so badly he'd developed some kind of writer's block.

Especially when he'd been doing so well since moving to Credence.

But the first thirty-two years of his life had been a cakewalk next to this. Even the darkest time of his career, when his dick had been splashed over every tabloid in the country, had been a walk in the park compared to getting down the last five and a half years.

It was as if his life had been divided into two. Before CC and after CC.

When had *that* happened?

He reached across his desk for his packet of Nerds and gave it his customary shake. He loved that rattle noise they made. Sadly, there was no rattle forthcoming.

Damn it. *Empty*.

He opened his desk drawer. *None*. He opened the one on the other side. *Also none*. He felt in his pockets and the pocket of his hoodie thrown over the back of his chair. Still nothing. He couldn't possibly have eaten his entire supply of Nerds, surely?

Wade stood, annoyed at his dependence on candy and even more annoyed at CC for supplying it—like some fucking drug dealer. Quickly, he shut his computer down. There wouldn't be any Nerds at Jack's, but there would be beer.

Wade strode into the bar ten minutes later. The customers had increased over the last month with more women staying at the boardinghouse in town, and Jack's had become the drop-in place for people to meet.

Tucker was happy as a clam. He'd even expanded his cocktail menu.

His big, stupid grin greeted Wade as he sat at the bar. Arlo and Drew were already seated. "Let me guess, you need a Grasshopper, right?"

Wade snorted. He wasn't that desperate for booze. He doubted anyone had been that desperate since the seventies. "Only if you fancy wearing cool, green sludge all over your pretty face."

Tucker laughed, unperturbed as he reached for a glass.

"He's still in a mood," Arlo said.

Drew nodded. "MSP'll do that to you."

Drew thought every adverse male mood could be accredited to *massive sperm pressure*. If he ever went on *Mastermind*, it'd be his expert subject.

"Well you'd know," Wade said.

Arlo and Tucker sniggered, but Drew plowed on. "Laugh all you like, buddy, I'm used to living with it. You, on the other hand, have been away from all those Denver honeys for quite some time…" He made a lewd motion with his hand. "I hope you're cleaning out those pipes regularly."

"Not if his current personality is any indication," Tucker said.

"Maybe he's forgotten how, with so many women catering to his hot quarterback needs," Arlo mused.

Wade flipped him the bird. "Fuck all of you."

The guys' laughter was swallowed up by a raucous burst of female laughter that had all of them turning in their stools. Wade noticed Winona and Della in a booth with two of the other women who had stayed on a couple of weeks ago.

He didn't remember their names, but his mother had said one was an electrician and the other some computer wizard. Credence had to rely on those services from nearby towns, so to have these two women had caused much excitement, and they'd both already done small jobs around town.

It didn't hurt they were single women in their twenties.

"So?" Tucker said, drawing everyone's attention back to the bar, fixing Wade with a look. "What in hell did you do?"

"Do?"

"Don't play dumb, man, you know what I'm talking about."

Jesus. *CC* again? "I didn't *do* anything." Three sets of eyebrows rose in unison, clearly calling bullshit.

"She was supposed to be here until the end of summer," Arlo pressed.

"Yeah. She was going to do a Facebook page for the funeral home."

Tucker nodded. "And the bar."

Fuck's sake. What in hell had CC been doing while he'd been at the farm every morning? Putting on her red cape with a huge fucking FB on it and connecting the whole town?

Enough with the Facebook already.

"She left early. Period."

"Right." Arlo nodded. "So what did you do?"

Wade put his beer down. "Aren't you supposed to be on my side?"

Arlo shook his head. "She's got a nicer ass than you."

Drew rubbed the stubble on his chin. "She wasn't the same after she came back from Nebraska."

Wade suppressed the snort. Neither of them had been the same. "Of course not. Her father had just died."

"Nope." Drew's brows beetled together. "Wasn't that."

"And you're the expert on these things, I suppose?" Wade demanded.

Drew shrugged. "Grief *is* my field."

"You're an undertaker. Not a fucking social worker."

"I'm a bereavement agent."

Wade snorted. "Make sure you put that one on your Facebook page, bud."

Tucker narrowed his eyes. "You slept with her, didn't you?"

Wade took a mouthful of his beer as he reached for his poker face. This was none of their goddamn business. "No comment."

Tucker reached behind and pulled out his wallet. He extracted a hundred-dollar bill and handed it to Drew. Arlo also put a hundred down on the bar.

"I said no comment."

"Which means yes," Tucker said.

Wade shot him an exasperated look. "It means no fucking comment."

Tucker shook his head slowly. "You couldn't keep it in your pants, could you?"

"He fucked up," Arlo said as if Wade wasn't sitting right beside him.

"Yup." Drew nodded his agreement in the three-way conversation that did not involve Wade. "He fucked up."

Wade opened his mouth to deny it again. But there was such a thing as protesting too much, and his friends already had his measure. "Yeah, okay." He sighed. "I fucked up. Are you happy now?"

"The question is," Drew asked, "are you?"

Wade rolled his eyes. What was the point in psychoanalyzing it—he'd slept with CC. Not his smartest move, even though it had felt right and natural and...*necessary* at the time. It'd happened. It'd been once, and now she was gone.

Move on already.

He lifted his beer to Drew. "More psychobabble from the bereavement agent?" And he set about draining his glass.

"How do you feel about her?" Tucker asked.

Wade wasn't sure how he felt about CC, but he did know how he felt about this conversation. He'd rather give back his Super Bowl rings. "Jesus." He glared at Tucker. "Are you serious?"

Tucker didn't answer. Just stared. So did Arlo and Drew. For three macho dudes, they were doing a good *Gilmore Girls* right now. But they clearly weren't going to let up.

Fine. What *was* she to him? Wade couldn't pluck out a suitable response from the soup in his brain. A soup of half-formed, ill-defined thoughts and emotions. "She's my PA, for fuck's sake. My…girl Friday. My left tackle. Christ, she's an *employee*."

"Really?" Arlo pressed. "Is that all?"

"Yes." Or at least she had been. *Until she wasn't.* Until he danced with her and kissed her and lived with her and comforted her and watched her puke rainbow vomit.

And slid inside her.

"You know how many people meet their soul mates at work?" Drew asked.

Wade's jaw tightened. *Enough with the soul mates crap already.* "I don't believe in that bullshit."

"Oh come on, man." Exasperation cloaked Arlo's voice. "Because of Jasmine? Because one chick screws you over a hundred years ago, you're just going to stay single all your life? Not even give yourself a shot at what Wyatt has with Jenny? Or your mom and dad have? It's okay to fall in love again, dude."

It might have been a long time since Jasmine's betrayal, and the acuteness of that sting had long since dissipated, but it wasn't hard for Wade to recall. He'd vowed back then he'd never give a woman the power to hurt him again, and he'd fucking meant it.

"Yeah, man." Tucker nodded. "That's just dumb."

"They're right," Drew agreed. "You're not always going to be this hot, you know."

The guys laughed, and Arlo high-fived Drew. "I'm not in love with her," Wade said, breaking into the merriment. If he loved her, surely he'd be the first one to know? "But I do feel bad." *Really fucking bad.* "About stepping over a line. About making it untenable for her to keep working for me."

"Did you say sorry?"

Wade opened his mouth to confirm that he had, then shut it again. He hadn't. In true Wade fashion, he hadn't mentioned it at all. Just tried to move on.

His friends looked at him with pity in their eyes. "So what are you going to do about it?" Arlo demanded. "For so royally screwing things up?"

Fuck if he knew. Where did he even start to make amends for what had happened between them? For crossing the one line she'd asked him not to cross.

Sure, she'd crossed it, too, but that didn't absolve his responsibility.

"You need a grand gesture," Arlo said.

"A what?"

"Something big. And splashy."

Tucker nodded. "Chicks dig that shit."

Wade liked the way they were thinking. It suited a guy with a lot of money and no clue. "Like what?"

"Shit, dude, I don't know." Arlo frowned. "Do I look like I know this crap?" He tipped his head in the direction of the table that was still laughing the loudest. "Go ask Winona, she's the romance queen."

Wade would rather have his testicles scooped out with a melon baller than ask Winona. He drained his beer. A grand gesture...he could do that.

Fuck yeah, he could.

• • •

It took Wade approximately three hours to think of the perfect thing. And another week to find, organize, and expedite everything. By the time he was knocking on CC's hotel room in San Clemente eight days later, papers in hand, he was feeling like the king of the fucking world. It may not be the most sociable hour to be visiting, given it was barely seven in the morning, but he'd just driven from LAX, and he knew CC was an early bird, and he didn't want to wait any longer.

He had the most perfect grand gesture, and he actually bounced on his feet as he stood at the hotel door. He couldn't wait to see the look on her face.

She didn't answer, and Wade knocked again. He knew she was here, her car was parked in front of the unit. He'd thought it'd be difficult to find where she was staying, given how she'd deleted the app off her phone within hours of walking out his door. But he'd emailed her last week to ask where she was staying so he could send her a termination contract, and she'd told him.

Keys jingled as he shoved a hand in his pocket and bounced a little more. It seemed like they were making a habit of this—hotel rooms. Although this kitschy little San Clemente number was classier than the highway motel in Nebraska. Better view, too, with the Pacific Ocean sparkling in calm early-morning splendor over his shoulder and seagulls wheeling overhead.

Wade wasn't prepared for the sight that greeted him when the door finally did open. He'd expected her to be up and about, neat as a pin per usual, the room flooded with light, ready to face a day of online house shopping, a pen and notebook neatly placed by her laptop. Or maybe in a sarong and bikini top having already been for a swim, her hair damp.

Okay…that one could just be wishful thinking…

Instead, he was staring into a black hole, her room so dark he half expected bats to fly out. She blinked at him blearily, squinting into the sunlight. He'd obviously woken her. There was a blanket mark on her face to match the cranky frown, and her hair was in disarray.

He was pretty sure there was a Cheeto clinging to it.

It seemed like they were making a habit of CC being far from her best in hotel rooms, too.

It should have worried the crap out of him, but Christ, it was so *good* to see her. Just setting eyes on her again was like a calming hand on his shoulder, like soothing fingers on a fevered brow. Like everything was *right* in his world again, and he hadn't even been aware that it had been wrong.

But, perversely, there was also a more *male* reaction. His pulse leapt at the sight of her in that Broncos T-shirt, the same one he'd stripped her out of in Nebraska. The one with his number on the back.

Christ. *Why that?* Anything but that.

His mouth went dry as sand. He was thirsty as hell, and he knew exactly how he wanted to slake it.

Those soothing fingers turned hard and hot and slid lower. *Way* lower. *Not soothing at all.* His heart might be out of action, but his body was definitely pumped.

It was official, he had the hots for his left tackle.

"Wade?" Her frown deepened as she shoved her hand into her hair and tried to finger comb it into place.

"Hey." It was a banal response, but her breasts were moving interestingly under her shirt and she wasn't wearing a bra.

"Ugh." She put her other hand up to block out the sun as she squinted at the papers in his hand. "I have no idea why you're here. You were supposed to be mailing that. Hell, you could just have emailed it if you only knew how to work the damn scanner."

Wade stifled a smile. She *was* in a mood today. Not even that was enough to stem the sudden flow of blood to his crotch. "That's why I had you."

Her lips thinned. "What do you want?"

Okay. *Dumb* thing to say. He gave himself a quick mental kick in the ass and forged ahead. "I have something for you. Something I owe you."

"You don't owe me squat, Wade."

It was cuttingly dismissive. But Wade hadn't come this far to be put off by CC in a foul mood. She didn't scare him. If anything, her whole cranky pixie act was turning him on. CC was the only woman outside of Credence who had ever spoken to him like his status in life meant nothing to her.

Her disregard for his social status was disturbingly hot.

"Well, I don't know about that. I think—"

"Wade." She sighed. "*God*, if you must talk at me at least come inside. I feel as if the sun is shining laser beams directly into my eyeballs."

She left him standing there as she retreated into the dark. And there was his number on her back. Like a brand. Taunting him with a wave of possession that was vicious in its intensity.

Dragging his eyes off her shirt, he followed her into the gloom, glancing around at the general dishevelment of her room. It was not in a state Wade could reconcile with the CC he knew.

There was crap *everywhere*.

Her bags were on the floor at the end of her unmade bed, open and well-rummaged-through by the looks of them. There were clothes on the floor and draped over all the chairs. Red Bull cans, presumably empty, littered every surface, along with empty beer bottles. Packets of Cheetos, both empty and not quite empty, were strewn over the coffee table and the bed.

The sink in the kitchenette was piled high with dirty dishes. More beer bottles and a few wine bottles and glasses sat on the drainer. What the hell? It was like a frat house during Greek Week. He half expected to see porn on the TV. Even in Nebraska, when she was grieving for her father, everything had been neatly in place, from her toothbrush to the used tissues in the trash can.

Wade glanced at CC, who was standing near a coffee table awash with real estate pamphlets and empty cans. Her laptop was under there somewhere, too, he could just see an edge and the cord trailing away. "Whatcha been up to, CC?"

"Nothin'. Just sleeping in and walking on the beach, watching Netflix. Trying to kick my Red Bull habit."

He raised an eyebrow as he scanned the room, his eyes dwelling on all her empties. *This* was kicking her habit?

"I'm weaning off," she said waspishly. "I'm not crazy enough to go cold turkey. Trust me, you *do not* want to see that."

Because she was such a delight right now?

She turned to search through the empties on the coffee table, flashing that number nine again. Grabbing him by the balls again. Wade clenched his hands by his side to stop from reaching for her, from spinning her around.

The backs of her thighs were exposed to his view as she bent over and the hem rose. She picked up cans, shaking each one like a junkie hoping to find a forgotten eight ball. She made a triumphant noise in the back of her throat as liquid finally sploshed in one, and she straightened and raised it to her lips.

The hem of the T-shirt rode up at the front now, flashing the tops of her thighs and pulling against her chest as she tipped her head back and swallowed.

He wasn't sure how watching CC drink the dregs of *who-knew-how-old* Red Bull could be classed as erotic, it just fucking was. He wanted to slip his hands under that shirt and lick her neck.

Satisfied the can was empty, she tossed it on the coffee table before glaring at him suspiciously. "Why are you looking at me like that?"

Wade didn't think *because I want to kiss you really fucking badly* would go down so well right now. And he hadn't come for that. To make things worse. He'd come here to apologize.

"You…have a Cheeto in your hair."

She frowned, feeling for it and plucking it out. She stared at it for a beat or two as if she was trying to remember how it got there. Then she shrugged and shoved it in her mouth.

"What?" she demanded as he continued to ogle her.

In his defense, he couldn't help it. She was like a

frat house wet dream right now.

"You're…" He dropped his gaze to the front of her T-shirt. "Wearing my number."

"It's seven in the morning. They're my PJs."

"Yes." Wade swallowed. "Of course." *Get a grip, dickwad*.

It wasn't like he owned the fucking number. The Broncos may well have retired it, but it wasn't like he had worldwide exclusive rights for its use.

Her frown faded as she searched his face, and even in the gloom he could feel her eyes on his mouth and his throat and his chest. His breath sawed in and out of his lungs, and the muscles in his neck corded in restraint.

She swallowed. "Wade."

It came out all low and breathy, slightly louder than a whisper, and it stroked like a feather all the way down the taut ridges of his abdomen.

"I'm sorry." He shook his head. He should just let this go. Throw the keys to the house he'd bought her down on the coffee table and leave. Before he had *more* to apologize for! But his temples throbbed and his chest throbbed and his legs throbbed and *God help him* his dick throbbed.

He couldn't have moved with all the will in the world.

"It's just…seeing you in my number…it hits me right here." He slapped his abdomen. "I'm not one of those guys who needs to *brand* a woman, but when I see you in that shirt it makes me want to get a big black Sharpie or a tattoo gun and mark it all over your skin."

Wade swallowed, trying to control the tremor he

could hear in his voice.

"I'm trying to concentrate on why I'm here, but it's distracting as fuck. *You're* distracting as fuck."

CC didn't say anything, she just stared at him. Wade wasn't sure if that was a good thing or a bad thing. He really hoped she was thinking of something sane and sensible to bring him back from the edge, or at least be contemplating a change of clothes.

She nodded slowly, and he swore he could hear her breathing now, too. "Is this better?" Before he understood her intentions, she'd grabbed for the hem of the shirt and reefed it off over her head, tossing it on the ground.

Fuck. No.

Wade's jaw dropped as she stood before him in a teeny tiny pair of purple satin panties and nothing else, her nipples hard and round as nickels. The papers slid from his fingertips, his cock just about shredding his fly to get out.

This wasn't what he'd meant about her changing.

It was his turn to stare now. And stare he did, his hands clenching and unclenching by his sides, his body swaying a little.

"For fuck's sake, Wade. Do you need an embossed handwritten invitation?"

Hell no. He did not.

CHAPTER TWENTY-FOUR

CC's heart drummed in her chest, and her hands shook as Wade strode toward her with absolute purpose in his eyes. She shouldn't be doing this. She *absolutely* shouldn't be.

But her common sense had been waging a war with her body since she'd opened the door, and it had completely deserted about the time Wade had declared he'd wanted to brand her with his number.

All she cared about was getting lost in him. She'd missed him so damn hard and the rest, right now, was bullshit. She knew having sex with him wasn't going to solve anything. That'd probably only make her cravings for him worse.

But she was a junkie, and Wade Carter was her drug of choice.

Their bodies sparked as they met, their mouths sizzled as they meshed. His groan was like jet fuel to her system, and she all but climbed him, locking her legs around his waist. He smelled like the ocean and tasted like coffee, and she kissed him deep and hard and long, her head thrumming to the frantic beat of her heart.

Somehow he made it to the nearby couch, collapsing onto it, his hands clamped to her hips as she unlocked her ankles and dug her knees into the cushions on either side of his thighs. A chip packet crinkled beneath her shin, but she paid it no heed as she rubbed herself against him, the deep throb between her legs craving connection, craving the heat and hardness of him. The hard ridge of his arousal felt alternatively good and bad. Relieving and stoking in equal measure.

"Christ." He tore his mouth from hers, his lips attacking her throat and moving lower, his tongue licking along her collarbones. "I missed you," he muttered into the hollow at her throat, his hands sliding from her hips to her ribs to her breasts.

CC moaned as they cupped and kneaded, and he pushed her back slightly to watch as he plucked and tweaked and taunted her nipples until they were hard as diamonds. He stared at his handiwork, licking his lips like they'd been sprinkled with Nerds, then latched on *hard*, first to one nipple then the other, switching back and forth in an endless pattern.

Delirium took hold. CC shoved her hands in his hair and held on tight, grinding her pelvis against his as he devoured her breasts. Then suddenly he was kissing her again, wet and deep and sloppy, his arms circling her back, pulling her close, the wall of his chest hard against the taut, wet peaks of nipples still tingling from the ministrations of his mouth.

It hurt a little. It hurt so damn good.

She reached between them then, hurting somewhere else a lot more, groping for his fly, shoving it down, her fingers brushing against his dick then reaching inside, freeing it from his underwear, palming him, squeezing him.

He groaned, and CC swallowed it up, her hands deft and sure as she guided his erection to the hot, wet heart of her, pulling her underwear aside with one hand as she centered him with the other, the thick crown of him notching into place at the slick heat of her entrance.

She was vaguely aware that this was their second time without a condom, which moved them from reckless to irresponsible, but she was damned if she was going to stop this ride now. Her heart was tripping, and her breathing was labored, and every cell in her body throbbed with the need for possession.

CC wasn't sure if she sank down or he thrust up. All she knew was that suddenly he was inside her. Deep inside her. And nothing else mattered but this man and this moment and this thing between them as she panted and moaned and moved up and down in time with his in and out and the pleasure built and built and built.

She kissed him, her mouth *needing* his, needing his *full* possession. Needing his taste on her tongue and his groans rumbling through her head and the harsh pant of his breathing. It careened out of control in a flash, her mouth hungry and reckless and greedy as he thrust higher and harder and deeper, pushing her over the edge.

Pushing them *both* over the edge.

The deep guttural groan of his pleasure was like an anthem in her head, and she rocked and bucked to its rhythm, riding it—riding him—all the way to the end, their hearts beating frantically in unison. The climax rolled over them like thunder, spinning them around and around, taking them to the highest high and leaving them gasping and sated and exhausted, panting and clinging to each other in the aftermath.

CC allowed herself only a moment or two to recover and another moment or two to revel in the tickle of his breath on her throat and the thump of his heart against hers. But no longer. That would be madness, and the longer she waited the harder it would be to let go, and she *had to let go* because she had no desire to be one of those sad, weepy women who called his new PA looking for some scraps of his time.

As soon as her legs felt able to hold her, she climbed off Wade's lap, crossed to where she'd dropped her shirt, picked it up, and dragged it down over her head. Calmly—more calmly then she'd have thought possible—she turned to face him. He'd tucked himself away and straightened himself up, but he looked totally wrecked, and damn if that didn't make her want to storm back on over to him.

She ground her feet into the carpet.

He eyed her warily. "Are you okay?"

"Why did you come?"

He didn't say anything for long moments, then he, too, stood and crossed to where he'd dropped the papers he'd been holding when he'd arrived. He moved with grace and power—such a pleasure to watch—and muscles down deep and low fluttered and stirred again.

She hadn't realized how much she'd missed *that.*

He scooped the paper off the floor, turning to her and saying, "How's the house hunting?"

CC folded her arms. "Wade."

"What?" There was a real edge to his voice. "It's okay to *fuck* you on your couch but not to want to have a *conversation* with you?"

Heat rushed to CC's cheeks, and she thanked Christ for those blackout curtains. She took a steadying breath. Fine, he wanted to chat like they hadn't just rutted like wild beasts within five minutes of seeing each other?

Whatever.

"I have an agent on it. There are a few places I like, but I want to check out the whole area before I decide. I'm going to see some more places this afternoon."

He thrust the paper in her direction. "That won't be necessary anymore."

CC frowned, taking it automatically. Now the sun wasn't blazing into her eyeballs, she could read, and it wasn't a termination contract. But it was a contract.

For a house?

"What's this?" she asked, her heart starting to thump hard and slow in her chest.

"It's yours."

CC blinked. "What?"

He passed over his cell phone and there, on the screen, was her house. Her dream house. With the white picket fence and the sweeping ocean views. Then he fished in his pocket and pulled out a set of keys, handing them to her. She took those automatically, too.

"I bought it. For you."

CC stared at him, then at his phone, then back at him. "It's not even for sale."

He shrugged, but for the first time ever he actually looked smug. "Everything's for sale, CC, you just gotta offer the right price."

Her heart beat harder, banging like a drum, re-verberating through her abdomen. Was he kidding? *Was he freaking insane?* It took about ten seconds for the shock and incredulity to wear off. And another ten for the red mist to fog her brain.

"You're serious."

He grinned and nodded. "As a heart attack."

Oh God. His face was a picture of triumph and excitement. Like he'd just tossed a forty-yard pass. Like a kid on Christmas Eve. He thought she'd be happy about this?

He actually thought she'd be *happy* about it.

"No." She thrust the contract back at him as her temper notched closer to DEFCON 1.

"It's okay." He held up his hands to ward off the papers. "I know you're going to say it's too much and you can't accept it, but it's not, it's nowhere near enough, and I insist."

"Dear God…" She shook her head at him, trying to swallow her anger, to contain it. But her voice trembled and her hand trembled. Hell, her whole body was succumbing to rage. "Your ego knows no bounds, does it?"

His grin faded. "What?"

Yeah. That got his attention. "I don't want your damn house, Wade."

"CC…" He frowned. "It's a done deal. I already bought it."

She shoved the contract at his chest, along with the keys and his phone. "Well *un*buy it," she snapped.

He clutched the items automatically. "But…it's what you wanted."

CC gave a hysterical laugh as she paced away. God…did he know *nothing* about her? Had he learned nothing from their conversation that night in the red sitting room. How could she have let him inside her body when he knew so little? "You have no clue what I want," she said, turning on him.

His jaw clenched, and CC felt momentarily triumphant that she'd hit her mark. But he wasn't about to take her criticism lying down.

"I know what you wanted five minutes ago. I know what your body wants."

CC shook her head and gave another slightly maniacal laugh. "That's just practice, Wade. Knowing what women want in bed is muscle memory for you. It's your…superpower."

His laugh was as mirthless as hers. "Oh please, don't beat around the bush, CC. Why don't you go ahead and call me a manwhore while you're at it."

CC shrugged. "If the shoe fits." She was breathing heavily now, so was he. The kind of heavy that had nothing to do with orgasms.

Unfortunately.

"For fuck's sake, CC. It's your *dream house*. I was trying to do something *nice*."

That did it. *Red alert*. Deploy missiles. DEFCON 1. "I wanted to pay for the house *myself*, jackass," she yelled. "With my *own* money, from my *own* bank account."

He threw the keys and contract on top of the mess on the coffee table. "It's my damn money in that bank account," he yelled back.

"Yes," she hissed. "But I earned it, I worked for it. I worked twenty-four freaking seven for it, for almost six years of my life, putting up with your whims and your phone calls at three in the morning and bearing the brunt of weepy women who think you're some kind of sexual savant."

Although they did have a fair point there.

"I *earned* the house I'm going to buy. This house—" CC pointed at the contract like it was a rattlesnake. "This house of...Wade's *oops-dear-I-fucked-my-PA* guilt? I earned this one on my back, and you can shove it where the sun don't shine, buddy." She scooped up the papers and slapped them at his chest. "You can't freaking buy me, Wade. In case you haven't noticed, I'm not like other women."

He snorted. "Oh, I noticed."

CC would have thought that a compliment not that long ago. She didn't think he meant it that way today. "Did you? Did you really?" she demanded, her pulse pistoning along now. "I don't think you have. It seems to me you just treated me the way my father treated my mother. Buying her what she wanted because she was too damn dependent on him to go and get it herself. I'm not like my mother, Wade. I don't *need* or want a man to take care of me. I can earn my own money and I can pump my own gas and pay my own bills."

Her voice was getting louder and louder because yelling was far less impotent than bursting into tears, which was her other option.

"And I can *buy my own damn house*."

CC could see the moment her words hit home. When Wade finally remembered their conversation that night rolling bedsheets into bandages and he realized how badly he'd screwed up. How he'd tried, albeit unintentionally, to take something from her she'd fought so hard her entire adult life to maintain—her independence. She sucked in some deep breaths to calm herself. It wasn't his fault, Wade was reverting to type, doing what he always did. Throwing money at his problems.

It usually worked, so…why not?

But knowing she was one of his *problems* was almost too much to bear right now. It was just adding insult to injury. "Just go, Wade. Go and never come back."

"Christ, CC." He shoved a hand through his hair, and she actually felt a bit sorry for the poor little rich boy. "I'm sorry. I know I fucked up back in Nebraska, and I was just trying to make up for it. But I can see I've fucked it up even worse."

"You don't have to apologize for Nebraska, Wade. What happened there was as much on me as it was on you. Just like it was on the couch before. It's fine."

"But you left early because of it."

Oh God, how could a man who had been with so many women still be so fucking clueless about them? "I didn't leave because we'd had sex. I left because of the blonde."

"The blonde?" Wade frowned. "What blonde?"

CC laughed. Yeah, there'd been so many over the years, she guessed he probably needed clarification. "At the lake. Skipping stones with you."

His frown smoothed out as he obviously located her in his mental book-of-blondes. "Oh, right. Yes. What about her?"

Sweet mother of pearl. CC shook her head.

"Nothing, don't worry about it."

He frowned again. "I was just talking to her. She came up to me, she knew who I was but she was cool, and we just…talked."

"And you showed her how to skip stones."

"Well…" He shrugged. "She was pretty bad at it."

CC rolled her eyes. "Probably not as bad as she made out."

"Don't be ridiculous, CC. I was just talking to her."

"I know that." CC sighed. "That's the point. There are always going to be women who are just talking to you. Who are smiling and asking for your autograph as they make goo-goo eyes at you and rub their boobs on your arm. There's always going to be another freaking blonde, Wade. And I'm just…not strong enough for that."

"Wait. But…" He shoved a hand on his hip. "What are you saying, CC? Why do you even care? Unless you have…feelings for me."

"No." CC shook her head vehemently as she lied, because right now was the worst possible time to realize that she *did* have feelings for him.

All the feelings.

She loved him. And that was why seeing him at the lake, why having that light bulb moment about the demands of his celebrity had been like a knife into her heart.

"I don't know how I feel, Wade." Another lie, but at least it gave her some wiggle room. "But I do know how *you* feel. About relationships. You don't do them. You're a serial dater. You change your women almost as frequently as your underwear, and fidelity is everything to me."

The angles of his jaw whitened as his mouth turned grim. "I have *never ever* cheated on a woman in my life."

"Yeah, but you've never had to, have you? You've never been with one woman longer than a few dates. What happens if you ever do decide to settle? When a few dates becomes a few weeks, then a few months? How long does it take you to get tired of monogamy, Wade?"

"I was with Jasmine for two years," he said through gritted teeth. "I can do monogamy just fine. I am *not* your father, Cecilia."

CC swallowed at the way he used her full name. He'd said it in anger, as a reprimand, but it still had that strange buzzing effect on her cells, making it hard to concentrate on what else he'd said. About Jasmine.

But Jasmine had been a long time ago, and CC would be a blind fool to ignore his track record since then, because she doubted she'd survive another man she loved leaving.

"But you haven't, have you?" CC folded her arms. "Done monogamy? Since then."

"I've never met anybody I wanted to go down that path with again."

Well, that was bullshit. Having met a lot of Wade Carter's women—usually at their expiration date— CC could confidently say there were plenty of possibilities. Wade might have gone for lookers, but few of them had been dull, vacuous, or boring.

And then there was her.

If he'd come here for her, if he'd bought the house *because he'd had feelings other than guilt for her*, this would have been the perfect moment to say, "Until you."

I've never met anyone I wanted to go down that path with again until you.

But he hadn't. Which was all she needed to know.

"And you don't want to." That's what this all boiled down to. He was determined to stay footloose and fancy free.

"Christ, CC." He shoved a hand through his hair. "The Jasmine thing…that hurt a lot."

CC nodded. She understood how hard it was to trust again when your heart had been smashed to pieces by someone who was supposed to love you. Looking back, CC realized she'd probably never really trusted a man who wasn't one of her brothers her whole entire life.

"Okay…well." There was no point going on about this. She picked up the keys and held them out for him. "Thank you for the thought, but I'm not taking the house. You have clever lawyers, I'm sure they can get you out of the contract."

He shook his head, refusing to take the keys. "I'm not taking it back. It can stay empty for all I care."

"Fine." She threw the keys back on the table. "Your money."

They stood awkwardly, staring at each other for long moments. It was hard to believe he'd been inside her fifteen minutes ago.

"Go home, Wade. Finish your book."

He shook his head. "I seem to have gotten another case of writer's block. Nothing's the same now that you've gone."

Oh God. The longing in his voice nearly killed her. What did he want from her? To be some freaking mascot? A cheer squad. His reliable *girl Friday*, taking care of him, stroking his ego but never expecting anything in return?

She needed more than that. More than he could give.

He had to go—now. Before she caved. "You can do it," she said briskly. "You *have* to do it. You just have to find a way back into it again."

She forced her legs to walk to the door, forced her hands to reach for the handle, to turn it, to pull the door open. She forced herself to stand and wait.

"I really am sorry, Cecilia," he said as he drew level.

She swallowed, her gaze fixed on his throat because she didn't trust what she might do if she looked into his eyes. "Me too."

And then he walked out the door.

CHAPTER TWENTY-FIVE

Wade sat in front of a blinking cursor for three days with CC's voice whispering inside his head. *Find a way back into it*. But the whisper came with an avalanche of memories *not* conducive to writing.

CC in his number. CC in her purple panties. The taste of Red Bull and Cheetos—his new favorite thing. The driving need to be inside her.

Easy, sexy, distracting memories.

But there were darker ones as well that tightened his chest. Their fight. Her palpable *and very understandable fury* over the house. A blonde he barely remembered.

Which hadn't been about the blonde at all. He knew that.

He just wasn't sure what it *was* about. She'd denied any feelings for him, so why in hell did she care who he spoke to?

She'd accused him of not knowing what she wanted, and, given what he'd done, Wade couldn't blame her. He must have been suffering a rush of blood to his head when he thought buying her dream house as a gift was a good idea. How could he have forgotten how growing up in the shadow of her mother's debilitating dependence had made CC so fiercely *in*dependent. How *taking care of herself* was paramount. Was something she wore like a badge of pride.

Yeah…he'd been a total dumbass.

Unfortunately, none of the memories made it easy to write, and he was growing more and more impatient with his lack of progress. He'd been short with his mom this morning at the farm and pissed off at Wyatt's goofy lovestruck face. Completely undeterred by Wade's irritation, his brother had just raised an eyebrow and asked with a smug cat-that-got-the-cream smile how long it had been since Wade had gotten laid.

Bastard.

Tucker had suggested last night at the bar that maybe they should all throw Wade an intervention after Wade had scowled his way through three beers. Drew had offered the sales display room at the funeral home for such a purpose due to its bright lighting, which apparently would help with openness and honesty. But having his friends all sit around trying to get him to talk about his *feelings* was creepy enough without doing it in a room full of gleaming cherrywood coffins.

He just had to finish the damn book, that was all. As CC had said, he *needed* to do it.

Okay. Enough. Wade placed his fingers on the keyboard. *Find your way back in.* Easy. Not.

The CC years were proving to be exceptionally difficult.

Squaring his shoulders, he forced himself to type the first thing that came into his head about how he'd felt the day he'd met CC. He'd been trying to get down *the facts* of that meeting for days and then deleting each attempt because it read too much like a Wikipedia entry.

Maybe he needed to approach it differently. Think

laterally or, hell, dig deeper?

Okay…

> *The first time I saw Cecilia Morgan, she*
> *was kicking her then-boss in the testicles for*
> *backing her into a corner and trying to kiss*
> *her. I fell in love that day.*

Wade snatched his hands off the keyboard, staring at what he'd written.

What the fuck? Where had *that* come from?

His pulse swelled in his head, reverberating like rotor blades. Wade "The Catapult" Carter didn't *do* love. He'd told his friends in the bar only last week that he couldn't have feelings for CC because she worked for him, because she was his employee, because it *wasn't like that.*

But it *was* like that. *Exactly like that.*

He'd been lying to himself because what he'd just written was absolutely true. He'd fallen for her hook, line, and sinker that first time—he just hadn't realized it until now.

But now that he had? *Holy. Shit.* It ballooned like a fucking mushroom cloud in his chest, swallowing everything in its path. He'd loved before, so he recognized the emotion, but this was so much *more* than what he'd felt for Jasmine.

Hell, he'd been clued in for less than a minute, and he already knew that.

Jasmine had been all the things a young guy had wanted in a woman. She'd been sweet and quiet and adored him. She'd looked good on his arm and was happy to let him lead, to be the man.

CC was none of those things.

In fact, over the years he'd known her, she'd been a pain in his ass for probably half that time, taking her job as his left tackle to extremes.

But he loved her anyway.

Christ. He shoved his hand through his hair as he stood, pushing away from his desk and pacing to the big windows that overlooked the street. What a fucking idiot he'd been. To have missed it. To have let something that had happened a decade ago snap freeze his heart.

He paced the room, a restless energy sizzling along his nerves as he pondered what to do now. Go and get her, of course, because what was his life if she wasn't in it? But *how* did he go about it? He'd already played the grand gesture hand and had fucked it up spectacularly.

What did he get a woman who'd already thrown back the keys of her dream house? He was a gift giver, and the women he'd known had loved that kind of thing. Wade didn't know how to handle a woman who didn't.

I'm not like other women.

That's what she'd said, and she was right. She wasn't like any other woman he'd ever met. She was rare. Unique. A one-off.

She was five Super Bowl rings. An eighty-yard Hail Mary.

And he didn't know how to win her over.

Panic set in at the thought. He didn't even know if she felt the same way. She denied having feelings for him, but had she been lying, too?

Jesus.

He paced back to the window and tapped his fingers against the frame, staring absently at the play of bright sunlight along the grayed, gnarly limbs of the big old tree between the house and the front gate. He hated not knowing, hated feeling out of his depth. Wade was a decisive kinda guy...that's what made him an excellent quarterback, he didn't prevaricate.

His cell phone chimed, and Wade's pulse leapt as he dragged it out of his pocket. CC?

No. A text message from Arlo.

> *Tucker wants to know if you need that intervention yet?*

Wade gave a half laugh, half snort. He shook his head, grateful for idiot friends looking out for him. He was going to miss these guys when he went back to Denver.

> *No. I need a kick in the ass. I am an idiot.*

He sent the text and waited for a reply, staring at the streetlight, the aroma of Red Bull and Cheetos so tantalizing he could almost smell them.

> *You live in the city. Of course you're an idiot. Come to the boardinghouse. Need some dumb muscle. I can kick your ass there.*

Wade smiled, shoved the phone in his pocket, and headed for the door. He sure as hell was getting nothing done here, he might as well be among friends.

• • •

When Wade got to the boardinghouse, he found Arlo and several pieces of furniture on the sidewalk, baking in the afternoon sun. From beds to couches to a huge oven and a massive fridge and freezer.

"These fall off the back of a truck?" he asked.

"Yeah, dude, this is what I do in my spare time. I deal in stolen goods."

Wade laughed. "Better be careful, I hear the chief of police around here is a real asshole."

"Pfft. He doesn't scare me." Arlo pointed to the nearest couch and bent to slide his fingers under. "This one first."

"Seriously," Wade said, also bending to grab hold of the other end. "Where'd you get this stuff?"

"Bob sourced it from somewhere. I didn't ask any questions."

Bob and Ray appeared suddenly as Wade and Arlo straightened, balancing the weight of the couch between them. Bob was holding a clipboard—no wonder CC loved him—and Ray had a tool belt slung around his hips.

Great. The Rat Pack.

Bob had probably been the loudest in his displeasure at Wade letting CC run away. She had apparently volunteered to help him format a local history book he'd been compiling for the last fifty years and load it to Amazon.

Wade wasn't sure Credence was ready for Bob Downey, published author, and he certainly didn't need the old coot busting his balls today.

"Afternoon, Mr. Downey, Mr. Carmody."

They nodded at him. "That's for the far common room," Bob said, consulting his clipboard. "Follow us."

Wade and Arlo followed. It may have been forty years since he'd been mayor, but Bob Downey was used to being obeyed.

"How's the writing?" Arlo asked as they maneuvered the couch through the front door and into the relative cool of the house.

"I wrote a whole paragraph today."

Arlo whistled. "Progress."

Oh, it had been progress all right. "Yes. A very illuminating paragraph, actually."

"Oh?" Arlo cocked an eyebrow as he walked backward along the hallway with Ray and Bob instructing him to watch his step.

"Turns out," Wade said, pausing for a moment as they edged the couch around the corner into the common room, "I'm in love with CC."

Arlo grinned. "Well, hell…give the man a cigar."

"Yeah, yeah." Wade bent his knees, and he and Arlo placed the couch in the spot where Ray was pointing, against the far wall. "I'm a little slow on the uptake, okay?"

"A little slow?" Bob snorted. "There are dead people quicker than you."

Wade shook his head. Eighty-something years old and the man had ears like a bat.

"So?" Ray looked at him expectantly. "What are you going to do about it, sonny?"

Arlo laughed. "Yeah, *sonny*, whatcha gonna do?"

But Wade wasn't in a laughing mood. "Well, buying her a *house* as a grand gesture didn't work, so I'm shit out of ideas."

"Who bought who a house as a grand gesture?"

Winona suddenly appeared beside Wade's shoulder.

She wore a colorful caftan, myriad thin bangles jingled on her wrists, and big hoop earrings swung from her lobes. Bob and Ray greeted her enthusiastically. Wade half expected them to break into a rendition of "That's Amore."

"Wade bought CC a house," Arlo said.

She whistled and nodded at Wade. "Impressive. Thinking big, smart man."

"Yeah. I thought so." Except it had been the worst possible thing he could have done.

"Ah." Winona nodded. "She turned you down?"

"Yep."

"Wait." She frowned. "You bought her a house and told her you loved her and she *turned you down*?"

Wade glanced uneasily at Arlo. "Not exactly."

"What does *not exactly* mean?" she probed.

When he didn't answer for a beat or two, she pierced Arlo with a raised eyebrow. "I don't think the L word was part of the whole scenario," he supplied.

Winona's face went through a comical display of emotions from disbelief to incredulity. She stared at Wade. "Did you take too many hits to your head in that football career of yours?"

She flicked her gaze to Arlo again. "What is wrong with men?"

"We're emotional dwarfs?"

She sighed before turning her eyes on Wade. "Listen very carefully to what I'm going to tell you now, okay?" She spoke slowly in case he really had taken one too many hits to the head. "A grand gesture is nothing without the *I love you*. The gesture is there to get her attention, but it's not the whole shebang."

"Right." He nodded. "Got it. So I could just tell her I loved her now and it'd be okay?" If Winona was here to give him some harsh truths he might as well pump her for pointers as well.

"*Not now that you've fucked it up—*" She paused for a moment to glance at Bob and Ray. "Pardon my language, gentlemen."

Bob laughed. "Oh, don't mind us," he dismissed. "Best entertainment we've had since that night we played strip poker in Hannah Moore's room and we got to see her brassiere."

He nudged Ray's shoulder, and they both laughed. Everyone else paused for a moment as they digested that morsel of information.

Winona recovered first and continued. "Now you've made it harder for yourself," she said. "Now you've got to make it *extra* special to make up for the last time. But keep it small."

Wade blinked. Great… So no pressure, then. "And how do I do that?" he demanded.

Winona shrugged. "I'm sure you'll figure it out. Just try and not screw it up this time, huh?"

She turned and walked away, disappearing into her room, leaving Wade none the wiser.

"So?" Arlo prompted. "Any ideas?"

Wade shook his head. Extra special but small. Any other woman he'd just buy jewelry—a necklace or a bracelet. But he didn't think Winona meant small as in size. He thought she meant it in a non-flashy way.

In a way that *spoke* to CC. That *meant* something to her.

It hit him then, in a blinding flash, and he stood

a little taller. He looked at Arlo, then at Bob, then at Ray. "I'm going to finish the damn book like she asked me to."

And the part he was writing right now? It was going to be a goddamn love story. *A fucking ode.* To Cecilia.

"Then I'm going to send it to her to read, and when she has, I'm going to go to her and I'm going to take George and that damn pig with me and tell her I love her and *get down on my knees if I have to* and beg her to be mine."

"That could work," Ray said.

Bob nodded. "Women like words. Poems and love notes and whatnot. And not just on Valentine's Day."

Wade sincerely fucking hoped so, because it was all he had now. "Okay then, c'mon." He headed for the hallway. "Let's get this furniture taken care of. I got a book to finish."

• • •

Wade wrote. He wrote into the night and all the next day. He wrote for ten days straight, stopping only to go to the farm each morning, even though his father was back to doing all the duties he'd been unable to do just after his pacemaker had been fitted. When he got in from the farm, he showered and went straight to his office and picked up where he left off.

Sally was worried he wasn't eating and always left him a prepared plate of food before she went home for the day, but Wade barely touched them. Mostly he just mainlined Nerds because he only had time for writing.

He'd found his way back into the book, and it was flowing like honey. Making him smile and laugh and grab at his heart as he related all the funny little incidents with CC over the last five and a half years.

The time she stopped an enraged six-foot-seven, three-hundred-pound linebacker from entering Wade's office with just the fold of her arms and the raise of her eyebrow. The time she'd sat with the girlfriend of Jimmy Robinson, his backup quarterback, when she miscarried their baby while the Broncos had been playing away that weekend. The time she'd sourced a snowplow driver at three in the morning willing to drive Wade through a blizzard to the airport in buttfuck Indiana.

So many anecdotes. So many times and in so many ways she'd been there for him in the background, smoothing his way, making everything easy.

And he'd taken it all for granted.

He put it all in the book, hoping like hell that when she read it, she'd understand it for what it was. Him pouring his heart out to her. A love letter to Cecilia Morgan.

Wade emerged into the light ten days later, finally finished. He was exhausted—his back ached, his shoulders ached, his eyes were gritty, but he was done. And it was good.

Or at least he hoped it was.

Normally, CC was the one who told him what was good and what wasn't, but he hadn't sent her any of the pages as he'd done through this whole process. He didn't want her to see the new bit until it was complete. Until he'd totally plucked his heart out of his chest and placed it bleeding at her feet.

He hoped like hell she got it. That she could read between the lines to what he was trying to tell her.

His finger hovered over the send button on his email. He'd composed a brief email to CC and attached the document, and his heartbeat picked up tempo as the enormity of what he was about to do hit him.

He hoped it wasn't in vain. He hoped she had feelings for him, too, despite the issues she obviously had with his celebrity. Not that he could blame her. CC had been hurt by a philandering father and was slow to trust. Frankly, he'd have a helluva hard time watching random dudes just come up and start talking to CC, too.

But, if she let him, he'd spend the rest of his life showing her that she was his one and only. That she was his forever. And it started with the book.

If she read it and didn't get it, he didn't know what he would do. But right now it was all he had.

He hit send.

. . .

CC opened the email the following morning. She'd put an offer in on a house yesterday afternoon and had finally found a PA for Wade who checked all the boxes. She was feeling damn pleased with herself. So pleased that when the email was there waiting for her in her inbox, she didn't even hesitate to open it. She'd been expecting pages from him for a while now and had been going to email him about the PA situation later today, anyway.

She was definitely better than when he'd been

here two weeks ago. His visit had been a wakeup call. To stop feeling sorry for herself. To get on with her life. Because whether she loved him or not, Wade was Wade. Adored, revered, desired.

And he didn't love her.

His email was brief, and she quashed the disappointment as she read it.

> *CC, book is finally done. Would appreciate your feedback soonest.*
>
> *Wade.*

CC almost laughed out loud at the brevity of the email. Typical Wade. What else had she expected? A *dear* CC? Maybe a *warm regards*, or a *best wishes* at the end? She supposed she was lucky he hadn't signed off WC.

That was something, right?

Still, whatever was lacking in the email didn't detract from the fact that the book was apparently done? Finished. Jeez Louise…he must have written around the clock. She'd been expecting to get dribs and drabs of pages, and when none had arrived she'd assumed his writer's block was continuing.

Obviously not.

Would appreciate your feedback soonest. Of course he would. Wade always did think his needs were more important than anyone else's. But she was exceedingly curious, and she did have a free day…

CC got up, made herself a green tea—she was down to one Red Bull a day with lunch now—and placed it beside the bed. Crossing to the coffee table, she grabbed the writing pad and pen lined up neatly

next to the remote controls. She headed back and
crawled on top of her made bed, dragging her Mac
onto her lap and settling against the pillows.

She planned to read from start to finish and
make notes as she went. With any luck she'd have a
full set of suggestions to send to Wade by some time
tomorrow. Maybe the next day, depending on how
much work she felt was needed on the new material.

Taking a steadying breath, she clicked on the
attachment.

Four hours later, CC was a total wreck. She'd made
two pages of notes—small things, mainly, from the
three-quarters of the book she'd already read. But all
her note-taking had stopped from chapter forty-nine
on. The chapter that began—

> *The first time I saw Cecilia Morgan, she*
> *was kicking her then-boss in the testicles for*
> *backing her into a corner and trying to kiss*
> *her. I fell in love that day. I was just too much*
> *of an idiot to know it.*

He loved her. *Wade Carter loved her.* He'd loved
her since that day?

That first day when she'd been sure she'd never
be employed again, given that kicking men in the
testicles tended to be a career-limiting move. But
he'd whisked her away to the bar instead, brushing
her off, pressing a glass into her shaking hands, and
offered her a job.

A good one. With more money than she'd ever seen in her life and amazing perks as well.

He'd loved her *since then*?

Her head was spinning. With every word he'd written he'd built a picture of his regard and affection and, yes, his love. She'd smiled and laughed and cried at his words, touched by the depth and emotion in his prose.

Wade Carter may be a kickass ex-pro quarterback with three Super Bowl rings to his name, but he could write the hell out of a love story.

All CC had wanted since her ninth grade high school trip was to live by the beach where the waves and the sand were forever and constant and people were happy all the time.

It didn't matter anymore. Now the only place she wanted to be was by Wade's side. Even in a god-awful white elephant of a house in ass-end Colorado.

Shutting the Word document, she navigated quickly to her web browser and bought a ticket to Denver.

· · ·

CC pulled up outside Wade's house at just past eight in the evening. All it needed was some Spanish moss hanging from the big old tree in the front and it'd be the full antebellum nightmare. In Colorado. *Crazy.*

But hell, she'd missed this place.

Her legs wobbled as she stepped out of the rental car. Any other time she'd have put it down to the two-hour drive from Denver, but they weren't that kind of wobbly.

They were *huge moment ahoy* wobbly.

She had no idea if he was home or not, but there were lights on inside so she hoped it was a good sign. By the time she got to the big front door, her heart was belting so hard against her ribs she could barely hear herself knock.

The door seemed to take forever to open, and her palms sweated, which was utterly ridiculous. Her palms had never sweated in her entire thirty-two years. Knowing her luck, she was probably going into spontaneous menopause now that it looked like she might finally be catching a relationship break.

She practically leapt out of her skin when the door did open. And then it just about peeled off, along with her clothes, as Wade stood there all rumpled and tired and haggard. He was shirtless, his jeans hanging low on his hips, his three-day growth more scruff than whiskers.

Dear God. She'd missed *him*. His face and his hair and sweet Jesus, that chest. She wanted to launch herself at him and never let go. But if she touched him now she wouldn't say the things that needed to be said, seek the clarifications that needed to be sought.

"Cecilia," he whispered.

The ragged note in his voice caused her to sway a little, and CC grabbed the doorframe to steady herself. Christ, it was this house. She was going to go the full Scarlett O'Hara and swoon all over him any moment.

"You love me, Wade William Rhett Carter?"

He gave a slow smile, which wrapped itself firmly around her ovaries. He still looked tired, but he looked sexy tired now. "I do. And you love me."

CC nodded. "I do."

He flat-out grinned then, not looking remotely tired suddenly as his hand slid up the doorframe and he leaned in a little closer. "Okay then."

"And you want to be in a relationship with me. A monogamous relationship with me? Forever? Because I deserve forever, Wade, and I'm not interested in any other version."

"You do." He nodded slowly, his gaze meshing firmly with hers, and there was so much honesty there she couldn't look away. "You do deserve forever, and so do I. We deserve forever with each other, and I'm not interested in any other version, either. I know it's hard being in the limelight like I am, but believe me, Cecilia, there will only ever be you. I want to marry you and have babies with you and make you happy for the rest of your life."

CC's throat constricted. She believed him. Sincerity blazed from his eyes and vibrated through his body.

"Where will we live?"

"I don't care. In California or in Denver or in Credence. Wherever you want to live is where I want to be."

"Maybe we can spend time in each?"

He nodded. "Done."

God, he was saying all the right things, but she needed to be sure. "I'm going to have my own bank account and checkbook. I'm going to pay the bills." Well, she paid his bills anyway, but CC was pretty sure he knew what she meant. "*And* fix the fences."

"Of course." He smiled. "I don't want to walk in front of you, CC." He reached for her hand and entwined his fingers with hers. "I want us to walk together, side by side."

Dear Lord…she wanted that, too. "I'm not going to be easy, you know. I'm not one of those yes-women you seem to like so much."

He chuckled, and CC swore she spontaneously ovulated. "This is not news to me."

"I'm Scarlett. Not Melanie. If you want a Melanie, you should tell me right now and I'll go."

"I don't want a Melanie."

"You should. Your life would probably be easier."

He laughed then. "I have no doubt it would be. But for some crazy reason…I only want you. I love you, Cecilia."

CC swallowed against the tightness in her throat. She was starting to tremble now. "I love you, too," she whispered.

He grinned then. A Super Bowl touchdown kind of grin. "Good."

He let go of her hands, and before she knew what he was even thinking, he'd swooped her off her feet and up into his arms. He kissed her, and she kissed him back, drowning in the smell and the taste of him and the glorious promise of a future in his arms.

They were both breathless when he finally pulled out of the kiss, and CC was glad he was holding her because her bones had completely dissolved.

"Mmmm," he murmured, his lips wet, his eyes satisfyingly glazed. He moved then, kicking the front door shut with his foot, and CC yelped a little and grabbed him around the neck as he strode into the house with her, crossing the lobby to the foot of the sweeping staircase.

"Hold on tight, baby," he said as he paused at the bottom. "I'm going up."

CC loved it when he called her Cecilia. When he called her baby? It melted her into a pile of mush. So instead of saying *don't be ridiculous you'll break your back*, she clung tighter and stared into his eyes as he effortlessly traversed the staircase to the top.

"Where now?"

"Now?" He shot her a wicked smile. "Now, I'm going to throw you on the nearest bed and then I'm *going down* until all of Credence can hear you screaming my name."

CC did not protest. In fact, it was her first lesson in *that thing he did with his tongue*, and she did scream— loud.

"I think they heard you in Kansas," Wade muttered half an hour later, his breath warm on her belly as he kissed his way up, a smile in his voice. "Give me some recovery time, and I'll make them hear you in Texas."

CC laughed. Smug. The man was getting *so freaking smug*. But he was all hers. All the time.

She could live with that.

EPILOGUE

Four months later. Carter family farm.

If it had been anyone else's wedding, any other bride, Wade would have been muttering about the ridiculousness of a hundred-pound hog with a pink ribbon around its neck and an eighteen-month-old Border collie with a blue ribbon around its neck walking down the aisle together.

But this was *his* wedding and *his* wife, and if she'd wanted a mariachi band and jugglers, she could have had them. She'd already turned their Credence house—one that didn't need any more attention drawn to it—into an indoor petting zoo, with several piglets at varying stages of bottle-feeding, an orphaned baby goat, and two fluffy bunnies she'd assured him were both girls—until they'd had babies.

And now there were eight fluffy bunnies.

But that didn't matter, either. All he wanted was his ring on her finger. And the fact it had taken four months to finally get here meant nothing right now.

Wade was a patient man. Unlike Wyatt, who had been like a cat on a hot tin roof for the month it had taken his mother and Jenny to organize their wedding. He smiled at Wyatt now while he waited for CC at the end of the aisle. His brother smiled back, but all Wyatt really had eyes for was Jenny and her very slight baby bump.

Henry came down the aisle next, looking very country-kid in his jeans and vest and cowboy boots, a ten-gallon hat pulled low on his head, throwing rose petals on the ground from a small basket. Jenny beamed at her son, as did Wade's mom and dad, who'd made it their mission in life to spoil Henry rotten.

The barn looked a picture. When Ronnie had suggested it for the ceremony, Wade had been doubtful, but he'd been wrong. It was big enough for all the guests, including the ones with giant celebrity egos, and with the long side doors open, crisp November sunshine flooded the space.

Suddenly, CC appeared on her brother's arm in a long, flowing dress, and Wade's breath stuck in his throat, his chest too tight for his ribs. It was a simple design—no frills, no lace, no fuss—but given that her preference had been jeans, the dress was a revelation.

He already couldn't wait to get her out of it.

And he thanked God for her douchebag ex-boss with the grabby hands. His loss had been Wade's gain that day in a Denver hotel lobby, even if it had taken Wade almost six years to get a clue.

Six years of professionalism, bickering, and friendship.

Best. Foreplay. Ever.

• • •

Several hours later, CC's head was spinning from the whirlwind of the day. She wouldn't have thought it was possible to be this happy, but her cheeks literally ached from smiling. And still, the best was to come. If she could only get a spare second with her husband, she was sure he'd agree. She'd been hugging this information close since this morning, and she was practically blowing a gasket keeping it to herself.

Spying her superhot husband in his sexy tux with a bunch of ex-jocks, she excused herself from one of Ronnie's *crazy Southern relatives*, as Cal called them. If she didn't do it now, they'd be sitting down to their meal and a bunch of speeches and she probably *would* blow her gasket.

Picking up her dress, she pressed through the crowds, ignoring anyone trying to gain her attention—she was on a mission and she was not going to be stopped.

"Ah," Wade said as he saw her approaching. "My wife, gentlemen."

There was general good-natured teasing as CC joined them, slipping her arm around Wade's waist. One of them shook his head and said, "Man, anyone tell you you're punching way above your weight?"

Wade dropped a kiss on her temple. "All the time."

CC laughed and said, "Excuse me, gentlemen, but I'd like to borrow my husband for a moment, if that's okay?"

She didn't wait for their permission, just slipped her hand into his and tugged.

"I hope you're taking me somewhere to have your way with me," Wade said close to her ear as he followed.

CC smiled. "I think you're going to want to see this."

"Mrs. Carter, are you not wearing any panties under that big ol' gown?"

She laughed. "That's for me to know and you to find out, Mr. Carter."

Finally, CC rounded a corner and they were blissfully

alone, the sun slowly sinking over the fields to the west. "I've got something for you."

He smiled and pulled her close, nuzzling her neck. "And I've got something for you."

CC shivered at the brush of his mouth before pushing gently against his chest. There would be time for distractions later. She fished down the front of her dress.

"Mmm." Wade nodded appreciatively. "I like where this is going."

"Trust me, you're going to love it." CC produced the test stick she'd shoved down there this morning after she'd changed into her gown. *Why didn't wedding dresses have pockets?* "In fact, you're going to be over the moon."

Her hand shook as CC passed the stick over, her heart beating loud in her ears. He took it and, for a second, looked at it uncomprehendingly. Then his expression changed as he stared at the small pink positive sign in the test window and realization dawned.

"Congratulations, Wade," CC whispered around a sudden lump in her throat. "You're going to be a daddy."

He smiled, tentatively at first, a little disbelievingly, looking at CC, then back at the stick, then at her again. Then he was grinning and laughing and then he bent her over backward and kissed the hell out of her until CC was breathless and half-crazed with lust.

"Thank you," he said as he righted her.

CC's heart ached in her chest, she was so damn happy. "Your turn to be left tackle now."

"Yeah." He nodded. "It is. And I'm going to be the best damn left tackle there ever was."

Then he picked her up and spun her around and around and around as the last golden rays of the day blended into night.

ACKNOWLEDGMENTS

It's taken a village to raise this book, and I'd like to thank everyone who had any little hand in it along the way.

Firstly, my thanks must go to the good folks of Entangled Publishing for all the behind-the-scenes magic. I know this book went through multiple hands and a lot of backing and forthing was done on the cover, as well as making sure this book got onto as many shelves as possible, and I thank you all! Most special thanks to Liz, who not only went to bat for this book, but who drove me out to eastern Colorado so I could get a real feel for my little fictitious town.

Thanks to Robyn Rychards, who read this book from cover to cover, checking it for American-isms, Colorado-isms, and NFL-isms. This rugby girl did not want to screw up the gridiron, so her input was invaluable and any mistakes are my own! It was fabulous meeting you, Robyn, in Denver, and I hope we meet again.

To Harper Kincaid—who I love to pieces—thanks for kicking around titles with me in the early stages, and my dearest Jane Porter, who gave me some useful information about housing prices in SoCal.

Thanks as always goes to my husband, Mark, who keeps me supplied with cups of tea or glasses of wine depending on how well the book is going. He did not fall in love with a writer, but considers himself blessed to be married to one. Nor did he want to pack up and move hundreds of kilometers away to the ocean. But he did it for me. And for that alone, I will love him forever.

And lastly, thanks to the two special women in my life who've known me the longest and who cheer every success and are there to pour wine for every setback. They are my absolute rocks. Thanks, Ros. Thanks, Leah.

Loved the small-town setting
and laugh-out-loud humor of
Nothing But Trouble?

Then you won't want to miss
Just One of the Groomsmen
from *USA Today* bestselling author
Cindi Madsen.

She's just one of the guys...
until she isn't.

Read on for an excerpt...

(And keep reading to find out how to get Amy
Andrews's *Playing By Her Rules* for FREE.)

CHAPTER ONE

The houseboat came into view and Addie's excitement level went from its already high seven to a solid ten. An emergency meeting had been called, and all the guys were going to be in attendance. Every single one, including the guy she'd been dying to see for so long that she'd almost worried their sporadic phone calls, texts, and messages were the only way they'd ever communicate again.

Addie pulled up next to the sleek compact car she'd have to make fun of later—right now it meant that Tucker Crawford was here in the flesh, and within a few minutes, the rest of the gang would be as well. She wasn't sure why Shep had called the meeting, but it took her back to high school, when so many of their evenings and weekends were spent here at the Crawfords' houseboat. Lazy afternoons and countless poker games; impromptu parties that usually got them busted for one thing or another; and nights spent celebrating team wins or commiserating over losses, whether it was the high school team that the guys had all played for, War Eagle football, or the NFL, on which they were a house divided—it'd led to some of her and Tucker's most heated exchanges.

The scent of cypress trees, swampy lake water, and moss hit her as she climbed out of the beater truck she often drove, and since she was hoping for a minute or two with Tucker before everyone else showed up, she rushed down the pathway, her rapid steps echoing against the wood once she hit the plank leading to the boat. "Tucker?"

"Addie?"

She heard his voice but didn't see him. Then she rounded the front of the boat, where the chairs and grill were set up, and there he was. Even taller and wider than she remembered, his copper-brown hair styled shorter than he wore it in high school, although the wave in it meant there were always a couple of strands that did their own thing, no matter how much gel he used.

A laugh escaped as she took a few long strides and launched herself at him, her arms going around his neck. "I'll be damned, you actually made it this time."

Using the arm he'd wrapped around her lower back, he lifted her off her feet and squeezed tight enough to send her breath out over his shoulder. "I'm sorry for accidentally standing you up a few times. It's stupid how hard it's been to get away this past year."

"That's what happens when you go and become some big city lawyer." She pulled back to get another look at one of her best and very oldest friends. She had so much to tell him that she didn't know where to start. Thanks to his crazy schedule, even their calls and texts had slowed to a trickle. Despite working at the law firm for nearly two years, he was still one of the junior attorneys, which meant he ended up doing all the time-consuming research for the partners. Before that, law school had kept him plenty busy, and while she wasn't usually the mushy hugger-type, she didn't want to release him yet, just in case she had to go another five or six months without seeing him.

Only now that she was focusing on every single detail, from the familiar blue eyes to his strong, freshly shaven jawline, to— "Holy crap, dude. When did you get so jacked? Is lifting bulky legal files muscle building? If so, maybe I should start recommending it as part of my clients' therapy regimens."

His gaze ran over her as well, most likely assessing the ways she'd changed—or more likely hadn't. "Isn't it about time for a new sweatshirt?" He yanked one of the frayed, used-to-be-black strings. "That one's looked ratty since our first year of college."

She gasped and shoved him. "Hater. Just because *my* Falcons made it further in the playoffs than your Saints did last season. And don't even try to tell me you've thrown out your beat-up baseball cap that practically grafted itself to your head during high school. Or maybe you don't wear it anymore so you can show off your fancy-pants forty-dollar lawyer haircut." She reached up and ran her hand through his hair, loosening the hold the gel had on it.

Much better. There was the boy who'd once landed her in detention because he'd dared her to put superglue on the teacher's whiteboard markers while he distracted him with a question. The boy who'd challenged her to a deviled-egg-eating competition at the town festival and then moped about her beating him—to this day, the sight or scent of a deviled egg still made her stomach roll.

He grinned, every inch the laid-back Tucker Crawford she'd grown up with once again, and just like that, all seemed right in Uncertainty, Alabama.

"Crawford? Where you at?" Shep's booming voice hit them a few seconds before he, Easton, and Ford rounded the corner and stepped onto the back deck.

"Murph!" they yelled when they saw her, and then they exchanged high fives, shoulder punches, and a few bro-hugs on their way to give Tucker the same treatment. Addie saw the rest of the guys around town here and there, but it was harder to get together now that everyone had careers and other obligations, and they hadn't hung out in way too long. Funny how in high school they couldn't wait to get older so they could do whatever they wanted, and instead they ended up having less free time than ever.

Shep placed two six-packs of Naked Pig Pale Ale, the best beer in all of Alabama, on top of a big planter that only held dirt, since the neglected plants had shriveled up and died long ago. "Before we get this party started, I guess I should let you know what we're celebrating."

The hint of worry Addie had felt since receiving the urgent text evaporated. The message had been so vague—typical guy, although her mom and sister accused her of the same thing.

Addie sat on the edge of the table, and when Tucker bumped her over with his hip, she scooted. The table wobbled, and Tucker's hand shot out and wrapped around her upper arm as she worked to rebalance herself.

He chuckled. "Guess we're heavier than we used to be."

She scowled at him. "Hey! Speak for yourself."

"Right. It must be all my jacked muscles."

Addie rolled her eyes. That's what she got for

giving him an accidental compliment. Every single one of her boys had egos the size of pickup trucks, and the many girls who'd fawned over them through the years didn't help any.

Shep raised his voice, speaking above the din. "So, you guys might recall I've been seeing Sexy Lexi, going on almost a year now."

"How could we forget?" Addie quipped. "You talk about her nonstop." She glanced at Tucker, who'd yet to meet Shep's girlfriend, thanks to busy schedules and his last canceled trip. "Seriously, we go to get a beer and watch the game, and it's Lexi this, Lexi that."

Shep didn't frown at her like she'd expected, grinning that twitterpated grin he often wore these days instead.

"She's actually very lovely," she added, then curled her hands around the table. While his Southern belle girlfriend worked to hold it at bay, Addie didn't think Lexi was her biggest fan. She hated always having to downplay her friendship with the guys in order to not upset the balance of their relationships. Hopefully a little more time and getting to know each other, and Lexi would understand that Will Shepherd was more like a brother than anything.

All the guys were, and thanks to the fact they'd both stayed closer to home the past few years, she and Shep were even more sibling-like than the rest. It wasn't the first time her friends' girlfriends were wary of her, and she doubted it'd be the last. Sometimes she worried she'd get left behind, just because she'd had the audacity to be born a girl. Being the only girl in a group of guys was merely a technicality, though. It wasn't that she didn't have female friends or that she didn't know a lot of great women; it was that she'd grown up with these guys and forged memories and they liked to do the same things she did.

It was why she'd gone by "Murph" more often than Addison Murphy, or any other variation thereof. Thanks to her love of comfy, sporty clothes, she'd been voted "most likely to start her own sweatshirt line" in high school, a title she was proud to have, by the way.

Easton had been voted "most likely to end up in jail," and ironically enough, he was now a cop, something they all teased him about. Which reminded her...

"Don't let me forget to make fun of your prissy car when this meeting is over," Addie whispered to Tucker.

He opened his mouth, assumedly to defend himself, and Shep cleared his throat.

"*Anyway*, last weekend I asked Lexi to marry me." A huge smile spread across his face. "And she said yes."

Not at all what Addie had been expecting—marriage was such a big step, and it took her a beat or two to process. But happiness radiated off Shep in waves, the guy who'd once rolled his eyes over "whipped dudes" long gone. She was glad he'd found someone who made him so happy, even as a tiny part of her wanted to press pause on this night while they were all together, before everything changed in their group yet again.

"You get to bang Sexy Lexi for the rest of your life?" Ford held up his hand for a high five. "*Bro.* I remember when you had to work your ass off to score her number at that bar in Opelika, and Easton and I had that bet about whether her amazing rack was real."

"*Bro*, that's gonna be his wife," Addie said.

"Yeah, have some respect," Shep said. Then he put a hand to the side of his mouth and stage-whispered, "They're one hundred percent real. I told you guys that, right?"

"Only, like, one hundred percent of the time you talk about her." This was the one downside of being the only girl. Sometimes things got a little too TMI about the women they were sleeping with or hoping to sleep with. Back in high school, Tucker dated nearly every cheerleader in the county, so Addie would walk past one of the human Barbies and recall way too many personal details about her. Even when the girls would sneer or poke fun at her choice of clothing or hobbies, she resisted using that as ammo, something she used to feel she deserved a medal for.

Everyone continued to offer their congratulations, and after a few claps on the back and obligatory jokes about balls and chains, Shep said, "I want you guys to be in my wedding. To be my groomsmen."

Addie's stomach dropped. "You guys" usually included her, but she knew the word "groomsmen" didn't. "*Ha!* Y'all are gonna have to wear stuffy penguin suits and take hundreds of pictures. Have fun with that."

Shep looked at her, and a sense of foreboding pricked her skin. "Before you go celebrating too much, you're in the wedding party, too, Murph. I told Lexi I wanted you as one of my groomsmen."

While his girlfriend—make that fiancée—was pretty patient and understanding of Shep's crazy, out-there ideas, she was also *extremely* girly. As in she wore a dress and heels more often than not—including to the local bar, which wasn't a dress-and-heels kind of joint—and belonged to one of those societies that threw things like tea parties and galas. "I'm sure that went over about as well as coming out as a vegan in the middle of Sunday dinner."

"She understands you're just one of the guys," Shep said, and a hint of hope rose up. She hated that she'd immediately felt left out, the same way she used to when a group of girls would show up at the bar and suddenly she'd be alone, no one to help with game commentary. "But she's also more traditional, her family even more so."

"I understand," Addie said. "I don't think I'd look very good in a tux anyway, and my own mother would probably die twice over it." All her life, Mom had asked why she couldn't be more like her sister; why she couldn't dress up more. Since Addie hadn't been on a date in a depressing amount of time, Mom had also recently given her this whole spiel about first impressions and how when men looked for a significant other, they wanted to feel needed.

Like she didn't want to feel needed? Or wanted? She'd just prefer a possible significant other want her the way she was, not because she donned a dress and acted helpless.

"Which is why…" Shep straightened, his hazel eyes locking on to her. "Lexi and I came up with a compromise. You'll be a groomsman in name and when it comes to all the usual pre-wedding stuff, but in order to be part of the wedding party, you're gonna have to wear the same dress and shoes as the bridesmaids." The rest of the words came out in a fast blur, like he hoped if he talked fast enough she might miss them. "And you might have to dress up one or two other times, like at the rehearsal and maybe even the bridal shower."

The guys burst out laughing. "Murph in a dress and heels," Easton said. "That'll be the day."

Addie picked up the nearest object she could find—a weather-warped coaster—and chucked it at his head. It bounced off, and, if anything, only made him laugh harder.

The table shook, and when she glanced at Tucker, he had a fist over his mouth in an attempt to smother his laughter.

"You, too?" Two seconds before Shep dropped the bomb, she'd been thinking about how much she didn't want to wear a dress and heels. Was karma punishing her? Was this what she got for being comfortable for most of her twenty-seven years?

"Please, Addie," Shep said. "I know it's not your thing, but I can't imagine you not being part of this." He shot a challenging glare at the group of them. "And spare me the jokes about actually caring about my wedding. I never thought I'd be this happy, but I am, and I need you guys with me on this."

This time, the "you guys" definitely included her. Which made it that much easier to say, "I'm in. I'll do whatever you need me to."

• • •

Man, it was good to be back in town, even if only for a quick weekend. Tucker had been working hours and hours on end, thinking that after putting in two years at the law firm, he'd have enough experience and clout to slow down a bit. It never slowed down, though, his workload multiplying at an impossible-to-keep-up-with pace. He'd had to cancel his past two trips home with lame, last-minute texts and calls, but now that he was seated around the poker table with his friends, all felt right with the world.

"You're bluffin'," Addie said when Easton threw several chips into the pot. She matched his bet, and then they laid down their cards, her full house easily beating his pair of aces. "Read 'em and weep, sucker."

She leaned over the table to gather her winnings, the sleeves of her two-sizes-too-big hoodie falling over her hands. Her familiar movements were nearly second nature, as much to him as her. From the way she shoved the fabric up her wrists so she could finish gathering the chips to how she flopped back in her chair and reached into the bag of Lay's for a different kind of chip. Her knee came up to rest against the table, rattling everything on top and boosting the time-machine effect, and she wiped her hand on her frayed jeans before reaching for the newly dealt cards. Her neon-colored gel sneakers, the one new item in her outfit, reminded him of all the times she'd lectured about how important the right shoes and changing them often were for your joints.

He cracked a smile again at the thought of her in a dress and heels, bouquet in hand. The image still didn't compute. It was kind of like animals wearing human clothes—it just wasn't right.

It wasn't that they'd *never* seen Addie wear a

dress; it was that she loathed them with a hatred he withheld for things like paperwork and blind refs who ruined games, and she'd once slugged him in the shoulder for even mentioning her dress-wearing at her sister's wedding. The skirt had been long and baggy, and the real tragedy was that she couldn't toss around the pigskin—her mom said it'd ruin her nice clothes, and added that it was an "inappropriate wedding activity, anyway." So then they'd *both* had to sit there with their hands folded in their laps for what seemed like forever and it was boring as hell, an emotion he'd rarely experienced around her.

"Your poker face is crap, Crawford. I know you're thinking about how funny it is that I just agreed to wear a freaking bridesmaid's dress, and if you don't want me to jam that beer you're drinking where the sun don't shine, I suggest you wipe the smirk off your face." She pointed her finger around the table. "That goes for all of you."

"I appreciate you going along with it," Shep said. "I told Lexi that you'd probably slug me just for suggesting it."

"Lucky for you, you were too far away and wearing that lovestruck grin that makes me take pity on you."

"When someone basically says thank you, maybe don't follow that up by insulting them." Shep placed three cards, face up, in the center of the table. "Just a suggestion."

"This is why so many guys in town are scared of you," Easton said with a laugh.

She clucked her tongue. "They are not."

The other half of the table nodded, and Tucker found himself nodding even though he hadn't lived in town for the better part of two years. It'd been like that since high school, with Addie intimidating anyone who dared cross her path, and the selfish part of him was glad no one had come in and swept her off her feet. Not that she would ever let some guy do the sweeping. A few had probably tried, with her completely oblivious. With her dirty blond hair that was forever in a ponytail, the smattering of freckles across her nose, her big brown eyes, and the fact that she was cool as hell, it was surprising she'd stayed mostly single.

Ford pinned her with a look. "Addie, when dudes come in to see you for physical therapy, you tell them to stop crying over something your grandma could do."

"Well, she could! My nonna is tougher than most of the crybabies who come in whining about their injuries. They don't wanna put in the work it takes to get over them and fully heal. Telling them my grandma could do the things I'm instructing them to do is motivating."

"Not to ask you out," Ford said, and snickers went around the table.

"Very funny. Being scared of me and being un-dateable are two different things."

"You're hardly undateable," Tucker said, the words similar to exchanges they'd had in high school.

"Yeah, but it's nearly impossible to find someone who doesn't already know too much about me—or me about him—and even if I manage that, then I introduce him to you guys, and things unravel pretty quickly after that."

"Maybe with one of us gettin' hitched, we'll be less intimidating." Shep dealt the turn and they started a round of betting.

"I'm sure it's me," Addie muttered. "Now, do you guys want to talk about my pathetic dating life, or do y'all want me to finish taking your money?"

"Wow, what great options," Tucker deadpanned. "Not sure why anyone would be scared of you. Couldn't be all the threats."

She turned those brown eyes on him and cocked an eyebrow. "Listen, city boy. Maybe you can just flash your shiny car and some Benjamins to get your way where you live, but here we still live and die by the same code."

He leaned in, challenge firing in his veins. "And that is…?"

"Loser buys beer next time. And/or acts as designated driver."

"And sleeps on the breakfast bar," Easton added, jerking his chin toward the hardwood bench they'd taken turns crashing out on at one time or another. There were only so many sleeping spots in the houseboat. Winner and runner-up got the bed, and third place landed the couch.

"Oh, man." Shep rubbed his lower back. "I don't think I've recovered from the last time I passed out there." He took the top card off the deck, revealing the river, and Tucker watched faces for signs of what cards they had or were hoping for and if they'd gotten it.

The guys folded after he doubled the bet, and then it came down to him and Addie.

"Poker's so much better with all of us here," she said.

"Trying to distract me?" Tucker asked. "'Cause it won't work."

She laughed. "No, just telling the truth. We've tried to play with people from everyone's respective jobs, or some other rando who wants in when they hear we play poker, and it always sucks. And it's never as interesting with just four."

Ford shifted forward in his seat. "Remember Buck? That guy never shut up."

"And thanks to you"—Tucker gave Ford's shoulder a shove—"we already have the loudmouth position filled."

Ford flipped him off and then let out a loud burp. "He also scratched his balls even more than Easton does."

"Hey," Easton said. "When you've got balls this size, it requires constant adjustment."

Addie took a swig of her beer. "Buck wasn't as bad as that Yank Shep brought over. That dude didn't even know how to play."

"That Yank happens to be my cousin," Shep said. "And it's not like I wanted to bring him. My mamma insisted, and it was easier to drag him along than argue with her."

"We explained the rules over and over"—Easton reached across the table to grab the potato chips— "and that dude still didn't know whether to check his ass or scratch his watch."

Whenever Tucker came home, he noticed the extra twang in his friends' voices—not to mention the more colorful sayings—and he knew by the end of the night, he'd pick it right back up, his own accent thicker for a few days before the city smoothed it out a bit.

"All right, let's see what you got," Tucker said, and he and Addie placed their cards on the table at the same time.

Then she proceeded to take the last of his chips.

They played until everyone was sober again and Addie had pretty much cleaned them out. One by one they left, save the two of them.

"Are you staying here at the houseboat tonight?" she asked as she gathered her keys off the table outside. "Because you know that my door is always open, and I even have a bed that doesn't sway."

That was Addie's way of offering him a place to crash without making him feel homeless. His parents had divorced his junior year of high school, which was extra fun in a small town where everyone gossiped about it. It became even more fun when Mom moved in with a congressman who owned a country estate all of two months later. Dad had always pushed him to get out of the small town and find a way to make some real money, but once the bank foreclosed on their house, he pushed Tucker even harder to go into a high-paying field. Losing his childhood home had left him feeling completely uprooted, something he'd only ever confessed to Addie. It didn't help that Dad sold nearly everything so he could move towns, and Tucker had to beg him to hold off selling the houseboat.

Halfway through law school, Dad claimed he needed money too badly to wait any longer, so Tucker drove to Uncertainty, took out a loan against the small plot of land his grandfather had left him, and bought the houseboat himself. He'd nearly paid it off, although he'd already seen repairs that would need to be made whenever he found spare time—so probably about three years from now. "I like it out here on the lake, and I don't mind if my bed rocks a little."

"Dirty," she teased, and he laughed. Although now he was thinking about how long it'd been. Work was getting in the way of every single aspect of his social life. If he loved his job, it would be one thing, but he was giving up a lot for a future of making a lot of money—right now he still had plenty of bills and student loans to worry about.

A smile curved Addie's lips as she ran her hand over the deck railing. "I love this mini-house and all our memories here."

"Yeah, those were definitely the good ol' days." He folded his forearms on the railing and looked out over the water. It'd been a long time since he'd been able to kick back and joke with people who understood him. A long time since he'd felt so relaxed. And while being with the whole gang was a blast, Addie had always been his go-to when he needed advice or wanted to get more real. Certain things couldn't be communicated over the phone, and no matter how hard they'd tried to keep in touch via the various forms of technology, it just wasn't the same, and now he was out of practice. So he stuck to simple. "Tonight was the most fun I've had in a long time."

"Me, too. Like I said, poker's not the same without you. Same with football games, whether we're both cheering for Auburn on Saturdays, or if you're spending Sundays being an annoying ass who talks trash about my team." She set her jaw. "Even you have to admit that the Falcons had a good season last year."

"I admit nothing."

"Stubborn," she muttered. As if she wasn't equally

as stubborn. She sighed and lightly punched his arm. "Night, Crawford."

He returned the gesture. "Night, Murph."

She turned to go, but then abruptly spun around and wrapped her arms around his waist. "I understand that your job is demanding, but don't be a stranger."

He squeezed her back, noticing that her hair smelled fruity, like maybe strawberry or raspberry, or something berry, anyway.

"At least with Shep getting married you've got another excuse to come down and spend more than a weekend," she said, and something deep in his gut tugged.

"Yeah, it's good to have an excuse." What he wanted was an excuse not to go back to his cold, generic apartment and mind-numbing job. Back to his serious life where he'd have to feel the loneliness he was doing his best to pretend didn't exist.

What he wanted more than anything was to return to his friends and the town he loved, and he wasn't sure how he could possibly go back and be satisfied with his old life after tonight showed him everything that was missing from it.

IF YOU ENJOYED THIS EXCERPT, LOOK FOR
JUST ONE OF THE GROOMSMEN
WHEREVER BOOKS AND EBOOKS ARE SOLD.

From New York Times *bestselling author Victoria James comes a poignant and heartfelt romance.*

THE TROUBLE WITH COWBOYS

by Victoria James

Eight years ago, Tyler Donnelly left Wishing River, Montana, after a terrible fight with his father and swore he'd never return. But when his father has a stroke, guilt and duty drive him home, and nothing is as he remembers—from the run-down ranch to Lainey Sullivan, who is all grown up now. And darn if he can't seem to stay away.

Lainey's late grandma left her two things: the family diner and a deep-seated mistrust of cowboys. So when Tyler quietly rides back into town looking better than hot apple pie, she knows she's in trouble. But she owes his dad everything, and she's determined to show Ty what it means to be part of a small town...and part of a family.

Lainey's courage pushes Ty to want to make Wishing River into a home again—together. But one of them is harboring a secret that could change everything.

How to Lose a Guy in Ten Days *meets*
Accidentally on Purpose *by Jill Shalvis in*
this head-over-heels romantic comedy.

THE AUSSIE NEXT DOOR

by Stefanie London

Want to read Playing By Her Rules
*by Amy Andrews for **FREE**?!*

- Visit Entangledpublishing.com.

- Add *Playing By Her Rules* to your cart.

- Enter code: **FreeRomance19** at checkout.

- Enjoy your free book!

ONE WEDDING, TWO BRIDES

by *NYT* bestselling author Heidi Betts

Jilted bride Monica Blair can't believe it when she wakes up next to a blue-eyed, smooth-talking cowboy in the middle of nowhere and with a ring on her finger. It had sounded like a great plan at the time. Get married, get revenge, and get her money back. So why is she cleaning out stables and trying to keep her hands off the hot cowboy helping her?

Ryder Nash would have bet his best Stetson that you'd never see him walk down the aisle. But when the city girl with pink-streaked hair and a frog tattoo hatches a plan to expose the conman who married his sister, no idea is too crazy. And even though Monica might be the worst rancher's wife he's ever seen, he can't stop thinking about the wedding night they never had.

What was supposed to be a temporary marriage for revenge is starting to feel a little too real...

The rules are about to change…

THE WEDDING DEAL
By Cindi Madsen

Former quarterback Lance Quaid just inherited the most losing team in the NFL. He's got only a few weeks until draft day to turn things around, and after firing more than half his staff, he can't do it alone. Thankfully, his HR manager is more than capable, if only she'd stop focusing on "due diligence" and stop looking so sexy while she's yelling at him.

Charlotte James has made a life out of following the rules. But nothing could have prepared her for Lance Quaid—he's a human resources nightmare. The man is brash, has no filter, and, as her new boss, is constantly relying on her to cover his ass. Which is admittedly quite nice.

When Lance begs her to join him on a trip down the coast for his brother's wedding so they can finalize details—on a strictly business basis—she agrees...after they fill out the necessary forms, of course. Away from the office, though, sparks start flying as the team starts coming together. But both of them know anything more than the weekend would be a colossally bad idea—after all, the extra paperwork would be a nightmare.